LAND OF OZ

*Also available from Titan Books*

## FANTASY

*Rogues*

*Wonderland: An Anthology*

*Hex Life: Wicked New Tales of Witchery*

*Cursed: An Anthology*

*Vampires Never Get Old: Tales With Fresh Bite*

*A Universe of Wishes: A We Need Diverse Books Anthology*

*At Midnight: 15 Beloved Fairy Tales Reimagined*

*Twice Cursed: An Anthology*

*The Other Side of Never: Dark Tales from the World of Peter & Wendy*

*Mermaids Never Drown: Tales to Dive For*

*The Secret Romantic's Book of Magic*

*The Hopeless Romantic's Guide to Enchantment*

## CRIME

*Dark Detectives: An Anthology of Supernatural Mysteries*

*Exit Wounds*

*Invisible Blood*

*Daggers Drawn*

*Black is the Night*

*Ink and Daggers*

*Death Comes at Christmas: Tales of Seasonal Malice*

## SCIENCE FICTION

*Dead Man's Hand: An Anthology of the Weird West*

*Wastelands: Stories of the Apocalypse*

*Wastelands 2: More Stories of the Apocalypse*

*Infinite Stars*

*Infinite Stars: Dark Frontiers*

*Out of the Ruins*

*Multiverses: An Anthology of Alternate Realities*

*Reports from the Deep End: Stories Inspired by J. G. Ballard*

*Revolution in the Heart: Stories Inspired by Ursula K. Le Guin*

## HORROR

*Dark Cities*

*New Fears: New Horror Stories by Masters of the Genre*

*New Fears 2: Brand New Horror Stories by Masters of the Macabre*

*Phantoms: Haunting Tales from the Masters of the Genre*

*When Things Get Dark*

*Dark Stars*

*Isolation: The Horror Anthology*

*Christmas and Other Horrors*

*Bound in Blood*

*Roots of My Fears*

*All Hallows' Eve*

*Unearthed*

## THRILLER

*In These Hallowed Halls: A Dark Academia Anthology*

*These Dreaming Spires*

# LAND OF OZ

## TALES FROM THE WONDERFUL WORLD OF L. FRANK BAUM

EDITED BY

MARIE O'REGAN & PAUL KANE

TITAN BOOKS

Land of Oz
Print edition ISBN: 9781835417478
E-book edition ISBN: 9781835417485

Published by Titan Books
A division of Titan Publishing Group Ltd
144 Southwark Street, London SE1 0UP
www.titanbooks.com

First edition: September 2026
10 9 8 7 6 5 4 3 2 1



A CIP catalogue record for this title is available from the British Library.

EU RP (for authorities only)
eucomply OÜ, Pärnu mnt. 139b-14, 11317 Tallinn, Estonia
hello@eucompliancepartner.com, +3375690241



Designed and typeset in Minion Pro by Richard Mason.

Printed and bound by CPI (UK) Ltd, Croydon, CR0 4YY.

# CONTENTS

# INTRODUCTION

**MARIE O'REGAN & PAUL KANE**

Everyone remembers the first time they saw MGM's *The Wizard of Oz.*

The way the movie shifts from black and white/sepia-toned to colour, the songs – over the rainbow, following that Yellow Brick Road – and the characters of Dorothy, Tin Man, Scarecrow and Cowardly Lion. But how about the first time you read the book, *The Wonderful Wizard of Oz*? Or should that be books, plural? Because there are fourteen in the original series, penned by L. Frank Baum, covering many more aspects of Oz than you think.

From *The Marvelous Land of Oz* and *Ozma of Oz* in 1904 and 1907 respectively (loosely adapted in the Disney movie *Return to Oz* from 1985, which also incorporated aspects of 1914's *Tik-Tok of Oz*), right through to *The Magic of Oz* (1919) and *Glinda of Oz* (1920), which was published posthumously and focuses on a treacherous journey Dorothy and Ozma undertake, as well as their rescue by the Good Witch of the South, these form the bedrock of all the adventures that came afterwards.

Of which there were many. Just in terms of books, after Baum's death, publisher Reilly & Lee carried on bringing out *Oz* publications written by Ruth Plumly Thompson, which – combined with the originals – formed what's known as the 'Famous Forty'. Then, of course, you have all the tales published by the International Wizard of Oz Club, precipitated by Jack Snow's short story 'A Murder in Oz' (1958) – where the Wizard himself takes on the mantle of detective – the officially recognised *Oz* sequels, such as *The Emerald Wand of Oz* (2005), *Trouble Under Oz* (2006), and *Sky Pyrates Over Oz* by Sherwood Smith (2014), and all the alternate *Oz* books, like those penned by Russian novelist Alexander Volkov in the '60s and '70s.

This is before we get to other films – ranging from a short silent adaptation way back in 1910, right up to Sam Raimi's *Oz The Great and Powerful* (2013), which sought to address how the Wizard got there in the first place and cast *Spider-Man*'s James Franco in the title role – and TV takes, like the *Tin Man* miniseries from 2007 starring Zooey Deschanel.

Then you have the musicals, such as *The Wiz* – an award-winning Broadway hit, with music and lyrics by Charlie Smalls (amongst others). It was itself also turned into a film in 1978, famously starring Diana Ross and Michael Jackson.

But, you'd have to've been living in Oz yourself to have missed the most recent movies based on *Wicked*, another hit musical which itself was loosely based on the bestselling novel by Gregory Maguire (who has written a good few more since). The excitement around director Jon M. Chu's two-parter, starring Cynthia Erivo and Ariana Grande, is just one of the reasons why Oz is even more popular than ever at the moment.

So, when we began thinking about how to follow up the Shirley Jackson Award-nominated *Wonderland* and *The Other Side of Never*, a British Fantasy Award nominee and #1 bestseller (both also from Titan), even before we'd delivered the latter book, this topic was obviously the first choice. The chance to add to such a rich and varied history, being the fans that we are, was an opportunity not to be missed.

And hopefully we've delivered on the promise of that idea, gathering together another hugely talented group of authors to give their own spin on the material, whether they be reworkings, coming at the material from right-angles, side-stories, situations or characters connected – however indirectly – to *The Land of Oz*.

Author of *Startup Hell*, Caitlin Rozakis, takes as her inspiration the long-lost love of the Tin Woodman (as he's known in the original books), while Paul Magrs (*Doctor Who: Dracula!*) draws on what Baum's original tale might have meant to one young boy in particular.

Adrian Tchaikovsky (*Bee Speaker*) delivers a sci-fi take you won't forget in a hurry, Simon R. Green (*Which Witch*) ponders what might have happened once Dorothy returned home to Kansas, and Ian Whates (*The Double-Edged Sword*) reveals the role a certain bird played in events when the girl first arrived in Oz.

The author of *House of Idyll*, Delilah S. Dawson, transports Dorothy to a twisted version of Oz, and Christina Henry (*The Place Where They Buried Your Heart*) reworks the story by way of a fortune-telling sideshow, but Robert Shearman (*Doctor Who: The Chimes of Midnight* and its companion,

*Doctor Who: Jubilee)* uses elements of the mythos to comment on grief and loss.

Louise Carey (*Downfall*) and M. R. Carey (*Outlaw Planet*) give us two tales with a distinct link; author of the NecroTek books, Jonathan Maberry, explores Dorothy's connection to her home in Kansas; and Una McCormack (*The Peacemakers*) discloses whatever happened to a certain famous general. Finally, creator of The Factus Sequence – Stark Holborn – investigates a bizarre Ozian crime with shocking consequences.

So get ready, because we're about to take you to the Land of Oz and back, and then some! Rainbows and Yellow Brick Roads optional.

MARIE O'REGAN & PAUL KANE
January 2026

# THE DOOR TO OZ

**SIMON R. GREEN**

Everyone knows the story of Dorothy. How she was carried away from her little farm in Kansas, to the wonderful world of Oz. But there is a fundamental problem at the heart of this story; namely, why did Dorothy want to go home? Why would she want to leave a world of magics and marvels and incredible friends, to return to a grey and desolate farm and a family that didn't seem to have much time for her?

She must have had a good reason.

It was 1920; a full twenty years since Dorothy had returned from her magical adventure. In that time she had left her old life behind, grown into an adult, and founded a charitable enterprise called the Oz Foundation, that ended up with branches all over the world. Dorothy ran the whole affair herself, which was quite an achievement in a country where women had only just been granted the right to vote. But no-one begrudged Dorothy her success, because she had so openly dedicated her life to raising money for good works; and now her foundation fed the hungry, fought injustice, and improved lives in every country there was. But Dorothy still worked every day from her main office in Kansas City, in her home state; on the very top floor of the tallest building in that now-bustling place. And it was to this office that the journalist Arthur Magister went, to interview her.

It wasn't his idea. He was just called in to his editor's office that morning and told he was going. At first he was excited, because until now Dorothy had always refused to give any interview that wasn't strictly related to foundation business, but on the twentieth anniversary of her return from Oz Dorothy had reached out to the editor of the *Kansas Star*, and declared she was finally ready to put on record exactly what had happened to her during her time in Oz. And she asked specifically for Arthur Magister to do the interview.

He had no idea why.

"Why me?" he said just a bit plaintively, to his editor, Mike Chandry. "I don't do celebrity interviews. I do business, and politics…"

"And all the other stuff everyone reads after they've read everything else," said Chandry. "Including the automobile polo scores."

He glowered at Arthur from behind a desk half-buried under tottering piles of paper, a large and imposing man in an ill-fitting suit, with a permanently down-turned mouth and an eye always fixed on the main chance.

"She wants you," said Chandry. "And only you. Or she'll

take her interview somewhere else. So, how are you going to approach this very special assignment?"

"Well," said Arthur. "I suppose she must have read my stuff, and decided I would give her a fair hearing, so…"

"To hell with that!" said Chandry. "She's finally ready to tell the world what really went on in Oz, and I want every damned detail! I want every dirty little secret she's been holding back all these years."

"What do you mean, secrets?" said Arthur, doing his best to keep up.

"I mean dirt! I mean scandals, and political dealings, and…"

"What makes you think she's been doing any of that?"

"Because no one is that good, and that squeaky clean. I need you to dig deep, persuade her to open up and talk about all the payoffs and political bargains she must have made, to get her foundation's offices into every country across the globe. I want you to find out how much of those charitable donations ends up in her pocket. Get me the facts I can use to bury her!"

"That really isn't the kind of thing I do," Arthur protested feebly.

"It is now," said Chandry, "if you like having a job. The interview has been set for midday today, so you'd better get a move on. Turn up on time, make a good impression, and Magister… I want the real inside story. Don't come back without it."

Arthur Magister stood before the Oz Foundation, and had to crane his head all the way back to see the top of it. In a city packed full of huge and amazing buildings, this had to be the most impressive. It had a strength, and a presence, that it almost certainly drew from people knowing who lived and worked there. The Oz Foundation was a beacon of light in a world that was often very dark. Arthur squared his shoulders and walked up to the front door like a man about to brave a bear in its cave.

The doorman was tall and broad-shouldered, and looked as if he were more used to manual labour than guarding an entrance, but he smiled easily as he opened the door for Arthur. His uniform was sharply cut and positively bristling with brightly-shined buttons. He waved Arthur through into a very impressive lobby, wide and open and airy, but still designed to be welcoming. Arthur walked up to the reception desk, where another gentleman in an equally impressive uniform greeted him with a smile. The receptionist's uniform seemed a little shabby compared to the doorman's, probably because there was something indefinably shabby about the man himself. But his smile seemed pleasant enough.

"I'm here to see Dorothy," said Arthur, trying his best to sound like he was someone important. "I have an appointment..."

"Of course you do, Mister Magister," said the receptionist. "We've been expecting you."

He struck a large brass bell with the flat of his hand, and the great ringing sound seemed to fill the entire lobby. A door flew open, and a big bearish type in yet another smart uniform headed straight for the reception desk. He had blond hair and steady blue eyes, and walked with a cat-like grace. Arthur thought he had the look of a man who could be dangerous, at need. He extended a large hand and Arthur shook it gingerly, but the man's grip was reassuringly brisk and controlled. He nodded easily to Arthur.

"Call me Leon; I'm head of security here."

"Is there much need for security?" said Arthur, falling back on his usual defence of diverting authority figures by asking them questions. "Given how generally beloved Dorothy is?"

Leon let loose with something that was as much a growl as a laugh.

"The nicer people are, the more enemies they attract. People who want to change the world for the better are often seen as a threat, by those with vested interests in the status quo. But I make sure no one gets near her without a good reason. The bad guys have to get through me to reach her and there aren't many who can do that."

Arthur scented a story. "There really are bad guys? Has Dorothy been attacked? I mean here, personally?"

"No one in this building would ever allow Dorothy to come to harm," said Leon.

Which, Arthur reflected, as Leon led him to the elevator at the back of the lobby, wasn't actually an answer.

The elevator doors opened directly onto Dorothy's office. A surprisingly small and even cosy affair with comfortable furniture, tall potted plants, and a single great window looking out over the city. Dorothy stood up behind her desk to smile at Arthur as Leon escorted him forward.

"The journalist, Miss Dorothy," the security chief said calmly. "Would you like me to stick around and...?"

"No thank you, Leon," said Dorothy, in a pleasant easygoing voice whose accent still held echoes of her rural Kansas upbringing. "I think I can handle it from here."

Leon gave her a resigned look, and then presented Arthur with a warning one, before returning to the elevator. Dorothy waited until the doors had closed on her security chief before waving Arthur to the chair set out before her desk. He settled himself comfortably as she sat down, and regarded Arthur thoughtfully. He found her steady gaze just a little unnerving, and so gave all his attention to the desk. It was simple and straightforward, without any frills or fancies, boasting only a single sit-up-and-beg telephone and a complete lack of important-looking papers. Arthur took this to mean Dorothy ran a tight ship. Though he did have to wonder whether the papers might have been carefully removed, just before he got there, to make sure he wouldn't see anything he wasn't supposed to. He took a moment to study Dorothy, with a respectful but direct stare. The lady might be rich and important and almost universally respected, but he was damned if he was going to let her know just how impressed he was.

Dorothy was a neat, slender woman, in a fashionable but unthreatening outfit, the kind women wore when they didn't want to overawe their guest. She had short-cropped dark hair, bright eyes, and a mouth that always seemed to have a knowing smile tucked away in one corner.

Arthur couldn't help feeling very small and ordinary, in the presence of someone who had achieved so much. Dorothy nodded briefly, as though to indicate she knew what he was feeling, and smiled at him cheerfully.

"I've read your work, Mister Magister. Very thoughtful, very incisive. You go after all the right targets, and show favour toward none. Which is a lot rarer in the newspaper business than perhaps it should be. I know you normally prefer working on in-depth pieces, rather than celebrity interviews, but I hope you'll indulge me in my belief that I have chosen the right man for the job."

"I go where my editor sends me," said Arthur. "And let me assure you, I have no axe to grind with the Oz Foundation. I'm just here to do the best job I can."

"I never doubted that for a moment," said Dorothy. "But didn't you wonder why I asked for you in particular, out of all the journalists working for your paper?"

"Because you liked my work?"

"That was part of it," said Dorothy.

Arthur waited, but she had nothing more to add.

"Why are you finally ready to tell the whole story about Oz?" asked Arthur.

"It seemed the right time," said Dorothy. "It's been twenty years, after all. And I promise you, it won't be the story you're expecting."

Arthur felt a sudden tingling in his stomach, as he realised for the first time that this was a story he really wanted to hear. Given all the many and marvellous details Dorothy had already shared about her most astonishing trip, he had to wonder what there could be left to tell. He felt a growing excitement at sitting before this young woman who had travelled so… Well, far wasn't really a strong enough word, was it? To the other side of the rainbow… He was struck by how at ease Dorothy seemed, and to buy himself a moment to regain his calm, he nodded at the framed motto of the Oz Foundation, hanging on the wall beside them; *What Would Glinda Do?*

"Glinda; that's the good witch, right?"

"Oh yes," said Dorothy, smiling in a way that suggested she was inwardly amused by something she chose not to share. "She's definitely very good at what she does. Though it should be remembered that in Oz, a witch is simply a person of power and influence."

Arthur's attention was caught by the simple green door standing next to the motto. There was no sign, no explanation; nothing to indicate why it was there or what it was for. Set flush with the wall, it seemed like the door would only open onto the long drop outside the huge window.

"Is that some kind of emergency exit?" said Arthur.

"Something like that," answered Dorothy.

Arthur was about to push the question when he was suddenly distracted by a small dog emerging unhurriedly from its basket by the desk, padding happily forward to be made a fuss of. It was a little black dog, with long silky hair and small black eyes. Arthur gave the dog's shaggy head a good rub, and a small tail wagged happily.

"You should feel honoured," said Dorothy. "Toto doesn't always take to people. It's almost like he knows you."

"I have that kind of face," Arthur said solemnly.

The dog returned to his basket, turned around several times, and then dropped down. He lay very still, studying Arthur with dark watchful eyes.

"Toto," said Arthur, just to show he'd been paying attention. "That was the name of the dog who went with you to Oz, wasn't it? I suppose you must have had more dogs since then. Were they all named after the original?"

"Oh no," said Dorothy, quite casually. "That is the original. Toto hasn't aged a day since he returned from Oz."

Arthur looked hard at the very ordinary-looking dog, and the dog stared steadily back. Arthur had a strange feeling that the dog understood every word they were saying. He pushed the thought aside, and concentrated on the practicalities.

"But that would make him over twenty years old," he said mildly.

"Everyone who returns from Oz comes back changed," said Dorothy.

"Including you?"

"Of course. It's not every little girl who grows up to run a global business."

The tingle in Arthur's stomach increased. He was on to something here, he could feel it; something really big. And for the first time he decided he was going to treat this as an important story; something the whole world needed to know.

"How did your going to Oz change you?" he said bluntly.

"I had my eyes opened," replied Dorothy. "And when

I decided to come back, Glinda presented me with a gift, to bring to the peoples of Earth."

"What kind of a gift?" said Arthur.

"We'll get to that," said Dorothy.

Arthur suddenly realised that he hadn't got any of this fascinating information on record. He took out his notepad and pencil, and laid them carefully on his knee.

"I'm going to record all of our conversation from now on, in shorthand; if that's okay. Do you want to bring in a secretary to do the same for you, so you can have your own record of what's said?"

"I don't see any need for that," said Dorothy.

Arthur raised an eyebrow. "Most people insist, if only to make sure they're not misquoted or taken out of context."

"I'm fine," said Dorothy.

"That's very trusting," said Arthur.

"Not really," Dorothy told him. "Things have a way of working out for me."

Arthur had to smile. "After everything that's happened to you, I can't really argue with that." He took a deep breath, and plunged straight in. "Let's start with an obvious question. What do you think of all the books, movies, even stage shows and merchandise, that have been based on your experiences?"

"I saw the first movie," said Dorothy. "The real Oz was far more magical. I sold all rights to my story to raise enough money to get my foundation started. And to do that, I had to give up all control over how the material might be used. I knew they wouldn't dare change things too much, for fear I would denounce them. The public has always been on my side. But, of course, I always knew they'd go their own way. They did promise me I'd be consulted, but even though I used to write to them when they got things wrong, or make suggestions on how to improve matters, they never responded. So I just left them to get on with it. All I really care about is that the royalties keep rolling in, to fund the foundation's work."

"At least you had enough sense to insist on royalties," said Arthur.

Dorothy sat back in her chair and grinned broadly. "I'm a farm girl, Mister Magister. We know all there is to know about how to squeeze a penny till it squeals."

"Given the sheer amount of money Oz has generated down the years, you must be very wealthy by now," said Arthur. He was careful not to push that, just letting the remark hang there on the air.

Dorothy shook her head. "The vast majority of it goes to the foundation. My needs are very simple."

"All right; let's go for a big question," said Arthur. "Something that's always bothered me about your story. Were you really transported to Oz by a tornado? I've read reports about the kind of destruction they can cause. Most people don't survive contact with them."

Dorothy frowned, and chose her words carefully. "It was never a tornado. The film people added that for dramatic effect. It was more like a storm, of a kind I'd never seen before. A disturbance in the atmosphere so powerful it broke the world. A crack in the sky appeared and my house fell up into the air, and took me and my dog through into Oz."

Arthur leaned forward. This was new. "What do you suppose caused this storm?"

Dorothy smiled briefly. "Perhaps my wanting so much to be anywhere except where I was."

Arthur knew an evasion when he heard one. He sat back in his own chair.

"Do you still keep in touch with your old friends from Oz? The Scarecrow, the Tin Woodman, the Cowardly Lion?"

"Of course," said Dorothy. "Sometimes they come through into this world; for a visit, or to help out in our branches round the world."

Arthur sat bolt upright. There had never been any mention of this before. He had a sudden vision of his interview making the front page on every newspaper in every country. *Have You Seen the People from Oz?*

"Don't they stand out?" he asked bluntly.

"They're different here," said Dorothy. "Everyone who comes to us from Oz arrives changed. It takes a toll on them; they're not what they were. But they all volunteered, and they paid the price gladly. They believe in the foundation, and what it's for."

"And they believe in you."

Dorothy smiled. "Even after all this time. We did go through a lot together."

"Let's talk about when you first arrived in Oz," said Arthur. "You were just a little girl. Weren't you frightened, to find yourself in such a strange world?"

"No," said Dorothy. "It was all so magical. Everything was big and bright and colourful, like a dream come true. You have to remember I came from a small farm in the back of beyond. Kansas back then was a cold, desolate place. Massive grey prairies stretched away on every side, and there wasn't a tree to be seen anywhere. Our nearest neighbours were hours away. I had no one to talk to, and no one to play with; apart from Toto, of course."

She smiled at the dog in his basket, and Toto wagged his tail as he heard his name mentioned.

"The fierce sun had baked the land into a parched grey vista for as far as the eye could see, with long, jagged cracks running through it. What grass there was, wasn't green, because the heat had burned the tops of the long blades until they were as grey as everything else. Even the paint on the farmhouse's walls had blistered away, until they were grey too. It was like living in a black and white world."

"And your family?" said Arthur.

"I was so young when my parents died that I can barely remember them. I was sent to live with my only remaining relatives, who took me in as a duty. Uncle Henry and Aunt Em didn't really know what to do with a child, except as another pair of hands that could help around the farm. The constant heat and the endless back-breaking work had beaten them both down. Aunt Em seemed as grey and hopeless as the land around her. Uncle Henry never smiled, and worked the land from morning till night. He had no idea what joy was. I think they both cared for me as much as they could. They just never had the time to show it."

"What did they think of your amazing adventure, and the great success that followed your return?" asked Arthur.

"I think they were proud," said Dorothy. "Though they never did understand about Oz. They both left this world some years back."

Arthur nodded slowly, and decided it was time for something a little more probing.

"When you arrived in Oz, the first thing you were told was that you'd just killed someone. How did that make you feel?"

Dorothy just looked at him, as if to say *I don't do ambushes*.

"I didn't kill the Wicked Witch of the East. My house fell on her. What kind of person is too dumb to get out from under a falling house? I can't take any credit for her death, though when I discovered some of the appalling things she'd done, I almost wish I could."

"So Oz wasn't all sweetness and light?" said Arthur.

"Of course not," replied Dorothy. "There was good and there was evil, just like everywhere else; but at least in Oz they were right out in the open, where everyone could see them. Motives were always clear and actions were always straightforward, so everyone always knew where they were." She smiled briefly again. "Not at all like here."

There was a sudden loud explosion from somewhere at the base of the building. Arthur almost jumped out of his skin, his shorthand pad and pencil flying through the air; but Dorothy remained calm and composed, almost as though she'd been expecting it. Even Toto only raised his head a little, before lowering it onto his paws again.

"What the hell was that?" Arthur exclaimed.

"It would appear my building is under attack," said Dorothy.

"All of it?" said Arthur.

"This entire building is given over to the Oz Foundation," said Dorothy. "Everyone who works here is a part of it."

"So this isn't just aimed at you?" said Arthur.

Dorothy shrugged. "There are powers and forces in the world that would celebrate my death, and the destruction of my foundation. Let's see what's going on downstairs, shall we?"

She gestured at the huge window, and it flickered briefly before showing a detailed view of the lobby. Arthur immediately became so fascinated by what was happening that he forgot all about how he was seeing it. The entire lobby was full of chaos and mayhem. Some great explosion had blasted the front door right off its hinges, and left it lying scorched but intact on the floor. A small army of winged demons, like gargoyles from some cathedral, had invaded the lobby, all of them armed with machine guns, and they were firing at anything that moved and many things that didn't. Clouds of dark smoke left over from the explosion drifted lazily on the air, as though uncertain as to what else was required of them. And a tall woman dressed in black leathers, with a gaunt, wrinkled face, a single blazing eye and a black eye-patch, came striding through the lobby. Grinning a grin with absolutely no humour in it.

The winged demons bowed their heads to her as she passed, and then returned to their assault. The lobby walls were already riddled with bullet-holes, and several small fires had broken out. The demons were twisted, ape-like creatures, with massive batwings spreading from their hunched backs. They leaped and soared across the lobby, bouncing off the walls and hitting the ceiling and falling back again, so they could find new ways to attack. Their faces were full of malice, and a terrible delight in destruction.

"Mercenaries," Dorothy said flatly. "The dregs of Oz. Happy to be paid to go where the killing is."

"Those things come from the wonderful world of Oz?" said Arthur, his voice rising just a little.

"I told you there was evil as well as good," said Dorothy. "The only difference is that in Oz, you can tell which is which just by looking at them."

It quickly became clear that the demons were facing stiff opposition from a much smaller army, consisting of three very determined individuals. The doorman, unharmed by the explosion but clearly outraged by the loss of his door, was now wearing a suit of shining armour, that easily deflected any bullet which came its way. He also carried a large and brutal axe, which he slammed into one winged demon after another. Bones shattered and blood flew under the heavy impacts, and the demons fell like wheat under a scythe. More of them flew at the armoured doorman, from every direction at once, but he just hacked them out of mid-air and sent them crashing to the floor in bloody ruins. One demon dropped from the ceiling to land right in front of the armoured man, and opened fire on him at point blank range, but the bullets just ricocheted back and cut the demon down.

The receptionist was now a scarecrow dressed in a shabby old suit of faded blue, complete with a small stuffed sack for a head with the features painted on, topped by a pointed blue hat. As Arthur watched, the scarecrow's smirk slowly spread, tearing open the cloth. It was a very unpleasant smirk. The shabby figure vaulted over the reception desk and threw himself at the nearest demons. He clubbed them down with vicious force, breaking necks and smashing heads, and he couldn't wait to get to the next one. The nearest demons didn't even pause for their fellow mercenaries to get out of the way; they all just opened fire on the scarecrow with their machine guns. He stood his ground with his cloth fists planted on his hips, and didn't even flinch as the bullets tore through him. He took no damage and felt no pain, because after all he was only cloth and stuffing. He laughed out loud, a terrible mocking sound, and waded into the demons before him. He slapped the machine guns out of their hands, punched their heads clean off their shoulders, and tore apart any who didn't back away fast enough. The scarecrow stormed on through the lobby, an unstoppable force with inhuman strength.

Leon, the head of security, had become a huge and terrible lion. He raged among the demons, tearing them apart with his vicious claws and crushing them in his powerful jaws. He roared fiercely as he cut a bloody path through the demons, and when they flapped desperately into the air to avoid him he just leaped after them, and bore them to the ground to savage them. The demons shot him again and again, and he didn't even notice.

The last of the winged demons leaped and soared around the lobby, firing their weapons constantly and trying to keep out of reach, but the three defenders just grabbed them in mid-air and broke their backs over their knees. Sometimes they picked up dead demons to throw them at the living, smashing them flat against the bullet-holed walls. Dead bodies piled up across the lobby, but the winged demons kept on fighting until there was not a single one left *to* fight.

They were demons, and mercenaries. It was all they knew.

The woman in black walked unscathed through all the violence, not even deigning to notice it. Blood and death surrounded her but she walked on, untouched and uncaring. The three defenders did their best to get to her, but there were always winged demons in their way, buying the woman in black enough time to get to the elevator at the rear of the lobby. The view from the transformed window moved in to concentrate on the woman's face, and she allowed herself another humourless grin; as though she knew she was being watched. The woman in black hit the button for the top floor, and the elevator doors closed on the awful grin. The window was suddenly just a window again. Arthur looked at Dorothy.

"I know who they are," he said slowly. "The three in the lobby. The Tin Woodman, the Scarecrow, and the Lion."

"I told you they came through changed," said Dorothy.

"At least they killed all the winged things," said Arthur.

"Oh, I've no doubt there will be more," Dorothy assured him. "To keep my friends occupied, while our visitor has words with me. But my friends will do all that's necessary to hold off the mercenaries and make sure none of them get any further into the building, to hurt the people who work here."

"Who was that woman leading them?" asked Arthur.

Dorothy raised an eyebrow. "You didn't recognise her?"

"Never seen her before in my life!" said Arthur. "How could you ever forget someone like that?"

"Not easily," said Dorothy. "She is the secret ruler of this world. The power behind all the forces that oppose the foundation. Because she likes the way things are. The death and the hunger and the suffering. She is the Wicked Witch of the West, come out into the open at last. She must have realised how much ground she's lost to the foundation, and all its good works. So she's come to attack me personally. For her, it was always personal." She looked calmly at Arthur. "She'll arrive soon. Which means, it's time for you to know why you're really here."

"I'm here to interview you," said Arthur. "My editor…"

"Hush," said Dorothy. "I chose your newspaper because you worked there. I promised your editor an exclusive interview, and he all but bit my hand off taking the bait." She smiled warmly at the reporter. "I said I'd tell you things I never told anyone else. And I will. It's time for you to remember who you are."

Dorothy rose to her feet and came out from behind the desk. Arthur stood up to face her. She reached out and took both his hands in hers, and Arthur was so confused he let her. Suddenly it seemed to him that he did know her, had always known her, but had somehow forgotten until now. Dorothy looked on him kindly.

"It's so good to see you again, my dear Wizard."

The word hammered through his head like the pealing of a great bell. He rocked on his feet, and clung to her hands as though only they could keep him upright.

"What are you talking about?" he said hoarsely. "You mean, like the Wizard you met in Oz? But he was just a cheat and a liar… And anyway, he was an old man when you met him as a child. God knows how old he'd be now, if he was even still alive!"

"I told you everyone comes back changed from Oz," said Dorothy. "Try to remember. When you flew your balloon back to Omaha, you reappeared in exactly the same location you left from; but many years had passed since then. There were tall buildings on what had once been an open plain, and you flew right into one. Your balloon crashed to the ground, and you were badly injured. You lost all memory of who and what you used to be. But your trip back from Oz had rejuvenated you, made you young again, and your new vitality allowed you to recover. You made a new life for yourself, as a newspaper reporter."

She smiled, and shook her head. "Just more of the same old humbug."

"That's why the three in the lobby seemed to know me," Arthur said slowly. "Even your dog recognised me."

"Do you remember who you were, now?" said Dorothy. "Do you remember *me*?"

Arthur slowly withdrew his hands from hers. He was standing firmly now, a restored strength rushing through him.

"Of course I know you, Dorothy. Oh, my dear, look how you've grown. And what you've grown into. I am so proud of everything you've achieved…"

Dorothy beamed. "You haven't seen anything yet."

"How could I have forgotten so much?" said Arthur.

"You don't think your crash was an accident, do you?" said Dorothy.

"Of course it wasn't," said a cold, amused voice from the elevator doors. "I never leave anything to chance."

Dorothy and Arthur turned to look at the woman in black as she strolled calmly across the office to join them. There was a power in her, and a deadly grace, like one of the awful bird-eating spiders of the Amazon rainforest, given human shape and form.

"It took a lot of planning, to take the Great and Terrible Wizard of Oz off the playing field," said the Wicked Witch of the West. "To make him a powerless nobody, just like everyone else. But then, I never did believe in competition. That's why I distracted my sister in the East at just the right moment, so she'd never see the house coming…"

She stopped, to study Dorothy coldly with her single dark eye. "Did you really think I'd let you threaten me, little girl? As long as you were throwing your money away on good works I didn't care; but I finally discovered what you've really been up to. Someone in your employ talked. Someone always talks, eventually. You've been very clever, I'll give you that; slowly and subtly setting your plans in motion, building up your foundation until it was strong enough to challenge my hold on this world. But I never give up anything that's mine."

Arthur looked at Dorothy. "What is she talking about?"

"Why would I leave the wonderful world of Oz, for a grey land and a loveless family?" said Dorothy. "I chose to come back, so I could find a way for everyone to go to Oz. So humanity could leave this cold, sad place, for a better world."

"But I like it just the way it is," said the Witch. She sneered condescendingly at Dorothy, ignoring Arthur. "Did you really think you could destroy a powerful witch like me with a bucket of water that just happened to be standing around? I used it to make myself invisible, so I could cling to your back like an unfelt stowaway when you returned here. Because I felt in need of a new world to conquer."

"I always wondered," said Dorothy. "Why do you have an eyepatch?"

The Witch shrugged. "I traded the eye for power."

"Like Odin?" said Arthur.

"Just like Odin," answered the Witch.

"You should have asked for wisdom," said Dorothy.

"You can't stop me!" blazed the Witch. "I draw strength from the suffering of this world, and I will not have that interrupted. All the corrupt leaders of this realm bow down to me, and carry me on their shoulders, as long as I keep them in power. Everything and everyone in this world is my property now. Did you really think I'd allow you to steal from me, little girl?"

"You don't have a choice," said Dorothy.

"Because you still have the silver shoes?" said the Witch, grinning unpleasantly. "I've spent years accumulating enough power to defy their influence."

"I know," said Dorothy. She turned to Arthur. "And that is why you are here. Someone in the Witch's employ told me she'd be launching her attack today; because someone always sees the light, eventually." She smiled on Arthur. "That's why I summoned you here, old friend. This is your moment. What are you going to do?"

Arthur looked steadily at the Witch. "You stole my

memories, stole my past, stole everything I could have been. But you couldn't steal my power. The best you could make me do was forget I had it. But now, I remember."

"You were never powerful enough to defy me!" screamed the Witch.

"But everyone comes back changed, from Oz," said Arthur.

He thrust out both hands and blasted the Witch with a lifetime's accumulated power; and under its implacable force she withered and melted away until there was nothing left of her. The Wizard turned, to smile at Dorothy.

"How about that? I'm not a humbug any more."

"Welcome back, dear Wizard," said Dorothy.

"Good to be back," said the Wizard. "Is it over now?"

"It's only just beginning," Dorothy informed him. "Let's just take a quick peek at what's happening in the lobby."

The window changed back to show the Tin Woodman, the Scarecrow, and the Lion clearing up the dead. They were being quite cheerful about it. The invasion was over, the winged demons had all been routed, and even the front door had been put back in place. Dorothy dismissed the view with a wave of her hand.

"The moment the Witch died, her power over the mercenaries died too. They only work for money. Which means we're free to get on with our business."

"But what business is that?" asked the Wizard. "What happens now?"

"You see the green door in the wall?" said Dorothy.

They both turned to gaze at it. The Wizard recognised that particular shade of green immediately. It was the same colour as the eyeglasses everyone had to wear when they entered his Emerald City in Oz. The colour spoke to him, and he could feel himself responding on some deep and primal level.

"That door was my gift from Glinda, to bring back with me," said Dorothy. "A door that opens directly onto Oz. The aim of the Oz Foundation has always been to put a green door in everyone's home, in every country. So the whole of humanity can leave this grey world and go to a land where magics and wonders come as standard, and good things happen every day."

The Wizard shook his head slowly. "I'm not sure that dumping all the quarrelling, warring people of Earth on a magical land is a good idea. The people of Oz wouldn't know what hit them!"

"Everyone will change, when they go to Oz," said Dorothy. "I was just a small girl when I left, and look at all the things I did. Oz was where I learned how to help people, and why it was important. The people of Earth will become better people in Oz, and make wonderful new lives for themselves."

"But there's no room for that many people in Oz!" said the Wizard.

"Oz is a world, not a land," Dorothy said patiently. "And because it's magical, it can expand to become big enough to contain everyone."

Toto jumped out of his basket and scurried over to lean heavily against the Wizard's leg, as though to assure him that everything would be all right. The Wizard reached down absently to pat his head.

"Oz is waiting, to help all the people of Earth be free of

pain and misery at last," said Dorothy. "In a world where everyone's dreams can come true, every hurt can be healed, and every heart comforted."

She gestured at the green door in the wall and it swung slowly open to reveal a magnificent view of the wonderful land beyond. And it was so much more colourful and magical than any fiction could ever suggest. Dorothy took the Wizard by his hand.

"Come along, old friend. It's time for us to go home."

# ROSE AND EMERALD

**CAITLIN ROZAKIS**

"I thought I had beaten the Wicked Witch then, and I worked harder than ever; but I little knew how cruel my enemy could be. She thought of a new way to kill my love for the beautiful Munchkin maiden, and made my axe slip again, so that it cut right through my body, splitting me into two halves. Once more the tinsmith came to my help and made me a body of tin, fastening my tin arms and legs and head to it, by means of joints, so that I could move around as well as ever. But, alas! I had now no heart, so that I lost all my love for the Munchkin girl, and did not care whether I married her or not. I suppose she is still living with the old woman, waiting for me to come after her."

– ***THE WONDERFUL WIZARD OF OZ***, **L. FRANK BAUM**

Rose lived in a great wood in Munchkinland, with an old woman who always said that, while she was not Rose's mother, Rose must treat her with all the devotion she would have treated her own dear Mama. Since Rose could not remember her own dear Mama, she did her best to pretend, for it seemed to her a terribly shameful thing to say that she did not love the old woman who stood in her mother's place.

The old woman had given her a pair of spectacles, quite the finest thing that Rose had ever seen, let alone owned. They were golden all around the rims, and the lenses were made of a lovely rose-colored glass, just like her name.

"You must never take them off, my dear," said the old woman. "For they are the key to your happiness. You will find that the world is much sadder and you much sorrier without them."

So Rose kept them on, day and night, sleeping carefully on her back so as not to bend or break them. She only took them off once a year, when the tinker came by to adjust them to fit her growing head. The world without her rose-colored glasses was indeed a much sadder place. When she wore her spectacles, she could manage to see the bright side of everything. Even cooking and cleaning and caring for an unpleasant woman she only pretended to love.

Once, she thought she did find out what it was to love and be loved. A sweet young Munchkin, a woodman by trade, stumbled into the clearing where Rose lived with the old woman. He looked at the dilapidated cottage, which was as homey as Rose could make it despite its occasional tendency to leak rain through the roof. He made a face.

Despite the look of disgust, to Rose's eyes, he was very much the handsomest thing she had ever seen. She fell in love immediately. He seemed rather taken with her, as well, coming by every day despite the old woman's complaints.

He helped her with her chores so she wouldn't fall behind (for the old woman was shockingly lazy and would not lift a finger to cook or clean for herself).

"You are the most beautiful girl in Munchkinland," the Woodman said to her one day. "But why do you wear those spectacles?"

Rose touched the bridge with one finger, surprised, as she had forgotten she was even wearing them. "Why, they help me see the world the way I would like it to be. Through my rose-colored glasses, everything is lovely and arranged for the best."

"But what if things are not arranged for the best?" he asked, careful not to look at the house or the old woman waiting querulously inside.

"Then there's not much I can do about it, so I'd rather not know," she said firmly. For she understood perfectly well that, if the old woman had not taken her in, there were not many places a respectable young woman with no family and no prospects could go.

At that, he looked distressed. A few days later, he came to her with a plan. He promised her that as soon as he had enough money to build her a better house, he would whisk her away to live with him.

She dreamed at night of a cottage of her own, in shades of purple and peach and clean, clean white.

But not long after, he had a terrible accident. While chopping wood in the forest, he slipped and cut off his left leg. The local tinsmith replaced it with a shiny metal one, nearly as good as the first and a lovely silver-rose shade through her glasses. But shortly thereafter, he slipped again, and again, and again.

After he'd had all four limbs replaced, he stopped coming by the clearing.

"Well," said the old woman with an air of satisfaction, "I suppose he was not so loving after all. And would you have wanted a life armed with an oil can, anyway? It was all for the best."

"It's always all for the best," Rose agreed sadly. She looked at the empty clearing through her glasses, and they showed how much more room there was without a third person bumbling about.

"Now fetch me my supper," ordered the old woman.

It was months later that, while tidying the never-ending piles of refuse the old woman seemed to generate, that she found the contract with the Wicked Witch of the East. The old woman had promised her two sheep and a cow if the witch could prevent the marriage between the girl and the Woodman.

"Oh!" said Rose, suddenly realizing that there lay a fine line between clumsiness and curse. Two legs and two arms gone, and the Woodman had still kept coming back for her. The only thing left to be chopped off that she could think of (for she was a good girl, and the old woman preferred to keep her innocent) was the head. No wonder her Woodman had never returned! She cried bitter tears, which sparkled in the sun like rose-colored quartz. Yet, she still had nowhere better to go. She wiped her tears determinedly and looked around at the cottage, noting the pretty pink daisies she had picked in their pretty pink cup, the jug of sweet rosy milk from the farmer down the road, the salmon-colored curtains she'd embroidered herself, the blush-colored jasmine she'd trained over the window outside. It was still the best she could hope for, so it was still all for the best.

> "While I was in love I was the happiest man on earth; but no one can love who has not a heart, and so I am resolved to ask Oz to give me one. If he does, I will go back to the Munchkin maiden and marry her."
>
> – ***THE WONDERFUL WIZARD OF OZ***, L. FRANK BAUM

News traveled fast in Oz, when the birds in the air and the mice in the fields could scamper along bearing tidings.

When the old woman heard of the fate of the Wicked Witch of the West, she stamped her feet in terrible frustration. "You mean that was all it would have taken to kill her? Some soapy water? Rose, you could have ended her yourself and then I might have had an entire army of flying monkeys at my beck and call!"

The old woman was so angry at the unfairness of the world that she died of apoplexy right there on the spot.

Rose, who had looked at their little cottage in the woods and thought that surely it was the best possible place to live, had not understood the old woman's wrath. But she knew she should be sorry that the old woman who stood in place of her mother had died. So she shed a dutiful tear and dug a large hole and placed a rose on the old woman's grave.

"I cannot help but think that this is the best of all possible outcomes," she said to the rose and the corpse below. "And surely you would have wanted me to think that, since you gave me the glasses to begin with. I did not appreciate your kindness!"

Then she shed another tear, this one more heartfelt.

The part of the story that had most interested Rose, though, of course, was that of the Tin Woodman who went to the Emerald City in search of a heart.

"No wonder he forgot about me," she told herself. "But then, it's for the best – as long as the old woman lived, I could never have left. But now I am free, and he has a heart once more, and now he will come back and marry me."

So she waited.

And waited.

And waited.

And then finally, one day, decided that even in the best of worlds, someone still needed to clean the privy and compost the kitchen scraps, and if she wanted her happy ending, she would need to find it herself.

"After all," she said, "he's been under one curse already. What if he fell afoul of another one?"

So she packed a rucksack with a sensible array of supplies, and headed down the Yellow Brick Road.

"'I am the Guardian of the Gates, and since you demand to see the Great Oz I must take you to his Palace. But first you must put on the spectacles."

"Why?" asked Dorothy.

"Because if you did not wear spectacles the brightness and glory of the Emerald City would blind you. Even those who live in the City must wear spectacles night and day. They are all locked on, for Oz so ordered it when the City was first built, and I have the only key that will unlock them."

He opened the big box, and Dorothy saw that it was filled with spectacles of every size and shape. All of them had green glasses in them.'

– *THE WONDERFUL WIZARD OF OZ*, L. FRANK BAUM

When Rose arrived at the gates of the Emerald City, there was some very nasty business about her glasses.

It was the last in a series of misadventures that had tried even the ever-optimistic Rose's patience. There had been some fantastically unpleasant crows and far too many monsters and a Lion who had shouted and strutted about most imperiously. It had been hard to take him seriously, as he paused halfway through his roaring to drink from a bottle he hid in his mane. The only thing that had kept her going was an encounter with some talking mice on the edge of a field of poppies, who had said they'd seen her beloved Woodman and that he indeed had been the kindest and gentlest of men despite his metal body.

"I knew it!" she'd cried, and had chosen not to wonder how he could be so kind when he at that point still had no heart and thus had not come back to her. She had skirted the field, going miles out of her way to do so, for anyone sensible knew better than to venture across a field of poppies, no matter how pretty the blossoms or urgent the need.

But upon reaching the City of Emeralds, tired and footsore and more than ready for a hot meal and a bath, she had been barred at the gate.

"But I can't wear the green spectacles," she protested. "They won't fit on my nose."

"No one may enter the city without them," said the officious little man. "By order of the Great and Powerful Oz."

"But I already have spectacles to protect me," she said, tapping the rose-colored glasses. "And besides, I thought the Wizard no longer ruled here?"

The Guardian flinched. "We… are under new leadership, yes."

After some argument, she managed to secure both permission to continue to wear her own pink spectacles instead of the emerald ones, as well as an invitation to attend the court of the Scarecrow, who apparently now ruled the city. She had tried pleading sweetly, and when that didn't work, had done her best impression of the old woman. She felt faintly disturbed at its effectiveness.

When she stepped into the city, though, she was more confused than anything else. She knew perfectly well what green looked like through her glasses – she'd been seeing the resulting brownish-gray in the forest around her for her entire life. To her surprise, though, the Emerald City did not live up to its name in the slightest. It was, instead, the purest shade of pink. Rose, in fact.

She had spent her entire life wearing colored lenses except for once a year, and had had more than enough practice in understanding how they affected the world. Despite its name, the Emerald City could not have been green in the slightest. And if the city had truly been made up of every shade of pink in existence, seeing it through rose-colored spectacles would have made it even lovelier, but a much deeper set of pinks.

"Oh," she said, looking at everyone around her wearing their emerald spectacles. "I suppose that explains that."

She was marveling at a fountain constructed of the finest pink marble (almost certainly white) when she bumped into someone.

"I beg your pardon!" the girl said, her pretty blush an even deeper pink to Rose's eyes. She was about Rose's age, with rose-gold hair and eyes the brownish-gray color that suggested they were a sparkling green even without the help of green glass.

"Let me make it up to you," Rose said impulsively, for it was the first time she'd spoken to someone her own age since the Woodman had left. "Can I buy you dinner?"

'The next morning Dorothy kissed the pretty green girl goodbye, and they all shook hands with the soldier with the green whiskers, who had walked with them as far as the gate. When the Guardian of the Gate saw them again he wondered greatly that they could leave the beautiful City to get into new trouble. But he at once unlocked their

> spectacles, which he put back into the green box, and gave them many good wishes to carry with them.'
>
> – *THE WONDERFUL WIZARD OF OZ*, L. FRANK BAUM

Tourmaline, for that was the name of the girl with the green eyes, warned her that the Scarecrow had taken his job a bit too much to heart.

They had stayed up too late drinking wine (which Rose saw as a rosé and Tourmaline insisted was light green, so it must have been the palest of whites) and Rose had ended up sleeping on Tourmaline's floor on a rug so plush her hand sank into it. They had agreed on so many things, from the superiority of pears to apples, to the importance of braiding one's hair properly before bed, to (much later at night and deeper into the wine bottle) their quiet fears that their devotion to their respective tasks might have cost them their chances at love. But no matter how hard Rose tried, she could not get Tourmaline to understand that the majority of her beloved Emerald City was, in fact, white. The spectacles that had been locked onto her head since birth included cunning hinges that allowed them to be adjusted without being removed.

"You've never seen any other colors?" Rose asked.

"Well, of course, the outside world has a great many colors," Tourmaline said primly. "But none so pleasing as the many shades of the Emerald City. But you say you wear yours even outside the City! Surely the outer world is not so brilliant?"

"Quite the opposite. I wear them because I'd prefer the world to be *more* brilliant," Rose retorted.

Rather than argue, they'd moved on to what Rose might expect from her audience.

"Just don't contradict him," Tourmaline said, looking worried. "Since the Good Witch Dorothy left, he is the smartest man in all of Oz and cannot bear to be contradicted."

"You knew her? Dorothy?"

Tourmaline's gaze softened as she looked up at the spires above them. "She was the cleverest girl I ever met. I'd rather hoped she would stay. But there was already a Good Witch in the North and the South, and anyway, I suppose her people must have missed her terribly. It's not like she would have wanted friendship with a maid like me, for all that she condescended to allow me to help her dress."

"It's surely all for the best," said Rose, eager to comfort her new friend. "Because if she had gone North or South, you still would have had to leave your beloved Emerald City to follow her."

But this did not seem like a new thought to Tourmaline, whose gaze turned far away.

"I suppose nowhere is as green as the Emerald City," she said wistfully.

Rose thought of the forests and fields she had traveled through. "Perhaps not *as* green," she said diplomatically. She couldn't help adding, "But there is plenty of green in the world, and other colors besides."

The next day, she hugged her new friend. "I'll make sure to stop by before I leave."

"I wish you could stay," Tourmaline admitted.

"Maybe we'll come back, the Woodman and I," Rose said. "After all, the Scarecrow was one of his closest friends. After I find him, maybe we'll find a pretty green house here."

"We haven't any wood," Tourmaline said.

"Nor cottages, but neither of us has to be defined by what we started out as," Rose said. Now that she had left the leaky roof and the smoky chimney and the familiarity of the old woman's scolding, she found it easier to picture a number of different lives that had never seemed possible before. Why, if one could face down a lion, however cowardly, one might do anything. "We'll find new ways of living, together. Perhaps the Scarecrow will make a position for him."

The Scarecrow was both very much like what she had expected and not at all so. Everyone had made much of his intelligence, so she'd thought he of all people would refuse to wear the green glasses. But his were held on, since he had no ears, with neat, tight stitches straight into the fabric of his head.

"And you are?" he asked, smiling widely. This might not have been to his credit, though, since his smile had been painted on.

"I'm Rose," she said, for surely her Woodman had spoken of her, at least after receiving his new heart. But when the Scarecrow's painted-on eyes continued to look blank, she realized that Rose was not so uncommon a name. She added, "From Munchkinland."

He cocked his head politely, still no sign of recognition.

"I'm looking for my dear Woodman?" she added, a bit desperate.

"Oh! You're that Munchkin girl!" the Scarecrow exclaimed. "Yes, he told us all about you. I apologize, my dear, I don't think he ever mentioned your name."

Of course he wouldn't, she decided. He'd have been protecting her in a world full of Wicked Witches.

The Scarecrow continued, "So you didn't want to live with the Winkies, then?"

"The Winkies?" she repeated, confused. She hated sounding like a fool in front of someone so well-known for his intelligence. Surely, he would scorn her as unworthy of his friend if he learned how little she knew of this world. All she could remember about the Winkies was that they lived under the rule of the Wicked Witch of the West, much as the Munchkins had suffered beneath the Wicked Witch of the East. She had no idea what the Scarecrow thought they had to do with her.

But instead, he seemed pleased. "Why, yes! They're a lovely people, now that the Witch is dead."

Before she could ask why they were talking about the Winkies, he launched into a history of their people: how the Winkie Country was not so different from her own Munchkinland, how they had first fallen under the Witch's dominion, and eventually, how he and the rest of Dorothy's companions had heroically freed them. He became terribly excited. He even brought out maps.

"So you see, my dear girl, when the Tin Woodman asked you to join him, you should have had no reservations, despite it being a land far away from yours, for they are very much nearly the same thing."

"But," she finally had the courage to insert a word or two into the great deluge, "he never asked me to join him."

"Nonsense!" the Scarecrow insisted firmly. "He always said that he wanted a heart so he would wish to marry you once more, and he received a heart from the Wizard, therefore he must have asked you to marry him. It's all perfectly logical, quid pro quo and habeas corpus. That's smart person language, by the way, for 'therefore' and 'as proven.' You must simply have misunderstood. It's understandable, if regrettable, as not everyone is as smart as I am, so you should not feel in the least bit bad. My learned opinion is that now you understand properly, the only reasonable thing to do is go to Winkie Country and let him know that I've explained everything and you're ready to join him."

With that, Rose found herself ushered out before she could even explain that she could not possibly have misunderstood as she had not so much as seen her Woodman for years. She found herself standing on the brilliantly sparkling street, faintly bewildered and holding an 'I had my problem solved by the Scarecrow today!' pin she'd been handed on the way out.

Somewhat dazed, she wandered back to Tourmaline's rooms to say goodbye. Tourmaline greeted her, eyes shining. "You have a pin!"

"I suppose he did solve my problem," Rose said slowly. "For I know where my Woodman is."

Tourmaline insisted that Rose tell her the entire story, which she did. As it unfurled, Rose's heart grew lighter, though Tourmaline's frown grew deeper.

"But he didn't solve your problem at all!" Tourmaline protested at the end. "Why didn't the Tin Woodman come back to you, if that's why he wanted a heart in the first place?"

"It doesn't matter," Rose said. It had come out all right, in the end. "I know where he is now and I can go to him!"

"It doesn't seem right to me," the other girl said slowly. "And Winkie Country is awfully far away, when you aren't being carried by flying monkeys."

"It's all for the best," Rose insisted. "This way, by the time I reach him, I'll understand his troubles and the Winkies themselves, and so we'll be even better suited for each other."

"But will he understand yours?" Tourmaline asked.

Rose knew her own troubles were small – all she'd ever known was a tiny clearing and travel across an Oz no longer plagued by Wicked Witches. Still, it was going to be a wearisomely long journey, and as one more day would scarcely change the outcome, she allowed Tourmaline to convince her to stay the night and set out fresh in the morning. Tourmaline insisted that she take the bed this time, since it had been ages since she'd slept in a proper one and might be even longer before she did so again.

To her surprise, Rose awoke to find that Tourmaline had assembled a pack of her own while she'd slept.

"I can't send you off on such a lonesome journey by yourself," Tourmaline said, fiddling with the strap of her bag and refusing to meet Rose's eye. "I've never been out of the Emerald City, and I think I may be ready to see some of these new colors you speak of. And perhaps how other places are ruled."

'They thanked him and bade him goodbye, and turned toward the West, walking over fields of soft grass dotted here and there with daisies and buttercups. Dorothy still wore the pretty silk dress she had put on in the palace, but now, to her surprise, she found it was no longer green, but pure white. The ribbon around Toto's neck had also lost its green color and was as white as Dorothy's dress.'

– ***THE WONDERFUL WIZARD OF OZ***, L. FRANK BAUM

"Oh!" Tourmaline said, when the Guardian unlocked her spectacles and she looked out over an emerald meadow sprinkled with gold and white under a brilliant blue sky. "How very queer all the colors are! Even the sky is strange outside the city!"

Rose thought it best if she did not again bring up the argument regarding the spectacles and the actual color of Tourmaline's home. Instead, she chattered about such unchallenging topics as raisin buns and whether it would rain later in the evening while Tourmaline adjusted.

"Oh!" her friend said again, an hour or two later. She held out her hands, alarmed. "My skin! What is happening to me, are the trees giving me a rash?"

Now Rose had quite the dilemma. To explain about the glasses would be terribly upsetting, and she did not know if Tourmaline would even believe her. But not to explain would leave poor Tourmaline thinking that she was taking very ill indeed!

"Tourmaline," Rose said cautiously, aware that even this much would betray something of what she thought. "Are you the kind of person who prefers the truth even if painful, or to stay comfortable?"

"In a lie, you mean?" Tourmaline looked troubled. "I think you are about to tell me something I shall be distressed to hear, and yet I would prefer to know. Tell me true – am I dying?"

"You're not dying, you're fine." Rose rushed to comfort her. And then, more slowly, she reminded Tourmaline of their earlier argument about the effect of the spectacles.

Tourmaline looked down at her delicate, white hands in wonder and a little alarm. "I've always been this color? I thought I was the most beautiful shade of new-leaf green!"

Rose tried to reassure her that she was still ever so beautiful, at least to Rose. Tourmaline looked at her as well, startled. "Oh! And I spent so much time staring at the sky and the flowers, I just realized – you're not green, either! You're the same color as that pretty tree trunk over there!"

And with that, she burst into tears.

Rose tried her best not to be hurt, as surely it was good that Tourmaline was now seeing the true colors of things, but it was hard to have someone exclaim that you didn't look like they thought you did and then sob. But really, the Wizard had much to answer for. It was one thing to convince a city worth of people that their white marble surroundings were emerald, and another thing entirely to have them believing people's skin could be green!

"I'm sorry," Tourmaline hiccupped. "It's not you, you're lovely. It's just so much to realize you've been believing things that weren't true all your life."

Rose patted her hand. "I should have thought of a better way to tell you."

"But the Scarecrow!" Tourmaline said. "He'd lived all his life before outside of Oz, and he's supposed to be so smart. Why didn't he tell us?"

"I'm sure it was for the best," Rose said.

"You keep saying that, and yet you refused to wear the green spectacles at all," Tourmaline said, her eyebrows pinching together. "So you didn't think *that* was for the best."

Tourmaline looked like she was going to go on, but Rose realized that without conscious thought, her own hand had risen to hold her rose-colored glasses against her face protectively. Her friend lapsed into silence.

They went to sleep early, of mutual accord; or rather, they lay down to sleep. It was a long time before Rose managed to drift off and Tourmaline's shallow breathing made her think the other girl had trouble sleeping as well.

In the morning, again by mutual accord, they said nothing of the previous night's discussion. Instead, they spoke of the trees and rocks and rivers they passed, and gave pleasant greetings to everyone they saw on the road, until by afternoon things felt almost normal again.

Days of walking passed, not entirely without incident. There were monsters and hazards and treacherous plants. But there was also glorious scenery and unexpected kindnesses. Tourmaline proved to be clever and brave, with an occasional wicked sense of humor. Rose began to wonder how she had ever managed to sleep without the warmth of her friend by her side. Rose had never been so grateful for an uneven paving stone in all her life.

They crossed into Winkie Country, where golden fields rolled on seemingly forever, and everyone wore shades of yellow. After so many days in the forest and wilderness, Tourmaline looked at the uniformity of color with dismay.

"Were we really so unimaginative?" she asked, making sure no Winkie was in earshot.

"Munchkins are rather over-partial to blue," Rose said, shrugging. She hadn't bothered, since blue was a terribly difficult color to maintain in the woods on your own.

"I'm glad I know," Tourmaline said shortly. "And I think it's hateful that the Scarecrow never bothered to tell us. I think, if your woodman is happy here, maybe I'll just stay in Winkie Country with you. After all, my hair is the right color even without spectacles."

Rose's heart sang and she squeezed her friend's hand in joy. Against her skin, Tourmaline's palm burned, but a pleasant heat. She reached over to straighten Tourmaline's braid so they would both look their best now that they were back in settled territory. For one brief moment, a traitorous thought flashed across her mind that maybe there might be more than one best version of 'all for the best.' She reminded herself firmly of how much she loved her Woodman – after all, she'd come so very far for him and what else was love? – and how lovely it would be for her dear *friend* Tourmaline to live in a cottage next door to them. Perhaps with a fine Winkie husband of her own. Rose ignored how her gut twisted at the idea and hurried them on into the village ahead.

The Winkies were hospitable, at least. A bit more hospitable than Rose would have preferred, since she was anxious to get to the capital and start a proper search. She knew the chances of some random family knowing what had become of her beloved was slim, since she understood perfectly well that he had been carried across this stretch of country by flying monkeys and so the charming villagers would have had no chance to meet them.

But Tourmaline had looked with such silent longing at the snug little cottages, shifting on her sore feet, that Rose couldn't bear to say no. So they agreed to stay the night and found themselves quite the local celebrities, since few travelers roamed Oz. The Winkie village laid out an enormous spread of every delicious yellow thing, from creamy corn chowder to crispy fried carp, to bright lemon curd. She and Tourmaline dug in with enthusiasm after weeks of traveler's rations, only pausing to look around when they were too full to move.

The Winkies were, it turned out, the most marvelous tinsmiths in the world, capable of making all sorts of cunning things. Rose would have feigned being impressed in return for such lavish hospitality, but she found she did not need to pretend in the slightest. Candlesticks and tea pots, soup tureens and shoe buckles, even wonderfully clever lanterns with delicate patterns of pinholes that twinkled like the night sky when lit.

"Oh," she said. "Perhaps that's why my Woodman returned here. For if he were injured, surely this is the country where he would most easily find someone to repair him." Which certainly explained why he had not returned to her.

"You know the Tin Woodman?" the Winkies exclaimed.

"Yes! Have you seen him? Was he gravely hurt? Will he come back to me soon?" Rose asked, too eager.

They exchanged looks amongst each other. Finally, one said, "Then you have not heard?"

> 'Turning to the Tin Woodman, she asked, "What will become of you when Dorothy leaves this country?"
>
> He leaned on his axe and thought a moment. Then he said, "The Winkies were very kind to me, and wanted me to rule over them after the Wicked Witch died. I am fond of the Winkies, and if I could get back again to the Country of the West, I should like nothing better than to rule over them forever."'
>
> – ***THE WONDERFUL WIZARD OF OZ***, L. FRANK BAUM

"And after all they'd been through, such a lot of them, I couldn't possibly have let that many people down. Not even for the sake of two people's happiness. It would have been heartless."

The Tin Woodman sat on the tin throne his subjects had built him, his tin crown atop his tin head. They had embellished him thoroughly, every inch swirled with tiny holes and engraved patterns, very like the tin lanterns Rose had admired so much. Her glasses gave all that silvery shine a rosy glow. Surely this was the best place for him, the place he belonged and deserved to be.

"You could have sent a message," she said, holding her voice carefully steady. It wouldn't do to cry. It would be unkind. "I would have come. I *did* come."

She saw the moment the realization flicked across his face. He hadn't thought to send a message; he hadn't thought of her at all. His new heart was full of the Good Witch Dorothy, and the Winkies, and himself. But he was too tenderhearted to break her own heart and admit that he had filled his with enough other things that it had no need for her anymore. He was going to lie. He was going to lie so as not to hurt her feelings, and tell himself that he had done it for her sake. The glasses gave his cheeks a blush she knew could never truly show on tin.

"I'm so sorry," he said, and her heart lifted as she realized she'd misjudged him and that the rosy view of the world she preferred was correct after all. An apology! "It must have gone astray. Oz is full of hazards, as you well know."

The throne room looked no different, full of rose-colored light. Just because she had preferred rose to emerald made it no more true. Perhaps choosing a painful truth would have been less painful in the long run. Dully, she wondered how much she had missed, looking for silver linings instead of coming out of the rain like a sensible person.

"But now you're here." He had continued talking. "And I can have the Winkies make you a throne of your own. They'd like that, they love to serve… where are you going?"

For her feet had turned, apparently on their own. They were walking her out of the shiny tin throne room, leaving puzzled Winkies whispering behind her.

Tourmaline had waited for her outside. "How did it go? Are we staying?"

Rose just kept walking.

"Rose? Rose, are you all right?"

She strode out the doors of the tower and looked down on the golden waves of wheat. The rose-colored glasses brought them into focus; without them, the grain would be uniformly yellow, but the rose tint gave them a shimmering quality that made them even more beautiful. It was all for the best, surely? If he'd married her back in Munchkinland, she would have never known how selfish he was. She would have stayed in the clearing, or a clearing very much like it, and she never would have seen the Emerald City or the forest or Winkie Country. Even if the Emerald City had truly been white and the forest had been full of cowardly monsters and the Winkies had been so enticing in their helplessness that a simple maiden in need of rescue could hardly compete.

She rubbed at the tears beneath her spectacles, careful not to smudge the glass.

"Do you want to talk about it?" Tourmaline asked quietly.

"Everyone is so ready to invite someone to think for them," Rose said angrily. "At least the animals are ruled by one of their own, for all that his courage comes out of a bottle. But the Winkies couldn't face the idea of life without a tyrant telling them what to do."

She stopped short, realizing how close she'd come to insulting her only friend.

But Tourmaline stepped closer to her and twined her fingers with Rose's own. She looked sad. "And in the Emerald City, we were so desperate for someone to replace our wizard, we picked a man whose head was filled with straw." She snorted. "And the wizard turned out to be lying the whole time, anyway."

"Why do people do this?" Rose asked. What would the world look like if she just looked at it? Had it always been this ugly and she just refused to see?

"Because looking truth in the eye and making your own decisions is scary." Tourmaline wasn't looking at her, just staring out over the grain. With her.

"I'm scared," Rose admitted. Staying with the old woman had been terrible. But she'd been so frightened of what it would be like without her. Of what it would say about Rose if she wanted life without her. "What if the world is just too ugly?"

"It is ugly," Tourmaline admitted. "And sometimes I wish I could go back to when I thought everything beautiful was shades of green. But now that I've seen for myself, I would miss gold and blue. And rose."

She turned to Rose and lifted her hands, pausing with her fingers a hairsbreadth from the frames of the spectacles. "Parts of the world are beautiful, too."

"No," Rose said.

Tourmaline's hands fell to her sides, her face only a little.

"No," Rose said again, "it's something one must choose for one's self."

She gently lifted the rose-colored glasses from her face and blinked in the suddenly brighter light. Tourmaline's hair was the same gold as the corn. Her eyes were so green, it hurt.

"Maybe it's all for the best," Tourmaline whispered.

# THE POOR WORKMAN

**LOUISE CAREY**

*It's all here as promised, Your Majesty. When I traded a life of drudgery for a place in your court, I promised you I'd crack every case you sent my way, whether it took an egg spoon or an ice pick. All that this business with Sir Drill required, in the end, was a single question, but I'll let him explain how it happened in his own words. He was around for the whole sorry affair, after all, while I only swung in for the grand finale – as you know I like to do – to sort out the big reveals and set off the fireworks.*

*So. Here it is. The witness statement of Sir Drill:*

None but those who have laboured in the hidden places of the earth, where there are no shadows because there is no light, can truly know what it is to be dazzled after long blackness by a shaft of unexpected sunshine. When it opened upon me, though the beam was no thicker about than a man's waist, it outshone the lamps of my eyes so brightly that I thought at first their glass had been smashed in, and I'd been blinded.

I was sitting in the mine's central cavern when the light broke in, so my next fear was that the mad things in the shaft of the damned above me had somehow come to life again, and it was their frenzied writhing that had opened a passage to the world above. We all feared those demented creatures worse than anything, so I called out for aid in a hoarse voice and set all of the drill bits at the ends of my arms to spinning as fast as they could go. I pointed them up towards the shaft of the damned, to meet anything coming down that way, but I could still see nothing but brilliance.

A low rumble in the tunnel behind told me that Rock Screen and Pick were coming to my rescue. As I backed out of the circle of light, the white sheet in front of my eyes began to fissure at the edges with forks of black lightning. Then I heard something fall out of the shaft to one side of me, and it hit the ground with a soft thump, like an armful of clean laundry dropped onto a shelf. The sound was so different from the skittering limbs and clockwork screams of the mad things that it gave me pause.

Still, I was on my guard: I turned to face the thing and jabbed one of my drills at it, to keep it from coming closer. The other four I spread wide about me, barring its way into the tunnels at my back. The thing leapt away from me, and a voice – soft, too, but with a hard edge underneath it, like water flowing over sharp rocks – said, "Oh, I wouldn't do, if I were you."

I knew then that whatever was speaking to me was sane,

at least, and no monster from the shaft, so I silenced my drills and dropped my arms to my sides. And for the first time since the light crashed in – for the first time in a good while, in fact – I felt hope, a raw, jagged thing that was worse than the fear.

"I'm sorry," I said. "I meant no harm. I was frightened, is all." And then, stumbling over the words, "Did the good doctor send you? Are you here to keep his promise, at long last?"

The rumble behind me grew, and Rock Screen and Pick tore into the central cavern in a crunch of scree and a hiss of hydraulics.

"What's the racket?" Pick asked, but Rock Screen only yelped and threw up her hands to shield what was left of her face. Two of Rock Screen's eyes were lamps, like Pick's and my own, but she had a pair of real, human eyes as well, perched on telescoping metal poles above the network of hoppers, hydraulic presses and sieves that stood in for the rest of her. They were green as emeralds, and they served her well in spying out those precious gems amongst the broken and jumbled rocks that she filtered through her body, but right now they were screwed tight shut. I think the light was even more painful to her than it was to the rest of us.

"A friend," I replied. "I think."

Gradually, the white sheet fissured away into fragments. In the gaps it left, a woman appeared. She was not like any woman I had seen before. Her eyes were silver buttons that glinted almost painfully in the light from the shaft. Her face was of particoloured cloth, all stitched together in a crazy patchwork, and her dress also. Locks of brown yarn, adorned with a gay profusion of ribbons and bows, spilled down her shoulders. Her felted mouth, filled with little pearls for teeth, was shaped in an open and quizzical smile. She squinted at us, raising one cloth hand to her brow as she tried to make out our forms beyond the circle of light. But despite her warm demeanour, we kept our distance for the time being.

She was like us – there could be no doubt of that – but where we had been reforged in a furnace, she looked to have been sewn together by hand. I could not imagine what manner of accident had resulted in her strange transformation, nor why she had been constructed of such flimsy materials.

"Did you lose your body, too?" I asked her, as tenderly as my grinding, metallic voice would allow.

The patchwork woman laughed. Her voice was like the hum of a weaver's shuttle. "I'm as lost as a body can be! But that's easily fixed, if you'll tell me where I am."

"Why, these are the mines beneath the mountain in the Blue Forest," Pick told her. "Did you not mean to come here?"

"I didn't so much as know that here existed, until I stepped foot in it," the patchwoman replied. "I was chasing down a lead in the Blue Forest when I happened upon yon shaft of frozen freaks." She hooked a felt thumb above her head. "It seemed like just the sort of thing I was looking for, so I climbed down, and here I am."

I did not like this light and dancing way of talking about the monsters in the shaft of the damned. With the new light pouring in, I could see them above us more clearly now, their bodies tangled together in the shaft in a crush of twisted limbs. I averted my eyes. Those contorted forms, stiffened into merciful stone, were a constant reminder to us of what the dark could do to a mind unguarded against its terrors. But the patchwoman was a stranger, and a guest in our mine besides, so I let her unseemly levity pass without comment.

In any case, that she seemed to have happened upon us by chance was not encouraging. Pick and Rock Screen must have been entertaining the same hopes as I had, for the one let out an involuntary sigh, and the other kicked the cavern wall with one hydraulic leg.

"You're not here to turn us back, then, as the doctor promised?" Rock Screen asked, the edge of tears creeping into her tone. "He *must* have sent you, for you're just like us – so it had to have been him that fixed you." She made to kick the wall again, but I laid my hand of flesh and blood on her arm of rubber tubing, and she stilled.

"If he has not sent you to relieve us of duty, do you at least carry some message from him?" Pick asked, with renewed optimism.

There was a long silence at that. The patchwoman peered at us with her head on one side. "Okay, someone here is barking up the wrong end of the mineshaft," she said at length, "and I can't tell if it's me. That's the second time you've mentioned this 'good doctor', and I'm only about eighty percent sure I know who he is. If I'm right, I've just come from his house – but I can't pass on a message if I don't know who it's from or for, now, can I?"

She turned a sudden, surreal cartwheel, ending on her hands, with her yarn hair flopping down over her face. Her silver eyes glimmered at us through the strands. "Seems to me we've got this conversation turned all topsy-turvy, so how's this? Enlighten me about who you all are, and how you came to be down here in the dark. Once you've told me *that*, I'll know which of my numerous intelligence reports concerning matters aboveground is the one you'll want to hear about."

I turned to Pick, who raised one of his curved blades in a half shrug. Rock Screen blew out a huff of air from her compression cleaner. We none of us relished rehearsing our misfortunes, which were of a private nature. Besides, what the patchwoman said was nonsense, for how could learning our histories provide her with any message for us that she did not have on her person already?

Still, she was a guest, and her manner of asking had been courteous, if strange. So, when it became clear that the other two were not minded to answer her, I did my best to oblige her myself.

"You can call me Drill," I replied. "Though I used to be a man of flesh and blood, and not the creature you see before you now. I lived in Munchkin Country, not far from here. I had a modest cottage with an adjoining pasture, where my wife, my daughter and I kept a flock of sheep."

I had hoped that by mentioning my dear ones in passing like this, I could skirt the chasm that laid me open every time I thought of them. It did not work. It was a perpetual source of astonishment to me that my memories of our life together, which existed only in my mind, could overtake me faster than a cave-in, and sit twice as heavy on my chest.

For a moment I could not speak, so to cover my discomfort, I crept to the very edge of the circle of light. Keeping my arms of jointed metal down at my sides, I held out my one arm of flesh and blood, displaying the simple gold band that still adorned the ring finger there. The engraved pattern of leaves and flowers had been worn away by decades of toil, but I cleaned it diligently every night, and in the light from the shaft it shone as brightly as the patchwoman's eyes. She looked at it solemnly, waiting for me to resume my tale.

"I can only tell you what happened next through the words of others, for I remember nothing of it myself." My voice, unlovely at the best of times, was broken as loose scree. "One evening, I kissed my wife and daughter goodnight and went out to the pasture alone, for it was lambing season, and there was work to be done by night as well as by day. I was resting on the hillside after a difficult birth. And then, between one eyeblink and the next – as it seemed to me – I was lying not on grass, but a stone bench, and gazing up at a blue gabled ceiling where the stars should have been. I was in the house of a renowned surgeon – one Dr Pipt, I was informed – and he had a sad tale to relate to me.

"The good doctor told me that wolves had descended on our flock that night. They all but devoured me; without his timely intervention, I would have been destroyed. But happening across the aftermath of the attack, Dr Pipt saw that I could still be saved, and by his efforts alone.

"It took him many months of labour to restore me to life. Most of my body was irrecoverable. Where flesh, bone and sinew had been lost, he supplied their places with metal plating, solder, bolts and wires. He used whatever came to hand, for time was short: I hung suspended over the abyss of oblivion by the slenderest thread, which any delay might sever. He persevered, and the thread held. The result was as you see."

I fanned out my long, many-jointed arms, each with its cruel tip of pointed metal. And for the first time, I scuttled into the shaft of light, so that the patchwoman could see me plain. To her credit, she did not flinch or cower, but I saw her stiffen, her bearing shifting from relaxed attention to something else. It was the attitude of someone poised on the brink of flight.

She did not flee, though I would not have blamed her if she had. I knew what I was: my body a concrescence of rusting plates held together by rivets and stained by the damp air of the mines, my limbs sprouting off it at all angles in a skittering tangle of indistinguishable legs and arms. My one human forearm protruded from their midst, palm open, like the friendly lure above the jaws of an anglerfish. No one could account the good doctor's handiwork beautiful.

"As soon as I saw my new form in the glass," I continued, "I knew that returning to my… home would be impossible."

A myriad of thoughts and impressions crowded up behind the words. My wife's smile, and the feel of her skin against mine. The fine, soft hair on my daughter's head when she was two weeks old. The scent of grass and the light sinking down behind our cottage at day's end. All things I hadn't felt or seen in more years than I could count. The memory of them made me ache in places I was not certain I still had. The thread of my life had held, and the cost had been my life – or the only life that I had known and cherished. I said none of this aloud; I did not want to be accounted ungrateful.

"Needless to say, I could no longer work as a shepherd,"

I told her instead, shaking myself free of these thoughts with a shiver of my many limbs, "but Dr Pipt offered me an alternative. There was a vast city building in the West, he told me – a city of emeralds – and at its centre there was to be a palace of green and gold, adorned with every precious stone the earth had to offer. The Wizard of Oz, our wise ruler, stood in sore need of labourers in the mines beneath the mountain in the Blue Forest to supply the materials for this great civic endeavour.

"Dr Pipt himself had been appointed as foreman over a corps of miners stationed down there for some months, but the dark and the isolation had affected their minds, first with discontentment and eventually with insanity. They had rebelled against their employment and Oz himself, and began tunnelling up through the mountain in a great host, clamouring for his head.

"To protect his king, the good doctor had been forced to employ his arcane powers to turn the workers to stone, on the very instant that they broke through to the surface." I gestured to the shaft of the damned above our heads. "They have remained here ever since, as a warning to us all about the seeds that darkness can plant in an unwary mind.

"It was at this point in our conversation that the good doctor asked me if I would consider taking their place. He needed new miners. My new limbs were peculiarly well-suited to the work, and if that work would keep me hidden from a world that could look on me only with terror and disgust, then so much the better. And there was reason to hope that my transformation need not be a permanent one. The Wizard of Oz was the most powerful magician who had ever lived, Dr Pipt assured me, and he himself very nearly the Wizard's equal in skill and erudition. If they combined their efforts, he was confident that the two of them would uncover some spell or potion to remedy my plight. In short, he promised me that if I worked for him hard and faithfully, he and the Wizard would not rest until they had found a way to transform me into a man of flesh and sinew again.

"So I went down into the mines with as good a will as any consigned to such dark and difficult work could have. I dug many of these shafts myself, expanding on the efforts of my predecessors, and in time I was joined by my two companions, both stout hearts who had lost their bodies in circumstances similar to my own. Pick and I seek out new seams and carve tunnels to reach them, while Rock Screen processes what we've mined, extracting the gems and crushing and separating the hewn rock into its various ores." As I introduced them, I gestured to each in turn; Pick waved, and Rock Screen bobbed up and down on her hydraulic presses in a shy curtsey.

"Together, the three of us make a formidable team, and though our work is neither easy nor pleasant, we take pride in doing it well. We make it a rule not to dwell on our pasts," I concluded, "but rather to look ahead to that happy future when our labours will be over and our true forms restored. There's no more to tell, so I have done. And perhaps now you'll return the favour, and tell us all who you are, and what has brought you here. You have less flesh on your frame even than me, so I assume your accident was a terrible one – though I will not pry into the details. Do you serve the good doctor, then, in your own fashion, as we do in ours?"

The patchwoman had listened to my tale with an expression of growing puzzlement and distress, but now she let out a short laugh, though without any mirth in it. "Now there's a dose of déjà vu! I haven't served your 'good doctor' these ten years or more – and never willingly. But thank you, Sir Drill, for explaining. It's a pleasure to make your acquaintance, all of you."

To my surprise, she stuck out one cloth arm and shook hands with me. My flesh and blood arm ended just above the elbow, so she had to draw close to me to manage it. If she was still afraid of my drills, she gave no sign of it. Her grip was firmer than I would have imagined possible for someone made out of felt and stuffing.

This done, she danced back, her silver shoes flashing in the light. "Now, to continue taking your questions in reverse order: what's brought me here is that I'm in a race to solve a case!" She drew herself up. "You're looking at the President, CEO and Senior Secret Agent of the Oz Espionage Office – it's a department of one at the moment. And my name is as raggedy as the rest of me, for I go by Scraps." She made us all a sweeping bow, her soft body folding nearly in half along the seam at the top of her legs. Still bent double, she looked up at us with a grin.

"Then you work for the Wizard?" Pick hazarded.

Scraps' smile faltered. "Not exactly," she replied. Her crazy mouth of red felt and pearls turned down at the corners, an expression that ill-suited her merry eyes and jaunty bearing.

For an instant, she looked as grim as we did, and twice as old. "Oh dear, this is a tangle that's going to be tough to unwrangle," she muttered. "You see, my assembled items of ironmongery, while you've been down here digging for diamonds, we've had something of a regime change upstairs. Oz the Great and Powerful, well, isn't – not anymore. I serve Queen Ozma. And the two extra letters have made more difference to how things work around here than you might think."

This was troubling news, and provoked an immediate commotion.

"If the Wizard is no longer our king, then does his promise still hold?" Pick asked.

"What about Dr Pipt?" I cut in. "Surely he—"

Rock Screen began to wail, drowning out my question. "Does that mean we have to stay like this forever?" Her green eyes leaked tears which turned to steam when they hit the superheated pistons of her hydraulic presses, and promptly evaporated.

Scraps the patchwoman looked from one of us to another, and for the first time since she arrived, appeared to be at a loss for words.

"Please, Mistress Scraps," I begged her. "If we are without hope, tell us so at once." I felt within myself the fortitude to hear any answer she gave us. I would not lose my mind, like the mad creatures in the shaft of the damned. If it was my fate to spend an eternity down here in the dark, I would at least have the memory of sunlight to warm me.

Scraps waited until poor Rock Screen's sobs had subsided into moist sniffles before she answered. "Hope is the thing with feathers, as the poet says, and being stuffed only with cotton myself, I don't feel it's my province to comment on it," she said, her voice uneasy. "As for what's been going on up above this mine so drear... Look, I think it'll make a lot more sense if I show you, but first, Sir Drill, I have to ask you a question. It's a question I fear will cause you pain, but I promise you, it's not unkindly meant. There's something I need you to understand, see, and I think it's the kind of snarled-up stitching where it's better to cut the whole thing out in one go than tease it out piecemeal."

It was an answer my destiny hung upon, not a question, so I had no fear. "Ask it," I encouraged her. "There's nothing you could demand of me that would pain me more than what I've already told you."

Scraps' face wrinkled like a puckered seam, like she was steeling herself for an unpleasant duty. "You mentioned you had a wife and daughter in Munchkin Country. Could you tell me their names?"

I opened my mouth to reply. I know I did, because I had not oiled the hinges of my jaw in some time, and now I heard them screech. But my answer did not come.

There was another noise instead, louder than the protest of the ancient metal. It was the white, crackling sound of a radio lost between stations. It filled my senses, drowning my memories of home. Its tendrils crept up our hilly pasture and in through the windows of our little cottage, and what they touched, they destroyed. My wife, my daughter; their names, their faces. The light Scraps had brought flooding in through the shaft of the damned had whited out my vision;

her question whited out my mind. Everything I had known from before was covered over in an instant with a thick winding sheet.

I sagged. Wrapping my metal arms around myself like a cocoon, I sank to the floor. I could no longer tell if the roaring noise was within me or coming from me. My dear ones. My twin lights in the long, lonely dark that was my life. What had become of them?

Scraps regarded me through her gleaming eyes, and her face was sad. "That's what I thought," she said, gravely.

"What did you do to them?" I howled at her, and my voice was a snarl of barbed wire. "Where did— How did you—?"

She did not cackle or gloat, as a witch should. And she must be a witch, I thought, to have plucked the memory of my family clean out of my head and replaced it with – with—

"It wasn't me," she said softly. "And I can't put them back. I'm sorry; truly, I am. Come with me, Sir Drill – all of you – and I'll do my best to help you understand."

She pirouetted on her left foot, silver shoes flashing, then brought her right foot down to meet it. There was a sharp click as she snapped her heels together – once, twice. I lunged at her, in bitterness and rage—

—and found myself somewhere else. My feet skittered as they made contact, not with the packed earth and rock of the cavern, but a floor of wooden boards. There was a sense all around me of light and air, though I could not at once make out anything more. The witch Scraps had transported us with her dark arts, that much was certain. We had moved in a blink, in a half-footstep, to another place. Then I began to recover myself, and look around me at the round, blue-panelled walls and the gabled ceiling – and I realised that, for the second time in my life, I had appeared in the good doctor's cottage.

Pick whistled, and Rock Screen gasped. The place was not as we remembered it. Every spare surface was encrusted with precious stones, a gaudy profusion of gems that explained why I'd been dazzled when we first arrived. They covered the ceiling in a mock galaxy, a field of deep blue sapphires scattered with diamond stars. The room itself was in disarray: the stone bench had been overturned, the chairs and worktable smashed, and the doctor's equipment turned out and flung across the floor.

Moving through the room, my eyes lit at last on the good doctor himself, his back to the grimy fireplace. He, too, was changed. A bruise ripened on his cheek, just visible between the long, crooked arms which were twisted over his face in a pitiable attitude of terror. Not only twisted, but bound: he had been trussed with rough cord at the wrists and ankles. When he saw who had come, he raised his eyes to us beseechingly. "My old friends!" he exclaimed. "As you can see, I have come to a sorry pass! Rescue me from this hag and you'll have my eternal thanks! I swear I'll—"

His pleas were cut off in a gurgle as Scraps kicked him in the stomach. "That's enough out of you," she said.

This could not stand. I was angry enough at the indignities Dr Pipt had suffered that for a moment they overwhelmed my own sorrows. I turned one of my drills side on – for even in my fury, I did not wish to *kill* her – and smacked it into the witch's chest, driving her away from her victim. She stumbled back in surprise. "Do that again and I will make you regret it," I warned her. "Let the good doctor go at once!"

"This man is a traitor and a charlatan," Scraps replied, "and before you leap to his defence, I'd suggest you hear me out as to why."

I was not minded to listen to her, but I could see that Rock Screen and Pick felt differently. Perhaps because she had not stolen their memories, as she had mine.

"I say we hear her story before we decide what to do," Pick said.

"Yes. I want to know what he's done that's so awful," Rock Screen agreed.

I nodded with reluctance. "But you must promise not to lay a hand on Dr Pipt in the meantime," I told the witch. "We all owe him our lives."

Scraps pouted. "If that's what it takes, I'll lay neither hand nor foot on him till we're finished here. But to understand the extent of his depravity, we'll have to go back a ways, so strap yourselves in and hold on to your hard hats, okay?"

Pick propped one of his curved metal arms against the side of the workbench and eased himself to the floor, while Rock Screen squatted on her haunches. For myself, I took up a position between Scraps and the doctor. My companions might be content to let their guards down, but I was not.

"Way back when Queen Ozma took the throne, she outlawed the use of magic without her express permission, to prevent skulduggery and the like. Old Pipt here ignored that edict."

Scraps crossed the room in her curious, skipping gait,

stopping before the great wooden medicine cabinet opposite the fireplace. Its doors hung skewed from its hinges, their glass panels smashed to flinders, but the bottles, jars and phials within were still intact. From the very back of the topmost shelf, she pulled out a drawstring bag, opening its mouth to show us the white grains inside.

Pipt hissed in a breath. "Be careful with that!"

Scraps continued as though he had not spoken. "He cooked up a wondrous concoction called Powder of Life, and he used it to conjure up me, Scraps, to be his not-so-willing slave. All that's old history now. Suffice it to say that Queen Ozma gave me my manumission, and gave Pipt a pardon – after he swore on his life that he'd only done it the once, cross his heart and hope to die, and never would again."

Scraps shot Dr Pipt a look of unbridled contempt. "So you can imagine Queen Ozma's surprise when she caught wind of a rumour that Pipt had not been entirely forthcoming with her about the extent of his magical dabbling. He hadn't even been threecoming or twocoming. He may, in point of fact, have been lying through his crooked teeth. Naturally, she dispatched me straight away. 'Scraps,' she said, 'there's a mystery afoot, and you're the only one I trust to untangle it.' I'm tangled myself, you see, and that makes me suited by disposition to untangle everything else. So off I skipped to the Blue Forest, to have a chat with my dear old dad.

"I never thought I had any composure to lose," she continued conversationally, "so no one was more surprised than me when it all went flying out the window." She gestured to the chaos around us. "I did quite a number on this place when I figured out what he'd been up to. I did manage to hold myself back from destroying the evidence, though."

She beckoned us over to the medicine cabinet, and Pick and Rock Screen drew closer to inspect its contents. With a mounting dread, I followed them. A tattered label on the second shelf, frayed and peeling away from the wood, read 'Brain Furniture'. Each jar was neatly labelled with its contents: 'Obedience', 'Cleverness', 'Self Reliance', 'Poesy'. The shelf beneath this bore the label 'Memories'. My lamps scanned the row of bottles, their twin beams illuminating 'Loving Wife', 'Adoring Daughter', and 'Quaint Shepherd's Hut'.

I had no guts to twist, no stomach to clench. Perhaps I never did. Perhaps it did not matter, because the feeling that rose in me then was one I had never experienced in any body, sinew or steel, in all my existence.

"You asked me before if the Wizard and the doctor would honour their promise to restore you to your original forms," Scraps said. "The sad truth of the matter is they can't, because you're already in them. That perfidious pustule in the corner *made* all of you, and he did a pretty shoddy job of covering his tracks. Gave you just enough from those bottles and jars to make you think you had pasts, but you don't – no more than I did, when he made me."

"You don't understand!" Dr Pipt cut in, his reedy voice rising to a wail. "I *had* to give them the memories – it was a kindness. Without something tethering them to the world above, the first batch went stark, staring mad!" He glared at Scraps mulishly. "You saw the things in the shaft. They were even crazier than you."

Scraps thrust her face towards him, though true to her word, she did not strike him, and he flinched into silence. "Now, now, Doctor." Suddenly her sing-song voice dropped a register into something altogether more sinister. "It's a poor workman who blames his tools. You made the four of us well enough, which is all I'll say in your defence. If our wills and wants appal you now, you know whose fault it is."

She turned back to me and my speechless companions. "You see what he is, now. He traded the gems you mined to Oz in exchange for royal favours for himself and his wife, and what the Wizard didn't want, he kept for himself. He has lived very comfortably on your labour these many years. You built the Emerald City indeed, though you have never seen it, and that's the only true thing this swindler and slave driver ever said to you."

Scraps paused, passing a hand over her patched forehead. And then, snapping back to the present with a smile, "I'm truly sorry to have deprived you of your wife and daughter, Sir Drill, but as you can see, you've gained a sister in the process. It's a poor enough trade, I'll admit, but I hope you'll agree that it's better than nothing."

In the silence that followed this account, I was glad for the first time of my monstrous metal carapace. No fleshly frame could have withstood the rage I felt; it would have melted skin and bone to a puddle of fat. It was an anger that burned pure and hot as a furnace, with no detritus of grief to sully the flame. How could I grieve what I had never had, what had never even existed? I started my drills whirring, a blur of sparks and sharpened metal. I turned towards Dr Pipt.

Scraps laid a soft hand on one of my arms. "If that's the way you'd like to settle this, Sir Drill, then I won't stand in your way. But the talking's not done yet."

"What more's left to say?" Pick's voice was rusty with sorrow and anger. "If your Queen Ozma is a just ruler, then she'll do something now to help… to fix…"

He trailed off. It was not a sentence he could end, for truly, what was there to be done? The wrongs we had suffered, the indignities, had no redress, because they were no more and no less than our very selves. There was only one form of justice left to us. But Scraps had promised me my chance at that if I would only hear her out, so I flashed my lamps at Pick, twice, then a pause, then twice again. It was the signal I used in the mines to show that the shaft ahead was unstable, and it signified that we must proceed slowly and with caution. Pick nodded and subsided. He and Rock Screen were used to following my lead.

When Scraps saw that she had our attention again, she continued. "You're absolutely right. Ozma's a ruler of action, not words, and there'll be plenty of it, I assure you. But we won't proceed recklessly. We'll have reck and feck and all of those other good things, to make sure we don't make the harm any worse than it is already. The first decision we've got to reckon with is what to do with the lot of you, which is a puzzle most perplexing indeed. And why I'd like to ask: knowing what you do now, what do you want to do next?"

We were gravelled by the question, simple as it was. After a long pause, Rock Screen asked, "If we're not needed in the mines any more, will you let us go home? To the Munchkin

Country?" The base of her hopper vibrated in a cough of embarrassment. "I understood what you told us about the powders and the memories and all that, but I'd like to go there, all the same."

Scraps sighed – a long, rustling sound like thread pulled through rough cotton. "I wish you could, Mistress Rock Screen. But the home you remember is not a place you've ever been, and I fear you'd not get the welcome you're hoping for there."

Rock Screen was the youngest of us, and her hydraulic pumps rattled up and down as she stamped them, making the cottage shake. "That isn't fair! We remember it as if we *were* there. It shouldn't make any difference!"

"It makes a great deal of difference," Pick told her, his grating voice as gentle as he could make it. "Nobody would know us there: we'd be strangers. Besides, what would we do in Munchkin Country? These hands are well-suited to cleaving a path through solid rock, but they won't till the earth or bring in a harvest. Perhaps Dr Pipt might be prevailed upon to swap out my picks for a scythe and a shovel? Then I might manage pretty well."

"That's all right for you to say," grumbled Rock Screen. "My whole head is a sieve for sorting out stones. Dr Pipt can't very well swap that out."

Scraps waved her hands in a kind of panic. "My dear gentlemachines, I think you're missing the point! Meaning absolutely no disrespect to any of you, but you have pistons for legs and rivets where your eyes ought to be. You can hammer your drill bits into scythes until the cows come home if it makes you happy, but it won't help you fit in any better at Mayor Munchkin's afternoon tea parties. Being bored to death *is* an occupational hazard at those things, but not usually in the literal sense. I do have another idea, though.

"It's true that the three of you aren't cut out to be farmers and shepherds, whatever your memories might have to say on the matter, but I can think of better work for you – work where being covered all over in razor-sharp pointy bits like a big, mechanical porcupine, is an asset rather than a drawback! I told you before that the Oz Espionage Agency is a one-woman show right now, so why not come and work with me in the Emerald City? You helped build it, after all. Wouldn't you like to see it?"

"If you think the Munchkins would find our appearances hideous, I cannot imagine the denizens of the Emerald City would feel any different," I pointed out.

"Queen Ozma would," Scraps parried. "She has a tender heart for freaks of all stripes and varieties, and a soft spot for those of us created by the Powder of Life in particular. There's a sawhorse in Oz who's even more peculiar than you three, and he's one of her trusted advisors. There's me, your own sister, her most suave and sophisticated super-secret agent – that's classified, by the way." She grinned at us, eyes glinting. "So, what do you say? It's not much, I know, but it's honest work – which is more than you've had before, for you've been in the employ of a liar all this time."

"I say yes," I growled, "so long as you'll let us begin our work with this weasel."

Scraps swept out a hand. "Nothing would make me happier."

The three of us walked in lockstep towards our creator. Rock Screen's pistons hissed and the great tray of her head swung menacingly from side to side. Pick raised the cruel metal points of his hands in readiness. Dr Pipt shuffled away from us, his arms raised in a gesture of supplication. "N-now, let's think carefully about this," he stuttered. "I gave you life, you know. It does not behove you to turn on your creator. I order you – I beg you to..."

He hit the wall and we kept advancing. I started my narrowest drill, the one I used for precision work, and raised it level with his face.

"Please," he whimpered, raw terror in his eyes. "Please..."

I moved it closer. I could push it straight through the jelly of his eye and into his brain, and out the other side again, red and wet and reeking.

Only I could not. He and I faced one another, less than an inch apart, his cold terror and my hot fury roiling, seething, and boiling off to nothing. The moment stretched, unbearable. And then the pleading expression dropped from his face like a mask, and he sneered at me.

"I know my tools better than you think," he snarled. He brought up his bound arms to the point of my drill, and the rough rope disintegrated with shocking suddenness. I thought he would strike me, but both of his long, twisted arms snaked off to the sides of the room, moving as though they had no relation to each other. One grabbed a fistful of bottles from the cabinet behind us, sending powders and liquids flying in an uproar of glass.

"Take cover!" Scraps yelled. She caught up one of the tin

saucepans that were littered across the floor and held it out before her.

She was right to do so, for on its way back from the cabinet, the doctor's left arm made a fling at her with a potion – a black, viscous fluid shot through with veins of grey and silver. It missed her, but splashed against her makeshift shield, and where the drops touched it, the metal calcified, turning to milk-white marble.

All was confusion, then. Rock Screen lurched sideways, away from the deadly liquid stone. Pick sprinted for the overturned workbench and dove behind it. I dug my drill bits into the wall and scurried up to the ceiling. The three of us knew all too well what it would do to us if we touched it – we had seen the creatures in the shaft.

Scraps was braver and had more presence of mind than any of us. Having parried the doctor's first attack, she lunged at him with the marble pan, making a swing for his head that would have knocked him out cold, had it hit home.

Of course it did not, for in our panic, none of us had thought to take notice of the doctor's right arm. This he raised, almost leisurely, to his lips, and it was then only that we saw the little vial he held, produced from who-knows-where whilst his legerdemain had kept our attention elsewhere.

He popped the cork with a crooked thumb and drank off the contents in a single swallow. It was dark blue, and had a sheen like oil spilled over water. Straightway, he rippled, as though his body had become the liquid he'd just tasted. There was a sudden sense behind him of a vast space, far larger than the little workroom could really hold. I heard noises coming from a great distance; a cold wind, flashing red and blue lights, a babble of voices. Into this cacophony of light and sound, Dr Pipt stepped as into an embrace. Scraps' swing with the pan passed right through him, his head parting like a wave and then cohering again in its wake. The motion made his sneer into something twisted and obscene.

Scraps abandoned the pan and flung herself at his fading form, but he had vanished, and her hands came together over nothing but empty air.

"Oh blast!" she yelled.

"Is he gone?" Pick asked, emerging from his hiding place. Rock Screen peered out from under his arm, quaking.

"The fault is mine." I knelt before them all. "If I had not hesitated..."

Scraps waved my contrition away with a breezy motion of one cloth hand. "Don't say that, Sir Drill. It was your first job. You were bound to be a little nervous."

"It wasn't that," I confessed. "When the moment came, I could not act."

"I felt it too," Rock Screen said. "It was... hard to hurt him. He looked so frightened."

"My heart bled for him," Pick added. "I can split rocks, no problem, but splitting a person's face seems to be quite a different matter."

Scraps puckered her felt mouth in a frown. "If that's how you all feel, then perhaps we'd better find different work for you."

We all clamoured as one against that idea.

"We've only just found you, sister!" Rock Screen cried. "We don't want to be separated again!"

"Besides, you and Queen Ozma rescued us. We want to repay your kindness," Pick added.

I said nothing, though I felt as they did. I was thinking about what had restrained me earlier. What had made me stay my hand. I had been taught as a child that— But I shook off the thought. I had never been a child. The doctor was the architect of our memories, and of our natures, also.

"If we are too tender-hearted to avenge ourselves against those who wrong us, then that was undoubtedly by design," I said slowly. "Pipt knew us better than we know ourselves. He wanted us meek, and obedient, and gentle. And so I want to be none of those things."

"He *made* us pity him!" Rock Screen said in disgust.

Scraps did not reply at once. She crossed to the cabinet and toed at the shards of glass on the floor with one silver-slippered foot. Then she pushed the doors open wider and ran a hand along the bottles and jars. 'Kindness', 'Courage', 'Resilience'. 'Malice', 'Anger', 'Cruelty'.

"If you're not happy with the natures you've been given, all the tools you need to do something about that are right here," she said.

I would like to state for the record that Scraps made no attempt to sway or influence us. It had to be our decision, she opined, for we had never had the freedom to decide anything before, and so we must make a start as soon as possible.

But in the end, it hardly felt like a decision at all. We were all of one mind, and that was to reject the minds we had been given, and build better ones ourselves. And so we ask that you accept us into your service, Your Majesty, not as we were, but as we have chosen to be. We promise to work for you honestly, so long as you are honest with us, to uphold your laws faithfully, and to protect all your citizens – save one.

*Final thoughts and the like.*

*By: Scraps the Patchwork Girl, Secret Agent*

*For the Eyes of: Her Majesty Queen Ozma of Oz (and her eyes ONLY. I am NOT KIDDING. Note to self: next time I write one of these reports, I need to send it via morse code or exploding cassette tape, or at least put it in an envelope marked 'CONFIDENTIAL' in big red letters)*

> *A mind is a terrible thing*
> *To mock-up out of stuffing and string*
> *But don't lose hope unduly: just look at yours truly!*
> *And if hope fails – revenge is the thing.*

*And that's really all that needs to be said, isn't it, Your Maj? Okay, look, I know what you're going to say. Everyone deserves a second chance, even that scrunched-up old toerag Dr Pipt; the better part of justice is mercy, and yada yada yada blah blah bloo blee. Saving your presence.*

*I know you, Your Majesty. You have a gentle heart, and it's to your credit. But being made out of cotton myself, I'm not burdened with any kind of heart at all, and I've never found the lack of it steered me wrong. Mercy's great and all that, and usually I'm all for it. But not always.*

*Well. For those times when mercy doesn't cut the mustard, you've got three new and loyal servants, tucked away in their quarters in the Royal Palace and awaiting orders. For myself, I'm off to track down the good doctor, wherever he might be roaming. My new colleagues are just dying to see him again. They've had a real attitude change since last he met them, and they're eager to catch up! When I get back, I hope very much you'll give me leave to organise a little reunion.*

# HEARTLESS

**ADRIAN TCHAIKOVSKY**

I'd been on crunch time for five days when Minty's call came in. That avatar of his, the gurning cartoon he'd made when we were working together on Heartless. Five years ago, seemed longer.

We'd called ourselves SimTactic. We'd delivered precisely one project. Our promises of being forever colleagues had lasted a week beyond the paycheque. We'd gone our separate ways.

I'd never hit the heights of Heartless again. Recently I'd been working on in-game reactive decision-making for virtual love interests. It all felt grimly sordid. The more *self* I imbued the virtual cheesecake with, the more I felt I was sex trafficking. The one thing the poor AI fuckers are programmed to never say is "no".

All of which meant a call from Allardyce Mintsner – 'Minty' – was a shock to the system. A reminder of actually doing something significant. His image had intermittent static patterns running through it, which I pegged as real-time intelligent security screening. Minty was still doing the real business. My heart picked up. A few questions I might have thought to ask fell away. Five years and he looked even more like that cartoon avatar. The long face, with the laughter lines that made him look older when he was young, and would make him look younger in the event he grew old. That grin, endlessly boyish, never to be trusted. "Jennet," he said. "How's *Final Romantasy Nineteen*? I hear it's going to be the Big New Thing in pretending to fuck anime boys."

I indicated with a single finger the extent to which I wanted to discuss the topic.

"Only I have this little bit I could use your help with," he told me, more white teeth as the grin spread. That was what he called the good jobs. *This little bit*. "You, me, the whole gang."

My heart, which had been racing, seemed to stop. "You're getting SimTactic back together?"

"One last farewell tour," Minty said. "Look, I know we signed everything away, in exchange for that extraordinary bag of money they gave us, but I'm assuming you didn't actually scrub everything from your brain."

"Someone wants a new Heartless?"

"Got an end-user wants a little advice. You know they never read the manual."

That suddenly sounded less interesting. Hand-holding some idiot executive was not developing world-changing programming architecture.

"I know that face," Minty burlesqued disappointment. "I've not sold it, have I? Look, I'm sending a number to you. It's a lovely number. You and this number can be very happy together."

He did. The number and I had a whirlwind romance in my imagination. We travelled around the world to all the best resorts. "You're mad," I said. "Your end-user's mad."

"You forget the sort of end-user who was going to *end up* using our product," Minty said mildly. I hadn't; I never had. That was why I was doing this, rather than working on the cutting-edge stuff for the cutting-edge people. The thing about cutting edges is they shed blood.

Heartless had shed a lot of blood.

But the number was very large. I was never good at keeping thoughts off my face. Minty's smile grew only broader.

He sent me an address, a time. *The gang all together again.*

An industrial unit, an empty one, tenanted for one night only under an arrangement that wouldn't be troubling anybody's records. The sort of place people get lured to shortly before pieces of them get fished out of the river. Pleasant thought. Honestly not inaccurate, if I'd known who Minty's *end-user* was, but right then the number was still front and centre in my head. And here was Minty, still lean, still wearing those beige suits and open collar shirts like he was someone's correspondent in the colonies. Striding forwards to pump my hand, clap my back, pull me into a one-armed hug. Nobody in the world was more hail-fellow-well-met than Minty. And the mood was on him when he was nervous, mostly, but I'd forgotten that.

Trailing in his ebullient wake was another old friend.

Number 3 of 5 on the Heartless team, Eldi Karkowitz. Small, olive, dark, wearing a new incarnation of her self-rigged AR specs like she was just back from a steampunk fair. She didn't do skin-on-skin contact but I got a little smile from her, shy, as if we were strangers. That was Eldi.

"The others?" I asked. Minty's grin slipped slightly.

"We're it. Losmann's in one of those R&D compounds in the Desert States," Minty explained. "You know, anti-industrial-espionage. No way I could spring him. And Kir..." He grimaced.

"Kir was shot," Eldi said. "Police raided his hacker farm. A lot of people were shot. Kir was one."

"So, it's down to us to set the world to rights." Minty clapped his hands together. "Jennet, I'm going to introduce you to our client, then we're going to get on a plane."

"I— What?"

"Boots on the ground, Jennet. They need us where they're deploying. It's not the sort of problem that's amenable to just sending over a software patch. The number, hmm? Remember that lovely number."

I did remember the number, but I felt conditions were eroding its loveliness. "You never said anything about *flying*—" Which was when *he* came in with his people.

The people were big people. Their suits must have been tailored for their biceps, and for the compact bulges under their armpits. They moved in unison, dark glasses, earpieces, eyes checking every corner. *He* walked in front of them, a man who knew how to make an entrance. I'm not going to name him. You know who. You've seen his face on the news.

The General, I'll call him. He deserved at least that. Not a man supposed to be in this country, but that's always a grey area with someone who's simultaneously wanted by international courts, and whose regime is a 'key ally in the region'. The General. You know who I mean. Let's leave it at that.

"This is your team?" he asked Minty, who made the introductions. I could see it now, the strain. The tautness at the edge of the grin. When Minty was up against the wall he exuded bonhomie instead of sweat.

"Honestly one of the most enthusiastic adopters of the Heartless system," he told us brightly. "Only they've run into some glitches while peacekeeping, and, well, one goes to the source, right? Who better to iron out the wrinkles than us?"

"Where," I said, "are we flying to?"

That grin, inching wider, until I thought the skin would split. He named the city, you know where I mean. That had been in the news a while back, when the bombs were falling. And now wasn't, because the global information cycle has attention deficit amnesia. That place.

I didn't want to go there. It was an officially designated peacekeeping zone. Meaning, paradoxically, it was where the fighting was. Heartless was a weapons system; that was exactly the sort of place you'd expect to find it. But the point about Heartless was it was fire-and-forget. Someone like me – someone who'd helped design it – wasn't ever supposed to get near where it would be deployed.

I looked at the General and the big men with the lumpy suits. I could say no. That was a word it was in my power to say. I wasn't sure whether I'd manage any words after that. I was someone with some money and status in my profession and a citizen of a nominally democratic country right here in the city I resided in, I wanted to register a number of complaints. I don't know if I'd have out-and-out gone with *This is kidnapping.* I don't know that it *was* kidnapping, at that stage. But I thought about those big men, and about the big number, and about 'key ally in the region'. The *No* I could have said got smaller and smaller in my mouth until it went away.

Really, the *No* I could have said, to stop it happening, was at the start, before we developed Heartless. We pay for our sins.

We called it Heartless because – well, okay, we called it Heartless because if you're designing a military drone program then you *have* to have some edgelord name for it, because all your potential buyers have the emotional maturity of twelve-year-olds. But it fit, too. A distributed drone network, because at the time the networks with central control were all falling over. Hit the central point, everything becomes random vulnerable robots that lack the autonomy to do what you want. Heartless had no heart, see? The computational entity directing the swarm was built constantly in real time between all the units you had in the area. Encryption-shifting, hardened comms, all very resilient. Capable of coordinating a mixed team of bodies from little flying spies to tanks. But what let Heartless win out over the competition was the learning algorithms. The Ninth Wave AI stuff, that was as much my work as anyone's. See, the problem with previous AI was, it couldn't take a joke. Or rather, it didn't know what *was* a joke, what was a fact, what was a figure of speech. Any dumbass can make you a prejudice-amplifying machine that tells you everyone of a certain demographic is a criminal, and if you're just a racist on a power trip maybe that's all you want. If you're serious about finding real bad guys, all you get are so many false positives that your actual targets get lost in the crowd. Ninth Wave AI is context-sensitive, that's the big innovation. A whole extra layer of analysis and cross-referencing so the system can understand not just *what's* being said, but *why*. A big step towards the elusive General AI. Also, a big step towards making an autonomous drone swarm useful in the field. You want it to police your problem area, track down the insurgents, work out who's talking about building bombs and who's just shifty, it can do that. For complex peacekeeping environments, Heartless is absolutely your ideal death-toy. A bombed-out city still harbouring a desperate remnant population including an unknown proportion of armed insurgents is one hell of a complex environment.

We flew out in a military plane – small, loud, cold, landing at an armed camp outside the ruinous suburbs; an airstrip and a lot of armoured prefabs behind several layers of fence. A lot of troops, armoured vehicles, and ranks of drone bodies. The rotary fliers, armed and unarmed; the segmented worms that could slither through rubble; the compact tracked bodies like tanks the size of a human; the two-legged walkers that we'd absolutely based off that thing from the film with the cop, but were insanely nimble, no falling down stairs for them.

On the flight, over our earphones, Minty explained the General's problem, for which we were receiving such a generous number. Attrition amongst the Heartless drones was way up past acceptable tolerance. Worse, some human peacekeepers had allegedly come under fire from their own drones. Our drones.

"It's fuckery," Minty told Eldi and me. "Someone's found a crack in our system, and they're getting their grubby little fingers all over our code. We need to get this sorted, double time. Because the General isn't the only one who's using our system in the field and, if this gets out, our collective rep is in the crapper."

The General gave us a little presentation about their work here. Virtual 3D maps with annotations in a language I didn't read. His commitment to peacekeeping was very serious, he explained. That was why he had bombed the city into rubble, as a pacification measure. However, this had not sufficiently weaned the surviving populace onto peace, and the place remained rife with insurgents. Foreign bad actors were shipping in a constant pipeline of weapons, the General said with a dolorous shake of his head. If left to their own devices, the denizens of the place would be spreading out into more civilised, peace-valuing communities. There would be bombs, shootings, acts of extremism. The General's people would be under threat. And the airstrikes had, the General was reluctantly forced to admit, done what they could. Everyone left was a desperate terrorist, dug into the foundations of the city. Action on the ground was needed to sweep them all up. His moustache and the skin under his eyes quivered with emotion as he explained this to us. Hence his peacekeeping forces had been entering the city, going street by street, cleansing the place of murderers. And ahead of them had been the autonomous, many-shaped force of Heartless, taking down bad guys and analysing information, feeding back so that the General could direct his troops. All working as intended.

I sat there through this presentation – honestly, you get used to this sort of thing. It's usually some executive outlining his corporate vision, graphs and things where the red lines go up. Here, the red lines mostly went down, but as the point of the peacekeeping was for there to be fewer insurgents, that was working as intended. There wasn't a graph showing increasing levels of peace being kept.

However you represented it, though, that graph line had flatlined. Heartless was no longer doing its job.

Minty, Eldi and I got together after to discuss. Firstly, attrition levels on Heartless units had spiked about two weeks ago. Someone had worked out how to run a mass takedown of the drones, all shapes and sizes. Either destroyed or their security compromised, but they had stopped reporting back in droves. That some had been repurposed to be used against the peacekeeping forces was obvious, though reports of hostile drone contact were sporadic: anecdotal reports from the front line.

"You have no idea how hard I've already been working to

assure the General we didn't sell to the opposition," Minty said with a smile. He noticed Eldi's frosty look. "What? We *haven't* been selling to the opposition. The opposition couldn't afford us."

"Ah," Eldi said. "Morality."

"If you're going to get snotty, I shall take my big numbers and go home," Minty said with exaggerated dignity. "What the bad guys *have* is expertise. Possibly some local wunderkind, maybe someone from over the border. They've found a weakness in our security that we need to identify and fix. Makes us look bad. Very angry man, the General. Now, I'm going to need to get you sized up for these." And he slapped something down on the folding table there. His grin didn't falter but it was notably more fixed.

"That looks," I said, "like a protective vest."

"Astounding perspicacity," Minty said. "The General wants you out in the field, with the kit, jumping on the shortwave swarm comms. He doesn't have the tech people for it."

"Wants me?" I asked. "Us? And you?"

"I did my stint before you came. It's safe. You're, what's the word, embedded. Going in with the troops. One of these, a helmet, and you'll be fine. You probably won't even see any shooting. But the thing about Heartless is that it's designed to be comms secure. You've got to be damn close to listen in, even with the kit we have here." And, when Eldi and I started to object, "Very angry man, the General. Plus a lot of other angry men who do what he says, in whose midst we currently are. Come on, team players, eh?"

The streets of a dead city. That was my first take. Inaccurate. Dead cities were at peace; they didn't need peacekeeping forces. We went out in an armoured car, me in the belly with a ton of comms kit. The General had people on foot and drone support with us. I had a liaison, the only one who admitted speaking any language I knew. The others looked at me a lot, talked to each other a lot in low voices. I had a translator earbud they didn't know about, so I caught more than I was supposed to. It was all discomfiting and ugly, but I reckon the General had put them on their best behaviour. Making me feel profoundly uncomfortable at all times was, I guess, their best behaviour.

I got to watch the streets through the car's cameras. A ghost town, I thought. Then they got me out of the car because they'd found a downed drone. It was signalling its location for pickup, as damaged Heartless units were supposed to. They wanted me to come look at it, and the car's own intrusion countermeasures were stopping me getting a fine enough reading, so I got to see all those dead streets with my own human eyes instead.

The drone was one of Heartless' air units, a flying saucer about thirty centimetres across. The soldiers spread out around me as I set up. This had been a street, just a regular street where people lived. Now it was a long slew of rubble, and all the houses had been reduced to jagged stumps and outlines of walls. As though the street was a jaw and all the teeth had gone rotten or been knocked out. Cheery thought.

The drone didn't seem to be a part of any wider network. Heartless units work by a complex friend-or-foe algorithm, and this one had been knocked out of the group chat and wasn't being recognised by its former comrades. I went through the complex chain of handshakes and safeguards to get into the system, which doubled as a check on whether the unit had been compromised by some enemy actor. Everything was working as intended. I had the soldiers strap the thing onto the back of the car. Further analysis could wait until I was safe.

I heard a shout, as I was overseeing this. I looked round, and there was movement out in the ruined houses. My heart nearly stopped. *A trap, bait, the drone* – I saw ragged, dust-coloured people bolting away. The desperate scrabble that said *escape*, not *attack*. Even as I registered it, the soldiers were firing. I was shouting, I'm not even sure what. My memory records my mouth open, sounds coming out, but the gunfire was so loud it erased my words, even from inside my head. Then they stopped, because there weren't any targets in line of sight, and I was shouting, "They were children! They were children!"

The liaison took me aside. "You must not get in the way," he told me, almost kindly. "When we are engaging with enemy combatants."

"They were children," I told him. "They were running away."

"They are combatants," he said confidently. "Everyone left in this city is a combatant, an enemy of the peace. Why else would they stay?"

"But—"

"Children." He shook his head, a reasonable man lamenting the wickedness of the world. "It is regrettable that these people will even turn their children into combatants. It is terrible, what they force us to do."

I got back in the car, then. I should have been working on the data architecture of the drone, to see if I could find any unauthorised fingerprints. Instead I was just sitting, numb, in the belly of the vehicle.

I hadn't gone to see if there were bodies. I hadn't had the courage for that.

Later, we did come under fire. Immediately before, there had been another encounter with local *combatants*. From within the car it was easier to believe it. The cameras put a layer of distance between me and what went on, the quality of the video making it easy to see guns in hands. The soldiers outside were shooting and I could see their postures: confident, strong, heroic. Defenders of the peace. And then suddenly they were scattering, all that courage broken into pieces. A couple fell over, and I only realised in retrospect that they were dead.

"There!" the liaison was saying. "There, your machine's there!"

I caught a glimpse of something moving, out between two ruined walls. One of the two-legged Heartless units, that's what it looked like. A lot of dust kicked up by then, and the cameras weren't great. You never get the kit you need, when you leave it to the client. A decade of frustration at cheapskate corporations shorting me is what led to me doing something stupid.

The hatch of the car was open – there'd been an officer sticking his head out, but he'd dropped down hurriedly when the shooting started. That was because, as a military man, he knew what he was doing. I, a civilian, just popped up and took his place. I had my own tablet out, recording video and comms frequencies – top of the range kit, better imaging than anything the General had. I was able to get precisely seven seconds of film before I ended up back down in the car's interior in a jumble of limbs. The liaison was shouting at me in two languages, my translator coming in a moment after so I was hearing everything three ways. I thought they'd just dragged me down particularly roughly. Later, I found a shiny scar on my helmet, where a bullet had come spectacularly close to scattering my brains.

Nobody mentioned my heroics back at the camp; probably for the best. Minty and I went over my sliver of recording. I'd detected seven Heartless units in the area. The electromagnetic signatures and my moment of visual recording confirmed the bipedal unit as part of the swarm sold to the General. I could zoom in on the chassis at fine detail, pick up the little square code badge there, identifying the individual body. One that was down on the books as lost in combat.

The General wanted to know where they were being controlled from. Minty and I promised him results. That was easier than telling him we didn't know. The thing about the Heartless system was, it shouldn't need to be controlled from anywhere. Someone had sectioned off and subverted an entire chunk of the swarm, that our remaining units didn't admit to. Turned our independent drones into puppets.

"A fucking schism," Minty complained. "Nobody should be *able* to pull this off. There's some loophole in our code that's let this happen. We screwed up."

By this point I'd been working on the problem for several hours. I'd had a dozen different code-crawlers going over my homework and no loopholes had presented themselves.

"Maybe someone out there is just much, much cleverer than we are," I said.

"I refuse to accept that," Minty told me. "I am the cleverest son of a bitch in this time zone and the only person capable of screwing me over is earlier me not doing a good enough job. We need another head on this. I'm going to get Eldi."

The grin was gone, when he came back. The patrol Eldi went out with had come under heavy fire. Eldi hadn't made it back.

We did what we could with the drone I'd recovered, plus a couple more that the peacekeepers had brought in. All heavily damaged, but we were able to reactivate various sections of their electronic brains, simulate functionality, test their decision-making and responses. The problem being that an individual Heartless unit wasn't much, on its own. The swarm was the thing, and the moment we added any of these units to the swarm under the General's command they would just be subsumed into the whole.

Minty was becoming more and more certain that someone had worked out how to puppet a Heartless swarm. The very lack of intrusive electronic fingerprints was convincing him, paradoxically. "Nobody's taking them and reprogramming them individually. We've enough left intact to see that," he told me, up to his elbows in disarticulated components. "But if you could crack the encryption, you could put yourself in between the units, into the," a spiralling hand gesture, "the ether, you know. Intercept the comms, unit to unit, insert your own commands. Isolate drones in a sort of hallucination where what you told them becomes their new reality."

"That's a *very* complete hack," I said doubtfully. "The rest of the swarm would keep resetting any unit that was given weird ideas."

"Very hard, at the start," Minty said. "Easier, as time goes on. As you get more of the swarm onside, they'd maintain the variant reality you wanted the drones to perceive. Friends to foes. Peacekeepers to enemy soldiers."

"Enemy soldiers to civilians," I said grimly.

Minty's grin strained. "I don't follow you."

"I was out there. I saw who they were shooting—"

"You didn't." His hand was abruptly on my arm, pincering hard enough to hurt. His eyes swivelled. We were alone in the little prefab they'd given over to us, but that didn't mean we weren't overheard. "You saw peacekeepers bringing peace, Jennet. To armed insurgents."

My eyes bored into him. That rictus grin tautened.

"They shot at you, in case you forgot. And they got Eldi. You think that was…?" *Unarmed children running away into the ruins of their homes.* "Let's get this done. Encryption countermeasures and our own command-level attack." To his credit he'd stopped talking about the big numbers we were supposed to receive. Without Eldi getting her share it would have seemed bad taste.

It was me going out with the troops again. It should have been Minty, but the General decided he wanted his chief drone wiz at his elbow during the action. Not, I think, for Minty's advice or his scintillating personality, but because the General wasn't a trusting man.

The force I was embedded into was four times the size of the patrol I'd been with before: multiple armoured vehicles and heavy weapons. Inside one such car I was listening, an algorithmic scanner sweeping all frequencies for the bands that the suborned Heartless network was using. We had our own swarm, too, and I had loaded them up with countermeasures and screens to keep them on-message and stop them sharing any troubling ideas with drones the enemy had interfered with. The General was short on faith as well as trust, though. The bulk of our firepower had a human finger on the trigger.

We started to encounter rogue drone signals almost immediately, far sooner than I was expecting. The enemy Heartless swarm had thrown a net over the whole ruined city, like a spider's web whose strands we were sending signals down the moment we entered. Which was how Heartless was supposed to operate, only I'd never expected to be on the wrong end of it. Using my newly rigged kit I could find the nodes in the network, information my liaison passed on to the lead vehicle. We began the mopping up.

We caught the first drone almost immediately. A flier, lifting off from a bed of rubble. I deployed the electronic assault we'd developed and was able to get past its screens, sending a cascade of shutdown orders through its architecture. It dropped from the sky and the soldiers around me cheered. Abruptly, I wasn't just deadweight.

I could detect the network reconfiguring around us, drawing back. An intelligent response, but once the enemy had enough Heartless units on-side, the drones would be making tactical decisions around whatever orders they were given. The soldiers brought me the downed drone and I wire-linked to it, looking for the enemy hack within its programming, like vivisecting a live brain. Back at base, Minty was receiving my data, commenting occasionally as we hunted down the vulnerability the enemy had discovered.

We took two more drones that morning. There were a lot more in the area, based on the traffic I was detecting, but they were eddying away from our advance. By noon I was putting on a confident front that I didn't feel. We hadn't been able to find the hack. The drones we'd taken were all working as intended, using our protocols, without any discrepancies in their logic or programming. No evidence of infiltration or tampering at all. If we'd turned them on, they'd have meshed seamlessly with our own units.

"I mean this isn't good enough, Jennet," came Minty's low voice over the radio. "Our friend the General, he's expecting to hear we've fixed this."

We were still pressing into the city. I'd detected a moving knot of drones within the rogue network ahead, and was guiding the assault towards it. "We've not found anything *to* fix," I murmured to Minty. "No sign of enemy infiltration."

"Except the way," he pointed out, "they keep shooting at our soldiers."

Someone in the car began barking orders. The enemy had been sighted. I leant over someone's shoulder to get a look.

I saw one of the stalking bipedal units first, and then a couple of the tracked tanks, heavier drone bodies than we'd run into yet. A handful of fliers danced overhead. There was an exchange of fire almost immediately. I heard the dull sound of bullets bouncing off our armour as the walker opened fire on us.

There was more movement out there, though. I saw a hurried scurry of shapes at the back as the drones deployed against us and sought cover. The liaison was shouting at me to take them down, but I stared.

People. Enemy combatants. For a moment I really did see them like that, as though the soldiers and the General had hacked *my* reality. But they were just people, running desperately for cover. No guns in their hands, no body armour, no fanatical insurgent's gleam in their eyes. Men, women and children, clutching a few meagre belongings and running. I was shouting then, trying to tell the soldiers my reality, what I saw. Overhead, the vehicle's guns kept firing. Then the liaison shook me until my teeth rattled.

"Shut them down!" he told me. "That is your job. Shut them down."

I dropped back into my seat, hands poised to deploy our electronic assault. Multiple drones, a subsection of the Heartless swarm, but I could isolate them, take them one by one. With each loss, the whole would become the sum of fewer parts, less able to react to us. The vaunted Ninth Wave AI capability, to read true context and meaning into the data, would get coarser and coarser until it was just dumb machines doing machine things.

I looked back at the screens, watching the drones advance, spread out, cover to cover, splitting our fire, drawing our attention left and right. The humans, the civilians, were fleeing. I saw the small flying units of the swarm hovering over them, directing them. Shepherding them.

Somewhere out there, the enemy was telling them to do this. The enemy who'd broken our perfect security, stolen our creations. That was the General's belief. That was what Minty and I had been working on. I threw open my investigations, all channels and frequencies, looking for that invasive signal, and it wasn't there.

"What are they doing?" The liaison was yelling in my ear, shaking me. I tried to tell him they were protecting the civilians, but in his world there weren't any civilians, and that wasn't what he meant. He meant the other drones. The ones we'd brought with us.

One of the armoured cars exploded, jolted off its wheels, flipped entirely upside down and on fire. I lost all connection with Minty, our channel flooded with white noise. All I could hear was the back and forth of the swarm. Heartless, an entity without a core, existing solely within the interplay of its individual units. No centre, *one* swarm. The drones out there and those we'd brought with us working together as a single whole.

A second car went, hit by some of the heavier artillery the tank bodies were carrying. Abruptly daylight seared into the interior of our vehicle. The hatch above was open. I watched dumbly as the soldiers began to scramble out. The car wasn't armoured enough to resist what was coming for it; that meant it was just a target. A second later my world took a colossal hit and I was crunched on my side in a seat that had been wrenched loose from its fixings, the liaison on top of me. I could hear explosions and shouting and screams but they were very far away. The liaison punched me and kicked me, and for a moment I thought he was trying to stamp me to death in a fit of rage because I hadn't done my job. He wasn't concerned with me at all, though. He was just trying to get out of the car. The hatch, that had been overhead, was now more conveniently positioned given the car was on its side. I saw him scramble out of it, dragging a handgun out of a holster, and almost immediately fall over and lie still. I hadn't even heard the shots.

Silence fell. I looked around. There were a couple of soldiers still in the car but they weren't moving and there was a lot of blood from where they'd been knocked around. Of those who'd been, or gone, outside, nothing. None of the cameras were working. I only had that window on the world through the hatch, into the bright sunlight. I could see several bodies there.

Slowly, I moved. Nothing felt broken; everything felt bruised. I inched my way to the hatch and looked out.

I saw one of the bipedal units standing there, its guns on me. Beyond I saw others, all the models of body we'd designed. Slowly, painfully, I slithered from the car and ended up on my knees. That seemed appropriate. I raised my hands. Ninth Wave AI, context sensitive. It was an attitude they would be able to interpret and recognise, though not necessarily respect.

The bipedal body stomped over to me, shunted into me so I went over on my side. I stared up at it. What stared back at me was not the body but the swarm. Heartless, strung between all these bodies.

I pushed myself to my feet, feeling every knock and joint complain. The bipedal unit nudged me again, giving me a direction and no choice. Taking prisoners was not something we'd specifically programmed them for, but that was the point of advanced drone swarms like Heartless. They evolved their own behaviour based on a context-sensitive reading of the battlefield. I'd been out-thought by our own creations.

There was a long, stumbling trek through the ruined city, the burning cars and dead peacekeepers further and further behind. I did occasionally try to ask questions of the drones, but they'd never been intended for verbal communication. After about an hour I caught up with a group of civilians, probably including those I'd seen with the swarm earlier. They also had little interest in talking to me and, though my translator earbud was still working, they couldn't understand me. Eventually one woman turned out to have enough English to bridge the gap. She'd been a schoolteacher, apparently. She certainly wasn't an armed insurgent now. I tried to ask her who was controlling the drones for them. She said she didn't know. They just came. They just did what they did. Nobody could talk to them.

The drones kept us walking all day. There were sporadic pauses – at first I assumed these were tactical, that the General's troops were in the area. By evening I'd worked out that they were simply to give everyone a chance to rest and pass round the water bottles. Machine learning had worked out precisely how far it could push its prisoners, how often they'd need a break, to get the optimum progress from them. I was still thinking of us – of the humans there – as prisoners. I was still thinking of this – the stewardship of Heartless – as hardship.

By evening we came to the camp. It was set under the cover of twenty blocks of bombed-out buildings. I don't think it would have worked, if it had been planned out by people. People cluster together, naturally. A nice concentration of body-heat and visible presence for the airstrikes. This camp was broadly distributed, individuals and families tucked out of sight. A masterpiece of planning, but easy if you were a distributed swarm of drones with a hundred points of view. By then there were drones everywhere, all shapes and sizes.

That was where I found Eldi.

She came rushing out of a leaning doorway, so suddenly I had a panic attack, hands up to defend myself, stammering appeasement in three languages. Then she had me in a fierce embrace and I realised who it was and hugged her back.

She was right there, a restored part of my reality. A reality which had just become a hell of a lot brighter.

She took me into the cellar where she'd assembled a little comms kit, some of the analysis gear she'd gone out with.

"You're still… working?" I asked. We were right in the heart of Heartless, surrounded by armed drones. "Have you met whoever's hacking the swarm?"

She gave me an odd look. "You're still on that?"

"That's the brief."

"And if the brief and the reality are at variance, what wins out?"

I thought about the big number, which dictated that the brief did. I said nothing.

"Jennet," Eldi said, "what's going on here?"

"The swarm—"

"Not that. *Here*. The General. His 'peacekeeping'." You could hear the inverted commas.

"The insurgency—"

"Jennet."

I bit my lip. "I mean," I said, "did we ever have any illusions about how Heartless would be used? I mean, it *is* a peace-keeping force. Designed for deployment in complex, inhabited areas like occupied urban terrain. Able to root out terrorists and armed insurgents from among a population, intelligently, efficiently. Top of the range."

Eldi kept looking at me, as though I was a slow student. "And what's going on here?"

"The General wants to crush the insurgency…" I said slowly.

“That’s not what the General wants to do,” Eldi said. “That’s just for the cameras, for the world. Not for here. Not where it’s happening.”

I couldn’t say it, in the end. No matter how complicit I already was, I couldn’t say, *The General wants to kill every last man, woman and child left in this city, so he can deliver the site pristine to his state.* Eldi saw it in my face, though.

“The General thought Heartless was the tool for rooting out his enemies,” she said. “Heartless can read the room, though, like previous-wave AIs couldn’t. Nobody’s hacking the swarm; there isn’t a rogue swarm out there. It’s all Heartless. The drones here in the city, with the refugees; the drones out in the camp.”

There was a fuzzy squawking from somewhere. We looked at one another dumbly for a moment. I realised it was coming from my phone. It had been dead all day but now someone had tracked it down. *Someone,* being the only person sharp enough to do so: Minty.

“Jennet, have I got you? Are you there?”

I exchanged a look with Eldi, brought it up to my mouth. A ton of encryption and signal-bouncing, pinging off just about every satellite in orbit. We probably had a few minutes before someone pinpointed my location.

“Minty?”

“Jennet, something seriously fucked is going on in the camp.” Minty’s tight voice. I imagined the grin.

“Minty, you have to surrender to the drones,” I told him. I could hear shooting in the background. Shouting; something going up with a *whump.*

"I have to *what*? Listen, Jennet, you've got to give me something. You have to tell me who's doing this. The General, the General will—"

"Nobody's doing it." Eldi was holding my gaze as I spoke. "Heartless is doing this. Heartless has seen what's going on here." All those people, from the General down to the lowest soldier, screaming *enemy combatants*. The global media, nodding along, *right to defend themselves, terrorists, insurgents*. But Heartless had seen the situation on the ground and drawn its own conclusions.

"Jennet, *please*," Minty said, and then I could hear someone else's voice, right there with him, shouting at him. The General demanding he shut them down, shut them all down. All the drones, all at once. The swarm carving through the camp from inside.

Three shots. Tinny, not even that loud over the connection. Minty's shrill voice suddenly cut off. The General, bellowing distantly, shouting orders that surely nobody was listening to anymore. Eldi and I just listened until the shooting and the shouting were all done, and there was nothing from the General's camp but the busy silence of a hundred ready drones, keeping the peace.

# THE BLUE JAY

IAN WHATES

A flock is never the quietest place to be, which might explain why, on this occasion, the jays failed to note the approaching threat until it was too late.

Blue jays are the most beautiful of all the birds; with their jaunty crests and dazzling blue plumage they put all their feathered cousins in the shade – everybody knows this. Especially the blue jays. An individual will declare as much to the world, in loud, raucous cries that are impossible to ignore: "Look at me! Am I not beautiful?"

Gathered in a group, the blue jays will mount a cacophony of song to mark their glory, bobbing up and down as they compete to see who can voice the squeakiest 'squeaky gate' call, cocking their heads to one side as each vies to outdo their neighbour in the intricacy of their 'whisper song'.

The cyclone struck without warning, howling through the small copse in which they had gathered, plucking hapless birds from the boughs, stripping away leaves and branches and even uprooting some of the trees themselves.

The birds were scattered in an instant and Blue Jay lost

sight of his fellows. Had he been able to spare a thought he might have hoped that they escaped the worst of it, but in truth he was fully occupied with his own plight. Blue Jay felt powerless as he was tossed and turned, buffeted upside down and back again, at the mercy of the malevolent wind. All sense of direction had been snatched from him in the first moment. Disorientated, terrified, his only thought was to stay alive, though he had no idea how to do so. Round and round he spiralled: panicking; flailing; failing…

Then it was over. The wind dropped so suddenly that it took him a moment to process its absence and accept that his wings were his to command once more.

By luck rather than design, Blue Jay had broken through to the eye of the storm: the calm at the heart of the chaos. Nor was he the only one here. Above him loomed a great dark object: a house, he realised, though unlike any he had seen before. His previous encounters with human habitations – seen in passing as he flew by, sometimes pausing to feed on seeds or fallen fruit – had invariably left an impression of cheery places: homely, with bright white walls, fresh paint, and neatly trimmed lawns that offered few places in which an insect might hide. This example, on the other hand, was dull and grey, as if the elements had taken their toll on the building long before the cyclone struck.

Slowly but steadily the house was still rising, forced upwards by the constriction of the wind on all sides. Blue Jay felt panic rise with it – the only hope of sanctuary was getting away from him. He flew swift and true, his wings beating as never before, all the while fearing that the fickle winds might reach inward at any time to drag him back into the maelstrom. In the base of the house he spied a gaping hole, an entrance that had once, perhaps, given access to a cellar space. He made for that, reaching it just as the wind resumed its wailing and started to tug at him with insistent gusts. He found refuge on a small perch of stone just within the lip of the hole and huddled there, pressing against the solid earth and willing this nightmare to end.

It took him a moment to appreciate that his arrival had not gone unnoticed. Glancing upwards, he found twin black eyes staring down at him through the darkness. He froze, wondering what new horror they represented. Then a mouth appeared, and a lolling tongue, and the apparition barked. A dog! Once, twice, three times its yips rose above the muted rumble of the cyclone. It was close, too close; Blue Jay felt that the beast could lean forward if it decided to and seize him in those jaws. Instinct urged him to take flight, to escape, but to do so would mean abandoning this meagre shelter, leaving him once again at the mercy of the storm.

"Toto, come away!" A girl's voice. "It's just the wind."

The dog, though, seemed reluctant to obey. "Oh, Toto, please come away. The cellar's not there anymore. Aunt Em and Uncle Henry aren't there anymore. We're all that each other has right now."

With a last baleful glare down at Blue Jay, the eyes withdrew. At the same time a wooden door closed above Blue Jay's head, shutting him off from the house, and his world grew a little darker still.

After this he was left alone, with the wind unable to reach

him for all its puff and bluster. He fluffed his feathers against a creeping sense of cold and stayed as still as he could, terrified that the slightest movement might tip him from his precarious perch and leave him exposed. He heard no more sounds from above, and suspected the girl and the dog felt much as he did and were cuddling together for comfort.

Events caught up with him and Blue Jay drowsed despite his predicament, waking with a start to the realisation that something had changed. He had no idea how long he had slept, and it took him a moment to grasp that the winds were slowing, the howl of their passage quieting to a murmur. More than that, he felt a strange lethargy creeping up on him, unlike anything he had experienced before. Alarmed, Blue Jay stretched, but the movement proved too vigorous, dislodging him. He began to fall. Panicking, he fought against the sluggishness and bent all his will to his wings. Every beat became a minor triumph as he arrested his fall and started to regain some altitude, but slowly, oh so slowly.

He drew level with the house once more and continued onwards, the cyclone's presence forcing him far closer to the building than was wise, but he was determined to escape now that the storm seemed to be abating. The dull grey walls gradually passed by, but he began to falter, as the effort to keep moving grew to be too much. Until abruptly it wasn't.

On reaching the roof, Blue Jay found himself rising above the storm's dark funnel. The pressure of the swirling winds must have lifted the house to the very top of the cyclone, so that it sat upon the funnel like a crown carried on a cushion. He had been this close to escaping the storm all along, without ever realising it.

As soon as he was free of the cyclone's influence, the sense of lethargy disappeared. His tiredness, however, did not. The energy required to make it this far had taxed his small body, leaving him desperately in need of sustenance.

In order to effect his escape, Blue Jay had climbed high into the air, so that now he could see the land for miles around. In the near distance he spied a cornfield, gold and inviting. Hunger lent him blinkers, so that all other aspects of the landscape paled into insignificance. Without hesitation, he swept down towards the field in a long, arcing dive.

Within minutes he arrived, to find that his destination was everything he could have hoped for: a vast swath of ripe corn just waiting to be eaten. He promptly set about doing so.

Barely had he begun, however, before a voice said, "That's it, just ignore me like they all do." He paused in his pecking and gazed up to see a tall figure with arms outstretched, perched atop a high pole – a man, or at least *almost* a man. The face didn't look quite right and the old blue hat that rested atop the head seemed to be an afterthought, as if it was only there because no one else had wanted it. The rim of the hat had slipped down at some point, as if to emphasise that it didn't really fit this head, and it now covered one eye.

"At first they wouldn't settle, flying away at sight of me," the voice continued. "The birds, I mean. Proudest moment of my life, which admittedly hasn't been a very long life. It made me feel I was worth something. But then this wily old crow didn't fly away. Instead, he stopped to take a closer look at me, even landed on my shoulder to show the other birds that I couldn't harm them. After that the game was up. Taking courage from the crow's example, the other birds came back. A great flock of them gathered at my feet, milling around and eating all the corn they wanted, with me powerless to do anything about it."

Realising that the figure posed no threat, Blue Jay resumed feeding.

"What use is a scarecrow who doesn't scare crows?" the voice lamented. "If it wasn't for this pole at my back holding me in place, I'd be off in a jiffy to seek my fortune, but..." He sighed. "It's very tedious, you know, being stuck up here night and day, not even able to take myself off to a different part of the field. I can't even *see* much of the field since that pesky crow sat on my shoulder – no, please don't go that way!" Blue Jay was shifting around in pursuit of more corn, oblivious to the scarecrow's request. "I'll lose sight of you," the scarecrow continued. "The crow pulled my hat down, you see, quite deliberately, so that it covered my larger eye, just to prove that he could."

Blue Jay didn't know how to respond, so kept eating. After sating his hunger, he studied the forlorn nearly-man, wishing he might do something to help. The pole that held the scrawny figure in place was beyond his capabilities, but perhaps there was something else he could manage. Blue Jay flew up and perched on the scarecrow's shoulder, chirping, "Friend!" to reassure him.

"What are you...?"

Blue Jay grasped the point of the lopsided hat and pulled, lifting it up to the crown of the scarecrow's head so that it no longer covered one eye.

Job completed, Blue Jay gave a cheerful chirrup – "There, at least you can see again!" – and then took to the air, leaving both the cornfield and its scarecrow behind.

"Oh, thank you, thank you!" the scarecrow called after him. "You surely are the kindest and most beautiful of birds!"

But Blue Jay knew this already.

With his energy levels restored, Blue Jay was able to take proper stock of his surroundings. He had no idea where the cyclone had brought him, but it was unlike any place he had been to before. The light seemed a little different – brighter, more vibrant than at home – and there was no denying the land was beautiful as well as bountiful. Tall, imperious trees, great stretches of green fields and ripe cereal, row upon row of flowers in every colour imaginable, a burbling stream whose surface rippled and sparkled with reflected sunlight, and a bewildering variety of birds, some with plumage so fine as to almost rival his own. Almost.

Yet everything struck him as a bit... peculiar, in a way that he couldn't begin to explain. Even the air tasted a little strange here.

Strangest of all, however, was the cyclone. It hung suspended in the air, a great grey cone, motionless and silent. Blue Jay could just make out the roof of the old farmhouse resting atop it. The most unsettling aspect had to be the silence. Strain as he might, all that he could hear was birdsong – not any song he recognised, but birdsong nonetheless. Where was the shriek that heralded the irresistible power of the wind? Where was any sound at all to signify a cyclone's presence? Yet here the cyclone was.

Curiosity drove him to fly towards the static storm, and as he drew nearer, further sounds came to the fore: a babble of excited voices and a soft tinkling as if many tiny bells were being rung at random. A small crowd had gathered beneath the frozen cyclone, gazing up in wonder, scratching their chins and gesticulating.

These had to be the oddest people he had ever seen. Short and squat, the size of human children yet with the features of adults. And all their clothing was blue – from grey-blue to green-blue, from deep military shades to palest cornflower and every hue in between. They wore nearly as many shades as Blue Jay's own plumage – though naturally none carried it off as well as he did.

They wore hats, too, round hats similar to the one that the scarecrow had worn, but theirs were festooned with tiny bells around the brim, which were the source of the tinkling sound.

Even as Blue Jay alighted on a nearby fencepost, curious to see what would happen next, an old woman appeared. Taller than those others present, she brandished a gnarled and crooked stick as if preparing to smite the onlookers. She was dressed plainly apart from her shoes, which were silver and sparkled in a way that Blue Jay could only admire.

"What are you gawping at?" she snapped at those watching.

They immediately started to disperse, hurrying away, some cowering down as if they'd been struck by that twisty staff before.

"I know that you Munchkins are shirkers," the woman called after them, "but laying down your tools in the middle of the day? Whatever next? Back to work, the lot of you. There are crops to be harvested, that fence to be mended..."

At this last, she gestured towards the post on which Blue Jay perched, evidently spotting him for the first time. "My, my, what a beautiful bird," she declared.

Had anyone else said this, Blue Jay might have preened to display just *how* beautiful, pirouetting to emphasise the striking blue and black bars of his tail feathers and the dazzling blue panels of his back. But the way this woman regarded him was so covetous that any temptation to show off disappeared in an instant. All he wanted to do was fly away.

Except that he couldn't. A strange tingling had enveloped his wings, spreading across his whole body and, try as he might, Blue Jay couldn't move. It reminded him of the lethargy that had crept upon him when he first arrived here, the paralysis that still held the storm and house at bay. For the first time it occurred to him that this woman, this *witch* – for what else could she be? – must be responsible.

He watched in horror as the woman strode towards him, crossing the short distance in long, vigorous strides that belied her apparent age. In mere seconds she towered above him.

"Now what have we here?" She grinned in a fashion that chilled him to the bone. It was predatory, causing Blue Jay to fear she might eat him on a whim.

"This is proving to be quite a morning," she said. "I came to the Munchkin Meadows to forage for wild herbs and spices for a particularly wicked spell I'm brewing." The cackle that followed convinced Blue Jay that he really didn't want to know what that implied. "And what do I find? First a cyclone threatening my Munchkin workers and now the strangest of birds…"

Her gaze intensified. "Not from around here, are you, my pretty?"

Blue Jay strained for all he was worth. He had defied the paralysis earlier when it struck the old farmhouse, surely he could do so again. But this compulsion seemed stronger, harder to break, perhaps because on this occasion he was the sole focus rather than just one component.

"That mosaic patterning on your back is quite exquisite," the crone purred. "What a pretty brooch it will make. Blue, too, which is the favoured colour of my Munchkins. It seems only fitting that, as their ruler, I should be adorned with something as blue and lovely as this, don't you agree? Rejoice, little bird, for you are to be honoured. Once you've been fully plucked I shall wear your plumes with pride." So saying, she reached out to grasp him.

Whether it was the prospect of being plucked bare or the horror of those taloned fingers coming towards him, Blue Jay could never be certain, but at last – with an almighty effort – he broke free of the enchantment and was able to move again. He launched himself from the fencepost, his heart and wings beating fit to burst as he skimmed low over the meadow grass.

Behind him the witch shrieked and cursed but he paid her

no heed, determined never to fall foul of her spells again. "Come back here, you—" Her voice cut off abruptly – in mid-yell – as there came a *whumph*. It wasn't an especially loud *whumph* yet it reverberated through the air. Still Blue Jay didn't look back, making for the safety of a tree at the near side of the meadow. Only once ensconced in its branches did he dare to peek.

Nestled in the meadow not far from his refuge stood the old farmhouse in which he had taken shelter from the storm. Of the witch there was no sign, and at first he assumed that she must have spirited herself away, but then something glinted in the sunlight and he saw her silver shoes protruding from beneath the house.

He was still considering the implications of that when the door to the building burst open and a girl appeared, stepping out into the meadow with a cry of wonder. She had a tumble of brown hair and wore a blue and white dress – the blue far too pale for Blue Jay's liking. At her heels scampered a furry black bundle on stubby legs with beady eyes that seemed to settle on Blue Jay immediately. He recognised them as the same eyes that had stared at him when he first sought respite from the cyclone. As if to confirm this, the dog gave a sharp yap and made a beeline towards him.

"Oh Toto, look."

The girl's words stopped the dog in its tracks. Four people were approaching the pair – three of the strange short men and a marginally taller woman with white, curly hair. In marked contrast to the men's blue attire, the hat she wore was also white, as was her pleated gown. Toto returned to his mistress, his fascination with birds evidently forgotten for now.

The elderly woman greeted the girl with deference and declared that she too was a witch. She had kindly eyes, which seemed to acknowledge Blue Jay in the tree and – was it his imagination? – smile at him, even as she continued speaking to the girl.

There followed some commotion among the men – Munchkins, the self-declared witch had called them – and the girl was given the silver shoes. Soon after, the witch conjured a slate with chalk marks on it, seemingly from nowhere, kissed the girl on the forehead, then spun around on the spot three times and… disappeared.

This set Toto barking once more, turning circles of his own, and left Blue Jay feeling lonely. It had only been a quick glance but a warm one. In that single look the woman had *seen* him in a way that no one else had since he arrived here. He was a long way from home and, inexplicably, felt that he had just lost a friend. Even the girl had her dog, Toto, for company, while he had no one. He watched the two of them walk away, the girl striding across the meadow without a care in the world and the dog trotting beside her. Blue Jay felt tempted to follow – here at least was a tenuous link to the land he knew – but before he could do so a voice spoke, startling him.

"Don't fret, dear bird. This is their path to tread, not yours." It was the kindly woman, who now sat on a bough close to him, though how she came to be there he had no idea. "I am the Good Witch of the North," she said, "and you are Blue Jay, the hero who distracted the Wicked Witch of the East to such an extent that a house came down on top of her."

Other birds, who had been hiding amongst the tree's

foliage, now emerged. They flitted over to sit close to the Good Witch, chirruping merrily, which reassured Blue Jay further.

The Good Witch's smile was quite disarming, and Blue Jay relaxed, feeling safe for the first time in a long while. "We are going to be the firmest of friends, you and I," she assured him. And he believed her.

"And that, dear children," said the Good Witch of the North as she closed the leatherbound book, "is the true story of how one small bird saved us all from the Wicked Witch of the East and restored freedom and happiness to all of Munchkin Country."

"Miss, miss!" A girl thrust her hand into the air.

"Yes, Nimmie?"

"How was Blue Jay able to escape the evil witch's spell and fly away like that?"

"That's a good question. No one knows for sure, but I suspect it's because Blue Jay doesn't come from Oz, and although very similar to our native creatures, the difference was just enough to ensure that the spell's hold on him was weaker than the witch assumed."

"Why did the house fall down to the ground when it did, miss?"

"Because keeping the house and the storm frozen in place required a lot of concentration, even for the Wicked Witch of the East, and when Blue Jay freed himself she was so surprised and so enraged that she forgot about them for a moment. That was all it took. Freed of her influence, the storm dissipated and the house… landed."

"On top of the horrible witch!" someone shouted gleefully.

"Indeed."

Once the merriment that followed had subsided, the Good Witch asked, "Now, who can tell me which of Dorothy's companions joined her in order to regain a heart…?"

The day's classes concluded soon after and the Munchkin children filed out, happily chatting among themselves, but one girl lingered. It was the same girl who had been so curious during the lesson. She shifted awkwardly from one foot to the other, clearly desperate to ask something further.

"Yes, Nimmie," said the Good Witch, "is there something I can help you with?"

"I was just wondering, miss, about Blue Jay. Did he ever get to go home?"

"Ah…" The Good Witch paused to collect her thoughts. "Therein lies another story, the telling of which is not for today. Suffice to say that no, he never found his way back, but then he didn't need to. Once word spread of the part he had played in ridding us of the Wicked Witch, Blue Jay became celebrated among birdkind throughout the land, and to this day he is welcomed and fêted wherever he goes. Therefore, he is perfectly content to make his home here in Oz."

"He's still alive, then?"

"Oh yes, very much so. If ever you're walking in the woods and hear a gate squeak when there is no gate to be seen, or should you hear the whisper of a song to which you can't quite catch the words, keep an eye out for a flash of blue among the branches. That will be Blue Jay. He can't resist showing off a little, even now, and who can blame him?"

"For he is the most beautiful of all birds!" Nimmie said, clasping her hands gleefully in front of her.

The Good Witch smiled. "Exactly so," she agreed.

# FINAL REPORT ON THE REX REMBRANDT AFFAIR

## (BY SCRAPS, THE PATCHWORK GIRL OF OZ)

**M. R. CAREY**

*And I mean final. No arguments or take-backsies, Your Majesty. This was a knotty one, a conundrum. It gave me heaaaches and stretched my seams, and now that it's done I want nothing more than to give myself a good shaking out and be done with it.*

> *I love a vexing puzzle*
> *Like a rabbit loves his hutch*
> *Or a bitey dog his muzzle*
> *Which is to say not much.*

*But let's see now. How to tell this? Because reports, when you come right down to it, are not really in my report-oire. I have no rapport with reports. But I am always in your service (not your tea service but your secret one) so I'll put on a solemn face like an owl or a secretary of state and do the bestest best I can. I'll use a solemn style too. I can do it when I need to.*

*Ahem. A report, by Scraps.*

Rex Rembrandt. A king. An artist. A winner in life's intricate and endless game.

And the game is of the kind called zero-sum. If Rex is a winner, it follows that whoever he's with in any given situation must be a loser.

The current loser is a man who, when asked, gave his name as Dr Oswald Pipt. He claims to be from Australia but this seems unlikely given his accent, which to Rex's well-attuned ear sounds like Czech or Polish laid over North African French. He's a curious specimen, age indeterminate, hair white and wild, body and limbs twisting as he speaks into configurations that seem ill-advised.

Pipt is unhappy. He has been ill-treated, it seems, by almost everyone he's ever met. By a controlling wife, a devious old hag, a feral cat, but most of all by the queen of his distant country (which sounds less and less like Australia the more he talks about it). Pipt would have Rex know that he is a scholar, a scientist, one of the foremost thinkers in his esoteric field. "Magic," he insists in a way that's somehow fierce and pathetic at once. "I am an adept in the art of magic. And I've made such advances, my good sir, as you could never imagine. Powder of Life! Liquid of Petrifaction! Condensing and decoction of the great pillars of human nature, as intelligence, courage, prudence, compassion, fortitude, ambition, generosity of mind and spirit, patience, moral principle – and of course their opposites which I will forbear to name."

The doctor (if he is a doctor) takes a sip of his beer and blinks a great many times as rapidly as a semaphore. His eyes roam around the bar, his expression furtive and hunted. "And for this I was banished," he hisses. "Forbidden to practise my mystery. Told that I would be executed if I persisted. Executed! In Oz, where life is eternal barring accidents and sorcerous interventions. Only think of it. Queen Ozma proscribes my magic and at the same time threatens me with her own! The sheer hypocrisy of it!"

"Shocking," Rex murmurs, idly stirring his cocktail. He only popped into this bar, the Stalwart Soldier on Warren Street, for a quick drink on his way back from a consultation. He was tired. He was disgruntled. He was frustrated and troubled by the continuing existence of a man named Kenneth Baskin. The wispy-haired grotesque sitting alone in the darkest corner of the room had drawn his attention, had seemed at the very least to offer a diversion.

So Rex had bought the man a drink. What's going on with you, he asked, and by asking had unleashed this torrent of rancid sorrows.

"And she still pursues me," Dr Pipt continues, choking back a sob. "Even here. I've forsaken Oz, I've stepped across the sundering divide into this…" His long fingers flex, indicating the bar or the city or perhaps the whole world.

"This nonsensical place, where magic is barely even acknowledged and sorcerers are accorded no respect at all. Where in order to live, in order to be granted the perquisites of life, a man must first amass and then disperse notional tokens of metal or oiled paper."

"Money," Rex interposes helpfully.

"Money, thank you. And where – strangest of all! – death is accepted as a necessity rather than as an inconvenience best avoided. I find it, to tell you frankly, baffling. I don't like it. I don't approve."

"Well, who would?" Rex demurs. He's had enough of this brain-rot. He's about to gulp down his dregs and take his leave.

But the other man is still talking. "And so," he says, "in order to get by, you understand. Though it's a profanation of my gift. Though my very stomach to a great extent rebels at it… needs must, you understand… and the amount in question… I refuse to haggle. You'll determine yourself what this marvel, this miracle deserves by way of exchange. What its value is in… in money. Yes?"

Rex waves vaguely. He lost track of that one, but the doctor has mostly been talking to himself this whole time so that's fine.

What happens next is puzzling. Dr Pipt takes a used matchstick from the ashtray on the table between them and proceeds to perform an ad hoc surgery on it. He uses his fingernails to split the pith with finicky care, peeling it back to left and right, top and bottom. When he's finished, the matchstick is a stick man with the black business end as its head and four splayed, splinter-thin limbs.

"Cute," Rex observes, but his lip curls with contempt. What has this man ingested besides ethyl alcohol? Whatever it is, it must be strong.

"And now bear witness," declares the doctor portentously. From his pocket he takes a small drawstring bag, into which he dips his right hand. When he brings it out again he holds a pinch of white powder between finger and thumb. Ah, Rex thinks, that answers that question.

The doctor sprinkles the powder on his partially dissected matchstick. "Bear witness," he says again, this time in a reverential whisper.

The matchstick man stirs. He sits up. He tries to stand, but since his spindly legs end in narrow points he doesn't manage the thing. Rex stares, transfixed, his boredom of a moment before a thing forgotten. "How...?" he manages. But the doctor doesn't answer. He picks up the little homunculus, bends back the end of each leg to make rudimentary feet, and sets him down again. The matchstick man walks with an odd, stumbling gait across the table, arms thrust out in front of him. He walks all the way to the edge, tips over and falls. Pipt makes no attempt to stop him or to catch him before he hits the floor. He's lost down there among the empty crisp packets and accumulated dust-balls.

"No eyes, you see," Pipt says. "The powder provides animation, the spark or vital force, but it effects no other changes. It can only work on what's already there. I wouldn't have you complain once our business is concluded that you'd been cheated or misled."

Rex has to parse that last sentence two or three times

before he realises what's happening here. His heart skips so many beats in a row that he thinks he's having an aneurysm. "That's very scrupulous of you," he says, keeping his voice steady with an effort. "And I'm somewhat interested in making the purchase. You say, though, that you're unfamiliar with our currency, which puts me in the position of having to make an offer which I think is fair. What would you say to a hundred million pounds?"

Pipt gives him a narrow-eyed, appraising stare. "Two," he says.

"One and a half."

"No. The powder is worth two."

"Done," says Rex. "As you pointed out earlier, haggling demeans us both." He takes out his phone. "Let me have your bank details and I'll transfer the funds."

The doctor hesitates. "I don't as yet… that is… Bank details?"

"No matter." Rex waves the problem away. "Where are you staying while you're here? I can have my man bring the cash around to you in a wheelbarrow."

"I have no lodgings as yet."

"Hmm." Rex puts the phone away again. "In that case we'll have to do this the old-fashioned way." He has his briefcase with him, and in one of the pockets of the briefcase is that venerable antique, a cheque book. Some of his older clients still believe in such things and he always comes prepared. He writes a cheque for the requisite sum, signs it and dates it and solemnly hands it over. "Take this to any bank," he says, "and they will give you the money. They may require you to open an account first, but that's not difficult. Congratulations, Dr Pipt. You're a rich man."

Pipt takes the cheque but regards it dubiously. "This isn't money, though," he says.

"No. It's a promissory bond – a cheque, in common parlance. The money is in my account and will be transferred to you on presentation of this document."

Pipt still hesitates. Rex gives an impatient shrug. "Do we have an agreement or not?" he demands. "I thought you were serious about this."

"I am," Pipt says. "Never doubt me, my fine fellow. Here." He hands over the bag of powder and Rex pockets it so quickly it leaves an after-image on the air. "Excellent," he says. "Pleasure doing business with you. Take care now. Enjoy your newfound wealth."

He leaves without a backward glance, which is just as well because Pipt would be sure to register the huge smirk on his face. There's a great deal less than two hundred million pounds in Rex's business account, but that's a side issue because the cheque is dated the 1st of October 1066 and he signed it with the name Scrooge McDuck.

Nobody could call Rex Rembrandt an amiable man, or a decent one. He's clever enough, to be sure – in some ways you could even call him gifted – but his wits have never made him rich enough to be happy or happy enough to know when to stop.

He was in his time a wayward youth and the marks of it

are written on his body. On his left arm is a tattoo of a skull with a dagger in its teeth, on his chest a pouncing tiger. These days he's much more respectable, at least on the face of things. He runs his own company, which offers interior design consultancy at the high end of the market. For the right price he'll turn your mansion from a tawdry pile into something really special, so you won't be ashamed to have the Russian oligarchs round for a poker game. Needless to say, the right price is so high there's no getting close to it without ropes and pitons and an independent oxygen supply. You don't hire Rex unless you bank with Coutts and use your own private jet when you pop out for a pint of milk.

So Rex is doing very well for himself, all things considered, but here's the snag. Every now and then he'll walk into some billionaire's pied-à-terre and see something purely lovely that he'd really, really like to own. Rex doesn't live in a mansion himself, just a six-bedroomed detached house in Monken Hadley, and truth be told that fact doesn't sit well with him. Why should the oiks who hire his immaculate taste because they've got none of their own get to sip the delights of every human culture while Rex sucks up the bitter lees?

He took to stealing. A Chimú sculpture here, a Graff diamond wristwatch there – anything that was small enough to be portable and beautiful enough to make the risk worthwhile. Sadly, however, he made a wretched thief. His fine eye was usually on the object of his covetous hunger rather than the rest of his surroundings. Hence Kenneth Baskin, a wealthy octogenarian who caught Rex filching a pair of emerald cufflinks when he was meant to be laying out swatches for a wall hanging. Panicked, Rex reacted as any reasonable man would in that situation and beat Baskin to death.

Or so he thought. But Baskin persists in a coma, stubbornly hanging on despite horrific injuries. If he recovers and points the finger, Rex is done for. This invidious prospect has sapped his spirits and cast a pall over his mood for weeks. Fear and fretfulness have left him so depleted he hasn't even contemplated any further thefts. He's been expecting the knock on his door, the reading of his rights, the ignoble end of all his joys.

But now things have changed. Now there's the powder. The threat of Baskin's waking still hangs over him but it seems he might have found a way to resume his acquisitions that carries no personal risk.

Rex experiments. He's seen how the powder worked on a matchstick, giving it locomotion (because it had legs) but leaving it blind (because it had no eyes). His first trial run is with a Matryoshka doll, a gift from his aunt that he finds hideous but has been obliged to keep on display in order to avoid reproaches and hurt feelings. He takes it down from the mantelpiece and places it on the living room table. He undoes the drawstring on Dr Pipt's bag. He dips his hand and takes the smallest pinch of the powder between finger and thumb. How much is too much? How little is not enough? Rex rubs finger and thumb very delicately together, letting a few grains of powder sift down.

The doll does nothing.

He releases a few more grains.

Still nothing.

Impatient, Rex smears the powder across the doll's painted face. The doll blinks and sneezes. "Боже!" it exclaims in a thin, reedy voice. "Как щекотно!"

Rex screams and jumps back, but he quickly regains his composure. He leans in, fascinated, to examine the thing. The Matryoshka regards him with a stoical, slightly wary gaze.

"You can talk," Rex says. "Can you understand me?"

"Ты мерзкий ублюдок," the Matryoshka opines. "И мне очень некомфортно."

"Speak English," Rex commands.

"I was only remarking," the Matryoshka says, "that I'm terribly uncomfortable. I think something's moving inside me."

Rex has an idea what that might be. He removes the lid of the Matryoshka, eliciting a murmur of protest, to find the next largest doll squirming and wriggling underneath. "Там было темно!" it exclaims. "Thank you! It was dark in there."

Rex explores further. Underneath the second doll is a third, under the third a fourth. He's never liked the Matryoshka enough to find out how deep it goes, but he makes his way down the stack now and counts seven in all. They gossip softly as he reassembles them, seemingly as comfortable when they're in two pieces as when they're put back together.

"Are you my mother?" the smallest squeaks, gazing up adoringly at the largest.

"I suppose I must be mother to all of you," the largest says, "for the family likeness is astonishing."

Rex flicks the smallest with his thumbnail, sending it rolling on its long axis across the table-top. With cries of dismay – "Little sister! Little sister!" – the others waddle off in pursuit. Their progress is slow: having no legs they can only rock from side to side on their bases, lurching a little further forward each time. It's really funny to watch, at least to begin with, but the more he sees the little limbless beans struggling to move, the creepier and more disgusting it looks. He sweeps them all off the table and kicks them out of sight under the sofa. He's drawn to beauty, and the sentient blobs are anything but beautiful. He'll have to tell his aunt the cleaning woman stole them.

But to Hell with all that! Rex sits back and gloats. The powder is everything Dr Pipt said it was – worth every last penny of the two hundred million pounds he didn't spend on it.

It's time to get down to business.

What Rex has in mind is something like the first act of a heist movie, the one in which the mastermind assembles his team one by one despite their vehement protestations that they're out of the game. But Rex's team will make no such protestations. Rex's team will be inanimate objects awakened to sentience by the Powder of Life.

They will, not to put too fine a point on it, be toys – action figures already sculpted or moulded into human shape and therefore possessed of all the relevant limbs and sensory organs. There would be no point at all in sending in the Matryoshkas, which are now skulking under Rex's sideboard, casting fearful or reproachful glances at him whenever he passes.

Rex outgrew action figures at age ten, but by pure coincidence he still has one. It's Sir Percival the Gold Knight, an antique manufactured by a now-defunct American toy company in the 1960s. Rex acquired it as part of a job lot at an auction and kept forgetting to trash it or sell it on. He anoints Sir Percival now, welcomes him to his new life and introduces himself as God. Sir Percival kneels and swears fealty on his plastic sword's hilt. Rex accepts this oath with due solemnity.

Sir Percival will be the leader of the heist team because his solid plastic core gives him some degree of heft. The other toys that Rex picks up on the cheap via eBay are of more modern manufacture and much flimsier build. There are two soldier dolls, a commando and an adventurer with ginger hair and a manly beard made of flock; a female superhero in a spider-themed costume that features a white hoodie; a squid-headed alien from a science fiction franchise; and a leggy blonde in a white mini-dress sporting a shocking amount of bling who is purportedly a Priestess of Power. Rex is clueless about popular culture and has no idea who any of these personages are. He chooses them with a single criterion in mind, which is points of articulation. He avoids Barbies and their ilk because their knees and elbows don't bend. He wants his miniature thieves to be able to run and jump and climb, flex and grip, wield a variety of tools.

He hits an early obstacle on that score. None of the toys have fully-functional hands. Their fingers are a single moulding with only the thumbs separate and opposable. Obviously this will severely limit their usefulness. Rex performs minor surgeries with a craft knife, slicing into the mono-block hands in several places in order to create more or less serviceable fingers – usually only two, sometimes three, but enough to make them capable of grasping and holding.

Of course that still leaves the question of what they will grasp and hold. He builds up a bank of equipment for them: strong twine, zip-ties, a miniature block and tackle from a model railway, a grapnel hook made out of twisted and folded paper clips. He glues LED lights to the chests of the two soldiers, taping the little pill-shaped batteries to their backs. He equips the female figure wearing the spider costume with a tie-pin and the squid-headed alien with a blade from a straight razor.

The toys have been pretty docile through all of this. None of them showed any surprise or alarm at their own sudden emergence into consciousness. There were no existential crises or meltdowns, which he'd been half-afraid there would be. As for his own status, Rex introduced himself to all of them as God, which (let's face it) might as well be true as far as they were concerned, and they didn't argue. He told them he was the greatest god there ever was and that they were his champions, his chosen ones, raised above all others because of their great virtue and courage. He gave them their own Eden too, a cardboard box with an old cushion wedged into the bottom. And in place of the whole don't-eat-the-fruit thing he ordered them never to leave the box without his say-so. Like the Matryoshka they unnerve him somewhat and he prefers to have as little to do with them as possible.

He notes that they have different personalities – the soldiers gruff and capable, the spider-woman sassy and bold, the alien a willing imbecile and the Priestess volatile but pragmatic. Does this reflect the natures of the original characters on whom they're based? Rex doesn't know and doesn't care. What matters is that they all do what they're told.

Their first outing is to an apartment in Knightsbridge where Rex has recently done a complete redesign for a crusty dowager. In the course of his labours he spotted and admired an aquamarine-and-diamond tiara which bears the unmistakeable and exquisite hallmarks of Peter Fabergé. Rex takes photographs, draws up a plan, briefs his team in obsessive detail about where they'll find the lovely thing – in the aforementioned dowager's jewellery box, which in turn is located in a drawer in her bedside table.

Sir Percival is troubled. "My lord," he protests, "is not theft a thing forbidden by your own commandments?"

"As a general rule, yes," Rex admits. "But this old lady has lived a very wicked life. In fact, she's a thief herself and has no claim to the tiara. She stole it from…" He's making this up as he goes along but there's barely a pause. "…From the rightful princess, who she locked in a dungeon. So that she could usurp her rule. And now the princess needs the tiara to prove who she is and take her rightful place on the throne."

"Such perfidy as never yet was seen!" Sir Percival cries, visibly shocked.

"That's my point," Rex says. "Don't let me down here, gang."

The toys promise that they won't.

Rex takes the Underground and then walks to the building, arriving just before midnight with a bright orange Sainsbury's shopping bag dangling negligently from his left hand. He has the access code for the street door, given to him by the old lady while he was working on her soft furnishings, but he doesn't know how often the code changes and in any case he's not so stupid as to let himself be seen on the CCTV cameras positioned both inside and outside the front entrance.

There is an ornamental screen of bay laurels to both sides of the door. Rex inserts his shopping bag into this screen at pavement level, making sure to thrust it well in among the roots of the juvenile trees where it can't be seen. With this done he simply walks away.

There is an all-night bar in the lobby area of the nearby Palgrave Hotel. Rex orders himself a glass of Cabernet Franc and sips it while flicking desultorily through the latest issue of House and Garden. There is an article by Calvin Gaynes about floral motifs that he finds entertaining but jejune.

After perhaps three-quarters of an hour he closes his magazine, pays his bill and retraces his steps. In his absence his little band of reavers should by this time have infiltrated the apartment by way of a drainpipe and an open window, found their way to the old lady's bedroom, located and rifled the jewellery box and returned – with the tiara – to their start point. Or else they will have miscarried, in which case Rex defies any police officer in the land to prove a connection between a group of enchanted toys on a crime spree and himself.

When he reaches the spot where he set down the bag he kneels as if to fasten an errant shoelace. This subterfuge allows him to retrieve the bag, which feels satisfactorily heavy – much heavier, in fact, than he had anticipated. He manages to resist the urge to examine the contents as he hefts it and goes calmly on his way.

At home he decants both his tiny strike team and their haul, dumping them all out directly onto his bed. He gasps when he sees what they've brought him. In addition to the tiara there are several rings and necklaces that are very fine, some gold and silver chains and an enormous quantity of earrings.

The toys pick themselves up and at Percival's signal come to stand in a line next to this treasure trove, facing Rex with their hands clasped behind their backs as though they're soldiers at parade rest.

"You went beyond your brief," Rex observes.

"My lord," Sir Percival reports, "when we found the jewellery box we saw that there was a wondrous deal of riches there. We reasoned that if the tiara was stolen then most likely these other pieces were too. We considered further that if this were not the case then we could at your command return the other treasures later. If we have overstepped and offended you, Lord, then the fault is mine and I pray you let the punishment be mine too."

"No, it's fine," Rex says. "You did good. Great, in fact. I'll, um, get these to the princess and tell her the good news. As for you guys…" He nods towards the box. Percival bows his head in acquiescence and the others all salute. They climb into the box and Rex closes the lid. He's exhausted from the night's excitement but much too wired to sleep. He sits up for more than an hour admiring the tiara from many different angles. Finally he dozes off, fully dressed, still clutching the wonderful thing to his chest.

This early success provides proof of concept, on which Rex is quick to capitalise. The targets now are not current clients but past ones whose security he was unable to penetrate at the time but whose treasures he noted and has yearned for ever since. From a retired stockbroker in Kennington the toys skilfully remove an early de Chirico and a blue period Picasso, cutting them neatly from their frames and carrying them away like rolled-up carpets. They divest a disgraced but still obscenely rich minor aristo of a lovely Anthony Caro piece in mahogany and cedar – too big and heavy to go through a letterbox, that one, so they lower it out of a window on pulleys while the duke snores like a chainsaw three bedrooms along. They purloin a Gasparo da Salò viola, among the first ever made, from the grace-and-favour house of a government minister who not only can't play but according to most authorities is absolutely tone sodding deaf.

They have, in other words, an absolute field day. They do for Rex what he proved unable to do for himself, bringing the wealth and wonders of the world under his roof where he can give them the adoration and worship they deserve.

Unexpectedly this proves to be a point of contention between Rex and the toys. One evening, when he has the full panoply arranged on and around his bed, he realises that he has an audience. Sir Percival has managed to climb up to the top of his box and lifted the lid to peer out. It's not quite breaking the commandment because he hasn't actually left the box, but it's pretty hard to ignore.

"Well?" Rex demands. "What is it?"

"My lord," Percival ventures, "did you not say that you

intended to restore all of these treasures to their rightful owners?"

Rex decides to head that one off at the pass. "I did say that," he replies, "and what I say I will do. Am I not your God? And isn't my word the only law you know?"

Sir Percival agrees that both of these propositions are true. His tone is meek and his eyes are downcast.

"Well then," Rex says, "what do you think you're doing, coming around here and poking at me with questions and insinuations? What does your lack of faith say about you as a person? Hmm? Maybe you'd prefer to serve some other god, in which case… you know, wrath, smitings, it could get ugly."

Sir Percival begs forgiveness and Rex says he will think about it. The toy slides back down inside the box. And there are no further questions after that, but to Rex's chagrin there are looks that amount to questions; looks that express doubts about his integrity, his goals and the very basis of the relationship he's forged with the toys. He expected absolute obedience, but it seems that's too much to ask these days even from entities that owe you their very existence.

But Rex is prepared to be magnanimous so long as there's no more backsliding. He can't stay angry for long when he's surrounded by so much beauty and perfection. He continues his routine, ending each day with a protracted adoration of the wonderful things he owns – a living, breathing hymn of praise to the human spirit and the maker's spark. Has anyone ever orgasmed from artistic appreciation? Rex certainly feels something quasi-sexual at moments like this.

But his blissed-out mood is spoiled again a few days later

when he learns from Kenneth Baskin's sister that Baskin has recovered from his coma. "He barely got to see the wonderful work you did on his study and drawing room, Mr Rembrandt! I feel sure the first thing he does when he can talk again will be to thank you."

No, Rex thinks grimly, the first thing he'll do is have me arrested. But that 'when he can talk again' offers at least a straw to clutch at. "Kenneth still isn't entirely awake then?" he asks hopefully.

"Oh, he's awake," Victoria Baskin assures him. "So far he's only moved his eyes, but the doctors tell me that he's getting stronger every day. And the best news of all is that there's no sign of brain damage. He'll soon be sitting up and chatting with us!"

And calling the police, to tell them that the man who replaced his drapes also swiped his cufflinks and beat him senseless. The whole thing is exasperating, especially now when Rex is riding so very high. He hates that his past actions persist in having consequences. He keeps Victoria talking, ascertaining as casually and indirectly as he can that Kenneth is still at the same private hospital in Hampstead to which he was originally taken. In a room of his own, of course, not on a general ward. That makes it easier.

Easier for what? Rex catches his own train of thought on the fly and rides it a little further. What is he contemplating here? When he assaulted Baskin it was an act of desperation. He hit out with no conscious thought at all and was a little queasy afterwards to discover that he was capable of such crude violence. It didn't sit well with his self-image. To be ruthless is one thing, but to clobber an elderly gentleman with a marble paperweight borders on the déclassé.

This – the thing towards which he's edging by the slowest and wariest of degrees – this will be different. Specifically, it will be murder. Rex will be suppressing Kenneth Baskin's testimony by suppressing Kenneth Baskin, permanently.

But honestly, what is the alternative? He can't be expected to throw up his hands and surrender to fate. He's building something for the ages, and if he's arrested his entire collection will go back to its original owners who are far less well equipped to appreciate it. Besides, a man of his sensibilities would wither in prison. It would be monstrous, a crime against nature.

He decides. Or rather he allows himself to acknowledge the decision he's already made. Kenneth Baskin has to die so that Rex Rembrandt can live and prosper.

There remains the question of how, but that's a question that virtually answers itself. He tips the toys out of their box and calls them to order. "I have a new mission for you," he tells them. "There is an evil man who has defied my commandments and compacted with the Devil. I've passed judgment on him, and it falls on you lot to carry out that judgment. He is to die. Not suffer, you understand, just die. We're going to do it painlessly by giving him an overdose of a painkilling drug. That shows wisdom and compassion, as you'd expect from a just and kind god."

There's absolute silence from the toys. They're staring at Rex like he's just told them he's going to take a shit in their box and then sprinkle some Powder of Life on the turd. "Do we understand each other?" he asks – quite mildly under the circumstances.

"We are to end a life," Sir Percival summarises.

"That's it," Rex says, relieved. "Okay, let's get down to the details."

When it comes to drugs, Rex has only ever done cocaine and weed, but it's not as though opioids are hard to obtain. Pills are easier than injectables but a syringe is what he needs and he's willing to splash a great deal of cash so in due course a syringe comes his way. Fifty milligrams of fentanyl, enough to kill the average man or woman twenty times over. He explains to the toys how to find a vein, how to sink the business end of the hypodermic in to the proper depth and depress the plunger. This will take three of them, two to hold the hypo straight and the third to lean in and do the dirty. He lets them choose who will carry out these roles because they know their own strengths and he's never really been a details man.

He makes them practise it again and again with syringes full of water, injecting into the cushion from the bottom of their box. And while that's going on he visits Kenneth Baskin in his hospital bed so he can get the lie of the land, memorising the route to his room. It's a risk, but Baskin is asleep when Rex arrives and he doesn't stay long. If he had been awake Rex would have found some excuse not to go into the room. "Come back soon," a cheerful nurse tells him. "He's getting better every day. I think he'll be sitting up and talking before the end of the week."

Rex steps up the practice drills. He makes the toys study his hand-drawn map of the hospital until they can recite by rote the route to Baskin's room. Details man or not, he's got to be absolutely certain they get this right. He notices that most times it's Squid-head and the Priestess of Power who hold the hypo and Percival who drives it home. The soldier dolls turn out to be curiously squeamish about such things.

Not that the others are happy. Percival asks Rex several times whether he's absolutely sure, sure beyond all fathom of possible doubt, that this wicked man has to die.

Rex gets prissy. "Of course I'm sure, Percy. Gods don't make mistakes. We pride ourselves on our infallibility. And the less infallible ones, well they just fall by the wayside. It's a god-eat-god world out there."

Sir Percival nods, his handsome poly-acrylic face lined with sombre thought and moral responsibility.

"Great," Rex says. "One more time from the top."

When he's satisfied that his little wetworks team is up to the job, he transfers them to their old plastic bag and takes a short drive over to Hampstead. As with the robberies he's chosen a quiet time, well after midnight when the streets are empty and there's no one to see him ghost up to the hospital's rear entrance. There's an ambulance bay that's still open, a single vehicle sitting in its cross-hatched spot in front of an up-and-over door that's raised just a crack. Light spills out from inside but there's no movement. Rex waits for a few minutes to be sure. Then he sets down the bag and chivvies the toys out onto the concrete verge.

"Don't let yourselves be seen," he warns them. "Spider-hoodie, you're the advance scout. Go ahead of the others and make sure the coast is clear. If anyone does see you just stand still and hope they mistake you for ordinary toys. That way you might still get a chance to complete the kill."

"My lord," Percival says, "if by any means I might entreat your mercy for this man, though he has deserved your wrath—"

"I'm going to stop you there," Rex says, "because it feels like we've been here before. Make up your damn mind, Percy. I mean seriously. What side are you on in this? The side of decency and right and divine law or the side of depraved, evil cunts who piss me off?"

He waits. Eventually Percival takes the knee and ducks his head. "My lord," he murmurs, "you round me right. I will take your words to heart."

"Thank you. Okay, off you go then."

One by one the toys go down on hands and knees and crawl under the corrugated steel door. When they're all inside Rex hands them the hypo and gives them his blessing.

They're not inside for very long, but lurking in the shadow of the lone ambulance Rex feels every second. When the toys come scuffling and sliding back under the door he bundles them into the bag in frantic haste, his hands shaking. Murder is new to him and he's not blasé about it yet. He has to force himself not to run back to his car, head ducked down inside his coat as though he can already feel the heavy weight of some policeman's hand clamping down on his shoulders to stop him in his tracks.

By the time he gets home and shuts his door against the world he's a nervous wreck. He drops the bag but doesn't bother to release the toys from it. He can't look them in the eye right then. He just asks one question. "Percy, how did it go down?"

"My lord," comes the barely audible voice from inside the bag. "I did exactly as you bid me do."

Good enough. Rex pours himself a stiff whisky and drinks it off in a single gulp. Then he staggers up the stairs, falls onto the bed fully-dressed and knows no more until morning.

Except…

It's not morning when he wakes. The light is coming from his bedside lamp, a sphere of radiance that ends at about the level of his knees. The rest of the room is in total darkness. Rex's wrists have been fastened to the bedposts with the zip-ties that he gave to the toys. He can't see his ankles but he assumes the same has been done to them because they certainly can't move. He's spread-eagled on the bed, immobile and helpless.

"Hey!" he croaks. "Hey! What… what's happening? Where are you?"

The toys step into the light. They stand in a line beside his head. Their manner is grave and solemn, as though they're attending a funeral. "My lord," Sir Percival says, "you must forgive these indignities."

"No I fucking mustn't!" Rex explodes. "Untie me! Set me free right now or I promise there will be wrath and smitings for everyone!"

"No," the Priestess of Power says.

"No smitings," the commando agrees. "Not yet. There are things we've got to get clear."

"Questions to be asked," says Spider-hoodie.

"Matters to be resolved," clarifies the adventurer, scratching his flock beard.

"Bollocks!" yells Rex. "Untie me! I fucking mean it!"

"You must hear us out," says Sir Percival. "We require this of you, and if it be presumptuous then you will deal with us accordingly. But I must say, my lord, that your being unable to free yourself unaided speaks against you."

Rex simmers down. He can see that he's in trouble here. He doesn't know why yet, but he can see the benefit of listening to what the toys have to say and then spinning it when he has a better sense of what's going on in their tiny minds. "Very well," he says. "Speak, my creations. Your lord is listening."

"Well, that's sort of the problem," Spider-hoodie tells him. "We're not sure that you are our lord."

"What?" Rex is indignant all over again. "Didn't I create you?"

"It seems you did," Sir Percival says. "But we saw how this was done. In the Bible we're told that God created the universe merely by speaking a word. You created us by sprinkling us with this powder." Squid-head advances into the circle of light, hauling the drawstring bag of Powder of Life from the drawer of Rex's bedside table.

"That's not yours!" Rex protests. "That's mine! I forbid you to touch it!"

"Then you admit that you're only a sorcerer, not a god?" Sir Percival asks. "That this is the source of your power?"

Rex hesitates. He'll really have to watch his step here. "No," he says. "Not at all. But it is the repository for my power, which means it's holy. None of you should go near it." He tries for a more authoritative tone. "I, your god, command this."

Sir Percival folds his arms.

"I said—" Rex blurts.

"Yes, my lord, I heard what you said. But it is for us to speak now. We have been thinking, and we have been talking."

"I didn't give you permission to do either of those things!"

"No. But we did them anyway. We were troubled by the tasks you set us. As the God of the Covenant you should be the embodiment of good and right and justice, but you commanded us to steal and then to kill. We could not reconcile these things."

"You don't need to," Rex protests. "You just need to obey!"

"We could not reconcile these things," Sir Percival repeats, "and so we looked elsewhere for guidance. We met a prophet, a sibyl, and we asked her to give us of her wisdom."

"She's a false prophet," Rex says at once. He has no idea what Percy is talking about but it's probably best to get that in early.

"Perhaps. Or it may be that you are a false God. How are we to know? We asked the sibyl this and she promised us guidance. She is come among us now to give it." The toys part, making a space between them at the very edge of the lamplit circle. Nothing happens. Nobody comes to fill the gap.

"I think your sibyl bailed on you," Rex scoffs.

The toys say nothing. They only wait. A few more moments pass, and Rex has another barbed comment on the tip of his tongue when something moves in the darkness, lumbering, uncertain, off-kilter.

The Matryoshka doll waddles into the lamplight.

"Behold," Spider-hoodie says, "the seven-in-one."

"Oh no," Rex objects. "Oh no no no. This... this isn't any kind of a prophet. She— they— whatever fucking pronoun it's using, she's not a sibyl, she's just a toy like you."

"I am mother and daughter both," the Matryoshka says. "Alpha and omega. Beginning and end."

"You're insane!" Rex corrects her.

"Disassemble me and see," the Matryoshka says. Squid-head and Spider-hoodie obey, moving in from either side to dismount the Matryoshka's upper half and set it on the duvet next to the lower body. The head of the second doll peers out.

"Disassemble me," it says, "and see."

The ritual is repeated five more times as the toys stand reverently by. When all seven dolls are free, Squid-head and Spider-hoodie reunite their heads with their bodies and step back into line.

"We are the seven in one," the biggest Matryoshka says. "The wisdom of the ages is ours, to know and to tell."

Rex can only stare in bemusement, not unmixed with admiration. Game sees game, and he has to admit that the Matryoshka knows how to work a crowd.

"Oh all-seeing one," the Priestess of Power says, "we stand in sore need of your counsel. Is this that calls itself Rex a god, a lord of creation who has the right to command our obedience? Or is it only some titan from Time's dawn, a being as flawed as any of us despite his vast size and awesome power?"

"Well, that's very much the question," the Matryoshka agrees. "Tell me, why do you doubt him? For certainly he has the power of creation."

"He told us to steal," Sir Percival declares. "And then to kill."

"To kill!" The Matryoshka's eyes widen and she purses her lips. "That's a shocking thing. Who were you to kill, and how?"

"A man named Kenneth Baskin," says the commando. "A giant like the Rex. We were supposed to kill him with poison."

"And do you still have this poison?"

"We do," Sir Percival confirms. "At the last we could not bring ourselves to end a life. Not without knowing for sure that it was our god that demanded it of us."

Rex can't stay silent when he hears of this betrayal. "You said you did as you were told!" he cries.

"I obeyed your final command to me, my lord," Percival replies with cold dignity. "You told me to make a choice."

"Bring the poison forth, then," the Matryoshka says. "I think I see an easy way to settle this."

The two soldiers go off into the dark and return a minute or so later with the hypodermic. They set it down at the Matryoshka's feet.

"What thing is this?" she asks Rex. "Speak. Is it what they say, a poison that will kill a man?"

And the rest, Rex thinks. He doesn't like how this is going at all. "It's a medicine," he hedges. "But sometimes… yes, it's been known to kill. Quickly. Painlessly. I'm a merciful god! Listen, you need to be really careful with that stuff. It's very, very strong!"

"This is what I suggest," the Matryoshka tells the rest of the toys. "Inject the Rex with the poison. If he survives then you'll know he's truly a god."

"But if he dies," Sir Percival points out, "then we will have committed the very sin we sought to avoid."

"Ah," says the Matryoshka, "but you have the Powder of Life. If he dies you can bring him back."

This is such transparent good sense that all the toys agree at once. Rex is the only one who objects, first commanding and then begging and finally screaming as Squid-head and the Priestess of Power bring the hypo up against his bound wrist. Spider-hoodie taps up a vein. Sir Percival drives the plunger home.

The titanic dose sends Rex into respiratory arrest almost immediately. He splutters, his face going red and then purple as he struggles to get some air into his stalled lungs. Then he dies.

The toys have their answer, but the sight of Rex's suffering leaves them shocked and dismayed. Quickly they deploy the Powder of Life to bring him back. They have no idea how much is enough, given his superhuman stature, but they intend to be cautious and try a little at a time until he stirs. That plan is moot when the Priestess of Power trips over the adventurer's foot and upends the entire bag into Rex's gaping mouth.

Rex revives. But the opioid is still coursing through his system and it hasn't lost any of its potency. He dies again.

And revives.

And dies.

And revives.

And dies.

And revives.

And…

"This is awful!" Squid-head wails. "What have we done? What have we done?"

"Nothing good," says the pouncing tiger on Rex's chest, for the Powder of Life has worked on his tattoos too. "He looks to be spiralling."

"Horrigle fing to shee," says the skull on Rex's arm, talking around the dagger.

"We can't let him suffer like this!" Spider-hoodie pleads. But really what other choice do they have? There's no intervention they can make that will put an end to Rex's suffering, since any attempt at a mercy killing will only be negated by the Powder of Life. All they can do is watch, hour after hour, as Rex is resurrected and succumbs again and again and again.

When morning comes he's still at it. Sir Percival leads them in a prayer and the Matryoshka tells them a fable about a man who hid his soul in a thimble and then hid the thimble inside an egg and the egg in a box and the box in a chest and the chest at the bottom of a moat. But she forgets the moral, and Rex is still dying noisily and repeatedly behind her as she tells the tale, ruining everyone's concentration. One by one they steal away, unable to look any more on what they've done. Rex may not have been the God of the Covenant but they've found their original sin.

*Postscript-appendix-epilogue-footnote thing*

*From: Me, Scraps*
*To: Her Majesty Queen Ozma of Oz*

*I'm a girl of shreds and patches*
*And bits of coloured cloth.*
*There's not one part that matches*
*And my biggest fear's a moth!*

*As Queen Ozma's faithful servant*
*I walk the wobbly border*
*Bringing hope and cheer and poetry*
*And law, and sometimes order.*

*All right, I had to make some of the background details up back there. I only had the toys' account to go on and they weren't the most reliable of witnesses. So I filled in the gaps with stuff that sounded right and on the whole I think I did an excellent job. Well done, says I to me. Good show.*

*But the last part, my queen, is one hundred per cent full of pinpoint accuracy because that was when I turned up on the scene. I'd already tracked down that wretch Dr Pipt and taken him into custody. He tried to bribe me with a cheque for two hundred million pounds but I was having none of that.*

*He told me about this Rex Rembrandt character who was*

*now in possession of the powder and I rushed off to find him, eager as always to do my duty. But gosh! And golly! I found it mostly done.*

*The thing that had been Rex Rembrandt was in a sad state by this time. The tattoos on his chest and arm were singing a dirge, but the man himself was just a squirming mass of tics and seizures. The powder was still working, dragging him up like a fish on a hook every time he died (death being a thing they do out here in the mundane world, although it's not a fashion that's ever caught on in Oz). He was having a very unhappy time of it. His whole life flashing before his eyes, I expect, but then un-flashing and re-flashing and on and on and on.*

*I did what I could. I took out Dr Pipt's other amazing invention, the liquid of petrifaction, and gave the living-dying-living man a good dousing. Little by little his convulsions stopped as his flesh and bone and sinew turned to solid marble. Good-oh, said I. Mercy hath rained all gentle out of Heaven, and its quality wasn't even strained.*

*I gathered up the toys and their fully-rounded sibyl and brought them home to the Emerald City. They've sworn the oath, saluted the flag, taken the shilling and signed the register. They're now part of your citizenry, so hooray! Sir Percival wants to atone for what he thinks of as unknightly conduct, so in due course I hope Your Majesty will consider issuing him a dragon from Central Supply.*

*Oh, and there's also a matchstick man who stands in want of eyes.*

*Funny thing. I had to visit London again a few months later, once more on Your Majesty's business, and while I was there I went into the British Museum because I really like to lie on my back and stare up at their big glass ceiling. They had a new item on display, recently donated by a property developer in Hertfordshire who had come by it in an estate sale. It was Rex Rembrandt's body, speculatively labelled as an Etruscan funerary monument.*

*So that's nice, isn't it? He doesn't get to admire and acquire any more but he's still in the game, so to speak.*

*As for the good doctor, I have a confession to make. I know I should have taken him to the chokey and turned him over to Tollydiggle Turnkey. But her mercies are so very, very tender, and besides I had a promise to keep. So I threw a party and I invited everyone who'd ever been at the sharp end of Dr P's wonderful inventions. It was quite a crowd, so I left early, but I'm sure everyone had the very bestest time.*

*Yours as ever*
*With bold endeavour*
*So quick and clever*
*I am:-*

*Scraps the Patchwork Girl, secret agent*

# THE WIZARD OF THE BOOKISH OMNIBUS

PAUL MAGRS

It was the year of the really hot summer, when we had the drought, and the wasteland at the edge of our council estate was dry and cracked like a jigsaw and the grass went yellow. Remember? And at the end of that summer there were the ladybirds? There were so many. It was a real infestation. "It's of Biblical proportions," said Maggie from down our street, who was very religious and gloomy. She slapped at her bare arms, squishing ladybirds who'd settled on her skin, leaving smears of bright orange like baked bean juice.

I remember being at school and all the kids screaming when the skies filled with low-hanging clouds of scarlet ladybirds. They weren't buzzing or stinging. They didn't mean us any harm, surely. They were only ladybirds, but it was unknown and it was frightening, especially to little kids who didn't know any better. We all went running back into school and the dinner nannies were going berserk. They were even more scared than we were, I think. We were all inside with the ladybirds clinging to us and, looking through the windows, we could see that the playground had gone dark with the swarm.

Then in the autumn the storms and heavy rains came.

And it was so wet that October the Cosy Bookish Omnibus almost got washed away. We were all aboard the library on the day when the rain was so crazy and the baked ground so soggy, it felt like the library was going to set sail. We were upstairs on a Saturday afternoon and the old man was reading to us. Well, it was hardly reading. Frank Mundy – the man who'd created the Cosy Bookish Omnibus – had learned that people listened better when he simply *told* the stories, rather than reading them straight out of the books. There was just something about the way he spoke that made us all catch on and listen to the details and stick with the story. It was so different to when he'd tried reading aloud in a boring, monotonous voice.

I remember that day, the thunder crashing and the lightning flashing somewhere in the skies above New Town. Not far from us! We were in the eye of the storm!

"By, it's been dramatic round here, hasn't it?" the old man said, grinning at the front of the top deck of his stationary double-decker bus. "We've had the drought and the swarms of ladybirds and now the storms!" By this time the rain was blatting down against the windows of the top deck. Really hard, like dried peas stotting off the roof and the windowpanes. The rain was running down in silver-grey sheets, but it was cosy aboard the Bookish Omnibus, with its colourful lamps and psychedelic walls. Here aboard, there were all the kids I knew from round our street and beyond, plus just as many grown-ups, come to listen to Frank Mundy doing his regular storytelling hour. The Bookish Omnibus was popular with all ages, just as Frank had intended it to be.

He had reached the part with the poppy field, and he took great relish in telling us how our friends in Oz became more and more tired as they tried to make their way through the long, swaying grass. They couldn't fall asleep! They knew it was deadly to do so! But still, they couldn't help yawning and pausing. Their eyes felt heavy and droopy, and they told themselves surely it would be all right if they could lay down for a little while…

Well, all of us aboard the Cosy Bookish Omnibus were agog, listening to this. We'd had the same characters in the same story from Frank for the past three story times and we were heavily invested in their fates. Even though the rain was slashing down and the thunder rumbled and shook the whole bus, we were all of us in that bright sunny field with the visitors to Oz and our eyes were smarting and our limbs were aching with fatigue and we too just wanted to lie down on the soft grass and go to sleep.

"But you mustn't!" cried Frank loudly, making us all jump in our seats, our beanbags, our wooden chairs. "It would be deadly to fall asleep in the field full of poppies!" His old, gaunt face took on a sudden, crafty look. "Do you know who would come and take you away if you fell asleep? Do you know who would come and get you?"

Suddenly everyone was shouting out. We were all calling out eagerly, "The witch! The witch! The wicked old witch! Her flying monkeys would come and get us!" We were all shouting, even those of us who didn't really know the answer.

The important thing was the shouting and the being part of it all. I looked around the deck and grinned to see how serious they all were, even the adults. I saw the DJ from our local radio station, Salty Jones, shouting at the top of his voice, just as caught up in the story as anyone: "It's the witch! The witch is coming!"

As if on cue there came an even louder, jagged crack of thunder and lightning and it felt like it was right above the wasteland now. There were a few screams from the littler kids, and also Mrs Taylor, with the popping-out eyes, who worked in the bakery in the precinct.

Frank Mundy held up his hands. "Now, everyone. Don't you panic! It's only the storm! It's right over the top of us now, but we needn't be afraid. We're very safe here aboard the Cosy Bookish Omnibus, aren't we?"

Everyone agreed loudly, but I was seven and I was in a sceptical phase. I didn't take the words of grown-ups on trust anymore, not since Mam and Dad had started having problems with each other. I knew that adults weren't always right. And wasn't it possible that this bus – standing exposed and alone on a little hummock at the heart of the wasteland – wasn't it very possible, even highly likely, that it could get struck by lightning on an occasion such as this?

"Oh, the storm!" cried Frank, like he was trying to distract us, pulling us back into his haphazardly-told tale. "Why, isn't it just like the storm that started our story in the first place? Do you remember, those of you who were here at the start? Was it last Saturday or the Saturday before...?"

We all shouted out again, how it was two weeks ago,

and he'd told us about it last week as well, because it was his favourite part of the whole story. "It bears repeating!" Frank Mundy cried. He whirled his skinny arms around his head and encouraged us to do the same. "It was the tornado! The tornado came to Kansas, didn't it? Where Dorothy Gale lived in an old wooden farmhouse with her aunty and her uncle. And the ground was just as dry and the grass was just as yellow as it was here. Do you remember? And everyone was running for shelter before the tornado came and carried them all away. Who remembers what happened next?"

Well, we all did, and we all shouted out loudly in response: "It carried the whole house away! It carried Dorothy up into the sky! It took her all the way to Oz and the wooden house squashed the witch!"

And here there was laughter, because everyone – especially the smaller kids – absolutely loved the bit where the witch got squashed flat under the house. "Eeeh, you bloodthirsty lot!" Frank laughed. "You're right! That witch got squished like a ladybird!"

It was when we were all laughing that the bus moved. There was that unmistakable lurch that brought us all up short. "What was that?" cried Wanda Baumgarten, who was one of our teachers at school, but lived on our estate. She had a Barbra Streisand perm and a floaty dress. "The bus moved, Frank!"

He shook his shaggy head crossly. "No, no, it can't! How can it? It's got no engine! The wheels are locked solid! The bus is rooted here in the wasteland forever! It can't go anywhere!"

But here it came again. That strange feeling. A teetering, lurching feeling. Like the bus was about to slide down the small hill. Still the wind was battering us and the rain was sliding down the windowpanes. Now Salty Jones was on his feet and looking worried as he peered out of the windows. "I think we're going to be washed away! I think the rain is going to turn into a flood and carry us off!"

His words caused a sudden panic. Kids were screaming and all the adults were in a flap. Everyone started running for the staircase and there was a scrum at the top. All of a sudden our friends in Oz and our concern for them were forgotten. Frank stood at the front of the top deck looking deflated. He looked like a worried old man now, and not like the storytelling giant he truly was. He tried to get through to us: "I'm sure there's nothing to worry about! Nothing at all! The Cosy Bookish Omnibus is rock solid! We can't be washed away by a bit of rain! Don't worry! You don't have to go running home yet…! Stay and listen to some more of the story…!"

But everyone was full of panic now. We surely hadn't imagined that sickening sensation of the bus starting to move by itself. Nobody wanted to be carried off in the storm, and so they all fled and pelted out of the bus as fast as they could.

I wouldn't have minded being carried off by the storm. I'd have liked the adventure of that, carrying me far away from home. But I ran with everyone else. I tagged along with the fleeing crowd. We left Frank Mundy and his Bookish Omnibus behind. We didn't even look back to see if it was safely staying where it was. We ran all the way home through the rain.

The storm that day kept up far into the night. It grew dark early as clouds rolled in from the sea and the whole of New Town fell uneasily asleep to the sound of those crashing cymbals and the thunder's big bass drum.

I stared out of our large picture window in our living room at the hill where the Cosy Bookish Omnibus stood. It had slid partway down its mount on the mud, but it didn't slide away. It wasn't completely disastrous. I held my breath and wished as hard as I could. I didn't want to see it getting washed away.

"Come away from the window and pull the blinds!" Mam urged me. "Your tea's going out, look." She was putting food on the table – pies from the town bakery and mashed potato. Dad was even at the table with us tonight, which was an increasingly rare phenomenon. His work kept making him late. His work was keeping him away from us.

There was an uneasy peace between my mam and dad that night as we sat down to pies and mash. They passed the gravy boat between them and were trying to be civil with each other, pretending that all the recent arguments were a thing of the past.

"What were you staring at that old bus for anyway?" Dad asked, quite snappishly. He rolled his eyes at the thought of local eccentric Frank Mundy and his rusted old bus parked on public land. "We should have it towed away," Dad said pensively. "I'm sure there's all kinds of violations involved in setting up something like that on his whim. People can't just do what they want to do."

Mam flicked out her long, glossy dark hair and looked thoughtful. "But he's doing it for a good reason. That's the thing. It's for everybody's benefit. That old man has spent every penny of his retirement fund to buy that bus and he's filled it with books for the whole community. He's invited everyone to share it with him. I think it's marvellous. All the kids love it. Everyone loves it!"

Dad glowered, munching on chunks of steak and onion. "*I* don't love it. Bloody eyesore, if you ask me. And I bet it's a death-trap. Rusty old thing like that. Just wait until there's an accident or a disaster. You'll see! You won't be so keen on that daft old devil then."

"You're such a killjoy," Mam sighed. The words were out before she knew it. "You never used to be like this. You've turned into such a misery-guts. What's wrong with you? You're only young. You're twenty-six but you sound like that old Chief Inspector at your station."

Dad grew angry, pushing his plate away. He had flakes of pastry in his moustache as he shouted: "Someone has to stand up for law and order! That's all part of the job! I believe in everything being done the proper way! Otherwise what have we got? Anarchy! That's what!"

Dad didn't read to me anymore. "You're getting too old for that now, lad. You can read to yourself, can't you?"

And more often than not, Mam had a migraine these days. She saw funny jagged lights and had to lie down in a dark room till morning. When I was really little she used to love to read to me. She read all the Ladybird fairy tales and I had the whole collection still in my bookcase, even though by now I knew them off by heart.

Dad didn't tell me stories but he'd sit on the edge of my bed and talk. That night he was leaning over me and talking in a sad, heavy voice about how he and Mam still loved me. They thought the world of me. But the thing was, these days, they just weren't getting on very well together. It was like they didn't love each other enough anymore. "Do you understand what I'm saying?" he asked. "It's hard for a kid to understand things like this. But grown-ups live in a different world to you. It isn't all stories and things turning out for the best."

When he kissed me goodnight his moustache was harsh and bristly. I fell asleep thinking of the hairy faces of the flying monkeys.

The next day was dry, but I couldn't dash out to check that the Cosy Bookish Omnibus was okay. There wasn't time. It was a day that Dad was taking me to see his mam and dad in South Shields, forty miles up the motorway. Mam never came with us because she couldn't stand them. "They shout too much! It's too noisy and smoky and argumentative. I saw far too much of those two when we had to live with them, back when you were just a baby!"

But I loved going to see my nanna and granda. Dad and I went racing up the motorway and the weekend was ours. We went to the pictures first and the Wimpy bar for burgers and chips. We bought American comics in the motorway services south of Tyneside. When we arrived at the house on Chaucer Avenue it was already in the usual Saturday night uproar, with aunties and uncles and cousins popping in for their tea. Everyone was dropping their kids off and then going out for a night on the town. The air smelled excitingly of aftershave, perfume and booze.

My little nanna greeted us effusively, as usual. "My lads! My lovely lads!" Her mouth was filled with hair pins as she fixed her jet-black wig in place. "Let me have a look at you! See how much you've grown in a week!"

My older cousin Martin was all the while doing press-ups and sit-ups on the living room rug right in front of her armchair. He was the sporty type and liked to show off. There was a pile of ten pence pieces in front of him: he got a shiny ten pence piece for every sit-up and push-up that he did. Nanna was egging him on: "Come on! Come on, you can do better than that! Keep going!"

Everyone had to do a turn on Saturday night at my nanna's. I wasn't about to do sit-ups or any of that rubbish. I'd rehearsed my act especially, and I'd brought Dad's mam's Abba record. I got him to put it on their stereo and then, with all the aunties and uncles and cousins watching I stood in the middle of the living room and lip-synched and danced to 'Dancing Queen.'

Nanna clapped and howled with joy at my performance. I'd memorised all the moves from *Top of the Pops* and gave a great bow of exhaustion at the end. But my dad took me out to the lobby where all the coats were hung up. He clipped me round the ear: "What do you think you're playing at?

Cavorting around like that? What the hell was that meant to be? Are you trying to humiliate me…?!"

But my nanna didn't care. She sat me with her for the rest of the evening when all the grown-ups went on their nights out. They were off to have a bop at the Chelsea Cat night club. My granda went out and bought us Saturday night supplies for watching the telly. He put on his pork pie hat and sheepskin coat and ambled up the road to the off-licence, returning with armfuls of sweets and crisps and bottles of pop.

My nanna listened to me when I told her about the Cosy Bookish Omnibus and how Dad didn't approve of it at all. "Ah, you've always liked your books," she said. "Not like the rest of them. Not like the rest of us lot!" And she listened when I told her about Frank Mundy, telling us the tale of Dorothy in Oz, and how he told it aloud so that the story went round and round, all in the wrong order as he lost his place and started off again, circling round the important bits. "He sounds like a strange old man!" my nanna said with a laugh. "But that story he's been telling you has reminded me of something. Did you know I used to sing in nightclubs? Before you were born? I used to love to stand on the stage and do a turn for everyone."

"Aye, yes, she did, uh-huh," said my quiet, gentle granddad with a nod, hearing this, and looking up from the Airfix battleship he was building. "She has a marvellous voice, your nanna. You doing your turn earlier was just like her, I thought."

"Listen to this," my nanna said. "I used to sing the song from that movie. The one you were talking about."

"What movie?" I asked.

"The one about the Wizard," she said and then, without

moving from her place in her golden tasselled armchair, she launched into 'Somewhere Over the Rainbow'. Her voice was shatteringly loud and tuneless, but it was wonderful to hear. She threw back her head and her jet-black wig wobbled as she sang her heart out for me. "What do you think of that then, eh?" she asked with a grin.

And then we settled down to watch the Saturday night movie, which was all about dinosaurs and cowboys.

That night I fell asleep on the settee. It was the law that us kids were allowed to stay up as late as we liked, even if it meant that we had to be carried up to our beds sometime after midnight. It was my dad, swaying with booze and tiredness, who lifted me up and put me into a zed-bed in the spare room. I dreamed of cowboys and furious dinosaurs being swept up by a tornado and carried through turbulent black-and-white skies. They flew with a swarm of scarlet ladybirds and a double-decker bus, swirling round in great fluttering loops before jolting back down to earth. And then I woke up woozily, listening to the adults talking loudly downstairs in the early hours. I came awake hearing them talking about my mam. "You can't just walk out on them, lad," my granddad was saying.

"It's her, it's all her," my nanna was saying in an upset voice. "She's pulling your whole family apart. She doesn't want you there. She wants you out. She's never wanted anything to do with us lot. It was only because of the boy that she's put up with you. She'll have you out on your ear! Just you watch yourself!"

My cousin Martin was on the other side of the bedroom,

in a blow-up bed of his own. I was getting up so I could go downstairs and ask what they were talking about when he threw a pillow at me. "Just go to sleep," he said, and I guessed he was tired after all his sit-ups. He couldn't understand what they were discussing downstairs. But I could. It was all about our family's future. It was all going wrong with every word they said, and it felt like the story of our lives was changing underneath my feet.

I lay awake and thought about that summer gone, and how it was like a different time now. Back before the Cosy Bookish Omnibus, before school started again. When we all went on day trips in the car to the Lake District and places like that. It poured down one day we were there. "It's been baking hot for weeks and weeks!" my nanna said with a laugh, sitting in the back seat with me and Granddad. "The weather's been wonderful! And look at this – when we come out to enjoy it, look what we get! Why, it's piddling down!"

"Aye, aye, it is an' all," my granddad added, chuckling himself.

And there we all were, stuck together inside our tiny car in a layby near Lake Ullswater. The rain was slashing down on the bronze-coloured lake and the adults were saying what a shame, what a terrible waste of a day out. All this way and no one even wanted to get out of the car!

We ate our picnic, crammed in there together. Mam opened a jar of hotdogs, which we ate cold in our hands. Granddad opened packets of some weird-flavoured crisps he'd found at the off-licence – sweet and sour flavour! "What a strange picnic!" said Nanna with a titter, lighting up a fag.

I sat with a hotdog in one hand and a fistful of sweet and sour crisps in the other. All the grown-ups were moaning but I had never been happier. I had my whole family around me and it was perfect.

When I was home again, back among familiar things, Mam was quiet and the air between her and Dad was stiffer than ever. I ran out to see how things were aboard the Cosy Bookish Omnibus, now that the rains were over and the sun was out above the wasteland.

It was a quiet Monday after school and only a few people were coming and going, choosing books and sitting down to browse or read quietly aboard the battered old bus. Frank's sour-looking wife Polly was working the pop-machine as usual, bad-temperedly offering me a drink as soon as I stepped aboard the omnibus. As an expert in awkward atmospheres, I could already tell that something was amiss when I arrived that teatime. There was an unaccustomed visitor and she was by the front of the bus, grilling Frank in unfriendly tones. I hung about, sipping pop through a straw, listening as this strange woman with an orange hairdo and a green tweed suit fired questions at the old man.

"None of them, I guess," Frank was saying haplessly. "None of the regulations or by-laws. I reckon I never really looked into any of that stuff before we started off with this whole thing." He gulped and his Adam's apple bobbed inside his skinny throat. He seemed quite upset. "Do you think I should have done more research first, Mrs Nye?"

The woman called Mrs Nye seemingly came from the County Council, and it turned out that they weren't very happy at all with some old gaffer simply adopting a parcel of public land and doing just what he wanted with it. Parking his kronky old bus in the middle of it and inviting everyone to visit and to have fun! "What were you thinking of, man?" Mrs Nye thundered. "Why, anything could happen. I bet you don't even have the right kind of insurance or anything, do you? What if someone fell down those steps and banged their heads? What if they fell out of the window? What if something terrible had happened in the middle of that storm the other day?"

Frank nodded, conceding that during the storm things had indeed looked rather dicey. "But we stopped story time early, in the middle of the tale, and sent everyone home. Before the bus got washed away in the flood or whirled away through the skies. Nothing bad happened, Mrs Nye! Everything was fine!"

She waggled her official-looking clipboard at him. "That's as maybe, Mr Mundy. But the council can't have the likes of you simply setting themselves up as librarians or anything of the sort. Where would it all end? People *pretending* to be things! Unofficial and untrained folk doing all kinds of proper jobs in a fallacious manner! Why, we have a perfectly good library in the town precinct, Mr Mundy. What is wrong with that?"

And here I found myself bursting out and shouting at her: "But… but you can't talk or say anything in there! You can't have fun or anything at all! And when my dad takes me to the library, he says I can't even borrow story books because story books are only for girls. He makes me borrow what he calls *informatio*n books!" Then I realised that Frank and this Mrs Nye were looking at me strangely, like I'd spoken out of turn.

"Ah, is that true, lad?" Frank asked me. "I'm sorry to hear about that. But he's wrong, you know. Story books aren't just for girls."

Mrs Nye narrowed her eyes at me. "Nevertheless, that is a proper library, with trained librarians. Why, I've heard that here, aboard this omnibus thing, you allow people to take away books and simply keep them, if they want? I've heard that you have silly, trivial things like comics, too? Plus a little bird told me that absolutely nothing is in alphabetical order? Everything is put out just any old how...?" She looked appalled.

Frank grinned at her. "That's right! It's pretty chaotic, actually. But that's how we like it."

"You have people playing guitars and making a racket! People over half a mile away on both Loki and Odin estates have complained about the noise!"

"Maybe we can try to be a bit quieter..." said Frank, looking more and more forlorn.

"No, no, it's no good," said Mrs Nye, tutting. "We really can't have anything anarchic and noisy and un-alphabetised taking up room on our wasteland. We have very great plans for this open patch of land. I'm afraid you're just going to have to clear off and vacate this spot." Then she handed him a large envelope that looked as if it must contain a very important letter. "I will bid you good day." With that, Mrs Nye from the council shuffled out of the bus, shuddering at all the colourful mess as she went.

Frank's wife Polly left her pop-making machine and went to commiserate with him. She wasn't very good at it. "Well, I told you, didn't I? You daft old man. You simply can't set yourself up as some kind of magical librarian in this day and age! People will laugh or say you're being ridiculous. High-up people will come and stop you doing all your ridiculous nonsense. You've stepped beyond the bounds of what an ordinary person should be doing, Frank. I knew it all along. I warned you, didn't I? I knew this whole thing was too good to be true!"

From that moment on Frank seemed to go into a state of depression. He looked defeated and hopeless as he wandered between his terraced house on our street and the Cosy Bookish Omnibus. For a while we thought he was just going to give in and close the whole thing down for good.

Then, one Saturday night we were all gathered for another story hour and, during the early part of the evening, he seemed to regain his spirit and determination. He was still telling us the story of *The Wizard of Oz*, and still the story was circling around and never quite moving forward in an orderly way. We were all gathered there, all the local kids and the usual adults – Salty Jones from the local radio, Mrs Baumgarten from our school, and this time even my mam was there. I'd talked her into coming with me for the first time to the Cosy Bookish Omnibus. She thought it was all a bit messy aboard the bus but I could tell that she really loved it. She sat with me and everyone else and listened patiently as Frank started telling his tale.

"Well, I guess last time they had arrived at the actual Emerald City, hadn't they?" he asked, with a frown, as if summoning the story up from somewhere deep inside his memory. "Now, there are two schools of thought on this point. Either the city was actually Emerald and all the houses and towers were built out of green glass, and all the people's clothes were woven out of bright green fabric, or it was all down to the special spectacles that our visiting friends were given on their arrival at their destination. So which do you think it is, hmm?"

As usual we all shouted out our thoughts and straight away a huge debate started up about whether everything in the Emerald City was actually ordinary-coloured and only appeared different through special lenses. Frank laughed happily at all the noise. "It's the age-old debate, isn't it? What's in the eye of the beholder, eh? Is it all inside our heads or is it really happening in the real world? Is it us, or is it the world? Perception or actuality?" He shrugged and beamed at us all. "Sometimes I think we'll never really know. So let us just assume, for the sake of argument and fun, that everything in the Emerald Palace was very, very green. The important point is that Dorothy and her friends – the Scarecrow, the Tin Man, the Cowardly Lion and her little dog Toto – were absolutely terrified when, eventually, they were allowed to proceed into the grand throne room of the Wizard of Oz."

I looked around at my mam to see if she was listening, and I saw that she was just as caught up in this as I was.

"And, as you know, they'd travelled all that way together for quite different reasons," said Frank. "They were each wanting things that they thought they needed. And they made themselves brave in order to walk up to that huge throne where the Wizard would be, in order to make their request."

There was a pause then, as everyone tried to recall what each of the characters had intended to ask for. Frank had, over weeks, confused everyone by sometimes mixing things up and getting them wrong. *The Scarecrow wants a heart! No, the lion! That's what the lion wants. What does the Tin Man want*?

"But none of that matters, in the end," Frank continued. "Because the Wizard – it turns out – can't really give them anything at all. Not a flaming sausage. He disappoints them all. It's a shocking state of affairs. Do you know why?"

We all stared at him, not liking the turn the story was taking. Frank was using something closer to his ordinary voice and not his storytelling voice, which was grander and full of fun. It was like he was coming out of the story and starting to tell us about the real world, like when our headmaster at school did assemblies and explained the moral of some parable he'd just read to us. "He was simply a humbug, wasn't he?" Frank sighed. "The Wizard was no kind of wizard at all. He was just some bloke. He'd come from Kansas as well, same as Dorothy. There was nothing magical about him at all. And suddenly everyone knew it. When they went to see him and asked him for their rewards for all of their adventures – why, that was when the truth came tumbling out. He was nothing special! Nothing special at all! Just some bloke. There was nothing he could give them that they didn't already have."

With this, Frank took a deep breath and then he fell silent. We waited for him to go on. But he didn't. He just looked back at us and his eyes widened slightly. There was an uncomfortable stirring in the packed audience at the top of the bus. People started murmuring. Was Frank all right? Had something happened to him? Maybe there was something wrong with his heart? Or maybe he'd had a stroke? He sat there rigidly, staring back at us. He didn't open his mouth for quite a while. Then he said: "So that's the end of my story, I reckon. That's it." He stood up abruptly. "Go on then, everyone! Get yourselves home! Story time's over for tonight! Story time's over – for good!"

Unbelievably, he started shooing us all out of there. He looked cross with us. He wasn't like himself at all.

As we hurried home in the dark from the Bookish Omnibus, Mam asked me, "Is it always like that? Does it always end like that? It was a bit weird at the finish, there…"

I told her: "It's never like that. It usually finishes with a singsong and laughing and everyone clapping!"

"Well, what's gone wrong tonight?" she asked. "Typical! When I'm there, it has to go wrong! That's just my luck!"

"I don't know," I said. But I kind of knew. I'd been there for that scene with the frightening Mrs Nye from the County Council, hadn't I? And I knew the things she'd been saying, and the officious threats she had made. I knew they'd had a real impact on Frank Mundy. I knew that she had somehow robbed him of his heart.

I wanted to know how the story ended. That idea went round my head for several days following the last story time. The days were dismal and Octoberish now, so there wasn't much chance of playing out or seeing anyone. I simply stayed in my room with my Busy Book – half lined, half empty pages – and tried to make up an ending for myself. I scribbled possible outcomes for the characters who were all still missing something.

Downstairs Mam and Dad were fighting, every chance they got to spend time with each other. Dad was on late hours, but whenever they coincided at home sparks would fly. I couldn't hear exactly what they said unless I went to sit on the stairs in the middle of the night.

I drew upon my memories of watching the old movie, but that was a long time ago. The Oz film was broadcast one Christmas when I was really small, when we first got a colour telly. I remember just me and Mam watching it and how we gasped when it all went bright and technicoloured. But how did it finish? I had an uneasy feeling that it was a bit of a let-down.

Did everyone get the things they were wanting? It was a film for kids, so I supposed they must do. They wouldn't want to disappoint the kids, would they?

At school there was a special assembly about the Cosy Bookish Omnibus, just like there was when it started up, when Frank Mundy had stood at the front of the school hall and whipped us all up with excitement. Back then he had told us that he'd spent all his retirement money on a broken-down double-decker bus. He told us that the Omnibus was going to be a library just for us – and some adults, too, if we'd let them aboard. It would have all the best kinds of books in stock, none of the rubbish, boring ones. It would have vampires, dinosaurs, spaceships, anything we liked. Everything was going to be free and we could come and go as we liked, and we could make as much noise as we liked. How we had cheered! It had sounded too good to be true.

This second assembly was a talk by Mrs Baumgarten, who stood in her crocheted shawl at the front of the stage and told us that our library was under threat. Everyone sat up straighter, not liking the sound of this at all. Mrs Baumgarten told us that we all had to work together to make sure the Cosy Bookish Omnibus survived. We had to stage a protest and let our feelings be known! Frank Mundy's friends hated the thought that the free library might have to close down – on order of the County Council – and so they were staging a day of protest and loud music in order to celebrate and cause a fuss. The idea was to hold a free festival with punk rock groups, folk singers, jazz bands, acrobats and anyone they could get to come and make a noise. It was all to get publicity to draw attention to how much everyone loved the Bookish Omnibus, and we all had to get involved.

At school, everyone was pretty excited, and soon set to work making banners and flags. Mrs Baumgarten had decided that our year was going to perform a piece of expressive dance. The festival was to be a week on Saturday, so everything was a bit tight and last minute, but that only helped with the excitement of it all.

In the middle of these preparations I asked Mrs Baumgarten, "Do you think Mr Mundy will ever tell us the ending to *The Wizard of Oz*?"

She smiled and said she hoped so, but she looked worried about him. "Once we make our point and we make sure the library can stay – then he'll be okay. He'll carry on with story time then, I'm certain," she said encouragingly, then clapped her hands to get everyone's attention. It was time for our 'Movement and Music' class.

At home when I told Mam and Dad excitedly about the planned festival, there was a strained silence. We were having what Mam called a 'funny tea'. That was when we just had a snack, really, with nothing cooked. A banana, a jam sandwich, some ginger snap biscuits. "What's this?" Dad asked with a frown. "Where's my dinner?"

I told them about how excited we all were about the punk bands and the folk singers and Dad glowered at me. "They'll get into bother if they're too loud. If they start causing an affray. You're not to go anywhere near."

I looked down at my plate, because there was no way I was missing out on our festival day.

"I think it's good that they're protesting," Mam said, with a quavering voice, like she was being defiant even saying this much.

"*Protest*," Dad scoffed. "What do they have to protest about? They could do with being a bit more obedient. People round here could do with following the rules a bit more. It's the only way things work properly, if people do what they're bloody well told!"

I found myself speaking up: "Mrs Baumgarten told us it's important that we always question authority. We have to ask: who are these people making our rules and laws? Do we trust them? Did we vote for them? How do we want to change our society? What kind of a world do we want to live in?" All these questions came out in a rush, fresh from Mrs Baumgarten's assembly that morning. "She said that we must always keep asking questions."

"No," said Dad. "No, you don't."

After tea I went upstairs to make up more of my Oz story. I was getting somewhere with my own ending, I thought. My characters were finding it wasn't so easy to get themselves home.

Downstairs Mam and Dad were fighting. At one point he called me down and stood me by the stairs. "Go in there and tell her you want me to stay. Tell her I have to stay right here, living with you both."

I went into the living room, where Mam was sitting in her chair and she was hugging a cushion, like she was cold in the near-dark. "Mam?" I said. "Let him stay, will you?"

She wouldn't look at me. I'd never spoken before without her turning to look at me with a smile. "No," she mumbled. "It's best for all of us if he goes. Right now. Tonight."

He was standing behind me, clutching his jacket and a small bag. "Right," he said. "Right then." He sounded bitter and furious. "I'm going."

And he went.

Mam and I didn't talk about any of this until the next evening, but I heard her crying very late in the night and didn't know what to do.

On the way back home from school the next day I saw that there were lights on in the Cosy Bookish Omnibus. Preparations were underway for the festival of protest. Salty Jones had brought his builder mates and a lorryload of timber. They were making a temporary stage for the bands to play on. People were hanging around to see what was going on.

Aboard the bus I found Frank Mundy, who seemed a bit perkier than he had for a few days. "Hi, lad," he told me. He could never remember anyone's names. "Have you heard about this festival? Have you heard about all the fuss we're going to make?" He shook his head. "Everyone wants to put up a fight. Everyone wants to make sure the Bookish Omnibus survives."

I nodded. "We all do."

He smiled broadly then. "I think books always bring people together. That's what I was hoping." Then he said, "Are you after a book tonight, lad? Are you looking for something?"

I told him: "Yes. I want to read the end of the book about Oz. I want to read it for myself."

"Good for you, lad," he said with a grin.

# THE LOST PRINCESS OF ZO

**DELILAH S. DAWSON**

There could be no doubt of the fact: Dorothy, the human girl who was such a favorite of everyone in the Land of Oz, was well and truly lost. She was quite certain she knew her way around the royal palace in the very center of Emerald City, and yet today she found herself walking down a hallway that seemed very determined to go on forever. The red and white tiles – which should've been green and white, but were possibly confused – stretched out so far that they blurred together on the horizon, and although the ceiling should've been quite high and perfectly straight, it appeared to be curving. Why, the hallway now looked very much like a tube, come to think of it, and even the floor was no longer quite so flat but was likewise forming a curve.

"Ozma?" Dorothy called. "Betsy Bobbin? Trot? Scraps? Toto?" There was no answer, and she sighed quite sadly. "Oh, if only Button-Bright were here. He knows a thing or two about being lost!"

She turned around, thinking to retrace her steps, for that almost always put one in a more familiar place, but it took ever so much energy, and her shoes slipped upon the tiles. When she'd gotten dressed this morning, her silver slippers had turned green, but things often changed their color in Oz, so perhaps they wanted to see what it might be like as emerald slippers. She had a difficult time finding purchase as she struggled to make forward progress. It was uphill in that direction, and so she turned back—

And found herself skidding downward, as if on a slide!

The palace no longer felt like a palace at all, and Dorothy tried to contain her shrieks as she slid faster and faster until she was no longer in contact with the tiled floor at all but was actually falling, falling down a hole. She was not worried about dying, for ever since Ozma had begun her reign, no one could ever die in Oz, but she was not currently wearing her jeweled belt and her shoes were misbehaving, and so she could not simply return to a place that felt familiar using her magic.

"I suppose I shall fall all day," she said, her stomach making a flipping sort of sensation in her middle. "And then we shall see what is what."

Dorothy did not, in fact, fall all day, for the space grew as dark as pitch and had nothing so nice as the sun to recommend it. When finally the falling stopped, it was because she landed on a pile of something quite wretched that felt like a cross between hay and fur and made a surprised sort of "Oof!" sound. She was not injured, at least, and so she stood and dusted off her dress as her eyes adjusted to the strange twilight world around her. She was in a wood, but not a pretty one. The trees all seemed to loom at odd angles, their branches sharp and covered in stiff needles. A smell hung in the chill night air, musty and sickly sweet.

"This is not Gillikin Country," Dorothy said to herself, for there was no one else to say anything, and something needed to be said so things might feel a bit less lonely. "Nor are these the Fighting Trees. What a strange place! And what is this thing I've landed on, I do wonder?"

She felt around the scratchy lump that had broken her fall and was horrified to discover that it was, or had been, a stuffed bear.

"Sir," she said, hunting about for a face to address. "Mr Bear, sir, are you well?"

But further prodding revealed that the stuffed bear had suffered some great distress, possibly caused by Dorothy's fall, or rather, her landing. The bear lay face-down, all of its seams split and spilling horsehair and sawdust, which explained the softness and scratchiness she had experienced. When her fingers played over round button eyes, she tried to flip the stuffed bear over, but instead, his head came off in her hands. Long threads dangled as she squinted into the squashed face, and sawdust poured out onto her green slippers.

"Oh, I am ever so sorry!" she cried. "I did not know where I was falling, or that I was falling, really, and I did not know there was anyone upon whom I might fall!"

The bear did not respond, torn asunder as it was, and Dorothy regretted that she had yet again fallen upon a strange personage by accident. If she could only find Ozma or Glinda, they could use their magic to help put this poor bear back to rights.

Closing her eyes, she clicked her silver – no, emerald! – slippers together three times, saying, "Please restore this bear to his former state and take me back to the palace in the Emerald City of Oz – that is my wish," but to her great dismay, nothing happened.

She was not transported back to her proper place, or even to Kansas. Whatever had happened to her shoes, they were not currently capable of their usual magic. Dorothy would need to take them to Ozma to discover what had gone wrong, but until then, all she could do was gently place the bear's head beside his neck and apologize repeatedly for her accidental transgression. Most problems in Oz eventually sorted themselves out, and Dorothy had faith that they would continue to do so.

"Halt!" cried a growly sort of voice, and Dorothy was not currently moving, but she held still so the speaker might know she was paying attention.

At first, Dorothy saw no one at all, but then a tall, brown, shaggy shape lurched out from behind a tree. It was another stuffed bear, bigger than Dorothy and holding a rather large meat cleaver. One round black eye sparkled in the low light, while the other trailed down the bear's face, held in place by long, dangling threads the color of old blood. Dorothy hurriedly stepped back, eager to get away from this creature, but she tripped on the arm of the fallen bear and landed on its raggedly deflated gray back.

"I told you to halt!" the brown bear said, holding his

cleaver up higher so that Dorothy could see rusty stains clinging to the blade, stuck full of little hairs.

"I did wish to obey," Dorothy said, not moving a muscle from the neck down. "But you frightened me so that I tripped."

"You *should* be frightened," the big bear said with quiet menace, "for you are my prisoner, and I shall take you to see the Cruel Burgundy Bear, and he will decide what's to be done."

"What's to be done?" Dorothy asked. "What can you mean?"

The shaggy bear snarled and stepped closer, engulfing Dorothy in his shadow. "Well, you are a murderer, and what's more, your head is all wrong. The Burgundy Bear won't like that a bit."

Dorothy felt around her head, which seemed perfectly normal, outside of the fact that it was currently existing in a place that wasn't very nice at all. "What's wrong with my head?"

The bear extended a paw, drawing a long, dark claw along Dorothy's cheek, leaving a hot scratch in its wake. "There's neither fur nor stuffing. It's exactly the wrong kind of head for a bear."

"That is because I am not a bear," Dorothy explained, flinching away from the cutting claw.

"You should do something about that before the Cruel Burgundy Bear sees you." The shaggy brown bear stood again, running that same claw over the sharp edge of his cleaver. "Or your trial and execution will go very poorly indeed."

"What do you mean, my trial and execution?" Dorothy asked. "No one can die in Oz. Jellia Jamb says so all the time."

To her great dismay, the shaggy brown bear smiled, showing sharp, crooked teeth. "I don't know where Oz may be, but you are in the Land of Zo, and here, everyone dies, often before they would prefer." He laughed, a deep and unpleasant sound. "You'll see. Now stand up and come along, for my city contains hundreds of bears, and they are all very hungry and bored."

Dorothy stood, and the bear turned around to lead her away. She considered running, but she was not particularly fast, and she did not know the area, while the bear was quite large and did. Instead, she reached for the fallen bear's head and pulled it away from the body, snapping the long threads that remained. It was half-full of sawdust, and as she shook it, musty brown flakes fell out until it was but an empty mask of gray fur.

"Hurry up," the bear said, "and know that if you run, I shall relish chasing you and stuffing you in my belly, for perhaps I am full of horsehair, but I have plenty of room for whatever you are, especially if I cut you up into nice little pieces first."

Dorothy slipped the gray bear's cloth head over her own, settling it so that she might see through the nostril holes. The world went all muffled and even darker, and she inhaled the unpleasant scent of wet horse and mildew. She did not know much of these bears, but if they disliked her head, then she would wear one that they found familiar, and then perhaps they would not be so keen to eat her like a roasted hen.

As she followed the shaggy brown bear through the forest, Dorothy couldn't help wondering if the bear had been correct in his assertion that this was the Land of Zo, which appeared to be nothing more than Oz spelled backward. She had not heard of such a place, and although back in Kansas, everyone died *eventually*, still the bear had made it seem as if people in this place died with more frequency and urgency. Certainly no one in Kansas or Oz carried around a bloodied meat cleaver, threatening to eat little girls – no one nice, at least. Oh, if only she had someone clever with her, like the Wizard of Oz or Professor Woggle-Bug or the Scarecrow! Dorothy did not feel that she lacked brains, but right now, her brains felt a bit scrambled. Perhaps it was from the fall, or from the taste of her own breath circulating in the moldy bear head, or perhaps because she had never been so frightened in her entire life. All she knew was that so far, this place seemed entirely contrary to Oz. People were cruel, her magic did not work, and everything looked and felt quite horrid.

The bear did not speak, but as they walked, he swung his cleaver as if practicing various ways to cut off a little girl's head. After some time, they came to a large, circular space among the trees, and in the center of it were four long pikes sticking up from the ground, three of which held a bobbing head in some state of rancid decomposition. Dorothy could not be sure if these were humans or Munchkins or some other species of Oz, but they were not animalistic in nature. She did not enjoy wearing the emptied-out head of a stuffed bear, but it was a state vastly preferable to losing her own in such a manner.

"This is the Hunting Ground," the shaggy brown bear said, "and I would say that you are welcome, but you are not, unless we decide to eat you, in which case you are most welcome indeed."

"But where are the houses?" Dorothy asked. "Where are the other bears?"

The shaggy bear snorted. "You have very few brains at all, it seems." He thwacked his cleaver against a tree and shouted, "Ahoy, bears! I've found a tender morsel!"

Heavy thumps shook the ground as more bears of all colors and sizes dropped from the branches overhead to land on the ground of the clearing. Some bears stayed on all fours, while others levered up onto their back legs, and all the bears, regardless of size, were quite menacing. All had long teeth and sharp claws, which seemed unusual in a toy bear, and many of them held knives or scissors or knitting needles, the metal dull with bits of hair and dried blood. The air trembled with their growls, and Dorothy trembled with it.

"What has happened, Corporal Ravage?" a deep, cold voice boomed.

"I've collected a captive, your majesty," the shaggy brown bear said. "It fell upon the Hungry Gray Bear, murdering him most violently."

"Ah, and that is why it has claimed his head. A fierce creature, this one."

The massive bear that appeared from the gloom was the color of blood in the moonlight, his coat so shiny it seemed wet. His eyes were little mirrors sewn in with crimson thread, and his teeth were so large and curved that they could not all fit in his mouth. Upon his head he wore a crown of bones, and in one paw he carried a scythe.

"His Majesty, the Cruel Burgundy Bear, our king!" cried the shaggy brown bear, and he fell down on all fours and bowed his head.

"Tell me, creature, what are you?" the Cruel Burgundy Bear asked, leaning close to Dorothy and sniffing the gray fur covering her face. Moisture was building up within the ragged cloth, and Dorothy could not stop herself from panting like a frightened dog.

"It is a freak!" claimed the shaggy brown bear.

The king turned to him, snarling. "This is a trial, and it may answer for itself."

Now, Dorothy did not like to lie, but she liked even less to die. Her only goal was to escape the awful woods and the fierce bears, with their foul claws and rancid breath that smelled like old meat.

"I am a bear," Dorothy said, trying to make her voice quite growly, "and I wish to return to my home."

"And where is your home?" the Cruel Burgundy Bear asked. "For all the bears I know live here."

"But surely there are other bears you don't know who live elsewhere," Dorothy argued. "You cannot know every bear in all the world. There are other lands than this, and other forests."

The bear sighed, his hot breath wet against Dorothy's arm. "This is true. But you do not look like a bear from the neck down, and you do not act like a bear. And what's more, you are a murderer. For all these crimes, I sentence you to death by execution, after which there shall be a feast." He leaned in close, and Dorothy saw the deflated gray bear's head reflected in his mirrored eyes. "And the feast is you."

"But sir, a trial must have a judge and jury—" she politely argued.

"I am the judge, and I am the jury, and I am the executioner!" the Cruel Burgundy Bear roared. "Now take this abomination away to the dungeon, for it hurts my eyes to look upon something so unnatural."

The shaggy brown bear pushed Dorothy's back quite rudely, and she walked in the direction he indicated. Part of her wished to explain to the Cruel Burgundy Bear that there was nothing as natural as a living person, but when one finds oneself amongst a variety of toys carrying bloodied weapons, such arguments lose their power.

"Walk," the shaggy brown bear commanded her, and so Dorothy walked, squinting through the nostril holes of her mask.

The farther she got from the Cruel Burgundy Bear and his many minions, the slower Dorothy's heart beat, and she found herself curious about what a dungeon might look like in such a forest. She did not have long to be curious, however, for soon she saw a great wicker cage, and within it, three shadows sitting quite still, as far away from each other as their confines allowed. A mossy green bear with red eyes sat with his back to the only door to this cage, and in his paws, he held a large pair of gardening shears.

"What is this?" the mossy green bear asked.

"Dinner," the shaggy brown bear replied. "Once the Cruel Burgundy Bear has regained his appetite."

The mossy green bear opened the cage door, and the shaggy brown bear shoved Dorothy inside, and she tripped and fell, skinning her knees. Without her magical belt or silver slippers or the tender ministrations of her many clever friends and their own magical accessories, Dorothy could only rub the dirt from her wounds and try not to cry. She wasn't terribly accustomed to feeling pain, and it was not a pleasant sensation.

"Do not attempt to escape," the mossy green bear warned her, "or I shall snip off your feet with my shears and swallow them whole, and then you shan't get very far."

"That won't be necessary," Dorothy murmured, her head sinking. "Although I do hope I should be allowed to argue my own case before the official sentence is decided."

The mossy green bear and the shaggy brown bear threw back their heads and laughed like this was a very great joke, and then the shaggy brown bear ambled away into the forest.

The atmosphere of the cage was quiet for a while, but then a tall figure strutted over, forcing Dorothy to look up from her seat on the ground. Before her stood a very large frog, which is to say, a frog the size of an adult man. He wore breeches trimmed in gold braid with a satin vest and swallow-tail coat, all in shades of acid green and the lambent yellow of a black cat's eyes. His red leather shoes turned up at the toes, and all his buttons gleamed like shards of glass.

"And what are you, pray tell, besides dinner?" he asked.

Wishing to be polite, Dorothy stood and dropped a curtsy, for all that her skinned knees smarted. "I am a girl, sir, formerly of Kansas and now mostly of Oz."

"And what, pray tell, is a girl, and a Kansas, and an Oz?" the fellow inquired.

Dorothy had to think about it for a moment. "Well, a girl

is this." She gestured to herself. "Except I am wearing a mask, because I was told the Cruel Burgundy Bear does not like people without fur. A girl is, I suppose, a sort of thing with a dress and pigtails and skinned knees, and she has friends and a dog named Toto and is, currently, very lost. Kansas is a place with lots of wheat and corn and tornadoes, and Oz is where I thought I was, but am not. It's a lovely place filled with magic where almost everyone is nice and no one ever really dies."

"That sounds wretched," said the frog, his wide mouth turning down. "For if no one ever dies, then there must be far too many people hanging about, with ever so many elbows jostling and feet being trod upon. Dying just makes sense. Keeps things nice and reasonable." He gave a bow. "I am known as the Manfrog, and I am also here because the Cruel Burgundy Bear is rather prejudiced against those who are decidedly not hirsute."

Another figure appeared from the gloom, and joy filled Dorothy's heart, because it was a familiar one. "Button-Bright! It is you! Oh, I am so happy to see someone from back home. I remember how King Renard IV transformed your head into that of a fox, but then you fell in the Truth Pond, and it changed you back, I do recall. So did you return to Foxville? Because if I am not mistaken, that is indeed the head of a fox."

The fox's black lips curled up in a sneer. "Who is this Button-Bright? My name is Bootblack, and this has always been my head. Heads do not change. Unless they are removed, like those fellows in the center of the clearing, and even then, the changing takes a few days as the flies settle in."

From the neck down, this figure looked exactly like Dorothy's friend Button-Bright, with his fine knickerbockers and stockings. But instead of a boy's roundish head with blond hair and blue eyes as bright as buttons, he had the head of a russet fox, with eyes as dark and hard as lumps of coal.

"Bootblack!" Dorothy exclaimed. "That isn't a very nice name, is it?"

Bootblack shrugged. "I am not a very nice Bootblack, I suppose."

"But Button-Bright is the kindest boy. A little lost and sleepy, but it never does any harm." Dorothy turned to the Manfrog. "And in my land we don't have a Manfrog, but rather, a Frogman. Oh, everything here seems quite backwards and upside-down, and I am very certain now that it is not Oz."

"As the wisest creature here, I can assure you that this is the Land of Zo, and that the concept of a Frogman is utterly ridiculous," the Manfrog said. "I should think that this Oz of yours is a very poorly run place, full of too many bodies and far too little fur."

"Oz is run by Ozma, and she does a very fine job indeed," Dorothy said tartly. "Although people do attempt to wrest control of Oz with a disturbing frequency, but that is only because people tend to be greedy."

"Did you say 'seedy'?" asked a new voice, which was slow and mumbly, like someone trying to talk with a mouthful of porridge.

"No, I said 'greedy'," Dorothy politely repeated.

A lump in the far corner of the cage quivered and rose up-up-up to standing, and Dorothy almost allowed herself to be excited, but then she remembered where she was, and how things tended to go here.

"I take it you are not my dear friend Jack Pumpkinhead?" she asked warily.

The tall, skeletal figure topped with a large, roundish blob staggered toward her, and she drew back before its long, pointy fingers could reach her mask-covered face.

"Squash," he slurred. "Jack Squash. But I have been in this cage for so long without a new head that I've grown quite rotten." His pumpkin head was all caved in and blackened around eyes that might have been kind and a mouth that had perhaps once smiled. The pulpy orange flesh sagged and puckered, and the top had sunken in at an odd angle. "I need seeds," he explained hungrily. "New seeds for a new head. Have you any seeds, girl?" The twig fingers reached for her, clicking and clacking, and she stepped back until she fetched up against the wicker cage, thorns pressing into her back.

"I don't have any seeds, I'm sorry to say, sir," she said, voice quavering.

He followed her with a slumping, drooping, desperate lurch. "Seeds like soft places to grow," he warbled. "You look very soft. Soft soil. Soft soil for seeds. Come here, soft girl thing, and let me see what has taken root in you."

Dorothy slapped his hand away, her cheeks burning. "That is a very rude thing to do and say," she informed him. "I will ask you to keep your distance." She looked to the Manfrog and Bootblack, but neither of them gallantly stepped in to her defense. Rather, they watched with an almost hungry interest, as if they, too, wondered what she was hiding behind her mask.

"It is not my fault that I am rotten," Squash observed, his head lolling as a leathery roach crawled out through a collapsing eyehole and skittered down the neck of his jacket. "I would prefer to have a nice, new, freshly-carved head. I feel quite certain that if I was given a large knife and something to carve, I should be back to my old self post-haste. Or perhaps – your head?" He again reached for Dorothy's head, and she ducked under his arm and ran to the other side of the cage.

Squash, Bootblack, and the Manfrog approached her cautiously, as if she were a dog and they a trio of dog catchers attempting to corner her. Dorothy looked to the door where the mossy green bear sat with his back to his prisoners, working his scissors with a sinister snicker-snee. She next looked all around the wicker cage and soon noticed a small hole in the weave that a girl might just be able to fit through. Hurrying to it, she dove headfirst. She was almost clear of the cage when her hips caught her fast, and she was suspended briefly by her waist, kicking her feet like mad.

"Oh ho!" said the Manfrog. "The girl-thing is stuck!"

"Tender little feet," Bootblack observed. "Meaty and juicy."

"The head," Squash crooned. "Save me the head!"

Long, amphibian fingers grasped Dorothy's ankle, and she kicked back violently, launching herself off from the Manfrog's body with enough power to break through the wicker weave. She landed on the ground on her hands and tumbled pell-mell until she fetched up against a tree. Like all the trees in the wood, this one contained a hole, and in this hole, she saw a small pink bear with a crank in its side. Of all the bears she had seen that day, this bear looked the most like a sweet little toy and not a bloodthirsty monster.

"Hello," she said to the little pink bear. "Are you a nice bear?"

The little pink bear did not answer, and so Dorothy thought perhaps it really was a toy, as every other bear had had much to say, all of it unpleasant.

"Hey, look! The girl is escaping!" the Manfrog called behind her.

Dorothy tucked the little pink bear in her pocket and dashed away.

She did not know in which direction she ran or what might lie ahead; she knew only that leaving the Cruel Burgundy Bear and his kingdom behind was the right idea. The forest seemed to be quite full of itself, as it went on longer than a forest ought. Dorothy was on full alert like Toto in a storm, listening for the ravenous bears galloping behind her with their knives, or for some new threat to appear before her. She wished most of all to see a pleasant village full of helpful Winkies or Munchkins, or at least a portion of the Yellow Brick Road. Alas, she saw nothing but trees caught in an infinite sort of twilight, and the sky was as dark and heavy as a blanket, starless and moonless and cold.

At some point, she had the bright idea to take off the mask she'd been wearing all along, and the moment the tattered gray fabric was off her face, she felt immensely better. She wiped moisture away from her cheeks, some mix of condensation and tears and blood that didn't invite too much consideration. Knowing there were still bears in the forest, and that she herself was still in grave danger, she did not discard the mask. She tried very hard not to think about the fact that it had recently been someone else's face, nor that she was the one who had brought about his untimely end.

Slowing to catch her breath, she could feel every heartbeat pounding against her ribs, every ache in her muscles, every skinned knee and every scratch on her palms. It was a terribly vulnerable feeling – pain. And with that pain came the worry that here, in this awful place, she might actually *die*.

She had not given death much thought since settling in Oz; not since her last visit to Kansas, really. According to Ozma and the Wizard, she would stay exactly her age forever, healthy and happy for as long as she dwelled in that magical land. But here, in the so-called Land of Zo, there were tears in her skin, aches in her bones, an unsettling pit in her stomach. No one was nice, and while Dorothy generally had excellent luck in Oz, here the wrong thing always seemed to occur. Landing on the Wicked Witch in Oz, she had been celebrated and lauded. Landing on the gray bear in Zo, she had been immediately branded a murderer—

And doomed to be eaten by bears.

What might dying be like, she thought? Would it be quite quick, like the feeling of falling asleep, only without waking? Or would it be more like when she'd had a fever in Kansas and the world went all swimmy and strange, time stretching out like honey? Would it hurt very much? If the bears started with her feet and ate their way up, how long would she be alive to watch?

She shook her head and looked down at the grimy gray cloth in her hands.

"Did it hurt when you died?" she asked the dead gray bear.

The dead gray bear did not answer, and that told her something.

As she continued to wander the woods, a horrible sort of loneliness set in. Dorothy was accustomed to dwelling in a beautiful palace in the Emerald City, surrounded by Ozma and Betsy Bobbin and Trot and Scraps and all her other friends. Why, she could hardly turn a corner in Oz without someone smiling at her! But here, she was all alone, and she did not know in which direction she might find the nearest friendly face. She had never felt so far from home in all her life, not even when her house had landed in Oz the first time. At least then, she'd had Toto. And then the Scarecrow, the Tin Woodman, and the Cowardly Lion. She was so lonely now she would welcome even a flying monkey!

And then she remembered that there was a mysterious little pink bear in her pocket. She held him up in the scant light and said, "I wonder what you're about," but he did not deign to answer. In fact, he gave every appearance of being a mere toy with no animation whatsoever.

But then Dorothy remembered her old friend Tik-Tok, and she reached for the crank sprouting from the little pink bear's side. After a few cranks, his black button eyes clicked back to reveal opaque white.

"Are you quite alright?" Dorothy asked him.

"I will be," he said in a breathy, whispery sort of voice.

"But what about right now? Your eyes look a bit odd," she pressed.

The little pink bear's neck twisted with a decisive click. "I only know the future, for the past is already dead."

"Oh! That might be very helpful." Dorothy smiled at him, hoping he would feel welcome despite his current discomfiting nature. "Can you please tell me how I will escape this place?"

The little pink bear did not speak, and so Dorothy wound his crank again.

"You will escape this place," he said, "by dying."

"And how will I die?"

She gritted her teeth while she waited for his answer, as she hoped that in discovering how she might die, she could simply do the opposite of whatever he suggested.

"You will die… *horribly.*"

Dorothy waited, but nothing more was said.

"That does not sound very nice," she admitted. "Can you please tell me, in great detail, the method of my supposed death?"

The little pink bear smiled. "There will be screaming, and the rending of flesh. Bright blood will splash out, hot and steaming, sticky and sweet. Meat will be torn from your bones, your eyes popping like—"

He went silent as his crank stopped spinning. Although she had more questions, Dorothy did not turn the crank another time but gently placed the little pink bear back in the pocket of her apron. After walking for a while, however, she realized that she had no choice but to do something unpleasant. She took the little pink bear out again and prepared herself as she turned his crank.

"…crushed grapes," he finished.

"No more on that topic, if you please," she said smartly. "I wish to know how I shall leave this wood."

"You shan't."

That made her stop, a cold chill creeping down her neck. "I shan't leave the wood? Not ever?"

"Oh no, not ever," he agreed, and then he laughed, and it was not the sort of laugh that one might hope to hear from a handsome little bear. When the laughter stopped abruptly, Dorothy again placed him in her apron pocket.

"Hullo?" someone called from the darkness up ahead, and Dorothy gasped and hid behind a tree to see what might come, saying nothing. Since she had not yet encountered anyone friendly or kind, she did not anticipate that this new personage might bring her anything but unhappiness.

The creature moving toward her wasn't walking or running, but moved in a sort of carefree dancing motion that Dorothy immediately recognized. "Scraps?" she called hopefully, peering around her tree.

"Yes, that is my name! But who are you, lost on your own in the Forest of Hungry Trees?"

Relieved to finally, *finally* hear a familiar voice, Dorothy stepped out from behind her tree—

And froze.

The Scraps she knew back home in Oz was an unusual sort of girl, formed of a colorful patchwork quilt with yarn for hair and buttons for eyes and pretty round pearls for teeth, and she delighted in dancing and turning somersaults and always had queer things to say. But this Scraps, while made of patchwork, was not a jolly girl.

This Scraps was, Dorothy thought with some pity, all wrong.

Instead of a patchwork quilt formed into a body, this Scraps was made of various body parts sewn together with rough black thread. She did indeed have the face of a little girl and even the head of a little girl, down to the neck – but it was sewn onto the body of a large man and walked on the legs of a cow. Her arms surely had belonged to a lion once, and a fox's gay orange brush tail twitched behind her. She was not dancing, as Scraps did, but rather struggling to move such a pendulous, awkward body.

Her rheumy silver-white eyes looked Dorothy up and down. "Well, what sort of thing are you?" she asked.

"I am a girl," Dorothy said, yet again. "A princess of Emerald City in the Land of Oz, and I am quite lost. Please excuse me. You remind me very much of someone I used to know, but I must be on my way."

Bobbing a curtsy, Dorothy attempted to walk around Scraps, but a heavy paw landed on her shoulder, the black claws digging into the fabric of her dress.

"Well now, wait a moment," Scraps said. "Don't leave just yet. Tell me: are you a wicked girl, Dorothy of Oz?"

Dorothy tried to shrug out from under the paw, but the claws were curled in so far that they were puncturing flesh. "I do try very hard not to be."

"Then why are you carrying the head of the Hungry Gray Bear in your hand?"

Looking down, Dorothy saw that it was impossible to hide the fact she was doing exactly that. "I found him," she said carefully. "Well, I fell on him – I am doomed to fall on people, it seems, but it is always an accident, not a habit. And then I was told that the Cruel Burgundy Bear did not like to look upon faces like mine, so I thought—"

"You thought you might wear your victim's face over your own?" The claws dug in deeper. "Why, that is very wicked, and I am surprised that the bears did not execute you, or at least put you on trial."

Dorothy's cheeks went hot with shame. "They did put me in a cage, but it was quite frightening and not at all safe, so I ran away. And now I want nothing more than to leave this wood and find my way back home. I can usually travel with my silver slippers, but now they are the wrong color completely, and they don't seem to work at all, and I don't know what to do."

The claws released her, and Dorothy let out a shuddering sigh and rubbed at her shoulder, where blood was now soaking through her favorite dress.

"I will lead you out of the wood, if that is what you desire," Scraps said, "for I don't like to think of wicked people like you just running about, doing as they please. Come along."

Scraps began walking, her gate halting and twitchy, and Dorothy had little choice but to follow. She had gotten all turned around in the wood and no longer knew which direction she had come from, but Scraps seemed to know the way.

As quietly as she could, Dorothy took out the little pink bear and wound his crank. "Where will Scraps take me?" she asked.

"To the ending you deserve," the little pink bear replied.

"What was that?" Scraps called over her shoulder.

"Nothing at all." Dorothy shoved the little pink bear back into her pocket.

As usual, this answer did not actually provide any insight. What ending did Dorothy deserve? Things usually turned out rather well on her adventures, but she also generally had friends and magic and luck on her side, and this time she was lost and all alone. No Toto, no Billina, no Jack Pumpkinhead. Oh, if only she had found one friendly ally in all the forest! She could not, by rights, call this Scraps an ally, as allies did not typically puncture the flesh of their friends and ruin perfectly nice dresses. If this place was the opposite of Oz, and the real Scraps was good and honest and kind, then what must this Scraps be?

With every step, Dorothy had to ask herself if Scraps was leading her out of the forest or back to the bears. Either Scraps was telling her the truth and helping her, or Scraps was betraying her, and the chances of each possibility were roughly equal.

"Where did you come from?" Dorothy asked.

"The woods," Scraps replied.

"Do you know who made you? And why?"

Scraps did not turn around. "Yes and no."

"Oh, that is very curious. What do you mean?" Dorothy prodded.

"I mean what I say," Scraps answered. "And that is all I will say."

Unsatisfied, Dorothy slowed her pace, falling behind as Scraps continued plodding forward on uneven cloven feet. When she couldn't wait a moment longer, Dorothy turned and ran in the opposite direction. She had watched Scraps move, and did not think that this patchwork creature could possibly be very fast, for cows are not very fast, and Scraps was not well-formed. Dorothy did not pause to see if Scraps had noticed her escape, nor did she look behind to see if she were being followed; she simply ran as fast as her legs would carry her. Her lungs began to burn, and her eyes watered, and her feet ached, for slippers were not meant for running, but she soon became quite certain that Scraps was not in pursuit. She ran as far as she could, and then she jogged, and then she staggered along, a hand pressed to the stitch in her side.

"There you are!" shouted a growly voice. "Here she is, just as the Little Pink Bear promised!"

The heavy thump of many bodies leaping down from trees thrummed up Dorothy's legs as she realized that she was running directly toward the very cage she had recently escaped from. Dozens of bears surrounded her, growling and drooling, their button eyes shining ravenously. She turned to run back toward Scraps, but it was too late. The Cruel Burgundy Bear was there before her, his mouth open to show his teeth.

"Your head," he growled. "What have you done to it? Take that hideous thing off at once!"

"I *can't* take it off," Dorothy squeaked, her body shaking with terror at his approach. "This is my real head, and I am just a little girl very far from home."

The Burgundy Bear put his great paws over her ears, holding her head like a ball, his claws pressing into her skull. "Oh, you can always take a head off, if you try hard enough.

Any body parts, really. And then you can make the most wonderful servants out of whatever you don't want to eat, just by sewing various bits back together and stuffing them with sawdust. I've taken off many heads, you know, even those belonging to lying little girls. I don't think this will prove difficult in the least."

The paws pressed and pressed, and as the world went dark around her, she heard the shaggy brown bear's voice, knowing and smug. "You see? You are not special. I told you – everyone dies here. And this is exactly what you deserve."

Looking into the mirrors of the Cruel Burgundy Bear's eyes, Dorothy clicked her heels together three times. "There's no place like home," she whispered. "There's no place like home. There's no place like home. There's no place—"

# HEART'S DESIRE

**ROBERT SHEARMAN**

Ever since the funeral, he hadn't opened the curtains in the house. It hadn't been a decision. It was simply the way things had turned out. He'd been to the church and sung the hymns and mouthed the prayers, and he'd stayed at the sorry pub wake for as long as seemed decent, and then he'd come straight home, and he'd locked the front door, and had drawn the curtains tight. And if someone had said to him that he wouldn't pull them open again the next morning he might have laughed, or called them a liar – no, he wouldn't have done either of those things, no accusations, definitely no laughter – whatever, he wouldn't have believed them. The next morning came and went and he didn't open them, and then the afternoon came and went too, and before he knew it, it was evening and there seemed little point in opening the curtains then. Not when outside it was so very dark. And cold. And empty.

The funeral had been on the Monday. It wasn't until late on Thursday he even gave the curtain situation another thought. He found himself staring at them, quizzically, as if he'd never seen them before, as if the very concept of curtains was a brand-new idea altogether. "In the morning," he said out loud. "Friday morning. I'll open them then." But Friday morning hadn't been a good morning at all, and he'd stayed in bed till long past noon, and he wasn't up to the challenge of opening a box of tissues let alone something as complicated as a pair of curtains. He decided to wait and see how he'd feel about curtains come the weekend – and the weekend turned out to be long and lazy, and there was no heart to it, on the Saturday it was as slow as death, and on Sunday he worked out that if he could only last the next twenty-four hours the curtains would have been closed a whole week, since the funeral. The house in black, its flags at half-mast. It would serve as a tribute to her. A little private tribute all of her own.

That had probably been the last time he'd consciously thought about the curtains, because after that first week of grief he'd found so many other things he had to ignore. The phone calls. The text messages. The cards of condolence that kept dropping through the letterbox. And the people on the television, whenever any of the people on the television were doing anything except taking part in a quiz show. He coped fine with the people on the television doing quizzes but he couldn't quite stomach them doing drama or comedy or wildlife documentaries or the news. Above all, not the news – he didn't want to see that the world was still going on without her, no better nor worse than before. He *knew* that was the case, he wasn't an idiot, but he couldn't stand the crass tactless evidence of it rammed down his throat.

He stayed at home in his dressing gown, and he'd eat his

way through the tinned food in the cupboards and he'd watch his quizzes and when he was tired he'd go to sleep and when he wasn't he stayed awake. Most of the tins were baked beans; most of the quizzes were easy. And the house was dark when he didn't have the lights switched on and it wasn't dark when he did, and he didn't like the sound the light switch made, he didn't like that hard click, and so he didn't have the lights on very often. He didn't go near the curtains. He kept his distance.

No, he didn't miss her. How can you miss someone you won't even think about? And he didn't think about her, so, no.

Besides, would she have missed him? Just consider that, had the situation been reversed? If he had been the one who'd fallen ill so suddenly, and he'd had to go through all those treatments. And the doctors had said they would make things better for her, hadn't they, they'd sworn blind, but they hadn't made things better, they'd made them so much worse and more painful and just *embarrassing*; what was the point? And before he took her to the hospital each time she'd ask him to help her with her make-up, and she'd say, "There's no reason not to look nice, is there?" She'd ask him afterwards if she looked all right, and how was he ever supposed to answer that, she looked as if she were *dying*. Would she have put on his make-up if he'd needed it, would she have lied to him every single time he'd asked her how he looked? Dear God, would she have missed him? If he'd been the one who had died. Would she have missed him at all? Maybe a bit, but not like this, never like this. Oh, by now she'd be answering the phone and watching TV dramas, she'd be flinging open the curtains every which way she fancied. She'd be over his death, she'd have turned off the grief as if it were a hard clicking light switch and she'd have moved on, out gallivanting with her friends from work, Cheryl and Liz, and that one with the horsey laugh, Zoe, her name was. She wouldn't miss him, she wouldn't miss him, so he bloody well *wouldn't* miss her, he would *never* miss her. He hated her a little. For making him the man he'd become.

One morning he sat bolt upright in his bed, and he could feel his heart hammering, and he was panting for breath – something was very wrong, what had woken him up? Had there been a loud noise, had the front door been broken down, was there a burglar? And then he realised what the emergency was. The curtains were open. They were wide open, and the light was *flooding* in, and there was no way to contain it, it was on the bed, over the wardrobes, it was on the best suit he'd worn to the funeral that he still hadn't hung away, he'd left it in a puddle on the floor. How could the curtains be open? – his mind raced, and he thought maybe there had been a burglar after all, some stranger had crept into his bedroom while he slept to make merry with his draperies. Because it wouldn't have been him, not even if he had been drinking again – to have the curtains open once more felt like an act of betrayal.

He leaped to his feet and rushed to the window, and at once he was struck from all sides by the beams of light, and he wondered whether that would hurt him, maybe he'd turn to ash like a vampire, or what was it that happened in that book his mum had read to him when he was a little kid? – "I shall melt away, I shall be all melted!" But he didn't melt, and his heart rate steadied, and he began to breathe more easily, and as he grabbed hold of the curtains to pull them closed he dared to look through the window at the world outside.

He stared down into his back garden.

*Their* back garden – she had always called the garden *theirs*. But it had been her garden, really. She'd been the one with the green fingers, she had a knack for making things grow. Whereas he could never tell apart the weeds from the flowers, from week to week he always had to ask her so he wouldn't pull up the wrong thing, and she never lost her patience and always found it funny. He didn't know why she even wanted him out there to help, he'd only ever get in the way – but she said she loved it when they gardened together. And he knew that when she gave him simple tasks like mowing the lawn it was a sort of gift. She was sharing with him her special passion.

The garden now was wild and overgrown, the grass would be up to her ankles. All the neighbours' gardens beside it were neat and trimmed, and in contrast theirs now looked starved of love. If she could have seen it like this, it would have broken her heart. "No," he said. "I can't be having that."

He supposed he must have cut quite the figure as he stepped out into the garden, wearing no more than his dressing gown and a pair of old Wellington boots. And had there been any signs of activity from his neighbours he would have bolted straight back to the safety of the house. But all was still. There was not a voice to be heard, not even a hint of birdsong. The sunlight hit him but he stood his ground bravely and gritted his teeth. He went to the shed and disinterred the lawnmower, brushed away the cobwebs. When he started up the engine it seemed so loud and rude, and then he realised he didn't care, he wanted the noise. Let it wake up the whole village! He began to mow the lawn. The grass was stubborn at first – it had grown thick and clumped, and it was heavy with dew – but he was just as stubborn back, and as he cut the grass down he almost started to believe he was enjoying himself.

And then – that awful scream.

Was it an animal? He thought it might have been. That he had run over something hiding in the grass – a hedgehog, a sleeping fox. The lawnmower stopped dead. He scrabbled about at his feet, dreading to find the remains of some poor creature he had cut in two. But there was no blood. The obstruction had been nothing more than a large rock. It protruded slightly from the earth. He turned over the lawnmower to see that its blades had been snapped off.

Ever since his wife had fallen ill he hadn't been able to let out all the rage that was within him. He'd felt it churning around his innards like trapped wind. Now he dropped the lawnmower, tilted his head to the sky, and he howled.

He waited for the rage to stop, and when it didn't, he turned it upon the rock that had spoiled his garden. He tried to pull it up, but it refused to budge. "You bastard," he told it. "You bloody bastard. I'll have you." He stomped off to the shed and came back with a spade. "I'll have you," he told the rock again, and he set to work, digging it from the soil. The rock was larger than he'd thought, but the fury drove him on, and he did wonder what would give out first, that fury or his own physical strength; still, though, he kept at it, he must have been digging away for half an hour or more and he never stopped for breath – "You bloody buggering bastard." And then, at last, the rock came free – it didn't even have the decency to give him any warning – it so suddenly released from the earth that the man toppled over flat upon his back. And there on the lawn he lay winded, and he wanted to laugh with the triumph of it, but he didn't, and he wanted to cry, and he didn't do that either. The rock lay on the grass beside him, almost listlessly, as if it were exhausted from the struggle too. At length he got to his hands and knees, and he examined it.

The top of the rock was flat, with equidistant ridges that seemed to have been cut into it quite deliberately. It was a brick, the man thought – this was no random stone, but an enormous brick. It was perhaps two feet deep, and tapered down into a sharp point. And the idea came into his head that this brick was also a tooth – that some strange giant monster had decided to take a big chomping bite out of his lawn, and the grass had been so rich and chewy that the tooth had been pulled clean from its socket and left behind.

It was yellow. Only now that the man considered it closely did he realise it was a sort of yellow he had never seen before. Not just a new shade, it was more than that – it was too bright, too colourful, too *sweet*, somehow. Looking at it made him feel a little sick.

He didn't know what to make of it. Decided not to care. All he knew was, very firmly, he wanted it gone. It was too heavy for him to carry. So, half-dragging it, half-rolling it, he managed to get it off the lawn and out by his back door. He didn't then know what to do with it. He wasn't strong enough to lift it into the rubbish, and he wasn't sure the binmen would take it anyway – he'd probably have to phone the council, and he didn't want to do that, and in an instant all those real-world problems came crashing down upon him. He stared at the brick. It seemed to stare back, cheekily, and he thought the yellow even gleamed a little brighter.

He fetched a tarpaulin from the shed and threw it over the brick. Then he went back into the house, kicked off his boots, went upstairs. He looked out of the bedroom window at his garden beneath him. He saw that his lawnmowing efforts had been quite useless, and he'd barely made an impression on the long grass at all. In fact, it looked a little worse than before – still overgrown, and now with a bloody great hole gouged into the middle of it. He sighed, and shut the curtains on it.

In the dark of the house he soon couldn't tell whether it was morning, noon or night. He ate half a tin of baked beans and watched a quiz on the TV, and then he decided to sleep for a while. And he didn't know how long he had been sleeping for, when he heard a familiar sound from outside.

It wasn't quite the scream he had heard before. It had that same earthy rasp to it, the sound of blade against stone. But it had none of the ferocity, really, it was little more than a whimper – some poor creature in the dark sobbing itself to sleep. It was pathetic. It wasn't loud enough to keep him awake, and he knew he could ignore it if he really tried, just closed his eyes tight and pretended it wasn't there.

But he couldn't sleep. So, fine, he *wouldn't* sleep. He would simply choose to stay awake. It could blub away all night long if it wanted. He knew one thing for sure. He wasn't going to open the curtains to look. Nothing whatsoever could induce him to open the curtains.

When he opened the curtains he didn't have the least expectation of what he might see. And so given the circumstances, he faced what had been done to his lawn with calm equanimity.

The worst-case scenario, he'd supposed, was that the brick had somehow slithered its way across the lawn and put itself back into the hole. That hadn't happened. He could make out the folds of tarpaulin and he supposed the brick was still underneath it, sobbing away like a baby. So, that was good. That brick at least had been dealt with.

The problem was all the other bricks. Because now there was a whole series of them studded deeply into the grass. Just as bright, just as yellow. They were neatly laid out side by side, and there were more than a dozen of them. They formed a pathway that began right up against the fence separating his garden from number 67's, and continued in a straight line right up to the hole he had dug. What upset him most wasn't the insanity of that, but the sheer *impertinence* of it. And then the travellers came.

The travellers seemed to step straight through the fence as if it had been made not of wooden slats but thin air. There were four of them. Three burly-looking men, and a little girl in front leading the way. He watched them as they followed the path right up to the hole. Then they came to an abrupt stop.

"Enough is enough," said the man. "Enough is *quite*

enough." And so once more he wrapped his dressing gown around him and heaved on his Wellington boots, and he set out grimly into the back garden to confront the intruders.

Before he had a chance to remonstrate with them, the little girl beamed at him, curtseyed most politely, and said, "Excuse me, sir, but can you help us? Is this the right way to the Emerald City?"

"No," said the man. They stared at him. "I don't know," he said. They stared at him. "This is my garden," he said. "You shouldn't be in my garden." They stared at him a little longer, and he wished they wouldn't keep staring, and he thought his voice sounded so feeble, it barely cut through the silence of the night – no birdsong, no rustling of wind in the trees, not even the sound of the brick whimpering. It was as if the whole world was holding its breath.

And then, suddenly, the girl spoke up. "Can you help us, sir?" And she was so polite and so lovely, and the world seemed to relax, and it was as if they were starting over and he hadn't said anything to her at all. "We're following the Yellow Brick Road! We're off to see the wonderful Wizard, and he's going to grant us our hearts' desires!"

The little girl smiled even wider, and as she did so, the yellow bricks she stood on blazed merrily, and she suddenly seemed to be bathed in a rich technicoloured glow. He looked at her properly. She had a sweet, earnest face that was framed by long pigtails, and she wore a pale blue dress with a prim, sensible skirt. Her cheeks were slightly dimpled and her eyes were sparkling, and she looked so thoroughly wholesome. He could imagine biting into her, and she'd taste of bran.

The only little incongruity was that pair of glittering silver shoes on her feet. They didn't fit the demure image whatsoever. He tried not to look at them, but now they'd caught his eye he couldn't resist: the heels were really so very high, and the silver was so provocative somehow, and the stilettoes seemed to point up her thighs, asking him to consider what other delights he might discover if he followed their trajectory and just kept on going – these weren't the shoes for a little girl, the man thought, not for a polite well-brought up girl who wore pigtails and a prim, sensible dress, these were the shoes of a woman of confidence, of sexual experience, these were the shoes of a *whore*. And he was so shocked by the word that he immediately clapped his hand to his mouth in case he spoke it out loud – he imagined again biting into her, taking one long, luscious bite. He dared to look back at the little girl's face, and he could see that she had watched him take in her thighs and she had *enjoyed* it. She was smiling as before, but all the innocence of it had drained away. There was something so old behind her eyes.

There was a warning growl. And he saw that in her arms she carried an ugly ferret-like dog. He could have sworn it wasn't there before. The dog made no attempt at politeness and bared its teeth at him.

"Why, I have an idea!" said the girl, with a laugh so light it seemed to tinkle like a bell. "Why don't you come with us to the Emerald City? You can join me and my friends on our great adventure! We're going to find our hearts' desires. We all have different hearts, and all have different desires. Scarecrow here wants a brain."

And he looked at the first man and saw that he was indeed a scarecrow, and that was a curious thing. "I desire a brain," the scarecrow said, and nodded emphatically, and dislodged some straw from his head in the process.

"I desire a heart," said the man beside him, who now appeared to be made of metal. His face creaked with the effort, and the scarecrow had to give him a little squirt of oil from a can.

"Courage! I desire courage!" roared the third man, who wasn't even remotely a man, who was a huge savage lion standing up on his hind legs. The man thought that was really something he should have noticed earlier.

"And I just want to be back home at the farm with Uncle Henry and Aunt Em," sighed the little girl. "It seems like such a very long time since I was there!" And then her face lightened, as if it just *refused* to be sad. "All my friends here I met upon the way, and I asked them to follow me on the Yellow Brick Road, and they just couldn't say no! And now we'll be friends forever, forever and ever, no matter what! Please, sir. Just tell me what you want. The thing you desire in your heart, most in all the world." She smiled, and she reached out a finger to him, he marvelled at what a very long finger it was. It touched him gently on the nose. "Boop," she said.

"What do you want?" asked the scarecrow.

"What do you want?" chorused the tin man and the lion.

"All I want," said the man, "all I want..." He thought hard. "All I want is for you to get out of my bloody garden."

The little girl looked genuinely surprised. "Oh," she said. "Well, we can't do that, sir. Not until we can continue down the Yellow Brick Road. And we seem to be missing a brick. Please, sir, have you seen it?"

They all looked expectantly at the man, and the girl was smiling, and all the monstrous creatures behind her were smiling too. They smiled with their teeth, and the teeth looked sharp, and he thought of the giant that had bitten so savagely into his garden lawn that it had left a tooth behind. He licked his dry lips. "No," he said. "I haven't seen it."

"You're sure?"

"I'll keep an eye out," he said. And at that, the man heard the orphaned brick start to whimper once more from beneath the tarpaulin. He hoped against hope that the travellers couldn't hear it as well. "If I find it," the man went on, "I'll be sure to let you know."

The dog didn't like that at all. It began to bark, and it squirmed in the little girl's arms – it wanted to jump and bite him, it wanted to tear his throat apart. "No," said the girl flatly, and the man wasn't sure whether she was speaking to him or to the dog – the dog clearly wasn't sure either, and it turned its head towards her and gazed at her questioningly. "No," she said again, no louder than before, and tapped its nose with that long finger of hers. The dog fell silent.

"This is my garden," said the man, and everyone looked at him in surprise, and he realised he was surprised he was speaking too. "I don't care, you see. I used to care about so many things, I think. Silly things that didn't matter, and a few things that did, and all of that's gone now. I don't care. I don't care about you. I don't even care about this garden. But it is my garden. It is *my* garden."

The little girl nodded, and then said, "Good night, sir."

He nodded back, and turned, and left them, and went indoors.

He went up to his bedroom. He looked out of the window. The travellers were all still there, standing on the very edge of the Yellow Brick Road. He watched them for quite a while. He knew that they realised he was there – and once in a while the little girl would smile up to him and wave. She'd wave at him to come down and join them. He wouldn't wave back. He wanted to close the curtains but he didn't dare. He stayed and watched them for hours and hours, until he really thought the night must be over, it must soon be dawn, surely a brand-new day would be starting soon? Hours and hours and hours, and he was so tired. And then eventually the little girl turned to her friends and shrugged. They turned around. They followed the Yellow Brick Road back where they had come from, and one by one vanished through the fence.

He went to bed, and he didn't know how long he slept. But he left the curtains open, and before long the daylight was so bright that it woke him up. He put on his dressing gown and his Wellington boots and went out into the garden. First, he checked on the lone brick underneath the tarpaulin. It was no longer whimpering, and it didn't glow, and its yellow was now muted and bland. Then he went to the lawn and poked about in the long grass looking for the other bricks. He'd dig them all up – he'd drag them out from the earth with his bare hands if he had to. But there were no bricks to be found. He fetched the spade. He worked long hours, and his hands blistered, and at last there was an ugly trench running from the hole all the way to the fence. And then he went back indoors, and he'd stayed so long in the sunshine that the house now seemed dark and stuffy and oppressive, and he opened up all the curtains so each room was full of daylight.

He ate a whole tin of baked beans and watched a quiz on the TV, but he was too distracted to get many of the answers right. And as soon as night fell he went up to his bedroom, and stood by the window, and waited.

He'd dared to hope that the trench would make a difference, and he was disappointed. The pathway of yellow bricks appeared on the lawn, blazing as brightly as before, and seemed to hover over the rough terrain. And at length the travellers came back through the fence again. The man went down to greet them.

"Good evening," he said.

There were now only two of them, just the scarecrow and the little girl. But she wasn't really a girl any longer, was she? Her face had sagged, and her body had swelled fat so it burst out of her little blue dress. Her hair was in pigtails, but it was grey and matted. But the eyes still shone brightly, her silver shoes shone even brighter. Time, too, had not been kind to the scarecrow – he was bent over, old and too weak to support himself, and his straw was writhing with worms.

Only the dog didn't seem to have changed. It recognised the man and bared its teeth at him viciously.

"The tin man has gone," said the girl. "He ran out of oil,

and we left him on the path a hundred thousand miles ago. If he had won his heart, maybe he would be with us still, who knows? The lion is dead. If he'd won his courage, maybe his death would have come more easily – but he cried and begged all through the night, he was so afraid, it was embarrassing." In spite of it all, the girl smiled. "Please, sir," she said. "Can you help us? Is this the right way to the Emerald City?"

"I don't know," said the man, honestly. "But I think maybe it is."

"We are following the Yellow Brick Road to gain our hearts' desires. The scarecrow wants a brain."

"The worms are eating me," said the scarecrow. "And the worms have worms that are eating them. And those worms have worms, and when they've eaten the worms, and they've eaten the worms that are eating the worms, then the worms shall eat me."

"And I just want to be back home at the farm with Uncle Henry and Aunt Em," said the girl. "Milking the cows and feeding the chickens. Fattening up the pigs for slaughter so I can turn them into pork sausages and use their innards as chitterlings. That is my heart's desire. What is your heart's desire, sir?"

The man said, "I have been standing over the garden all night. I have thought long and hard. And I once had a heart's desire, and she's gone. I no longer have desire in my heart."

The girl laughed; the scarecrow groaned; the dog barked and strained to bite him. "Join us on the Yellow Brick Road," the girl said, "and you'll *get* a heart's desire. Until he stepped upon the path, the scarecrow didn't know he wanted a brain.

I didn't know I wanted my chitterlings. Join us. Join *me*. And you'll have desire, I promise you, more desire than you'll know what to do with. You'll yearn again, there'll be no end to the yearning!" Once more she stretched out a long finger and reached for his face. It danced a little before his nose, playfully; would it press it again, *boop*? And then instead it changed direction. It made for his mouth. The girl traced her finger over the man's lips, back and forth, so gently. Teasing at the entrance, trying to find a way in – the man clenched his teeth and clamped his lips together tight.

She seemed to play with his lips forever, but at last she pulled away, and he dared open his eyes. His eyes were wet, and he realised he'd been crying. He looked at the girl, and she looked a little dismayed – but he thought that she was young again, behind all that age and the cellulite and the liver spots and all that swelling fat she was young.

"Please," she said softly. "If you won't take your heart's desire, then at least let us find ours. You are a kind man. I can see you are a kind man. We have been travelling such a long time. Help us find the brick that will complete the Yellow Brick Road, so we can journey to the Emerald City and be free."

And the man could hear the whimpering from the brick start once more, and it sounded so plaintive and so desperate.

The man said, "I have your brick. But I am not a kind man. I thought I was kind once. And when not kind, nice. And when not nice, at least sort of decent. But now I think… I think, I *know*… it was really always her. She was the kind one. She was nice and decent, and her kindness reflected on me. She made me a better person. And now she's gone, and she's taken all that away, and I have nothing left inside any more. I have your brick. But I will not help you."

He turned his back on the travellers and walked away. And the brick was screaming now, no longer in self-pity but in absolute fury, and the dog was barking so loud and he was wondering whether the girl would release it and it would come charging after and attack him, and he thought maybe he'd deserve that. But he wouldn't turn round to see – he walked calmly to the door of the house, he opened it, and he went inside.

From the bedroom he looked down upon the Yellow Brick Road. And at length the dog stopped barking, and at length the brick stopped screaming. And all was quiet. And at length the scarecrow lay down upon the path, and he didn't get up again, and the little girl stooped down beside him and gathered the straw into her arms, and raised it to her face, and kissed it gently. The wind rose up and the straw blew across the pathway and around the garden and across the fence into number 67's, and pretty soon there was no trace a straw man had ever been there. And at length, at some final length, the girl stopped crying, and she picked up her dog, and walked back down the path, and she was gone.

The man didn't go to bed that night. Instead he stayed at the window, the curtains neatly folded away now, and he gazed out at the world, the whole wide expanse of it, and waited for the dawn. It seemed to come so suddenly – a burst of yellow in the far distance, such a yellow burning away across unimaginable space, how extraordinary that yellow would have been close up. To have travelled so far and with such power – and then in a few short minutes the light was everywhere and it was day.

He ate some beans, and watched just one quiz show on the TV. Then he walked out into the garden, sat down upon the lawn, and waited.

The night stole upon him; it was dark before he realised it. And for the final time, the Yellow Brick Road appeared. Upon it, the girl. But she was no longer walking the path to the Emerald City – she was on her hands and knees. The knees were bleeding, and there was a thin trace of blood running all the way back down the path through the fence and beyond. She seemed exhausted, and yet she was relentless, she just kept going, dragging herself along by sheer force of will.

The dog rode her, sitting on her back with its head held high in pride. And the man wanted to shoo it off, but then he thought that the dog was encouraging her, and the pride it showed was for her strength and her courage. The dog glared at him, as if daring him to challenge that simple fact – that his mistress was remarkable and he loved her alone above all else in the world. And the man didn't. He couldn't.

Her pigtails were gone, most of her hair was gone, the doctor's treatments had taken care of that, he knew. And she was so old now, the illness had come so suddenly and had seemed to age her, that was what had been so cruel – but her eyes had never lost their sparkle. It was *her*, of course it was her, and he supposed he had always known that really.

He ran onto the path. He didn't think twice about it.

"Please, sir," she croaked. "Is this the right way to the Emerald City? All I want is to be home."

"Oh, sweetheart," he said, "oh, my poor darling," and he wanted to put his arms around her, but he was afraid it might hurt her – "you *are* home. This is your home."

She managed to shake her head. "Not any longer," she said. "Please. I need to finish my journey. I need to be home at last."

He ran to the back door, pulled the tarpaulin off the yellow brick. He had to lift it up, but it was still too heavy. And it was heavier, wasn't it? He thought it was heavier, that in the days since he'd found it, in the years since his wife had started walking the pathway, it had put on weight. "Hold on, darling, I'm coming," he called. He put his arms around the brick, dug in his fingers. The stone was sharper than he remembered, and it sliced his skin and broke his nails – and he didn't care, bit by bit by aching bit he heaved the yellow brick back onto the lawn. "Don't go anywhere, darling, I'm nearly there!" he'd shout, and he didn't know how long it took him, and he didn't dare look at her in case it was too late, in case she'd dragged herself away, or worse, her body had given up at last, or worse, it had turned to straw and been lost to the wind forever – "I'm coming, I promise you!" – and he wouldn't know how to deal with the grief a second time. It would swallow him up and he'd be lost forever too.

Every part of his body was hurting, his muscles strained and his skin cut to ribbons – and he tipped the brick into the hole, and it slid in so neat and smooth as if it were home at last. As if to say, *Really, what was all that fuss about?* – and the yellow beamed at him cheekily.

He went back to her, and now he was on the path the Yellow Brick Road seemed to stretch onwards forever in both directions. And the skies were painted a deep blue and the fields to the side were a warm green, and he couldn't see his house any longer.

"Please, would you help me with my shoes?" she asked. Because they had come loose back along the way. He went to fetch them, and one after the other he put the shiny silver slippers on to her feet. "And can you help me with my make-up. There's no reason not to look nice, is there?"

He gave her a little smear of lipstick, smoothed some colour into her cheeks. "Do I look all right?" she asked him.

"You look fine," he said.

"Liar," she said, and laughed.

He helped her to her feet; the dog dutifully jumped off her back as she stood up, and he could hear her poor stiff bones crack with the effort. She pointed. "Is this the way to the Emerald City?"

"I suppose so."

"Then come on."

Together they walked the Yellow Brick Road. For a while he took her weight and she leaned against him, and he liked the pressure of her body against his, and it made him feel needed again. And along the way she seemed to recover some strength, and she didn't need him to support her any longer – but she took his hand, and he was grateful for that, and he didn't let go. He would look at her sometimes and she was a sick woman turned old so young, and then he would look at her again and she might be a young girl with her hair in pigtails – and he loved both of them, because both of them were her.

They walked for many days and they never had to rest, and they sometimes danced and they sometimes sang songs. They passed through fields of poppies, and forests teeming with fighting trees and winged monkeys. And it took an age to reach the Emerald City, and the journey was over far too soon.

She stood at the gate and she was old and sick and as beautiful as he had ever seen her. "You could come with me if you like," she said.

And he was so happy, and he nodded, and was surprised when the word that came from his mouth was no.

"Why not?"

"Because," he said, "I'm afraid."

"Oh, baby," she said. "Oh, baby, it's all right." And she put her arms tight around him, and she gave him a big kiss. He felt her there against his lips for the longest time, and he didn't want to open his eyes because he knew she'd then be gone forever, and he'd be standing in his own back garden once more. And he was right.

The night was still. The moon was out, and there was just the faintest breeze. The brick road had gone too, the Emerald City forgotten. He waited for the grief to come flooding back and to crush him hard deep into the earth. And it didn't.

Down at his feet he heard something bark. He looked, and there was the little dog. "Oh," he said. "I'd forgotten about you. What am I supposed to do now?"

The dog didn't like him. He followed him into the house warily. "Are you hungry?" the man asked. "What would you like to eat?" The dog watched balefully as the man looked through his cupboards, but all he seemed to have were tins of baked beans. "Well, that's no good, is it?" he said to the dog. The dog barked in what might have been agreement, and pissed on the floor.

The man mopped up the piss and then got dressed and set off down the high street to the supermarket. He hadn't been shopping in a long while. It seemed almost alien at first, the neon lights, and all the trolleys, and all the people pushing the trolleys. He went to the pet food section, and bought several varieties of tinned meats, some in gravy chunks, some in jelly. While he was there, he also bought some tinned food for himself. He'd grown ever so tired of baked beans. Tonight he'd make himself a proper dinner. His stomach growled at the thought of it.

When he got back home it was to find that the dog had pissed on the floor again, so the man sighed and set off back down the high street to find some sort of litter tray.

That afternoon the man took the dog to the vet. "You've got a beautiful dog," said a woman waiting in reception with a poorly guinea pig. "It's not my dog," he replied. The vet gave the dog a thorough check, and said it was in good nick. "It's not my dog," the man explained. "I found it. Would you take it off my hands, please?" The vet said that he could put the dog up for adoption, maybe, but in the meantime it would be most helpful if the man could look after it. The man grumpily agreed. "He's got the most beautiful markings, hasn't he?" said the vet. "In the light he looks almost monochrome!"

The man would take the dog for a walk in the local park. If he timed it right, and they got a bit of a sprint on, he could fit the walk in between the early afternoon TV quizzes and the late afternoon TV quizzes. Lots of people took their dogs to the park too, and he began to recognise them: the old man with the two poodles would nod and smile, and so would the woman with the Alsatian. If the walk had been a particularly brisk one, he would reward the dog with an extra helping of chunks in gravy. The dog never seemed to appreciate this, and every time he fed him the dog would growl, every time he'd put on his leash, every time he'd fill his bowl with water. But the dog never bit him, and the man decided not to take the growling personally.

The woman with the Alsatian was called Jennifer. She told him her name one day when they found themselves sitting on the same bench. Her Alsatian was large enough that it could eat his little dog in a single gulp, but they seemed to get along well. "What's your dog's name?" Jennifer asked.

"It doesn't have a name."

"Why doesn't it have a name?"

The man shrugged. "You can give it a name if you want to."

Jennifer beamed. "Really?" she said. "What an honour! May I really?" And she thought for a little while, and then she gave the dog a name that was absolutely perfect and exactly the one you would hope she would.

One afternoon, while watching one of his quizzes, the dog

jumped up onto the sofa beside him and went to sleep, and the man began to cry, and he had no idea why.

He would regularly meet Jennifer on the bench. "Lots of single people come to the park to walk their dogs," said Jennifer. "Funny, isn't it?" The man had never considered himself to be single. Jennifer told him it was a new idea for her too – she'd been widowed five years ago, and she was still getting used to it.

"When does it get easier?" he asked her, and she thought about that seriously.

"I don't know if it ever gets easier," she said. "But it stops getting harder. So there's that. I think it gets… different. You'll see. Eventually, everything becomes different."

One day the vet phoned to say they'd found someone who would be prepared to take the dog. "No, that's all right, thank you," he said. "He's my dog, and I'm going to keep him." The vet had called right in the middle of one of his quizzes, and the dog looked as put out by the interruption as he was. The dog liked to sit on the sofa and bark whenever the man got one of the answers right.

"Would you like to come over for supper one night?" Jennifer asked him suddenly. "Nothing special, I just like to cook, and cooking for one's so…" The man said that would be nice. "And you can bring Toto with you if you like," she said. "If you want to stay late." And she blushed.

They left their dogs downstairs to sleep, and Jennifer took the man up to her bedroom. For a while they pretended there wasn't even a bed, they'd just gone there to get a better view of her back garden. They stood at the window and looked out at it. He said he admired all the pretty flowers she had. "Yes," she said. "I like to garden. I've got tulips and crocuses and so many daffodils. We don't have to do anything, you know." And she kissed him, and he kissed her back.

He didn't love her, but then, he was pretty sure she didn't love him either. But he thought he might like her an awful lot, and that was a bit like love. It was different. She got into bed, and he made to close the curtains.

"Oh," she said. "Do you mind if we keep them open?" She laughed, a little embarrassed. "I know it's silly, but ever since Simon died… I've just left them open. I don't know why. I suppose, I just don't want to miss anything."

"Of course," he said. "That makes perfect sense."

And they made love, and Jennifer went to sleep, and he held her in his arms for a while. Then he got up, and he looked out of the window. And for a moment he thought he glimpsed on the lawn the hint of a yellow road, but it was just the daffodils.

# THE OTHER FOOT

## STARK HOLBORN

"'I am General Jinjur," was the brief reply.

"Oh!" said the boy surprised. "What sort of a General?"

"I command the Army of Revolt in this war," answered the General, with unnecessary sharpness.

"Oh!" he again exclaimed. "I didn't know there was a war."

"You were not supposed to know it," she returned, "for we have kept it a secret."'

*THE MARVELOUS LAND OF OZ* – L. FRANK BAUM

I was at the bottom of a quart of lacasa when the job came through.

Bobsy Pother, the bartend, had been blethering on since I stepped in the door. He hadn't stopped for breath once and didn't now, even when the crow began to slap the window with its wing, leaving greasy feather-marks on the glass.

"Murder," Bobsy said, fumbling for the catch, "that's the word, isn't it. Murder of crows. Don't see them round here.

No call for them, not much call, caw, haha, they can't get the work, can they, people send jackdaws, prefer jackdaws, even with all the stealing, never mind it was years ago they worked for old Mombi, don't remember it myself, back in my grandfather's day it was, and the thing about him was—"

I wasn't listening. I wasn't looking at the crow either. It had a card in its mouth. I didn't like that. Cards and crows, both bad news. Instead, I let the last of the lacasa coat my tongue. Bobsy made the best in the city. Poured it into vats and let it ferment secretly in his attic until it turned sour as sweat and made you forget your troubles.

That's assuming your troubles weren't standing on the bar, shifting from foot to foot and staring you in the eyes.

"No," I said.

I hadn't spoken all day. My tongue was sticky with liquor.

The crow tipped its head and dropped the card onto the bar. I peered down. Green ink. Of course it had come from the city. Covered in pictograms: a cross, an eye, a knife, a… cat? Who the hell knew. It was too early and anyway, I didn't care.

"I said no. Don't do that work anymore."

The crow let out a ragged *grawk*, jabbed the card hard enough to leave a dent and took off out the window, toppling glasses in its wake.

Fucking crows. How the hell had it found me, all the way out here in Quadling Country? Bobsy was going on about crows and damage. I let the noise wash over me, like rain on leather, like grit under heel. Everyone thought I was mad for living in Rig City, aka Tattle Town, the Big Ear-Bleed, shut in with the Rigmaroles and their non-stop chatter, day and night; walls ringing with anecdotes and the sound of people screaming *and another thing* into each other's faces. For most, it's torture. For me, well. I have my reasons. My hearing's never been great, so the noise doesn't bother me much. And for all that the Rigs talk, not one of them has ever asked me a single question. Useful thing in my line of work.

Bobsy was staring down at the card now, and I could tell he wanted to ask about it, but his demented tongue was off on another story about someone called Grimbal and wouldn't be stopped for hours. I sighed, contemplated dropping the card over the city walls into the river. Hopeless. River would probably burst its damn banks to deliver the thing back to me on a wave of stinking silt. Green ink was like that. Persistent.

I turned it over. It was signed with a single word.

*Dyna.*

"Bobsy," I said over his yakking. "Pour me another."

It was going to be a long day.

Red Brick Road always brought back memories. Bad ones. So I didn't walk. I paid some mad bastard of a cartwheel to roll me all the way there. Had its advantages. One, he didn't chat. Two, the passing scenery became a blur. Best way to travel Quadling Country, let me tell you. It's an advert for all that magic legislation Ozma came up with; perfect example of the disconnect between *could* and *should.* Sentient donuts from Bunbury, hungry rabbit lads from Bunnybury – balloon heads from Loonville, Utensians, Scooters, Skeezers, Dicks – you get the picture. Not that I could talk. I mean, I could *literally*, unlike some of them. But that didn't mean I liked it out there.

It was a long journey. Didn't get to the gates of EC until after nightfall. Small mercies. Green looks black in the dark.

Felt the Love Magnet that hung above the gate start pulling at the hobnails in my soul, but as usual I didn't give a shit – about it, or anyone else. After a while, it gave up.

The crow was waiting for me, like I figured it would be. It took off, coasting thermals of chimney smoke, landing and preening while it waited for me to follow. I got nothing more than a mildly interested stare from the green-whiskered guard at the gate. Part of me wanted to turn around and ask him if he'd ever fought, if we'd stood toe to toe before, if I'd tasted his blood or spit, but I didn't. No point. All he'd do was cry and I didn't fancy getting salt-stains on my toes. So I carried on.

EC. The place got in my eyes, insinuated itself in whatever shine was left on my skin. I shrugged the reflections away and made for the shadows, following the crow away from the sticky yellow main drag and into the artificer's quarter. Not so bad there, so long as you remembered not to breathe any fumes.

Crow landed on the peak of a house, gables like candy-cane twisted one too many times, and twinkly-winky windows and pots of lime-y flowers and a dark wooden door. A verdigris-crusted plaque beside it.

*Dr Nikidik.*

Sounded Munchkin to me, but never did to assume. I leaned against the door and when it didn't open, hammered it with my toe.

There was a soft shuffle on the other side: someone already

standing there waiting. Not sure what I was expecting but it wasn't a Paper Man. He stood folded in the doorway, all sharp angled suit and a look that could cut. Concertinaed eyes that took me in, heel to tongue, before finding mine.

"Hell are you?" he asked.

No subject. Safest bet, sometimes, when you don't know whether you're addressing a *what* or a *who*.

Didn't blame him. I wasn't much to look at. I barely came up to his knee, my skin cracked and scuffed by the weather, worn down at the heel, tongue still sodden with lacasa, eyes just holes punched in flesh.

"Jack Buskin," I said. "Here for Dyna."

"She's expecting you." He grunted. "Didn't know you were a gumboot."

"I'm not."

I shoved past him into the narrow hallway. Waited as he pushed the door shut behind. He had to use all his weight to do it.

"'s way," he said.

The stairs were dark, lit only by false green flames in sconces. They shone right through him in parts, the bits worn thin. Showed the mends. Hands, knees. Neck.

"This Dyna, she Doctor Nikidik?"

His paper tongue slid in his mouth. "Nah."

"She make you, then?"

"Nah. Her aunt did."

"Powder of Life, right?"

"Uh huh." Half-turn of his head. "You?"

"Yeah."

His silence asked the questions people usually did. *There just one of you, then?* Swiftly followed by: *why?*

I sighed. "Was made by accident. Someone stepped in a pile of Powder."

"Shit." He sounded almost impressed. "You do the eyes yourself?"

"With an awl."

"Alright," he said. "We're here."

Here was a dim landing with a half-open door. That was never good. Usually meant someone had left in a hurry. Or wanted to. The paper guy hung back so I did the honours and nudged it open.

If I'd wondered what kind of quack Doc Nikidik was, one glance at the room gave me my answer. Shutters closed tight over the windows. Thick rugs nailed to the walls and ceiling as well as the floor. Soundproofing. Cluttered workbenches, sacks and jars of stuff, alembics and phials, books and scrawled notes. Empty lacasa bottles and old lunch and dinner pails piled around the trash. Half-welded *things* propped in corners. A glitter in the air. I knew that glitter, and even if I hadn't, the signs were there. The whole place stank of sentience.

A body lay face-up in the middle of the floor. An old man with long, crooked limbs that twisted around him like the rays of a fallen star. He wore a hairy green cardigan over a worn suit, patches bleached pink. Yellowed whiskers surrounded his mouth, sagging open beneath his eyes, which—

Were gone. Missing. Two dark cavities in the skull-like head. Optical nerves lying shrivelled on the cheeks. Surprisingly little blood.

I'd been expecting something bad. No one came looking for Jack Buskin for a missing hen or a Winkie prank. But this… I swore blue.

"Yeah," Paper Man agreed, folded in the doorway.

I edged forwards a step. Glass crunched under my sole and I winced. A lacasa bottle, nothing more, probably broken in the struggle. The place didn't look as though it had been ransacked. Not a theft then.

"Who was he?"

Paper Man's eyes slid past me.

"He was my uncle."

She stood in the doorway that led to the bedroom. I hadn't heard her approach, but like I said, my hearing isn't great. First thing I saw was her shoes. Usually is. Call it bias. Wrong to call them shoes. Slippers, more like. Sort of a thing worn by people who don't need to walk fast or far. Silver, of course. Some fashions never die. She was dressed like most young women did these days – Fairy of the Killing House style – in a checked dress, neat white blouse fastened at the throat, hair slicked into severe braids that hung down her back like dark rope. White stockings and those moon-shine shoes. I looked at her face. Saw at once she was older than she dressed. Twenty-five, I reckoned. Maybe thirty.

"Dyna?"

She folded her arms. "Mr Buskin."

"You called."

"You came."

"Not much choice. You wrote in green."

"I had to. I need your help."

"With this?"

She nodded. "No one else will listen."

"You reported it?"

"Yes. To the Army of Oz. He was sick in his hat and started crying and had to be taken home. Told me to drink a forgetting potion."

"You didn't agree."

Her jaw tightened. "My uncle was murdered and someone stole his eyes, Mr Buskin. No, I didn't agree."

I shuffled back, took another look at the room. "He have any enemies?"

"Why?"

"I'm guessing he didn't have a permit to be doing any of this magic."

"So? He's hardly the only one in the city."

I nudged an empty pail. "He live here?"

"Some of the time. He and my aunt have a house in the country. He usually goes home for weekends, at least. When he didn't a few nights ago, she got worried. Sent me to check. And I found him…"

Eyeless. I stared at the holes in his head, remembering the feel of the awl punching through the leather of my face, the bewildering and terrifying sensation as light rushed in for the first time. They never prepare you for that.

I leaned over the body. Wasn't unheard of for people to take bits of other people. Hearts, guts. Hell, I knew a guy in Quadling Forest made of four other guys stitched together. But that was mostly skin. Eyes are weird, though. Eyes are bad magic. Gave me that itchy feeling.

"So you'll take the job?" Dyna asked.

She knew I'd take it, but I gave her the satisfaction of pretending to think it over. "My services aren't cheap."

"Neither is that bootleg lacasa you like so much."

Damn crow snitch.

"I charge by the day. Results or no results."

"Fine."

"Starting this morning."

"Fine."

"And I'll need expenses."

She almost laughed at that. I liked the way it made her face alive. She reached into a knapsack that hung over the chair and pulled out a little chipped painted wooden box with a slot in the top. She tossed it to me. "Here."

"What is it?"

"Suggestion Box. Should get you out of trouble. If you run into any."

"Oh yeah? How does it suggest I fend off a killer with an eye fetish?"

The box made a noise, almost like a clunking purr, and spat out a strip of paper.

*Suggest kicking*, it said.

"It isn't always so caustic," Dyna said. "And it knows how to reach me. Now if you'll excuse me…" She looked down at her dead uncle. "Page? Show Mr Buskin out."

The Paper Man unfolded himself from the doorway and slipped sideways into the hall. I followed, the stench of magic clinging to my sole.

Spent the night under the table of some dive bar at the edge of town. Didn't make sense to haggle for a bed and anyway, there was something about being down there that I liked. Familiar. Sometimes I even caught myself pressing up against a stranger's leg just to feel the beat of blood in their veins. Sometimes, I rested – just for a minute – against the quiet leather of another boot. Not for long, though. The illusion wore off quick, and it always left me feeling lonely and sick.

Was woken by some asshole of a broom jamming me in the ribs and hollering for me to move on. I sloped out into the street, squinting in the sickly green light.

The suggestion box chuntered beside me.

*Suggest get to work.*

"Fuck off."

*Suggest fuck self.*

I watched the scrap of paper blow away. The box was right, I was delaying. But that's because I knew eyes meant a visit to the one place I swore I'd never return to.

Hadn't been totally honest with the Paper Man. Hadn't done my eyes myself. Back in the days after I'd first woken up, I'd wanted sight and all the trimmings; peripherals, colours, depth, not whatever mockery the Powder of Life could conjure up. So I'd gone to the person who could give it to me. She'd driven a hard bargain. One I regretted. But there was nothing for it. I'd have to go back to Luz, which meant going back to Oriel.

Took a Mechanical Pony east out of the city, down the

YBR and across Winkie River. The Mech Pony only went as far as Truth Pond, last stop, so from then I had to walk. Hated walking. Shanks' pony. The road ran out and so did the sun and the light was gone by the time I crested a hill.

And there it was.

Grey to the horizon. Grey as bonedust. Endless dunes. The Deadly Desert. Touch it and perish. Death lipping at the edge of Oz held back by… who knew. I stared at its shifting sands. Not for the first time, wondered what it would feel like to lay down and turn to dust.

*Suggest not*, the box said.

"Yeah well, we don't have a choice. Come on."

Robert's place sat on its own, more tent than house, walls and ceiling made from the remains of a hot air balloon. A loonhead living inside a balloon – explain that one to me. I'd never asked Robert about it because it seemed rude and anyway, he was insane.

He'd deflated some since last I'd seen him, wrinkled patches spreading across his head and cheeks. He bobbed low in the doorway.

"Who's there?"

"Customer. Need a lift."

"Over the desert?"

"Halfway. Need to get to Oriel."

He looked at me properly then, or tried to, inked-on eyes smudged at the edges. "When?"

"Tonight."

He bobbed silently for a while. "Can't do it. Not enough air."

That was obvious. The box whirred and spat out a bit of paper.

*Suggest handsome payment*, it said in large letters.

Robert eyed it before bobbing back inside. "Jeff," he called. "Customers."

The place was a mess of empty helium canisters and string. Scraps of rubbery flesh in dark corners. Tried not to look at them.

A monkey sat at a table. His wings were a mess, old army jacket stained and torn. The floor around him was littered with laughing gas canisters. He was not laughing.

Robert swayed over to him. "This guy needs to get to Oriel."

Jeff looked down at me. "Cost ya."

"We can pay," I said.

"When?" he asked.

"Tonight."

He picked up an inhaler, took a long drag. "I'll get my bag."

Didn't much like the thought of being carried over the Deadly Desert by a junkie veteran, but didn't have much choice either.

I stepped into the bag he held out. "You drop me there'll be hell to pay."

Not sure he even heard.

Hard to tell time when you're being carried in a sack. We flew high enough to avoid the dust clouds. Even though I couldn't see I felt the distance below. The fall might not have killed me, but the desert sure would. Could smell it through the hessian. An odour like empty rooms. Like sour electric.

Jeff flew steady enough, taking regular huffs of his gas. Couldn't judge him for that. Who knew what he'd seen in the army. Same shit as me but from above, I guessed. By the time we touched down in Oriel he was shaking.

"You need a lift back gonna have to wait until morning," he said.

"Sure, man."

He shambled off unsteadily towards the door.

For a while I didn't move. Just stared. Oriel sprawled up and out across its ledge of rock, built out of flotsam and held together by magic and spite. It might have been a sanctuary; an oasis of solid stone in the deadly, shifting sands. Maybe that's how it started. That's not what it was anymore. Now, people came to find what they couldn't in the rest of Oz. But here's the thing: people don't always chase what's good for them. Rarely do. And you could chase down all sorts of bad in Oriel.

Alcohol and narcotics were outlawed – never mind, folk always find ways to get high. Robert used to work out here, letting junkies like Jeff suck air out of his face. No violence? Fine, there was always some hammerhead around willing to dole out a bit of pain, not to mention the whispers about what went on in the basement, through the door with the stained handle. In a place as eccentric as Oz, getting what you wanted meant some weird shit. But that was all side hustle. Mostly Oriel dealt in one lucrative commodity.

The business of sight.

Problem with the Powder of Life. No one thinks about sentience the right way. Bring a cauldron to life, sure. But with no mouth to talk, no eyes to see, no ears to hear – you've created a prisoner, trapped in their own flesh.

Mouths weren't so difficult. A splash of ink, a rip in cloth. Ears too. Flap of rust or a couple pinpricks seemed to do the trick. But eyes were different. They were tricky. Painted on they'd work okay, but if you wanted vision, real vision, you had to come to an expert.

Her name was Luz. She ran Oriel like it was her own kingdom. Some said she was a daughter of Mombi. Some said she'd blown in from the other world, like the Fairy of the Killing House. No one knew if she was human or Munchkin or Winkie or what. All people knew was that she was a witch and she gave them what they wanted.

And if anyone knew why a killer would cut a man's eyes out of his skull, it would be her.

*Suggest make this fast*, the box said. It had obviously never been here before.

The lights above the doors flickered red and yellow and blue and green. All welcome, they said, whoever you are. We've got what you need.

The bar was crowded. So many different kinds of folk it was like someone had chewed up an almanac of *Citizens of Oz* and spat it out again. A one-eyed goat with blood on his horns, bellowing out a challenge to fight. A loonhead like Robert, nearly deflated in a corner. The Lonesome Duck, quacking on to a flathead who ignored him while pouring something thick and black into his brain can. A magical mimic on the red-lit stage, shifting between shapes in mockery of the half-wasted audience. It smelled of ditch-weed and spilled lacasa and lust.

I hopped up onto a stool at the bar. The Scare who ran the counter limped over, misshapen flesh and oozing strings of viscera.

"Jack," she greeted, dropping a slimy glass before me.

"Trixie."

"Social call?" A few of her eyes went to the box beside me.

"Work. She here?"

"With a customer. Won't be long."

I reached for my pouch to pay, but Trix brushed it aside. "On the house."

Nodding, I took a sip of lacasa. Sweet and burning. I'd found Trix's missing lover, who'd gone off to Nome looking for work. Hadn't been a happy ending – never is when someone's turned to stone – but Trix hadn't blamed me for that. And she'd paid on time.

I'd finished the glass of lacasa and was thinking on another when Luz appeared. Spark and polish in her silver suit and reflecting spectacles. She moved through the bar like a dark mirror. Even her black hair shone. Clocked me right away.

"Mr Buskin. Back again. What's it to be? Arms? Hands? Something… more personal?"

"Eyes."

"A deal we already made."

"Not for me. Man was found dead in EC a few days ago. Crooked conjurer called Nikidik."

She shrugged, throwing spangles. "City business."

"Sure. Only someone took his eyes. Was hoping you'd know something about it."

"I know a lot of things." She brushed my front with a fingertip. "Say I had heard a rumour. What would it be worth?"

"What would you want?"

She slid the glasses down her nose. I got a glimpse of one eye, multi-faceted like an old cut gem. "A favour."

She knew what she was doing alright. Unsigned favours were risky business in Oz. Never knew what they could be used for. Didn't have a choice though, so I nodded.

She smiled. "Follow me."

Luz led the way below stairs, into Oriel's creaking, vice-sodden heart. Tried not to think about what was going on behind all those closed doors. Her parlour was a windowless room guarded by a rag-man. Pearls for eyes. I looked away.

"Who's your friend?" she asked. She meant the box.

*Suggest mind own business*, it spat out.

"Cute," she observed, before taking a seat at her desk. The room was half study, half laboratory. Shine everywhere. Mirrors and broken glass, crystal and tin. Beakers bubbling. Silver liquid dripping through intricate pipework into a single flask. Behind a beaded curtain, a bed. A cabinet full of blades and spikes.

The sensation of awl punching hide.

"These eyes," she asked. "You'd know them if you saw them?"

"Probably. Why?"

Smiling, she lifted an icebox onto the desk and opened the lid. "Take a peek."

Vapour billowed from the ice box. Inside, neatly stacked, were dozens of pairs of eyes. Pink bunny eyes, wet, black tortoise eyes. A single yellow goat eye. Eagle eyes. Snake eyes. Munchkin and Winkie eyes. Stone Nome eyes. They all watched me, following my movements.

"Where did you get all these?"

"I buy what people sell."

"And has anyone been selling lately?"

"A few days ago, in fact. A fine pair of Munchkin eyes. Used. Antique, I'd say. An acquired taste. But some people like such things."

The box grumbled unhappily. *Suggest explain*, it said. I wished it hadn't.

Luz indicated the lab set up behind her. "Eyes hold what they see. Imprints of memories. Usually we distil it out, back to pure sight. That's what we use for clients like Mr Buskin here. But some people like the flavour of another person's sight. The flashbacks. The seasoned recollections. It's like doubling the life you've lived, and your knowledge. Or so I've been told."

The pupils of the eyes dilated as I leaned over them.

"Which are the antiques?"

"Back left."

She was right, they looked used. Yellowed whites, broken veins, a fog of cataract on one. And they were green, so dark they were almost black. Could easily have been the dead man's eyes. Or some other poor bastard's.

"Who sold them to you?"

"Broker from EC. Where he got them…" She spread her hands.

"How do I know these are the stiff's?"

"One way to find out."

At my nod she lifted the eyes out of the cold box and took them over to the workbench. I didn't want to watch but couldn't help myself as she picked up the right one, held it between a chrome-tipped finger and thumb and began to squeeze.

The eye started to weep. A single tear that dripped into a silver dish.

Even the suggestion box was silent as she brought the dish to my face and let the dead man's tear slide into the ragged hole of my eye.

I wasn't a stranger to sordid substances and vile fluids; hell, my soul was stained with the blood and effluence of half of Oz. But there's something about getting another man's tear in your eye that nothing can prepare you for.

Sympathy. Revulsion. Bad familiarity.

Tried to swipe it away but it was too late. Luz's study was melting and telescoping into a different room – Dr Nikidik's – pain blurring the light to a smear and a figure was looming over me. The tip of a knife filled my vision and beyond its shine I caught a flash of gold and green brocade. A symbol I recognised. An elegant, stylised *OZ*.

Then sunder and pain and black.

I was back in Luz's study, she and the suggestion box and all those dozens of pairs of eyes staring.

"Well?" she asked, placing the eye back in the box. "You see who did it?"

"Nah. Just a knife. But those are my dead guy's eyes alright."

I was lying and she knew it. But she handed over the box like we'd agreed and let me walk on out into the night.

*Suggest trouble*, Box said in tiny writing as we stepped into the bar.

Trouble was goddam right. Because I knew that insignia like my own heel. It was the flash of Queen Ozma's private guard.

Which meant that whatever I had stepped into here, it was far, far worse than I'd imagined.

Tipped Jeff extra to take us to Truth Pond, but still, the way back to EC took all day. Wasn't at my best, either. A night of slugging lacasa and trying to avoid the worst of Oriel's temptations had left me sweaty and limp. If any of Ozma's hoods had come for me during that journey I'da put up no more fight than an old sock. Who knew what Box had got up to the night before. When I asked it how it was doing all that emerged was a faint *suuughhrrrrrrrrrrrrr* so I let it be.

By the time the Mech Pony clunked up to the city, the sun was setting through the jewelled turrets of Ozma's palace. Verdigris and pond slime. Burning sage and bottle glass. I kicked Box until it woke up and slowly cluntered out an answer when I asked where to find Dyna.

Followed its directions to a cheap hotel on the city's west side, close to the outer gate. Sorta place where so many folk came and went that even the walls could be paid to forget a face. Dyna had means – that much was obvious – so the fact she was staying in some no-name joint told me she already knew her uncle had been into some serious shit. Assuming he even *was* her uncle.

Whoever he was we were connected now, and by more than tears. I had the feeling that if I didn't get to the bottom of whatever was going on, it'd come get me.

So I went up the five flights of rickety stairs, past rooms filled with wailing Winkie families and fighting Hyups, all the way to her door.

She was expecting me. No Killing Fairy checks this time. She was wearing a grey-green dress, her dark hair down on her shoulders. No shoes, long slim toes on the boards. I looked at her face.

"Well?" she said.

I nodded inside. Waited until she'd closed the door. Box slumped onto its side against the wall, which I guessed meant it was asleep. Dyna looked at it for a minute before turning to me.

Slowly, I bent down and let the container with the eyeballs inside slide out onto the floor.

"They're his," I said.

She was pale, but she didn't scream. "How do you know?"

"Saw it. Out in Oriel. Where I found 'em."

"You saw the killer?"

"Say I did. And say I told you it'd be better for you not to know. To go back to that aunt of yours and make paper men and forget what you came to EC and found. What would you say?"

"I'd tell you to go fuck yourself, Mr Buskin."

Of course. "Sit down."

Felt better when we were both on the floor. Nothing to do with the power dynamic, more that it would be harder for any bats or moths or goddam sentient cobwebs to overhear us.

"He was murdered?" Her breath smelled like dark berries.

"Assassinated."

She went still and didn't speak.

"You knew, then?" I asked.

"Suspected."

"His name wasn't Nikidik, was it?"

"No. It was Pipt."

My turn to freeze. Dr Pipt. The Crooked Magician himself. Inventor of the Powder of Life. Genius. Madman.

"Pipt died years ago," I said.

She shook her head. "Faked. He knew he'd never get out from under Ozma's gaze so long as he was alive. She stripped him of his powers once. It nearly killed him, getting them back."

"Well, he's dead now."

"At Ozma's hand."

"We don't know that."

"You said it was assassination. Means it was political." She leaned towards me. "It was her, wasn't it? Ozma?"

"All I saw was a uniform."

"So that's a yes. I knew it. She's wanted to be rid of him for years." There was a candy-apple colour to her cheeks. "He was going to talk, Jack. He'd been acting strange lately. Kept saying he had to restore the balance. He said people needed to know."

"Know what?"

"He wouldn't tell me. Aunt Margolotte, either. Said it was too dangerous, that we'd be safe so long as we didn't – know, that is. Whatever he saw, whatever he knew, he was killed for it."

Together, we stared at the box of eyes on the floor. They stared ceilingward and didn't meet our gaze.

"We can't."

She touched the ridge of me, where the leather creased. "We have to."

Saw her wrist close up for the first time then, without the lace or ruffles. Saw the tattoo, faded in the flesh. Two knitting needles through a bisected circle.

The insignia of the Army of Revolt: the legion of young women commanded by General Jinjur. The Army that took Emerald City without a single drop of blood spilled. As if that was any metric to measure loss of life.

"You were in the AoR?"

Her face looked old and tired and trusting and sorry. "I was young."

Did I recognise her, or was I imagining it? Did I know the scent of her, the salt of her sweat, the funk of her shed skin, the weep of her blisters? Is that why I felt so drawn to her? Had I once been hers, at one time?

"So was I," I said.

"You were…?"

"In the Army. Like you. Saw battle. Battles. Don't know how it happened but my soldier stepped in a few grains of Powder in an armaments tent. Here I am."

Her eyes travelled over me. "So we might have…?"

"Worked together. Maybe."

She sagged back against the wall. "Shit." The container sat beyond both of our toes. "Are we going to do this?"

"Guess so."

"How do we…? You know."

"Bottoms up."

Thought she would refuse. She didn't. She was some woman. Instead she eased open the box and hovered her fingers over her uncle's watching eyes. "Shall I?"

Closed my eyes and nodded. Felt the skin of her wrist touch my throat and then the slide, wet and cold and wrong, of the eyeball down my gullet. In the moments before memory took her I heard her swallow, the jerk of her body as she gagged on her uncle's eyeball, the hard grip of her hand across my middle as she fought to keep control of her guts.

Then we were gone and we weren't we, we were he. Me. I was looking out across a battlefield, watching an army – *my* army – throw itself into the arms of the enemy. Raw magic seared my eyes, the acrid smell reaching even up here high above the war zone.

A company of pitchforks marched forwards to be blasted into splinters by Ozma's magicians. A company of bandsaws took their place. And everywhere the sentient army died, their dead-quick-dead flesh turned to sand, bodies leached of everything that had once made them alive. So many had died that dunes were beginning to build up, clogging the grasslands that separated Oz from Nome. And still, they kept marching. And still, they kept dying.

There was a soldier at my shoulder, saluting, telling me they needed more Powder of Life and what was I to do?

Refuse? When the only way to save the beings we had made and sent to fight was to make more – or surrender?

So into the weaponry tent. Back to the alembics. Industrial scale. Powder by the barrel. Bring 'em to life, boys and girls. Bring 'em all to life. Let's see Ozma's squaddies fight their own possessions.

On and on it went. Past sense. Things requisitioned quick as made. Things made live quick as requisitioned. Things dead quick as live. And the dust blew. And the dunes grew. And how many dunes make a desert? And what is that desert but the presence of countless never-should-have-liveds, thrown to the slaughter? What is the Deadly Desert but our shame?

And when it was over we agreed to forget. We all agreed to forget because the truth was too horrible to acknowledge and carry on living. But anything built on a lie will crumble eventually – even empires. Especially empires. Which makes memory dangerous. And those who possess it enemies.

Someone was touching me, shaking me out of the visions from Dr Pipt's memory, right back into my own flesh. Dyna was slumped beside me.

Through my awl-punched eyes I saw green and gold brocade, and the tips of swords levelled at my throat. Ozma's guards.

"You're both under arrest," they said.

She was waiting for us at the palace. Even though it was late she was fully-dressed, wide awake in her private rooms, working at a huge desk. Did she never sleep? I stood on the plush sage carpet, filthy and sick in body and brain. Dyna stood beside me, trembling but defiant.

"Mr Buskin," Ozma said, rising like a candle flame, all halo of gold hair and shimmering robes. "And Miss Dyna. Thank you for coming."

"Your invitation didn't leave much room for demurring," Dyna said.

"It was intended as an escort, nothing more." She came forwards. "I am sorry about your uncle."

"You had him murdered."

"I had a threat to the peace and safety of my people removed. Believe me, my dear Dyna, it was a decision I did not want to make." Her beautiful face was a picture of sorrow. "We tried everything to reason with him over the years. I had hoped that without his magic, he might learn to live a peaceful life."

"You deprived him of his reason for being."

"I gave him a chance. He rejected my offers of reconciliation. He really did leave me with no choice."

"Why the eyes?" I asked.

I could still taste the slick saltiness of Dr Pipt's vision in my throat.

Ozma smiled sadly. "I couldn't risk his memories falling into the wrong hands."

"Like Luz's?"

"A mistake. One of my guards decided to dispose of the eyes in a, um, gainful manner. I am glad you retrieved them, Mr Buskin."

Of course. She'd known what I was up to all along. Probably watched while I did it too.

"My uncle was going to expose the truth." Dyna was vicious. "He was going to tell everyone what their precious Oz is built upon. But now we know. You can't silence us all."

"Oh, dear. I'm afraid I can."

Ozma's sparkling eyes flicked over Dyna's shoulder. Nothing I could do to stop the guards coming forward to seize her arms and push her to her knees. Our eyes were level for one awful moment before a guard grabbed Dyna's face, forced open her jaw and emptied a flagon of liquid into it. I lunged forwards but another guard grasped me by the scruff and hauled me back away from the splash and patter of the liquid. That's when I realised what it was.

Water of Oblivion. Drawn from its golden basin in the palace. *Don't swallow*, I begged Dyna silently. But she was choking, her throat working, and I saw the moment the Water took effect. She stopped struggling. Her lips dropped open, her eyes cleared of anger, turning wide and innocent. Total amnesia. Forgetting everything that had happened. What she'd seen. Who she was.

"Take her out to Oriel," Ozma told a guard. "Have Luz remove the eyes and burn them." She watched sadly as the guards took Dyna by the elbows. "Ask her to replace them with something nice. Crystal, I think."

Then she was gone. But of course, the Dyna I'd known – quick and inquisitive and angry – was already lost.

Ozma leaned down towards me, hands on her knees. Scent of blossom and sour magic.

"Mr Buskin. I know you paid dearly for your sight. I would hate to remove it. So, I trust we won't have a problem?" She stroked my tongue. "You'll forget what you saw, won't you, Jack?"

"Yeah," I said turning away. "I always do."

# SILVER & GOLD

CHRISTINA HENRY

Dorry leaned against Essie's legs, breathing in the scent of old lavender and damp tea leaves. Essie's silver shoes glinted in the gloom, catching the small rays of light that seeped under the tablecloth. Dorry loved those shoes. They had a stacked heel and a single strap that went over the instep and buckled on the outside with a shiny silver buckle. Whenever she saw them she felt strangely comforted, because they meant *Essie* to her and Essie was the most important person in the whole world, the one she loved above all others.

Dorry didn't mind being under the table. It felt cozy in there, with the draped folds of cloth all around and the shoes winking like treasure in a cave, like the booty in the stories Essie told her about pirates on the high seas. Essie reached under the table and patted the top of her head, like she was a dog. Dorry wished she had a dog, one with black button eyes like a teddy bear, one small enough for her to pick up and carry in a basket. But Essie said a dog was another mouth to feed and they had enough trouble sometimes feeding just their two mouths, so there was no dog. Dorry circled the floor on all fours, pretending she was a puppy hunting for a bone.

A thin wall divided the caravan and she heard Essie's sister, Wessie, reading the cards on the other side. She cocked her head, still a dog, listening intently. *The Page of Wands*, she thought. Wessie was telling the person – likely a young woman, as those were a fortune-teller's best customers, always – that she could expect good news soon.

Essie's shoes moved, tapping restlessly. She was always irritated when her sister had a paying customer and she didn't.

Their real names were Esther and Wesleya, but nobody ever called them that. They had to be a rhyming pair, even if they were not entirely identical twins any longer.

There was a squeak outside as someone stepped up on the wooden stairs that Essie placed outside the door each day, alongside the sandwich board that read: **Your Future in the Palm of Your Hand! Readings 5 Cents.**

The door opened, bringing with it the faraway aroma of popcorn and grilling onions and, of course, the dust. Always the dust. The dust blew everywhere outside all the time, crawled up her nose and made it itch, seeped between the strands of her hair so that when she unbraided it once a week to wash the red waves were streaked with it.

"Hello?"

Dorry didn't need to see the woman to know that she hovered, hesitant, at the entrance, letting her glare-blind eyes adjust to the gloom inside the caravan. Essie only kept a couple of candles on the table, allowing the deep shadow to create a sense of mystery. Essie's silver shoes disappeared as she stood, calling to the customer, "Come in, come in" in her light and clear voice. Her white dress and blonde curls would be like a beacon in the dark.

The soles of the customer's shoes made hardly a sound on the carpet as she crossed to the table. Dorry stayed perfectly still. She could be very, very quiet when she needed to be.

The woman chattered nervously, saying she never did things like this and her husband wouldn't really approve, but their farm wasn't doing so well and of course, no one's farm was with this dreadful drought and she was only hoping for some *good* news for a change, hoping for something she could pin her lights on as she looked down the road.

"Can you *really* tell the future?" she asked, and Dorry could practically see the plaintive expression on her face.

"Of course, my dear," Essie said. Essie always took on a motherly air with the customers, even though she wasn't much older than many of them, and sometimes younger. Dorry had seen a copy of her birth certificate once, folded up in Essie's jewelry box, and it said 1899, which meant she was only thirty-six. It was very grown-up to Dorry but not old at all, because Essie was still so beautiful. She hoped she'd grow up to be just as beautiful, but she knew she wouldn't. Her face was plain and sort of freckly and anyway, she would never be tall.

The desperate farm wife clinked a nickel against Essie's gold rings. Dorry watched as the customer's legs rustled the cloth and she sat.

"You'll need to put your bag down, dear. I must look at both palms."

"Oh. Oh, of course," the woman said.

Dorry imagined her fingers circled tight around the

handle, pulling it into her lap before reluctantly placing it on the floor. The customer's shoes peeked under the tablecloth, brown leather and as worn out as the undercurrent in her voice. The toe of the left shoe was separating from the sole.

*Would have been better off going to the cobbler than the fortune-teller*, Dorry thought, but she was also smart enough to know that without rubes like this she and Essie would never earn their own bread.

She lay herself flat on the carpet without even a rustle, breathing in the hot scent of the dust. Above her, Essie was doing her patter, keeping up a continuous stream of talk to disguise any sounds Dorry might make. But Dorry never made a sound. She was a quiet little mouse in the shadows.

Her clever fingers lifted the cloth, just a bit, just so she could see the farm wife's cheap purse balanced a few inches away. Dorry's bare toe reached back and tapped Essie's shoe, their signal that Dorry was about to begin the lift.

"Oh. Oh, my goodness!" Essie exclaimed.

Dorry felt the farm wife lean forward in her chair. "*What?*" she said, her tone a mixture of hope and alarm.

Dorry tuned out the talk then, because all her focus was on sliding the bag, oh-so-carefully, until it was under the table. She eased the clasp open and looked inside, not expecting much based on the woman's shoes. Still, a handful of coins would be a handful they didn't have already, so Dorry looked.

There was just enough light for her to see a folded handkerchief, a coin purse, a worn enamel compact that might have been worth something once but wasn't anymore. And an envelope. Her heartbeat quickened.

She squeezed the envelope between finger and thumb and felt the thick press of paper inside. *The mortgage payment*, she thought. *Jackpot.*

The temptation to take it all was strong, was always strong. But the first thing the farm wife would do upon standing would be to peek inside her bag, making certain the envelope was still there. Dorry contented herself with removing one bill from the back of the stack. The farmer and his wife would assume they'd miscounted the money, no matter that they had probably stacked up the bills on their kitchen table and counted and recounted them twenty times.

She folded the bill and tucked it under her body, closed the flap of the envelope, clicked the purse together very, very softly and pushed it right back out to its starting place. Then she rolled over and sat up, grasping the bill in her hand. She tapped Essie's ankle twice, letting her know all was well.

Essie went on for a few more moments, really buttering up the farm wife, who found herself in receipt of a 'free' charm to keep away bad spirits. These little poultices were made from one of Dorry's old gingham dresses and filled with dried lavender and sage.

The farm wife stood and thanked Essie. Dorry heard the click of her purse opening, the little rustle as she assured herself that the envelope was safe inside. Dorry grinned. So predictable, these rubes.

The door opened, and the dust and the smoke and the cries of folk gasping in wonder seeped in again, before the door slammed shut. They waited a minute or two, always cautious that the rube might return or that another would quickly follow. There was no noise from next door, so Wessie didn't have any customers. It was getting on to midday. Anyone at the circus or the sideshow would be looking for their lunch, probably. Essie seemed to think the same, for Dorry saw her silver shoes disappear. Her heels *click-click-clicked* over to the door and Dorry heard her open it and flip the sign to 'BACK IN 1 HOUR'. Then she latched the door and said, "Well?"

Dorry scampered out from under the table, still pretending she was a dog. She crawled over to Essie, who shook her head at her. Dorry sat back on her knees and barked.

"All right, little puppy. What have you found?" Essie said, patting her head.

Dorry unfolded the bill and Essie gave a little *whoop* as she snatched it from Dorry's hand. "Ten dollars! That's my girl, that's my *girl*!"

Dorry stood and leapt in her arms, just a child again, and happy that she'd made Essie so happy. Essie was the whole world, the closest thing she'd ever had to a mother.

Essie and Wessie had found Dorry toddling on the edge of a cornfield in Kansas about nine years before.

"No sign of your people," Essie said when she told Dorry the tale. "We never knew if they got sick and died, or they left you because you were another mouth to feed, or they stopped for a picnic and plumb forgot you altogether.

"Me and Wessie were driving along. She was complaining about some such thing, the way she always is—"

"I was not," Wessie said, cutting in, but Essie bowled right over her as if she'd never spoken at all.

"I saw your red curls just bobbing alongside that corn and told her to stop."

Dorry didn't know how to imagine herself that way, small and alone. She only remembered her life with Essie and Wessie, but mostly with Essie.

"I got out of the car and chased you right down before you fell in a ditch and hurt yourself. As soon as I picked you up, you just snuggled into me like you'd been waiting for me. Wessie said we should drop you at an orphanage—"

"I did *not,* I said we should look for your people. Essie just wanted to take you away like you were a doll she found on the side of the road."

"—but I knew you were our own girl and you belonged with us."

Dorry was maybe five when they told her this story. They'd already been running a 'lost daughter' scam to great success. They'd go to a fairly large town or city and find a good busy place, one where people weren't paying real close attention to the folks around them. Dorry would run off into the crowd. Essie would watch from a distance and when they saw a likely mark – a moderately well-to-do woman who looked like she'd respond with compassion – Dorry would burst out crying. The woman would stop to help, offer to help find her mother.

Essie, some small distance away, would turn on the waterworks herself and head in their direction, calling for her lost lamb. The woman would assist Dorry to Essie, who'd shake her hand and embrace her and while the kindhearted lady was being jostled by this activity Wessie would lift her wallet or coin purse and disappear into the throng.

They'd made a lot of money that way, and they'd made a good team. They'd never been caught, either. But that was before the Bad Time, when Wessie stole away Essie's guy and Essie tried to kill them both.

She took Wessie's left eye out with her little knife and the guy disappeared. Dorry couldn't remember his name – it was something on the tip of her tongue, sometimes, but she couldn't call it up. She remembered that he used to give her rides on his shoulders. He was tall and strong and he had a mouthful of white teeth and chestnut hair that curled around his ears. Dorry had liked him, but she didn't like him as much when he hurt Essie's feelings.

He gave Wessie a gold bracelet, a thin chain with one gleaming green stone in the center of the links. The bracelet went missing that night, too, along with Wessie's eye.

Essie and Wessie never spoke except to snipe at each other now, though they couldn't seem to separate. Dorry said once it would be better if they went off on their own, without Wessie, and Essie had looked at her sharply and said, "Whatever she's done, she's my sister."

Dorry thought that really Essie just wanted to rub it in Wessie's face forever that she'd driven the guy away, and that Wessie hadn't gotten him off her. Wessie, she knew, wanted to stay so she could blame Essie for everything.

They were identical twins, and there was a time when you could hardly tell the difference between the two. You'd always know which was which now, on account of Wessie's eyepatch.

Essie thought it prudent to read a few more fortunes that day, so as not to arouse suspicion, though the ten dollars would have her and Dorry in clover for a while. She cautioned Dorry not to bother with any other purses that day unless they looked especially prosperous. Dorry did find an especially nice jade comb that she couldn't resist, and it was the sort of thing the lady might think she dropped accidentally, anyhow.

After they took in the sign for the day, Essie said. "Let's go out on the town, Dormouse."

Dormouse was Essie's special name for her, one that she'd given her when Dorry was young because she was "so small you could fit inside a teapot". Even now, when Dorry was maybe ten years old or thereabouts – without sure knowledge they just guessed at her age, and celebrated her birthday on the day they'd found her – she looked much younger, closer to seven. She never answered to her real name, and only Wessie called her that anyway, pronouncing all the syllables one by one – "Dor-o-thy". Essie said they'd named her after their mother but that it was too much name to give to such a little child.

When Essie said, 'Go out on the town' she meant going over to the circus side. They didn't often have money for the food and games in the main area, but Dorry loved to go when they could. The fortune-tellers were part of the sideshow, only loosely attached to the main draw. The circus folk – the acrobats and elephant riders and clowns – went town to town by train, and their arrival was often heralded with a parade.

The sideshow folk followed in their shadow in trucks and

caravans, sometimes stopping at places the circus didn't go because there was no train depot nearby. The people in these places were mostly amenable to gawping at the Alligator Man and the Bearded Lady and having their palms or their cards read. Sometimes, though, they'd encounter a town of suspicious, squinty-eyed scripture lovers, and they'd move on quickly, keen to reattach to the big top, which brought some degree of respectability.

Dorry and Essie washed their hands and faces in the basin and Essie put on a fresh dress, though she didn't change out of her silver shoes. She never wore any others, and only took them off at night. Sometimes Dorry would step her much smaller feet inside and try to buckle the straps around her ankles. Essie would laugh and kiss her and say, "You can have them when you're all grown up."

Then she'd add, "Just make sure Wessie doesn't get them. Though I'm planning to outlive *her*."

Essie gave Dorry's braid a tug and descended the steps of the caravan. As if waiting for the bang of Essie's door, Wessie emerged from her side. She wore a plain black dress and shoes but her eyepatch was a glittery gold, the same material as the sparkly gold cap that rested on her blonde curls.

Dorry noticed that she, too, had taken in her sandwich board for the day. That meant she'd either had a good day of earnings, or she'd had a bad day and didn't want to admit it to her sister by leaving the board out for extra business.

"I'm going to the big top," Wessie announced, clattering down her steps. The ever-pervasive dust soiled the tips of her black shoes almost immediately.

"A newsflash I did not ask for," Essie said in a bored voice. "Come on, Dormouse. Want some popcorn?"

"Oh, yes," Dorry said. It was her favorite treat. After that she liked caramel apples the best, though the only time she ate one was when they were up north where the apples grew.

"I made two dollars today," Wessie said.

"Ooh, what absolute riches," Essie said, and slung her arm around Dorry's shoulders.

She steered her through the sparse foot traffic of the sideshow. People stood here and there, watching the snake charmer playing a horn or rooting for Hector or Jan to win their wrestling match.

The sun was going down, and the shadows were doing their work. During the day the sideshow was like an old woman trying and failing to cover her wrinkles with powder. The down-at-heel trailers and shoddy-looking tents gave off an air of tangible desperation. But at night the darkness settled over everything except where the lamps chose to shine, making everything young and lovely and mysterious again, full of magic and adventure.

From the midway came shrieks of fear and delight as the Ferris wheel creaked in a slow circle, baskets shaking when customers kicked their feet into the open air. Men's voices pattered everywhere, asking for boyfriends to win a prize for their ladyloves by swinging a hammer or knocking over targets with an air rifle. The dust didn't go away, it never did here, but it seemed to Dorry that it settled at night, became harmless sparkles from a fairy's wand.

The sugar-sweet aroma of cotton candy on the air mixed

with the sweat of the crowds, even though most had washed off their farmers' grime and put on their best clothes. It would be so easy, in the busyness of the crowd, for Dorry to slip her hand into a pocket and come away with a few coins or even a dollar bill. But there wasn't any need for that today. Today, they were rich.

Essie frowned as she noticed Wessie tagging along behind them. "I thought you were going to the big top," she said, flicking her fingers so Wessie would go away.

"I am," Wessie said. "There's a new ringmaster, and I want to see him. Mathilda says he's very young, and very handsome."

Irritation flickered in Essie's eyes. She hadn't known about the new ringmaster, and she didn't want to ask Wessie about it, so she snapped out, "I don't know why *you're* rushing over there, then. Nobody young and handsome would be interested in that face."

As usual, Wessie rose to her bait. "My *face* is the same as yours."

"Not quite," Essie said, tapping her index finger under her left eye.

"And whose fault is that?" Wessie said, her tone spitting venom.

"Yours," said Essie. "He was mine, and you shouldn't have taken him."

"You shouldn't have left him alone so that he *could* be taken," Wessie said. "And speaking of things that are *mine,* I know you have my bracelet. He gave it to *me,* and I want it."

Essie rolled her eyes. "Stuff your nonsense. Don't you think if I had that stupid thing I'd have sold it long ago? Me and

Dorry would be kicking it up in California, our road paved with gold."

"You have it," Wessie said. "I know you do. And I'm going to find it."

"Suit yourself," Essie said in her bored voice. The thing that always made Wessie maddest was when Essie was nonchalant, so of course Essie did it all the time.

"You think you've got everyone fooled. You've even got little Dorothy fooled. But I'll prove it. Wait and see."

Wessie stomped ahead of them, her gold cap bobbing through the crowd. Dorry only realized that Essie's hand had bitten hard into her shoulder when Essie's grip relaxed.

"*Her* bracelet," Essie muttered, because it was fine to show her irritation once Wessie was out of earshot. "It was only her bracelet because she stole him in the first place. And she never made two dollars today. She'd have had to tell forty fortunes, and there wasn't nearly that much foot traffic."

Dorry didn't say anything, for Essie was in a mood now and so was she. She didn't like to think about that night. They'd been staying in a motel, for it was before the caravan and sideshow days. She was asleep on a little cot in the corner and she woke to the sound of screaming, everybody screaming, and the silver knife was flashing and there was blood, so much blood. Wessie on the ground with her hand over the hole where her eye used to be and Essie's hands so red it looked like she wore scarlet gloves. And Dorry huddled under her blanket, not wanting to see but needing to see, and then…

"Oh!" she said, because she remembered something then, something she'd somehow forgot. The man, the one they'd fought over, staggering backward and the blood pouring out of a smile in his throat where no smile should be.

*Essie told me he left. She's always said that.* But Dorry didn't think that man could have gotten very far, bleeding like that.

"Oh, what, Dormouse?" Essie asked, smiling.

Dorry looked at her and the memory of blood must have still been in her eyes because Essie's smile faltered and she said, "What's wrong?"

Dorry shook her head. Maybe she was remembering it wrong. That happened sometimes. She'd say this or that had occurred, and Essie would say, "Oh, no, Dormouse, don't you remember? It was like this instead." And Dorry would believe her, because she loved Essie so much and she didn't think Essie would ever lie to her.

*But there was blood. Lots of blood.*

"It's nothing," Dorry said. "Can I have a red hot?"

Essie's eyes narrowed, like she knew Dorry wasn't telling the truth. But she was happy about their unexpected windfall and Dorry knew she wanted to get back into a good mood after the encounter with her sister.

"All right," Essie said. "Then we'll get some popcorn and go off to see this young, handsome ringmaster. What do you say?"

"Yes," Dorry said, and tried to forget the blood she thought she remembered.

A little while later they were ensconced on a bench across the big top from Wessie, who was pointedly not making eye contact.

"That gold cap is like a stupid beacon," Essie said. "Makes it easier to avoid her."

Dorry had a paper bag of popcorn in her lap. She shoved handfuls into her mouth as a beautiful lady in a pink dress did tricks on a white horse. Dorry didn't know her name. A lot of the circus folk were from faraway places she couldn't imagine, Poland and Prussia and other countries she couldn't even say. They mostly talked amongst themselves, the sounds of their speech strange and musical.

After the horse lady, the clowns came out and tumbled around while the acrobats prepared the nets and swings and tightropes for their act. Essie tapped one foot against the other, a sure sign that she was getting impatient. Then the clowns cleared away, and out he came.

Essie sat up straighter. Across the main ring Dorry noticed Wessie do the same.

Then he began to speak, and Dorry was caught, too. She'd never heard a voice like that before, deep and rich and resonant. It seemed to come from nowhere and everywhere all at once.

He was dressed all in green, from the top of his tall hat to the cuffs of his velvet suit. His black boots were polished so bright they seemed to reflect the faces in the audience, and Dorry wondered how he managed to keep the dust off them. He had a square jaw under a straight nose and a mouthful of white teeth that made Dorry think of that man, the one who went away (*was killed*) on the bad night.

He talked, and he said the usual things that ringmasters say about dangerous feats of derring-do and what they were all about to witness. They were just regular sorts of words and Dorry didn't understand why when he said them they seemed more magical.

*He's putting a spell on us*, she thought, and she looked to his eyes to see the trick there, and was astonished to find she couldn't see his eyes at all. His eyes were covered by spectacles with green lenses, and they kept whatever was behind them hidden.

Then the ringmaster stepped out of the ring, and the promised feats of wonder began, but Dorry found she wasn't so interested in the acrobats tonight. She felt like shaking her head to get the wool out of it. Essie squinted after the man in green and murmured, "I wonder where he came from."

"Through the air in a balloon," Dorry said, and Essie laughed and pulled one of her braids.

"What made you think of that, Dormouse?"

"I don't know," Dorry said, and it was true. "I could just picture it somehow. I don't think he would travel like an ordinary man."

"He's an ordinary man," Essie said, but she wasn't looking at the ringmaster now. She was watching her sister, who was watching the ringmaster with her one good eye.

When the show was over for the evening, Essie said to Dorry, "Let's go see where this man came from, and where he's going, and if he'd like to have dinner with me tomorrow."

"Better hurry," Dorry said. "It looks like Wessie has the same idea."

"Of course she does," Essie said, watching Wessie's gold cap bob against the flow of the crowd as she determinedly headed in the direction of the emerald-clad man. "She never wants anything unless I want it first."

*But aren't you the same?* Dorry thought, then she banished it quickly. It seemed disloyal somehow.

She and Essie slipped out of the big top and in the direction of the little tents where the performers slept when the circus was set up in a town. It wasn't that they weren't *supposed* to go there. They were a part of the show, too, and a fair number of them knew Essie and Wessie by sight, if not by name. But Dorry always had a sense that they were going up in the world, country mouse in the city, whenever they crossed over to the circus side. They were just a little cut above the seedy sideshow, folk with actual skills instead of fake fortune-tellers and human freaks.

She and Essie moved through the night, away from the tired crowds making their way home to their dismal, dust-filled farms. The barkers tried their best to make them stop, play one more game, win one more prize. The shadows folded over them as they moved away from the bright lights and frantic motion.

Dorry gripped Essie's hand tight. Suddenly she didn't want to go see the ringmaster. The path ahead seemed fraught, dangerous, as if something wild and bloodthirsty could leap out of any pool of darkness. She remembered the ringmaster's white, white teeth and thought, *He's the kind that can bite.*

"Let's go back," she said, pulling on Essie's hand.

"What?" Essie said, trying to tug her fingers out of Dorry's insistent grip. "What's gotten into you?"

"It's not safe," Dorry said. "We should go back."

"You're being a silly goose," Essie said dismissively. She was intent on the ringmaster and wasn't listening to Dorry at all.

But Dorry's spine shivered and her knees knocked and she knew something was wrong, wrong, wrong.

Essie stopped to cadge a cigarette off one of the animal handlers, who pointed her toward the tent at the very end of the row, a little apart from the rest. It seemed ominous, that separation. Dorry didn't say anything, though. Essie didn't want to hear it, and Dorry didn't want to go back through the growling dark on her own. She was a sideshow baby; she'd never been afraid of the dark before, but she was now. Every step they took closer to the solitary tent felt like a collision waiting to happen. Something big and terrible was about to run them down.

When they reached the tent, Essie peeked inside the flap to assure herself that he hadn't beaten them there. "Spare as a monk's tomb," she remarked.

Dorry peeked around Essie to see. A single lantern hung from a ring on a pole in the center. There was a cot with a wool blanket folded up at the end of it. At the foot of the cot was a great brown leather trunk, so big Dorry could fit inside it easily, small as she was.

"Well, well. To what do I owe the pleasure of two lovely ladies standing on my doorstep?"

He strode along the path like it belonged to him, like everything in the world belonged to him. A lantern swung from his hand, but carelessly, as if the light hardly mattered. It made the darkness dance back and forth, like it moved to his whim. His voice was modulated, less impressive than it had been in the ring, but Dorry still thought it was hardly a regular voice at all. It made her feel confused, that voice, made her want to trust him when she knew she shouldn't.

Essie moved toward him in a flash. Dorry trailed behind, holding a handful of cloth at Essie's waist. She heard Essie say, "I'm Esther Gale, the fortune-teller in the sideshow."

"But surely…" the ringmaster said. "I met another young woman who said that *she* was the fortune-teller?"

"My sister," Essie said, and though her tone stayed light and pleasant Dorry alone knew she was irritated by the mention of Wessie.

"Of course," he said, looking her up and down in a way that Dorry did not like at all. "Twins!"

His tone was meant to convey surprise and delight, but Dorry heard something Essie didn't hear. He already *knew* she was Wessie's sister. Had Wessie told him? Had he walked the sideshow and asked about them? *How would he know otherwise? But why would he pretend* not *to know?*

"And who is this?" he said, turning his attention to Dorry.

She shrank back. He still wore his emerald-green glasses despite the dark, and she couldn't see his eyes, but she knew his gaze was on her – questing, questioning.

"This is my girl, Dorry," Essie said.

"Prin-*cess* Dorry!" he exclaimed. "What faraway land did you come from, princess? Kalamazoo? Alakazam? Abracadabra?"

Dorry thought the nonsense words were meant to make her laugh, and for most kids they probably did. But she did not believe he was sincere. She thought he was a showman, a humbug, and she didn't know why Essie was so interested in him. Essie frowned down at her when she didn't respond.

"Say something, you goose."

Dorry shook her head, but the ringmaster knew his job and he said, "Of course, of course, royalty doesn't speak to the likes of me. But let me offer you a favor, princess, and I beg you to accept it."

Dorry had seen plenty of sleight-of-hand tricks in her time. Jack Crawford, who was skinny as a scarecrow and twice as smart, did the three-card monte on the midway sometimes and he'd taught her how it worked. But even she was stunned to see the emerald-green rose appear in the ringmaster's hand as if he'd summoned it from air.

He thrust it toward her. Dorry felt Essie's glare, and knew she'd have to take it from him. She clasped the stem gingerly between her fingers, as if it were a snake about to strike. The petals were made of some silky material that gave off a faint sheen.

"Why do you wear green glasses?" she asked, and she didn't even know what made her ask it.

He smiled, and perhaps it was because he'd coaxed her into speaking despite her obvious reluctance. "Everyone wants rose-colored glasses, but my world has a different tilt, and a different tint."

This sounded like a riddle, a riddle that made Dorry feel stupid, so she just curtsied her thanks for the rose and left things to Essie.

After several minutes' conversation Essie had discovered his name was Oscar, that he was from Nebraska, that he was all alone in the world and that nothing would delight him more than to have a meal with her tomorrow evening. Dorry scratched at the dirt with the toe of her shoe and wished to be back in her little cot, snuggled up under the blankets with the door shut.

"And will Princess Dorry join us tomorrow?" he asked, and Dorry felt his questioning gaze on her again.

"That will be past her bedtime," Essie said smoothly.

They made all their arrangements, and Essie said goodnight. Off they walked, back through the rows of tents now filled with the tired chatter of weary performers and the scent of their dinners cooking over fires. Dorry felt an itch on the back of her neck and looked behind her. Nobody was there, but she was sure that Oscar the ringmaster had been watching them.

That night Dorry dreamed of the bad time. She'd never dreamt of it before. There had been a big black mark where that night was in her mind, with only little flashes around it.

She was peeking out from underneath her blanket, just a little hole big enough for her to see, big enough for her to breathe. Wessie and that man had come back to the motel room late, late, late and while they were standing outside the door, Essie had opened it and yanked them both in. Essie started yelling and the man was trying to calm her down and suddenly there was the knife, the little silver knife that she kept tucked in her garter. Essie swung out at the man and Wessie stepped in between, her hands up, pleading. She said that they were happy and couldn't Essie just be happy for them? She was sorry for Essie but that was just the way it was.

And Dorry remembered that Essie said, "No, it's not. It's the way I want it to be."

The silver knife went into Wessie's eye quick as lightning, and then Wessie was on the floor crying and the man charged at Essie. The silver knife flew out again, left to right, and the man staggered back and the blood flowered from his neck like a red, red rose.

Dorry gasped and Essie turned to glare at her. Dorry had never seen Essie like that before. She was cold, cold as the east wind blowing hard from the ocean in winter, and there was no kindness in her.

*A witch*, Dorry thought. *She looks like a scary witch in a children's story.*

"Go back to sleep," Essie said.

Dorry covered up her head with the blanket, but she couldn't sleep and she could still hear. She heard Wessie's wails taper off into snuffling sobs, and Essie hissing that they must get rid of him somewhere.

She heard the sound of something heavy scraping, dragging across the floor. Then the door slammed, and she was alone in the room. She was afraid to look out, afraid that if she did Essie's silver knife would come for her, too.

The morning after that night, Essie told her that Wessie had an accident, that she'd fallen and hurt her eye. She said that the man who first Essie, and then Wessie, was going to marry had been nothing but a grifter and he'd run away with Wessie's emerald bracelet and most of their money.

When Dorry tried to tell her that she'd seen something else, Essie had tugged at her braids and said, "Don't be silly, Dormouse. That must have been a bad dream you had."

And Dorry believed her, because Essie never lied to her. Never.

Oscar the ringmaster came for Essie at the prescribed time, and off they went in a car that he had borrowed just for the occasion. Wessie stood on her steps with a sour expression and watched them go. Dorry stood on their steps and tried not to show the anxiety on her face.

Dorry had hoped it would rain and prevent their meeting. Essie hated the rain, hated the way it ruined her hair and makeup. If it rained then she would make an excuse and Dorry would have a chance to work on her, to convince her she shouldn't go out with that man and his white, biting teeth.

But it didn't rain. All day long clouds had gathered and lingered, smoking over the blue sky until there was nothing but a mass of heavy gray. The air was thick and humid and Dorry tasted electricity on her tongue, but the clouds just kept swelling and swelling, refusing to burst.

She went inside and paced back and forth, back and forth. On the other side of the wall, she heard Wessie pacing back and forth, back and forth. Dorry peeked outside. It wasn't raining, but the threat of rain had kept most of the crowds away. Those clouds pulled the night over the sideshow like a blanket, and Dorry peered out from a little hole in that blanket like she had the night the bad things had happened.

*Something bad is going to happen again. Essie, come home.*

She curled up on the floor in front of the door and bit her lip and tried not to cry.

Dorry must have fallen asleep, because she woke to the sound of voices outside the door, angry voices like the ones she'd heard on that other night, in that other time.

"...don't know what you're talking about," Essie said, and Dorry heard the dismissal in her voice. "If that boy *was* your brother, as you claim, then I don't know what you're doing here bothering me about it. He stole my sister's bracelet and some of our money as well, and ran off with it. Go look for him somewhere else. When you find him, get my money back."

"Don't lie to me," Oscar the ringmaster said. "They found him in a reservoir with his throat cut, and the last two people he was seen with were a couple of golden-haired twins with funny names. It took me four years to track you down, but it was you. I *know* it was you. What happened to my brother?"

*Brother. Brother. That man. He was the ringmaster's brother and Essie killed him.*

Dorry stood, and pushed out onto the steps. Oscar and Essie stood a few feet away, and their voices weren't as loud as they'd seemed to her inside but they were still angry. Essie saw her come out and fixed a smile on her face and said, "What's the matter, Dormouse? Have a nightmare?"

"Yes," Dorry lied, and waved at her to come in. She wanted

Essie away from him, away inside where she could be safe.

"It's been swell," Essie said to Oscar, and she turned her back on him.

Only when Dorry saw her face full on did she realize that Essie was scared, scared out of her wits. It was there in the lines of tension around her eyes, the clench of her white fist around her little silver clutch purse.

Wessie burst out of her side of the trailer then, screaming, "Liar! Liar! That's all she does is lie, all the time. She told that little girl we found her by the side of a cornfield but she stole her, stole her right out of a baby carriage in a nothing town in Kansas because she liked the look of her and wanted a toy doll to play with."

Dorry stared at Essie. It couldn't be true. It couldn't. Essie loved her. Essie had saved her. Essie couldn't have stolen her away from her people, from a mother and a father and a home.

"She lies all day telling fortunes and makes that little thing steal money from the marks for her. And no matter what she says to you, she killed him. She took out her silver knife and slit his throat because he wanted me instead of her. She killed him! She *killed him*!"

Essie turned her head toward her sister, mouth open to rebuke. Dorry felt frozen to the spot, her stomach turned upside down.

Something appeared in Oscar's hand, quick as lightning, just as real lightning flickered overhead. For a second Dorry thought it was another rose, but then there was a flash, and a bang, and Essie's lipsticked mouth filled with blood. Thunder rumbled. Essie staggered forward. Oscar leveled the pistol, and again there was a flash and a bang. Essie fell to the ground, rolled over once, half her body disappearing under the trailer.

Wessie flew at the ringmaster, her gold eyepatch glittering in the white scream of lightning. She pounded his chest and his impassive face with her fists as the sky opened up and the rain poured down. "You killed my sister! What did you do that for? You killed my sister!"

Dorry ran down the steps. All she could see of Essie were her stockinged legs and her silver shoes. The heel of the left shoe had broken when she fell, and something gold shimmered there.

Dorry dropped to her knees, feeling in the darkness, the cold rain soaking her down to the marrow, down to the place where she thought Essie had loved her. Her hands closed around the thin gold chain. She brought it up to her face, listened to Wessie wailing and beating the ringmaster, saw the emerald winking at her. Wessie's bracelet, hidden inside the heel of Essie's silver shoe.

Dorry's fist clenched around the bracelet. She stood up, her bare feet squelching in the mud, and took off into the night. She heard the ringmaster call after her, heard Wessie's anguished cry.

She ran and ran, the emerald bracelet tight in her hand. If she ran far enough and fast enough, maybe she could make it all the way to Kansas.

# GENERAL JINJUR'S LAST STAND

UNA McCORMACK

Everybody knew that a witch lived up on Sugar Farm. That was one of the things that everybody knew, including the grown-ups, although they were tight-lipped about the whole thing and didn't say anything other than, "Keep away from Sugar Farm."

Of course, nobody had ever seen her, although one of the older boys, Tag, said that he'd been going by on his bike one fall evening (he never explained why he was all the way out there) and that he'd seen bright lights flashing behind the house. Also, there was a long row of pumpkins along the fence, each one with a face carved into the flesh, and spiked into the posts. "Like the heads of her enemies," said Tag, and indeed the thought of all those poor pumpkinheads, stuck on their spikes and left to rot, was more than some of them could take. "There was a crow pecking at one of them," said Tag. "Pecking at the hole where its eye should be." At this point one of the babies burst into tears and someone ran out from one of the houses and they all got told off mightily for teasing. Nobody mentioned Sugar Farm, though. Everyone kept away from Sugar Farm.

Still, what else were they supposed to do, given that there was an honest-to-goodness witch living within a hop, skip and a jump of town – or, at least, a short bicycle ride along a couple of country lanes. There was no harm in talk, was there, and there wasn't a rule against that. And so they talked and talked and talked, particularly as the year drew on and the days grew shorter and the leaves began to drop and settle on the ground.

For Tansy, it was a trying time of year. Tansy was a practical girl, who liked things to be clear-cut and well explained, and she found these kinds of stories rather wearying, and more so as the years went by and she thought that perhaps some of her friends should have long since grown out of them. Perhaps they couldn't help it, Tansy thought; seemed like most of the older folks around here still believed these tall tales. What chance did the children have? So every year, she gritted her teeth, and tried to put up with the nonsense, until the year she couldn't put up with it any longer.

School had finished for the day, and the sun was still warm enough to sit outside, so a big gang of them had gone over to Fleebee Flyte's. Fleebee wasn't the nicest kid in town, but her folks had a huge garden with many interesting highways and byways, and they didn't mind a whole gang of them hanging around and playing their games, and sometimes, if she was feeling generous, she let you have a go on her swing. If anyone was In Charge, it was probably Fleebee, to which Tansy had long since resigned herself as one of the many small and inexplicable injustices which went on in the world.

This afternoon, Fleebee was most definitely not sharing her swing, and was bashing it backwards and forwards with great energy. The huge tree from which it hung shuddered slightly with every push, and each time a few more golden leaves drifted to the ground. The talk today turned, as it often did in the fall, to the old woman who lived up at Sugar Farm.

"My *ma*," said Fleebee, "says she's lived up there for ever. And my ma's lived here her whole life and that's years and years and *years*. And *my* ma says that when *her* ma's ma was little, the old witch was very powerful, and she cast a spell that made everyone march around for days and days and days, until the Good Old Queen appeared and put a stop to all that kind of nonsense. And the old witch was so angry that she came back here and built a horrible old house and hid behind its gates to plot her revenge. One day she'll burst out and fill the whole land in a cloud of steam, but until then, she sits in her horrible old house, except that sometimes, during the fall, she tricks people onto her land, and takes them into her house, and she offers them treats, and then, and *then*..."

"Go on," said Tansy, who was getting bored. "What then?"

"And then she *eats* them!" said Fleebee, with relish.

This, thought Tansy, was going too far. "Don't be ridiculous," she said. "People don't eat people." And then, since she was a scrupulous young woman, she added, "At least, not commonly. And certainly not in these parts." She reflected on that. "At least, not that I've seen."

"So what does she do with the people she steals?" asked

Fleebee, and before Tansy could point out that there was, in fact, *not a shred of evidence* that the witch at Sugar Farm had ever stolen a single soul, the stream of lurid suggestions had commenced.

"She puts the bones of her victims in her garden, and grows her wicked treats there, and she offers them to people who get too close! They're eating *bones*!"

"She casts spells on passers-by!"

"She turns their heads to vegetables!"

"She turns their arms and legs to metal!"

"She turns their brains to straaaaaaaaaw!"

This last (which had turned perilously close to a wail by the end) came from Poppy, one of the youngest in the group. Tansy, seeing how Poppy's eyes were filled with tears and her lower lip was wobbling, said briskly, "What nonsense! All bafflegab and cabbage leaves, like Granny Clapboard used to say. None of us have any idea who lives up at Sugar Farm. We don't even know it's an old lady. We certainly don't know it's a witch!"

"Of course it's a witch!" cried Fleebee. "What other kind of person would put out pumpkinheads for the birds to peck at?"

"Maybe she likes the way they look," said Tansy.

"They look creepy!"

"Maybe that's what she likes about them."

"Then *she's* creepy!"

"Or maybe she's a lonely old woman who's gone odd and strange because her nearest neighbours have decided to get in a tizzy about her. But a *witch*?" Tansy scoffed. "There aren't any witches! Not these days! There's no magic done these days – not in Oz!"

One thing that Tansy had yet to learn in her young life was that people didn't much like to be contradicted, particularly not when you tried to prove them wrong with good strong facts. And people who thought they were In Charge didn't like being challenged, particularly when you were in their garden sitting next to their swing. Fleebee jumped to her feet, and squared up to Tansy.

"You're just talk, talk, *talk*, Tansy Tarsnip!" she said, her eyes flashing and her hands upon her hips. "If you're so sure, I say you go out to Sugar Farm and knock on that sweet little old lady's front door, and then come back here and tell us your tale! If you *can*!"

"Don't be ridiculous!" said Tansy. "I'm not hauling myself all the way out to Sugar Farm just because you've scared yourself stiff with some stupid story—"

"I'll lend you my bicycle," said Wilna, one of the quieter girls.

Tansy, who had never yet had cause to be annoyed by Wilna, had a feeling that the girl was trying to be helpful, so she didn't bite her head off. "No, thank you."

"I dare you," said Fleebee.

There was muttering around the circle. The Game of Dares was held in deep reverence. Tansy started to get the first inkling that things were not turning out to her advantage. "Don't be silly, Fleebee," she said, "we're getting much too old for that game—"

"Scaredy!" said Fleebee, the gleam of victory in her eyes. "I don't just dare you – I double dare you. No – I double dare you with knobs on!"

There was a collective gasp. Tansy, looking round the group, realised that she was in something of a pickle. However much she might privately think this whole business was *very silly indeed*, everyone with whom she must associate on a daily basis took the Game terribly seriously. To refuse a dare – a double dare, a double dare with knobs on – would consign Tansy to oblivion. And everyone needed company, even company as ludicrous as this.

"When?" she said, grudgingly.

Fleebee smiled in triumph. "Within the week."

"All right, all right…" Tansy took a deep breath and said, "*Dare dealt; dare done.*"

The ceremonial words of acceptance issued, she and Fleebee formally shook hands and sealed the deal. Fleebee, darn her, had a big old smirk on her face. With the ritual complete, the group started giggling and chattering to each other, conjuring up between them lurid accounts of Tansy's imminent fate. Tansy sat on the edge of the circle and steamed. After a moment or two, she felt a gentle tap on her arm.

It was Wilna. She gave Tansy a kind but rueful smile.

"You can still borrow my bicycle."

"Not tonight," said Tansy to Wilna. "I have to practice my bassoon."

"You said that last night," said Wilna. "And the night before. And the night before that."

"Well, I'm not very good on the bassoon," said Tansy.

"Tansy," said Wilna. "The week's wearing on."

Tansy scowled and scuffed the toe of her shoe into the ground, digging an ever-deeper hole.

"You're not scared, are you?" said Wilna.

"What?" Tansy glared at her. "Of course not! There's nothing up there!"

"All right," said Wilna. "You're just… taking your time, that's all."

"I'm taking my *time*," said Tansy, "because this whole thing is *stupid*."

"Uh-huh," said Wilna.

"And worse than that, it's *mean*," Tansy went on. "Going all the way out there to bother some old woman, all because some kids don't have enough to entertain them. It's not *nice*."

"Uh-huh," said Wilna.

"And… and…"

There was a long pause, broken eventually when Wilna said, "Shall we go and get the bicycles?"

"Not tonight! I'm *busy*!"

Wilna waited.

"Did you say *bicycles*?" said Tansy.

"Well," said Wilna, "I'm hardly going to let you go out there all alone, am I?"

Wilna, it turned out, had cut a deal with her older brother Parker not to tell their ma and pa that he was spending most of his evenings canoodling with Glaudia Bushels and not playing kickball with his pals like he'd said. Thus she had secured unlimited use of his bicycle. It was a big old beast of a thing – Parker being something of a sporty type – but Tansy wasn't the kind to be intimidated by a bicycle. You shouldn't, in her opinion, be intimidated by things that were made by people. You should work out how they were made so that you understood them and knew what to do about them. Magic and spells were something else, but there wasn't any cause to be bothered about that kind of thing these days. Not in Oz.

Wilna's bicycle was a smaller affair, and had a wicker basket on the front, with a little garland of dried flowers twined through. "Don't," she muttered, seeing Tansy look at the flowers. "I didn't choose it. I've tried and tried but they're stuck on."

Tansy figured she would be able to find the right adhesive remover in a trice, but they had other business to contend with first. They wheeled the bikes out onto the lane, and soon were on their way up to Sugar Farm. Tansy's plan was there and back again. Fleebee had dared her to knock on the door; she hadn't said anything about hanging around for a chat. With luck and a following wind, she and Wilna would be back home long before anyone thought to ask where those two blessed girls had got to this evening.

The night was clear and crisp. Town was lit by the porch lamps, but, once they were out on the country road, they relied on the lanterns strung to their bikes. Tansy liked to be moving around, and as they cycled along she even started whistling. What was better than to be out and about with a friend, enjoying the fall, having an adventure? Well, perhaps the only thing better was for the adventure to be done, and to be back home in front of the fire with a mug of something hot and already embellishing your tale.

"We'll tell them she chased us," said Wilna.

"We'll tell them she waved her stick at us," said Tansy.

"We'll tell them all the pumpkinheads shouted at us as we made our escape," said Wilna.

In this fashion they laughed all the way to Sugar Farm.

At the fence, their spirits went into freefall. It was just as Tag had said: a long row of pumpkinheads, each one with a horrible face carved into the flesh so that they seemed to scream and jeer and howl. What Tag had failed to mention was that the heads were lit from within. Tansy, hopping off her bike, went to look closer.

"No candles," she said. "How has she done that?"

"Tansy! Don't get too close!"

"What? Why?"

"There might be a spell on them. They might be here to trap us—"

"Don't be silly, Wilna! They're just a bunch of old gourds. Still," she said, thoughtfully, "I'd like to know how she's made them light up."

She glanced around. Everything was very quiet. Not even a crow to keep an eye on them, or report back on their progress. They propped the bikes up against the fence, and, carefully, Tansy opened the gate. They both looked round, expecting something or someone to jump out. Nothing. Just an open gate, and a path, leading up to the dark huddle of the farmhouse. There was a single lamp lit, hanging in the porch.

"Right," said Tansy. "Let's get this done." She glanced over at Wilna, who was white-faced and trembly. "You can stay here if you want. I'm going to knock on the door and then run like the clappers."

"I'm not letting you go up there alone, Tansy Tarsnip!"

Tansy squeezed her arm. "You're a good pal, Wilna."

They crept up the path in the direction of the lamp. Nothing and nobody stirred. When they reached the porch, Tansy whispered to Wilna, "Come on, let's go round the back."

"What? Why?"

"I want a peek inside."

"Tansy—"

But Tansy was already making her way round the side of the house. They stumbled through a vegetable patch, muttering and whispering, and came more or less quietly to the back, where Tansy stopped to look out across the fields.

"What is it, Tansy?"

"Tag said he saw flashing lights behind the house," she said. "I wonder what that was…"

"Casting spells," said Wilna. "I know, I know – no such thing these days. Not in Oz."

Tansy moved towards the kitchen door and reached out for the handle. Wilna, beside her, stuck out her hand to stop her. "What are you *doing*?"

"We have to go in," said Tansy.

"No we most certainly don't!"

"Fleebee won't believe us if we come back and tell her that we came here. We have to bring proof. So I'm going to slip into the kitchen, find something, and come back out again. I'll be there a minute at most. You can stay here if you like."

But Wilna was beside her all the way. Tansy tried the handle; the door wasn't locked, and it opened with a muted creak. She crept into the kitchen, Wilna close behind.

"Tansy," she whispered, "I don't like this..."

Tansy didn't either, but there was nothing else to be done. She looked round, quickly. What would be good enough for Fleebee? Maybe the carving knife on the table? She reached her hand out to take it, pausing for a split-second to wonder, *Is it magic? Is there some spell on it that makes the pumpkins laugh and glow...?*

Suddenly, from near the door that led to the hallway, there was a *click*, and the room was filled with light. Wilna let out a short, sharp scream. Tansy, rubbing her eyes to help them cope with the unexpected brightness, turned and saw a figure in the doorway.

It was an old woman, with her hands shoved deep into the pockets of her black trousers. Those trousers were jammed into huge rubber-soled boots. She wore a baggy white shirt; over this was a black waistcoat, embroidered round the edges in a white thread. A pipe stuck out of one of the waistcoat's pockets. She stared at the two girls, and said, "Intruders, eh?"

"The witch," whispered Wilna. "The witch of Sugar Farm."

"Eh?" said the old woman, with a scowl. "What did you just say?"

"Wilna," said Tansy. "*Run!*"

She was old, so very old. But, my goodness, she moved like the wind. She was skirting round them and shutting and locking the back door and popping the key in the pocket of her trousers before either of the two girls knew what was happening.

"Are you… are you a witch?" asked Wilna, in a faint voice.

The old woman stared at them for a moment, and then she broke out into a raucous laugh – a *cackle*, that was the only word for it – that nearly had the pair of them diving under the kitchen table.

"A witch? A *witch*? Is that what they're saying now? Ungrateful bunch. I wish I *was* a witch. I'd cast a spell and turn their heads to pumpkins." She stumped over to the stove, muttering away under her breath. "A witch. A *witch*!"

She set the kettle to boil, and looked back over her shoulder to where Tansy and Wilna were standing clutching each other for dear life.

"Oh, sit down," she said. "We'll have a cup of tea." She peered at them both, then nodded at Tansy. "You," she said. "You look less likely to faint. Go over to that cupboard there," she pointed, "and get out the plate of macaroons. May as well have something sweet too. You get to my age, you don't pass up the chance for something sweet."

Five minutes later, they were sitting around the kitchen table, drinking hot tea and eating the most delicious macaroons that either Tansy or Wilna had ever tasted.

"Your grannies and your grampas," she said, "when they were your age and smaller, they used to come here all the time to eat what I made for them. This time of year was best, when the leaves started falling and the evenings turned sharp. They'd come to see the pumpkins and the lights, and take away buckets full of macaroons and cream-caramels and all sorts of delicious treats. And then over the years people stopped coming. I don't know why. Maybe it went out of fashion. Things do, eventually." She sniffed. "Anyway, I'm done with that business. I'll be gone soon."

"Gone?" said Wilna, alarmed. "But, ma'am, you look fit as a fiddle!"

"I'd say," said Tansy, stoutly. "I bet you'd give Granny Walnut a run for her money."

"What?" said the old woman, and then she got what they meant. "I said '*gone*', child, not '*dead*'! I've no plans on dying, not for a while yet. I've got some things I mean to do first." She refilled her cup. "Granny Walnut," she muttered, as she piled in the sugar and stirred the spoon. "I remember Lila Walnut toddling up here when she'd only just learned to walk. Plump little legs like tree trunks, bless her, and sticky little hands all over my table. You'd better believe I'd give her a run for her money." She eyed the girls. "And what do those grannies and grandpas think they're doing letting it get about that I'm a witch? That ain't kind!"

"We're sorry about that," said Wilna. "I guess stories have a way of taking hold, don't they?"

"Could have caused me a world of trouble. And all I ever did was make 'em sweets and hand 'em round! Sticky little hands all over my table. You think of that next time you see Lila Walnut."

She took out her pipe and lit it. "So," she said, "what do you two want? You haven't come here for treats, have you?"

Tansy and Wilna exchanged a look.

"Was there a dare?"

"Yes," said Tansy, after a moment, with some reluctance. "I was dared to come up here and knock on your door."

"And you?" The old woman nodded at Wilna.

"I brought the bicycles," Wilna whispered.

"Important job," said the old woman. "But rather than knocking on my door, you decided to pop into my kitchen. Risky, wouldn't you say? What with me being a witch and all."

"If I went back and said we'd done it, Fleebee Flyte wouldn't believe me," said Tansy. "I needed proof."

"Proof!" She puffed on her pipe. "Is that kind of thing important to you?"

"Well… of *course*," said Tansy. "You need proof, don't you? If you're going to believe something. How else can you be sure you should believe in it?"

The old woman stared at her, and then began to laugh, quietly. "You're not wrong," she said. "You're not wrong at all." She chewed on the pipe stem. "Fleebee Flyte," she said. "I knew her granny. Terrible show-off."

Tansy and Wilna looked at each other. This was all turning out very differently from how they'd planned. And yet – better, somehow. Tansy, summoning up all her courage, asked the question that was preying most on her mind.

"Ma'am," she said.

The old woman asked, "Do you mean me?"

"Well, yes…"

"Never been called that before. What?"

"I've been wondering – how do the lights work?"

The old woman stared at Tansy, as if seeing her properly for the first time. "You like that, do you? You like the lights?"

"I think it's amazing. But how does it work?"

"What would you say if I told you it was magic?"

"I'd be disappointed," said Tansy. "Because I know it isn't, and you know it isn't, and you know that I know it isn't. And I still wouldn't be any the wiser."

The old woman jumped out of her chair. She went over to the doorway, and summoned Tansy over. "Your hand," she said, beckoning, and, when Tansy put her hand out, she grabbed it and moved it towards the wall. There was a switch there. "Go on," she said. "Try it."

Tansy, feeling that old hand upon hers, realised the woman was trembling with excitement. She tried the switch. The room was plunged into darkness. Wilna yelped. Tansy tried the switch again, and the room was flooded with light once more. The old woman squeezed Tansy's hand between both of hers. She was… she was *happy*, Tansy thought.

"Electric lights," she said. "That's what they're called. Making sweets wasn't the whole of it, you know. It wasn't even the main part of it. What? You think I sat here all year stirring pots of treacle on the chance that some children would come wandering my way each fall? I was a friend of Ozma the Great, of Dorothy… in the end! They'd come to my farm when they were stuck, and they'd sit at my table and talk to me, and then off they'd go and set the Land of Oz to rights! Making sweets!" She laughed out loud. "Wait till you see what I've got out there!"

She marched over to the counter, grabbing a hat – a high cap with a visor and a jaunty feather on the top – and stuck it on her head. She rummaged around for a while in one of the drawers, bringing out a strange cylindrical object, shaped like a rolling pin, but shorter. Then she strode to the back door, unlocked it, and swung it open.

"Well, come on!" she cried. "Get moving!" She aimed the cylinder out into the darkness, and a bright light shone from it, pointing the way. "I've got things to show you."

"Ma'am?" said Tansy.

"Come on!"

The girls jumped up and followed her out (Tansy for one wanted a closer look at that light cylinder). On they went, deeper and deeper into the fields, chasing the light and the feather on the old woman's cap. "Ma'am indeed," she grumbled to herself, as she led them into the darkness. "If you're going to call me anything, you can call me General."

They walked for about five or ten minutes, the ground rising steadily in front of them. The General, seeing Tansy's fixed stare, handed her the light-cylinder.

"It's called a torch," said the General. "Take care of it. We'll need it to get back safely. Don't want to fall over in the dark."

Near the top of the hill, the General said, in a warning voice, "Tread carefully, now. Don't want you falling in."

"Falling into what?" said Wilna. And then: "Oh. I see."

The valley on the far side of the hill was transformed, the

whole bowl of it filled with lights – electric lights, as Tansy now knew to call them. They flickered and winked on huge pieces of equipment, and some of them were strung up, like lights on a tree, showing the way through. But in the heart of the valley stood a huge machine – the most beautiful thing Tansy had ever seen; the kind of thing that she dreamed about sometimes. A huge, sleek, metallic cone of emerald green that rose up and up – higher than a barn, than two barns – narrowing to a rounded snub-nosed point at the top. Around the base, three huge fins kept the vessel upright, and the whole was decorated with golden trim. A porthole winked at Tansy like an eye; beneath it she saw a crest, bearing a symbol which, if Tansy had been pressed, she would have sworn were two crossed knitting needles.

"Well," said the General, unable to keep the pride out of her voice, "what do you think *this* is?"

"I've no idea!" admitted Wilna. "I've never seen the like in all my life!"

"What about you?" said the General, to Tansy. "You, the one who likes things to be explainable and proved?"

"I think…" said Tansy, slowly. "I think it's something you might travel in. To go a long way away from where you are."

The General narrowed her eyes. "Go on."

"I think… that with the right kind of engine and the right kind of fuel, you can send that thing a very long way from here. I think someone could go on a great adventure, in that thing."

The General favoured her with a wide and toothy smile. "And you'd be quite right."

"This is what you've been doing here, this whole time?" said Tansy.

"There's only so much of the day you can fill making macaroons," said the General. "And when the children stopped coming, I got bored. I thought – I'm not hanging around here any longer. I'm the General! I knew Ozma the Great; Dorothy herself! Why shouldn't I have one last adventure? Whoever said adventures were only for the young?"

"So you're off," said Tansy. "Where are you going?"

"I don't know," answered the General. "Wherever it takes me. Follow a star, follow a comet – who knows where I'll land? Not an adventure if I know where I'm going, is it?" She looked at Tansy, and her eyes gleamed brightly. "Want to come along? Give me a day or two. I can make space for someone else."

"Oh…" said Tansy, very softly.

"I don't know where we'll go," said the General. "But I bet it'll be wonderful."

"Tansy," said Wilna. "Your ma! Your pa!"

"I know," said Tansy, grumpily. But it was tempting, so very tempting. And perhaps, on another occasion, Tansy would have said, "Yes, yes, *yes*!" But tonight? Tonight, they heard the sound of voices – a hue and cry – coming towards them on the night breeze. The townsfolk, it seemed, had decided to pay the General a visit. Standing at the top of the hill, they watched the fiery torches draw closer and closer. The General chewed on her pipe. "Thought I'd wait for the shortest day to leave," she said. "Guess I'll have to make do with Samhain."

She strode off, briskly, leading them through the maze of equipment until she reached a console with a huge emerald green button. "When I give you the sign, one of you needs to press this."

"Is that it?" said Wilna.

"No need to make a big fuss about these things," said the General. She looked at them in turn, and cleared her throat, gruffly. "Can't stand goodbyes," she said. "Wish you two had dropped by sooner, though! I liked you." She patted Tansy on her arm. "Sorry you're not coming. You're a good 'un, I think. I'd've liked you in my army." Then, to Wilna, "As for you… Don't *worry* so much, girl! And speak up! Nobody'll speak for you if you don't speak for yourself!"

"I'll try my very best, General," Wilna promised.

"Good girl," said the General. "Now – wait until you see me wave from the window. Then hit that button – no, not that one; that one, there, yes." And off she stumped, into her great rocket ship, and sealed the door behind her. They saw her – feathered cap still on her head – in the porthole, and she waved, and, together, Tansy and Wilna pressed the button.

There was a huge roar that rose and rose, shaking the grass and the corn and the two girls who grabbed on to each other as they watched. The rocket, gripped by mighty forces, began to shudder and shake and then – slowly, steadily, with great and engineered precision – it lifted from the ground.

Oh, what a beautiful sight! Tansy watched with her mouth wide open and tears in her eyes, and she thought, *I'll build something like that one day... I'll build machines that can whizz around the land in no time... And I'll have a great adventure, and Wilna will be right by my side...*

The rocket pushed on, up and up, growing ever more distant, becoming a star in its own right. The General was gone, on her last great adventure.

The girls stood in silence for a while. In the distance, they could hear shouting and yelling.

"Well," said Tansy, with a sigh. "I suppose we'd better find out what that lot want."

They walked slowly back down to the farmhouse. "I wonder how they knew where to come looking for us," said Tansy. "Fleebee Flyte, I bet, trying to wriggle out of the dare. She knew I wasn't scared. Not really."

But it was Wilna, in fact, who turned out to be the weak link. Parker, her big brother, had forced her to tell him why she wanted to borrow his bike, and Wilna hadn't been able to resist bragging.

"We're off to see the witch," she told him.

"What witch?"

"The one up at Sugar Farm."

Parker had rolled his eyes and thought, *kids' stuff*, but when it started to get dark and Wilna hadn't come home and it turned out Tansy Tarsnip was missing too, he thought he'd better have a quiet word with his ma. He regretted that immediately; she went into a tailspin, and set off running down the lane to the Flytes' place. If there was anyone who knew how to raise a posse it was Flora Flyte, and before Parker knew what was happening half the town, carrying lamps and flaming torches and whatever else they had to hand, was heading up the road to Sugar Farm.

Parker and Wilna's pa, hearing the ruckus, heaved himself wearily up from his chair and put on his jacket. "Next time, son," he said, "come speak to me first."

Parker wasn't going to miss out on the fun, so he followed his pa, and that meant he was on hand to see exactly what happened when the posse got to Sugar Farm. They'd been working themselves up into a tizzy all the way over (he told Tansy and Wilna later), but when they reached the fence and saw that row of pumpkinheads, all lit up from inside and grinning at them, they went berserk.

"My, they didn't like the look of those pumpkins," he said. "You'd've thought it had cast a spell on them or something. They all shouted, yelling and hollering, and some of them started pulling at the fence posts. I think they would have yanked the whole thing down and turned it into a bonfire, given the chance."

Fortunately there were cooler heads around, like Parker's pa and Tansy's ma, who between them most likely had more sense than the rest of the town put together, and after a fair amount of yelling and hollering and quarrelling, it was agreed that a small deputation (by which was meant Parker's pa and Tansy's ma and maybe Granny Oakleaves, if she was willing) should go up to the farmhouse, knock on the door, and politely ask the resident whether she might have seen a couple of girls who had not come home as expected in time for supper.

"Well, Granny Oakleaves wasn't willing," said Parker. "Not to begin with, at least. She said she'd only come along to see what happened, nosiness being the prerogative of the old, and she didn't see why she should be pulled into this kind of nonsense, and if people just left other people in peace to get on with their lives rather than bossing them around, then the world would be a happier place, and wasn't that the whole point of Oz anyway? And she took particular umbrage, she said, at people bossing old ladies around and good luck to that old witch was what she said. Anyway, Pa had to promise her that he'd milk her old cow, and she agreed to go up there with him and your ma, Tansy." Parker sucked his teeth. "I bet I get saddled with the milking," he moaned. "Even though this is all your fault, Wilna."

"All right," said Wilna. "I'll help. Just carry on with the story."

So they'd watched the three of them go past the fence, with all those pumpkinheads jeering at them, and walk (slowly, in Granny's case) up towards the farm. About twenty minutes later, they came hurrying back. ("And let me tell you," said Parker, "even Granny Oakleaves was going at a fair old lick.") They were waving their arms about and shouting, and telling everyone to take cover. But it was hard to hear them at first, because there was a strange noise in the air, a sort of whooshing and roaring that was getting louder and louder by the minute.

"Well, that was enough to get most of us to move a way away from the fence at least," said Parker, "and just as well."

Because after that, he told Tansy and Wilna, the air started to get hot and steamy, and that roaring noise turned into something more like a scream, and people yelled and covered their ears, and some fell to their knees.

"Magic, someone said," Parker told them, and that got passed around – although everyone knew there wasn't any magic done these days. Not in Oz.

By this time, more than half of the posse was running like jingo back towards town, but those who stopped and stayed and stood their ground, and kept looking up, up at the clear night sky with its friendly stars smiling down, were treated to one of the great sights of the cosmos: a huge green vessel lifting off into space. They saw it rise and rise, pushing up from the empty fields behind Sugar Farm, shooting higher and higher, on its journey to who knew where. And when it had gone, and everything started to become quiet again, they looked at each other and shook their heads, and said, "Well, now, wasn't that a marvel?"

"And it was," said Parker. "It was marvellous."

There was some concern, nevertheless, about what might have happened to the girls, if they really had been stuck in the middle of all that, but it wasn't long, Parker said, before they saw two small figures, both pushing bicycles along beside them, coming out from behind Sugar Farm towards the road.

"That was you two," said Parker. "In case you weren't sure."

"Ma!" said Tansy, when she saw her mother. Her eyes were shining and there was a smut on her nose. "I just sent a rocket into space!"

"That's my girl," said Tansy's ma.

They got into some trouble for being out late, but since Wilna had let Parker know where she was going, and everything had turned out fine, it was hard for their mas and pas to remain cross. And since there wasn't a witch at Sugar Farm any longer and probably never had been (not to mention that there was some good land going free), everyone was satisfied.

Fleebee Flyte was very impressed, and the next time the gang gathered in her garden she shook hands gravely with Tansy, called a truce, and said Tansy could use the swing whenever she wanted. "And Wilna," said Tansy.

"And Wilna," Fleebee agreed.

Several years later, Tansy and Wilna went off together to study in the Emerald City. Tansy was going to learn how to build bridges and towers and good long railways to connect Munchkin to Winkie Country and Quadling to Gillikin Country and all points in between. She was very good at this kind of thing, and people liked to work with her, because whenever they hit a difficulty she would laugh and say, "We can work it out. It's not rocket science!" One day there would be a bridge and a tower and a good long railway named after her that whizzed right the way round the Land of Oz.

But Wilna was more interested in finding out about how Oz used to be, and what the people who used to be said and did. So of course Wilna was the one to find the book in the library and bring it home for Tansy to see. The book was bound in rich green leather, with golden text on the cover which read: *Oz in Transition: The Last Days of the Scarecrow and the First Years of the Reign of Ozma the Great.*

Ozma the Great. The Good Old Queen, Best Friend of Dorothy, during whose reign the great Land of Oz changed beyond recognition into the bright, forward-thinking and friendly place that it was now. But those early days, said Wilna, after the Wicked Wizard was banished, were an odd old time, with all kinds of strange creatures running around with vegetables for heads and metal for limbs and straw for brains. What a funny old time that was, like the dream of a child stuck in a world that was dusty and sad and dying.

Right in the middle of the book, the author had reproduced a handwritten account of a very interesting episode, at the very start of Ozma's reign. Turned out that the Scarecrow had been deposed for a while, by an army of girls who were fed up of being treated badly, and didn't see why Oz should be left in the hands of men, and who marched on the Emerald City and took over the place in next to no time. Their revolt didn't last long, but then they were all very young, Wilna pointed out, and with a little more experience they might have turned Oz round much sooner. It had taken Ozma and Dorothy much longer to sort the place out, and, if you thought about it, you could say that they got what they wanted because Ozma was in charge for years after, and Dorothy was her best chief counsellor. So the girls did get to run Oz after all, for years and years, and a fine job they did of it too.

There was a drawing from the time, of the leader of the rebellion, and Tansy and Wilna agreed that she looked mighty fine, in her high boots and frogged jacket and high feathered cap, with her army of girls behind her, brandishing their sharp knitting needles. The picture was captioned:

*General Jinjur, leader of the Army of Revolt.*

"Jinjur," said Tansy. "General Jinjur…"

"Read on, Tansy. The next part's interesting."

After the revolt stood down, and Ozma took the throne, General Jinjur retired to Munchkin Country, it was said, where she ran a farm. And a fine place it was, fine enough that her friends Ozma and Dorothy would sometimes drop by and they would cook up their plans for the Land of Oz, and people from far and wide would come to sample Jinjur's wonderful wares. She had a reputation for making the finest sweets, you see, and who doesn't like that sort of thing?

"Treats," said Tansy. "She made treats. She handed them out to people who came to see her."

"And if that rocket was anything to go by," said Wilna, "I bet she had a few tricks up her sleeve too."

"Oh, Wilna, do you think it was her?"

"Who knows," said Wilna. "Not as if we can ask her, is it? But I'd like to think so."

"Imagine," said Tansy. "A great general, a great inventor, a great *heroine* – living right up the road from us all that time. Building her rocket. Making her plans. Dreaming big. Imagine that!"

The whole length of their good long lives, Tansy and Wilna would talk about what happened that night up on Sugar Farm, about General Jinjur and her last great adventure. They never forgot her, of course. Who would?

"I wonder where that rocket went," Tansy would say. "I wonder where she landed."

And Wilna would answer, "Maybe one day, when we're old and grey, we'll go and see."

# THE LITTLE HOUSE ON THE KANSAS PRAIRIE

JONATHAN MABERRY

## 1

The first thing you need to know is that when Dorothy Gale went home, the house was already there waiting for her.

That's the problem, you see. It shouldn't have been there.

Dorothy thought it was a new one, built by Uncle Henry after the cyclone, but no one could build a house that fast. Not in the time it took Dorothy to go on her adventure.

No.

It was the same house with a fresh coat of paint. And Aunt Em and Uncle Henry smiling and swearing it was all new.

Dorothy even believed it.

At first.

## 2

The cyclone came tearing across the Kansas plane, gouging the fields like the dagger-point of God's knife. Or maybe the Devil's staff. No one stopped to consider which metaphor really fit.

The Gale house was a box – a single big room with kitchen in one corner, table nearby, a couch and some chairs clustered around the hearth, a big bed for the grown-ups against one wall and a little bed for Dorothy against another. That was all. The privy was out back. No attic, very few closets. It was a fragile wooden box in the middle of a wide, flat farm.

In the center of the living room floor, covered by a rug, was a heavy oak door with a big iron ring inset flush. Below that was a cramped place Uncle Henry called a storm cellar, but it was mostly used as an apple store and a place for Aunt Em to put her home-canned goods and jars of preserves.

For a while it seemed as if the cyclone was going to pass by a mile or so off. Uncle Henry watched parts of the O'Keefe place spring up into the air, whirl around, and then vanish into the tall stalks of corn.

"Will it come for us?" asked Dorothy, clutching her dog to her chest.

It took her uncle a long time to read the wind and make a guess. "No, sweetie, I don't think so."

He had been right so many times before that Dorothy assumed he was right this time. Henry was like that – rarely uncertain and often right.

But he was wrong that day.

He was quite wrong indeed.

As they watched, the giant pillar of whirling gray wind and debris *turned*. It was as if it heard the certainty in Uncle Henry's voice and took it as a challenge.

It came.

Oh, how it came.

Dorothy only barely remembered the alarms and excursions that sent them all running, often in the wrong direction first, then in the right direction but without flashlights or supplies, and then Aunt Em and Uncle Henry climbed down into the shelter, calling for her.

Yelling.

Then screaming.

But by then the winds had found the house. With tentacles of force it pulled at the shutters until they tore away from their hasps, ripped free of their hinges, and went sailing off into the spinning void. The back door blew in and the front door blew out and Dorothy was shoved away from the trapdoor.

"Quick, Dorothy!" wailed her aunt. "Run for the cellar!"

"Get in here, girl," bellowed her uncle. But the words were blown away, their meanings torn to nothing by the howl of the storm. Still holding the yapping, cringing, yelping Toto to her body, Dorothy tried to bend into the wind, but it was like walking uphill through the mud.

Toto was gone somehow, and she had only a vague memory of him running for safety under the bed. Dorothy stepped toward the cellar while reaching for the dog and in both things she failed utterly.

And fell.

Her last moments of awareness were of the house spinning. The bed seemed to remain where it was but the house spun like a top. Or… maybe it was everything outside spinning.

Or the house spinning with the speed of the cyclone and all of it was an illusion brought on by terror. She screamed for Toto.

She screamed for her aunt and uncle.

She screamed and screamed and screamed.

Then something struck her and all of that noise and movement and terror went away.

## 3

Then, of course, there was the strangeness of waking up.

Realizing to her astonishment that she wasn't dead and was sure she should be.

Dorothy staggered to her feet, dizzy and sick to her stomach. The room seemed to swirl around her in a drunken Maypole dance, but Dorothy shook her head like Toto would and things cleared. Then she ran to the trap door and pulled it open, but the cellar was….

Empty.

No Aunt Em, no Uncle Henry.

All the apples and potatoes and garlic and onions were present in their baskets. All of the canned vegetables and mason jars by the dozen filled with pickles and carrots and preserves. All there, but no people.

Dorothy called for them, but she was alone. Only Toto was there and he whined and his tail drooped and he cast very nervous glances at the open windows and swinging doors. When Dorothy paused to look outside she was shocked to stillness. Her heart nearly turned to ice in her chest.

Where were the corn fields? Where was the wheat? Where was the kitchen garden with the thyme and rosemary, sage and parsley?

Where were the cows and chickens and…

Everything.

Where was everything she knew?

Outside there were green fields rising and falling over the soft curves of rolling hills. There were crops planted in neat rows, but Dorothy couldn't recognize the shapes or colors of the leaves. Nor could she easily identify most of the trees and shrubs. They were exotic in ways that might have delighted her in a picture book or viewed from a train when going on trips with the grown-ups. And the flowers! They shouted their colors as loudly as the storm had growled its power. Every color and shade and shape, a riot of beauty that edged every planted field.

"What…?" she asked. Toto came and stood next to her as she stared through the open back door. "Where *are* we?"

The little dog's only reply was a nervous whine. Then something made him turn and Dorothy watched as Toto crept over to a spot just left of the open door, near one corner of the big room. The animal crouched and sniffed the floorboards, scratching at the wood floor as if trying to get at something beneath them, but Dorothy picked him up to comfort him. And to take from that closeness whatever comfort she could get. There was very little comfort on offer, though.

Everything outside was wrong in one way or another.

The odd little people in odd little round hats with pointed crowns and small tinkly bells around the brim. All of the men wore blue hats, and all the women wore shades of blue. But to Dorothy, they didn't really look like grown people. They looked like children playing dress-up as adults. Even the side-whiskers and beards looked comically fake. She wondered if they were dwarves, which she'd heard about but had never met any in real life.

But so many…?

And why were they in Kansas?

"Toto," she said in a trembling voice, "I don't think this is right. I don't think we're home."

The little dog looked at her, out the window, and back to his mistress. His tail hung limp with confusion. He sniffed the air and uttered a low growl, but that turned into an insecure little *yip*.

"Where's the barn?" asked Dorothy. "Where are the cows?"

Another yip.

"Oh, Toto… I'm afraid something bad has happened. I think the cyclone picked us up and set us down in the wrong place. That's not our farm out there. Those aren't our neighbors. Oh dear…"

She stood there until the room and her head stopped spinning. That helped the nausea, but the fear was there. Oh yes, she had enough of that and to spare.

It was then that she realized the floor was very slightly off. Tilted. As if the corner of it was resting on something.

"I think the twister moved the house, Toto."

The dog glared at that slightly raised corner and growled again. This time without a yip. This growl was more certain. It was *meant.*

"It's okay," soothed Dorothy. "Maybe those people can tell us what happened."

Carrying Toto, she stepped through the open front door and into another world.

## 4

Another world it was.

And you know the story as well as I do.

Munchkins, a kindly old good-witch from the North – wherever North was in such a place – a scarecrow, a metal man, a semi-ferocious lion, monkeys with wings, dangerous traps in a field of poppies, the Queen of the Field Mice, very angry trees, a glorious City of Emeralds, glasses with green lenses, armies of crows and wolves and bees, and two very bad witches.

And Dorothy becoming a multiple murderer.

The first time was when her house landed on the Wicked Witch of the East, crushing the life out of her there in Munchkinland. Though, a case can be made that she did not have anything directly to do with that death, a counter-argument can also be raised that it was her destiny that brought her to Oz in the first place. If the witch hadn't been one of the really bad ones – one of two who had troubled Oz for many years – maybe more blame would be hurled at Dorothy instead of the wild praise she received.

The second time was the Wicked Witch of the West. No relation to the crushed one, but equal in power and malicious intent. That witch had made things awful for Dorothy, her dog, and the companions she made along the way. During a struggle where the witch stole one of the silver slippers Dorothy had acquired. It was not meant to do anything but pour cold water on heated fury. But, that's the nature of magical beings – you never know what gives them strength and you can never guess what will kill them.

A bucket of water. Ordinary water. No spells, no poisons or acids. Just rainwater in a pail.

Yet lethal to witches. So lethal, in fact, that one does wonder why the witch had such a thing just loitering about. It would be about the same as someone allergic to bee stings having a hive in their living room.

But… the point is that witch melted away, and as a result of this and other misadventures, Dorothy was granted her greatest wish – to go home. Back to Kansas. Back to her aunt and uncle. Back to what she knew and understood.

End of story.

Right?

## 5

Hardly.

## 6

When the good witch told her she could go home just by wishing it so – and tapping the heels of her magic silver slippers together – Dorothy's reaction was that she wanted to punch her. She almost demanded to know why she had to go through all those adventures, all those horrors, all that death and violence, when all she had to do was tap her heels. Those words nearly tumbled out in a shouted rant, but Dorothy bit them back, pasted on a smile, and tapped.

A moment later she reappeared in Kansas beneath the glaring sun, with air so dry it was hard to breathe. Toto squirmed out of her arms and stood by her ankle, sniffing the air and making small nervous yips. Dorothy looked around and realized she was on a prairie at the edge of her family farm and it was in the middle of another in a long series of Kansas droughts. All the grass looked withered and it was clear there hadn't been a drop of rain in days. Or weeks. She wasn't yet sure how long she'd been away.

On impulse, Dorothy took off her silver slippers and studied them, surprised they were real. Because if they were real, then Oz was real and everything that had happened to her was real. The relentless pursuit by the Wicked Witch of the West was real.

She shivered and set the slippers down on the ground, pushing them out of sight behind a withered bush. There would be time to show them to her family later. Now she just wanted to go home.

Then she froze. There *was* no home. The cyclone had taken

it to Munchkinland and dropped it on the witch from the east. It was still back there. All that would be left of it here in Kansas, she reckoned, would be sticks and debris and…

*God*, she thought with a dreadful start, *what about Aunt Em and Uncle Henry?*

But… it was Aunt Em who found her out there on the prairie.

She came running out from behind the stand of oaks that blocked her house from view. Most of the oaks still stood, though a few were broken or leaned crookedly. Em ran to Dorothy and hugged her and scolded her and asked a thousand questions. At first Dorothy just said she'd been lost, mostly because she had no idea how to tell the tale. How to say it without being called a liar or a foolish, over-imaginative little girl?

Em pulled her along and as they rounded the trees, Dorothy saw the house.

*Her* house.

Right where it should not – *could not* – be.

"Auntie, how is the house back?" she cried. "It blew all the way to… I… I mean it blew away in the storm."

Em smiled at her. "Oh, it's not the same house, silly! Your uncle built a new one after the cyclone."

"A… new one…?" Dorothy couldn't make that make sense. Uncle Henry wasn't young, and even if he was, could he really have cut down trees, sawed all of the timber into useful lumber, let the boards dry and cure so they wouldn't warp with the change of seasons, then built an entire house, and accomplish all of that in a few days or, at most, a week or so.

*How?*

The Gales were never a wealthy family, and everything about building a house cost money. The crops were still in the field, which meant that the loan Uncle Henry used to buy seed could not have been paid back yet. Paint, however, was cheaper and as they approached, Dorothy could smell that very clearly. Even so, outside and inside, the *new* house looked suspiciously like the old one.

It looked so much like the house that had fallen on the Wicked Witch of the East.

It looked *too* much like the house that should have still been in Munchkinland.

At no time during her adventures did any of the witches or wizards promise to return her house to Kansas. Glinda did not promise it while she was summing up Dorothy's adventures and telling her how to get home with heel taps.

Not a word.

And that was part of the problem.

How *did* it get there? What made it return? And why?

More importantly, why would Aunt Em and Uncle Henry lie and say it was all new? Did they think it was some way of comforting her after being lost? That almost made sense, but not when she looked at the idea closely.

Dorothy thought she wanted to know the answers to those questions, and asked, being quite bold about it, insisting they tell her the truth. Aunt Em and Uncle Henry kept telling her she was wrong. She had hit her head after all. She had been out of her mind. She was a kid. What did she know about such things?

## 7

That first night, Dorothy told her family about her adventures. Not every detail, but the bones of it. She left out the part about what the house did as it landed. That felt too gruesome and nasty. Nor did she bring up the slippers. They were hers and after seeing how much trouble they caused, she didn't want to bring them home, or even into part of the conversation.

Aunt Em and Uncle Henry sat and listened to her tale. They smiled all the time. Big, jack-o'-lantern smiles. Dorothy was surprised at how much her return filled her family with joy. Until then she'd always felt like a burden – an orphan child dumped on elderly farmers who struggled with bills.

She told as complete a story as she could, and Em and Henry smiled and smiled.

If those smiles were a bit too broad, too bright, and lasted too long, Dorothy put it down to the delight at discovering that the cyclone hadn't killed any of them. That there was a happy ending.

The silver slippers remained hidden and unmentioned.

Life settled down into the same kind of bland pattern it had been before the cyclone. The drought persisted, drying everything to dusty drabness. The paint on the house dried and even cracked in places.

And her uncle and aunt kept smiling.

Every day. Every night.

Those smiles.

## 8

Experience is a great teacher, and Oz was quite the classroom for cultivating a new and broader worldview.

As Dorothy settled back in at home, her experiences in Oz, the fights between good and evil, the deceits and trickeries and surprises all informed how she thought about things. She sat on her bed, holding her dog, staring at her aunt and uncle as they slept. Even deep in their dreams, they kept smiling.

And every day and every night, Toto growled quietly at the corner of the house that had been tilted up a bit in Munchkinland. Tilted because of what it rested upon.

All through one long night Dorothy sat up, trying not to look at those smiling faces of the sleepers across the room. Trying, often failing. But mostly looking into the shadows at the corner of the house that had landed on the Wicked Witch of the East.

"How did the house get back here?" she murmured to Toto, but all the little dog could do was shiver in terror.

## 9

In the morning, Dorothy was up before the first rooster.

She dressed quickly and very, very quietly, and slipped out the back door with Toto. It was still dark but there was a glimmer of light far off to the east, and the sky was troubled by gathering storm clouds in that direction. The stillness of the last few days was being blown away by winds. That unnerved her, because it was how the day started when the cyclone came and blew the house away.

Dorothy did not want another twister, that was certain. If there was some easier way to return to Oz, she felt open to it, but not in the same way. Heavens no. Maybe something gentler, less of a life-or-death thing. She studied the sky, which was slow to brighten, as if the sun was afraid to see what was happening on the Gale farm.

Dorothy was scared, too.

But she was also curious, and that's killed more than cats.

She took a lantern with her, a screwdriver from a drawer, which she put in her pocket, and one of Aunt Em's rolling pins, and crept around to that corner of the house. From a distance the house looked flat and level and normal. But then a lot of things look normal from a distance. A bumblebee and a wasp look a lot alike from far enough back. Green leaves don't look like poison ivy until you're close up.

Dorothy had just come back from an adventure where there was deadly danger at every turn. She'd lost count of all the times she nearly died. Her level of fear was a lot less than it had been before the cyclone, and that gave her a measure of confidence. Not a lot, but at least a generous dollop.

As she approached the corner, a gust of wind nearly knocked the lantern from her hand. She turned and looked off into the east and saw that the dawn was now hiding behind those roiling dark clouds.

*Rain would be nice,* she thought, *but that's it. No cyclones need apply, thank you very much.*

Toto, with his black fur, was nearly invisible in the gloom, though when he snarled, his teeth were white and very sharp. Dorothy took comfort in that. She wasn't one of those people who thought small dogs had meaningless bites. There were a couple of ornery farm cats who could attest to that.

With the lantern held out before her and the rolling pin ready in one tight fist, Dorothy approached that spot where she had last seen the stockinged feet of the witch poking out.

That memory – the image of it – brought it all back to her. The way the wicked witch's legs folded into themselves and then turned to dust, leaving only the silver slippers. Dorothy looked down at the farm boots she wore. The previous afternoon she'd snuck back to the edge of the prairie, retrieved the slippers, wrapped them in cloth, then in a box, and buried it where no one but her and Toto could find it.

Dorothy did not want to show the slippers to Aunt Em and Uncle Henry. Not to anyone, really. Her reluctance was inspired by Aunt Em's smile when she found Dorothy sitting among those drought-stricken shrubs.

Last night before bed, her aunt and uncle asked her to tell them again about her adventures in Oz. They hung on every word, and even seemed ready to believe her wild tale.

But Aunt Em had made a small mistake.

Dorothy retold the part about the cyclone landing in Munchkinland, about the Yellow Brick Road, and many other adventures. Aunt Em interrupted and asked, "But what about the witch's shoes, dear? What happened to them?"

Except… Dorothy never mentioned the witches of Oz. None of them. Her guardians in Kansas were very religious, and Dorothy didn't think talking about witches – evil or good – would go over very well with them.

Nor had she yet mentioned the silver slippers. Not a word.

How, then, did Aunt Em know?

"Witch…?" Dorothy replied. "Shoes?"

Em's smile flickered, a bit like a candle in a small breeze. "Did I say witch? I meant, which way did you go? And shoes? Land sakes, I meant to say, what happened to your shoes? Your little socks were all stained with mud and grass when I found you the other day."

"I guess I lost them," Dorothy said. Then she told her she had a headache and wanted to go to bed. Her aunt and uncle smiled their concern, and smiled as they gave her warm milk. They smiled as they watched her say her prayers and smiled as they tucked her in. They smiled as they went across the room to their own beds and went to sleep. And they smiled *as* they slept.

If they were really sleeping at all.

Dorothy lay there as the world fell into silence, thinking about Aunt Em's questions and the smiles she and Henry seemed to always have. Very wide smiles. Very happy smiles, unless you saw them from a certain angle – a bit behind and to one side. When she saw that profile smile from an angle where there was no direct eye contact, the grins did not look at all happy. At the time, Dorothy was too young to know the word 'leer,' but she had seen those kinds of smiles in Oz. It was how the witch of the West sometimes looked at her.

A leer. A nasty smile, as she thought of it at the time. Mean, sneaky, and… wrong.

Earlier yesterday Dorothy saw Aunt Em turn away to look for Henry's approach. His face was beaming and happy, but Em's was not. It wasn't the smile she'd worn before turning. Now it was that jack-o'-lantern grin. A wolf smile. A rat's smile.

There and gone, and when Em turned back to Dorothy, it was a happy smile again.

Maybe the Dorothy who was whisked away by the cyclone would have been fooled by it, but the Dorothy who came home was older. Not so much in years but in experience. And that Dorothy did not like those smiles one little bit.

## 10

That was last night. Now she placed the lantern on the ground near the corner of the house, angling it so the brightest glow illuminated the newly painted wood. All the hair on Toto's back stood up straight as a bristle brush. He bared his teeth at the house.

The wind was getting stronger and she could feel dampness in it. Would it be only a nice, soaking downpour? Good for the crops. Good for a lot of things. Or, would it be another twister?

"*Please*," she prayed.

Dorothy leaned close and ran her fingers over the paint. It was dry but oddly tacky, as if it was only recently painted. She'd been home for two weeks now and in this dusty climate, with all that late summer heat, it should have been completely dried.

She angled her head to look at the boards and something

made her frown. The paint farthest from the corner looked different, and when she touched it that portion of the outer wall *was* dry. Only the area right at the corner and right at the bottom was tacky. When she bent and sniffed, the paint smell was stronger there than anywhere else.

"Now that's strange," she told Toto. The dog gave her a nearly pitying look as if surprised she was just now realizing that. Toto took a tiny, challenging step forward and growled. Not loud but with clear meaning. This Toto was, like Dorothy, different than before the Yellow Brick Road and all that had happened.

Dorothy considered for a moment, then set the rolling pin down and dug the screwdriver from her apron pocket. It was small, a bit rusty, and would never make for a weapon, but that wasn't why she'd brought it with her. With a tongue sticking out of the corner of her mouth, she bent forward and pressed the flat blade against the damp paint. It sank in a bit, and she nodded to herself.

"Thought so," she murmured. Then, moving very carefully and slowly, she shoved on the handle. The blade pushed up a curl of half-dried paint from the wood an inch above the ground. She made sure not to gouge too deeply, working with very little pressure until a strip three inches long and as wide as the screwdriver's blade fell away. Then Dorothy moved the lantern closer and looked.

The wood was dark and discolored where it was exposed. It wasn't the white of the rest of the house, nor the tan of fresh pine. This wood was old. Years old.

"New house indeed," she huffed.

She placed the driver's end next to the section she'd peeled back and repeated the action. Again and again as the sun crept tentatively over the edge of the hills. When she stopped once more, there was a roughly square cleared place as wide as her palm. Dorothy sat back on her heels and studied it, letting what she saw tell its story to her.

The dark color did not cover all of the wood but was instead irregular. It was almost chocolate brown and looked like someone had splashed a bit of coffee against the side of the house.

It wasn't coffee, though, and she knew it.

Toto sniffed it and whined, then backed up a pace, crouched low, and snarled at it.

Dorothy was young but all of her years – except for a few weeks in Oz – had been on a farm. Even though Uncle Henry grew vegetables, there were other things Aunt Em put on the table. Fresh meat or cured meat or smoked meat or dried meat. There were turkeys on Thanksgiving and a whole chicken every Sunday after church.

As a farm girl, she knew there was always some killing that needed being done on the farm. That was how it was. She herself had broken more chicken necks than she could count. She'd helped Aunt Em cut fresh meat from spring lambs and, once a year, a cow.

She knew what dried blood looked like. And when she bent and took a long sniff, she recognized the familiar coppery smell.

"This is where you died," she said. "This is where my house landed on you."

Toto kept growling.

And growling.

"What are you doing down there?" asked a voice.

Dorothy whipped around and saw two figures standing there. Uncle Henry held a big hunting knife in his hand. Aunt Em had a carving knife in hers.

They were both smiling in all the wrong ways.

## 11

Dorothy got slowly to her feet, her back to the house but not daring to actually lean against it. Toto moved to stand between her and the two knife-wielding smilers. His teeth were bared but his tail tucked tightly under. He was as scared as Dorothy, but like her, he was not going to give up without a fight. Neither of them would have survived Oz had they been ready to lay down and die of fright.

Dorothy held her screwdriver tightly and wished she had thought to pick up the rolling pin.

"You're under a spell, aren't you?" she asked, surprising herself with how calm her own voice sounded.

"Spell?" asked Aunt Em as casually as if they were discussing the weather on a calm spring morning. "Whatever do you mean, sweet girl?"

"Don't call me that. I'm a girl, but I'm not sweet. And you two can stop smiling because you're not happy. Not really. Those are fake smiles."

"Oh, no, sweet girl," said Uncle Henry, "we're very happy to see you. You're our niece and we love you."

"Oh? How come you both have knives and came sneaking up behind me?"

They looked down at their blades as if surprised to see them.

Aunt Em beamed at her. "We thought we heard a prowler and came to see."

"That's right," said Uncle Henry. "A sound in the first light of dawn. Very suspicious."

"There's enough light to see by now," said Dorothy. "Even with the storm clouds. You could have seen me easy as soon as you stepped outside."

They said nothing, merely smiled. The weak sunlight that escaped beneath the ceiling of purple clouds glimmered on their sharp knives.

"And you didn't build this house."

"Yes I did," said Henry. "With my own hands."

"The whole house," said Em.

"While I was away?"

"Sure," said Henry. "We had to make it all nice for when you came home. We missed you soooo much."

"We did," agreed Em. "We cried every night and prayed for you to come back safe."

"Prayed?" Dorothy narrowed her eyes. "Prayed to who?"

Another blank stare. Their hair and clothes snapped in the freshening breeze. Far away there was a chuckle of thunder. It sounded mean and cruel and hungry.

"You can't even say it, can you?"

"We prayed and prayed," said Henry.

"To who?"

"To the all-powerful," said Em.

"Really? 'Cause I was just in a place where someone said he was all-powerful but he was lying."

"The wizard..." they said as one, turning the Z into a hissy S sound. Like snakes.

"People there knew about a lot of all-mighty folks. Not just wizards, but sorceresses and witches. Like Glinda the Good."

The smiles flickered again, nearly going out this time.

"She is a monster," snarled Em.

"She is a demon," growled Henry.

"She *helped* me," snapped Dorothy.

Toto gave a sharp bark of agreement.

They looked at her and did nothing. Just smiles that now looked more strained than genuine.

"She came to help me after the house – this house, *our* house – landed on the Wicked Witch of the East and crushed her flat."

Nothing. But the smiles were leaking slowly away.

The rising wind blew hair in Dorothy's face and she brushed it away. "And you know what happened when she died? Do you? I never told you, but I think you know."

"We know," said Aunt Em.

Only it wasn't her voice. Not really. It was a woman's voice, to be sure, but it sounded both younger and older at the same time. A strange voice, with a slight accent. It sounded familiar, though not exactly like someone else she met in that faraway place. A voice she'd heard for the first time in Oz. Not the voice of a guard or even the voice of the false wizard. No, this was very much like the Wicked Witch of the West.

Not exactly the same, but close enough for Dorothy to be certain that her guesses were correct.

"You're not my aunt," she said.

Em – the thing that wore her face – spread her arms and looked down at her own body. "Don't I look like her?"

"Not in the right way." Dorothy quickly squatted and came up with the rolling pin in her other hand. As she rose a really stiff wind knocked her back against the side of the house. She yelped and leaped away because that newly painted area seemed to move as if there were bugs just below the surface. She shivered in disgust, but then tightened her grip on her weapons.

That chased the smile away.

Aunt Em stood straight and took a step closer. There was still enough sunlight shining out under the ceiling of clouds to make Em's shadow fall across Dorothy. It was cold in that shadow. Very cold indeed. Deep woods at sunset cold. Locked in a cellar cold. Midnight when the fire burned out in the hearth. That kind of cold.

"You are being a rude child," she said. "You need to apologize."

Dorothy tried to make a defiant face, but it felt awkward and soon fell away.

Lightning forked in the sky and thunder boomed only a moment later. A storm was coming. Would it take her and her family to Oz? Or would it drown the whole prairie with flash floods? At that point, either option was better than standing in the shadow and seeing those smiles.

"This is wrong," she said.

"You are being impertinent, young lady," snapped Uncle Henry. "I ought to take a switch to you. Mmm. That's a good idea. Cut a nice switch and see if it will help teach you to mind your betters."

His voice no longer sounded like Henry's. It was oddly female. It was almost the same as Em's. Neither was right. Both made her skin crawl.

Another flash of lightning burned the sky, and Em and Henry glanced nervously up, their smiles once more fading a bit. They turned back to Dorothy.

"For punishment, you will close all the shutters and then go inside and think about what you've done."

"What *I've* done?"

"Yes," snapped Em. "Scraping fresh paint away. What were you thinking? Now we have to repaint that section and do it quick before the rain starts."

Dorothy glanced at the exposed wood, at the dark stains. Then back at Em and Henry, and their knives.

"I… I'm sorry," she said.

Henry glowered at her. "You should be."

"Now git. Close those shutters nice and tight, and lock all the windows," said Em. "We can't let the rain in on the nice new house your uncle built."

Dorothy gave a contrite nod, backed away, shoved the screwdriver and rolling pin into her apron pockets, turned and began running around the house, closing the shutters, pinning them tight. When that was done, she ran around back and entered through that door with Toto – angry and confused – at her heels.

Once inside, Dorothy tossed the rolling pin and screwdriver onto a table, then closed and locked the back door. There were shutters outside, but also shutter-panels for the inside. Double protection for families living in the path of so many storms and tornados.

Then Dorothy went to the front door and looked out. The clouds were now black as midnight. Aunt Em held the lantern while Henry was on his knees with a paint can beside him. He had no brush but was frantically scooping out handfuls of white paint and smearing them over the exposed stained wood.

Thunder boomed and boomed.

"Hurry, you old fool," snarled Em. "Cover it. Cover it all up. Hurry!"

Dorothy nodded to herself.

Then she closed the front door. She did it very quietly but pulled it firm. And, silent as a mouse, she turned the lock. Both doors had upright brackets and beside each was a flat length of sturdy oak. In really bad storms, that was the only way to keep the doors from blowing in. As Toto watched, Dorothy lifted the bar to secure the front door, and then the one to seal the back door. Now, no matter how bad the storm would get, the house was as snug as possible.

Safe and sound.

"Henry, *hurry*! *Hurry for* her *sake!*"

Overhead she heard splats as the storm's first fat raindrops fell.

She picked up the screwdriver and held it like a dagger.

Ready.

Waiting.

Em's words echoed. Hurry for *her* sake.

She knew Em wasn't referring to her niece. Or herself. Through the walls she could hear Henry's desperate hands slapping paint on. Thunder drowned it out.

It did not drown out the screams.

Those high, terrible screams.

It did not drown out the pounding as Em and Henry ran around the house, clawing at shutters, hammering at the doors, trying to get in.

To get in out of the rain.

The corner of the house began to steam. It wasn't fire smoke. It was the same hissing sound that the witch of the west made after Dorothy doused her with the bucket of rainwater. The screams were like that, too.

The screams went on and on for a long time. The storm lasted for hours. Torrents of runoff swept past the house. Soaking it.

Dorothy and Toto sat down on her bed, enduring the noise, the screams, the horror.

## 12

Dorothy didn't remember falling asleep.

As soon as she was awake, she cocked her head to listen. The storm was gone and the air was filled with birdsong. She opened her eyes and looked around.

The house was different. New, but clearly hastily built. Poor construction done with cheap materials. There were stacks of lumber against one wall. It was a work in progress, and not bad for an older farmer who could not afford much help.

Across the room, curled together in a loving embrace, were Aunt Em and Uncle Henry. Exhausted from long days of building and farming and grieving for their lost niece. Toto sniffed the air – the corner of the room and then the sleeping adults. His little tail began to wag.

Dorothy got up and stretched. She put the screwdriver back, then walked over to wake her aunt and uncle to tell them that she wasn't lost. She was alive.

She was home. *Her* home.

It did not belong to any witch.

Then, or ever.

# ABOUT THE AUTHORS

**Simon R. Green** lives in the small town of Bradford-on-Avon, in the south-west of England. It was the last Celtic town to be invaded by the Saxons in 504 AD. Simon has worked as a shop assistant, journalist, bicycle repair mechanic, actor and Chippendale dancer. That last one may not be entirely accurate. He has written a great many novels, including the Deathstalker SF series, the Ishmael Jones books, and the Gideon Sable mysteries. And one film; *Judas Ghost*.

**Caitlin Rozakis** is the *New York Times* bestselling author of *Dreadful*, *The Grimoire Grammar School Parent Teacher Association*, and *Startup Hell*. Her contemporary romance novella *Leah's Perfect Christmas*, written as Catherine Beck, was adapted as the Hallmark Channel Original Movie *Leah's Perfect Gift*. She lives in Jersey City with her husband and son. Visit her online at caitlinrozakis.com.

**Louise Carey** has been writing since the age of 15, when she co-authored the graphic novel *Confessions of a Blabbermouth* with her father, Mike. She has since co-written two fantasy novels with her parents, *The House of War and Witness* and

*The City of Silk and Steel*. Her debut trilogy of novels, *Inscape*, *Outcast* and *Downfall* has been published in two languages, and the French edition of *Inscape* was shortlisted for the 2024 Prix Utopiales. Louise read English at University College, Oxford and has a master's in Psychology from Oxford Brookes. She currently divides her time between writing and running an escape room company, which she founded with her partner and brother. When she's not penning stories or designing puzzles, she enjoys reading horror and DMing for a group of rowdy but well-intentioned adventurers.

**Adrian Tchaikovsky** is a British science fiction and fantasy writer known for a wide-variety of work including the Children of Time, Final Architecture, Dogs of War, Tyrant Philosophers and Shadows of the Apt series, as well as standalone books such as *Elder Race*, *Doors of Eden*, *Spiderlight* and many others. *Children of Time* and its series has won the Arthur C. Clarke and BSFA awards, and his other works have won the British Fantasy, British Science Fiction and Sidewise awards.

**Ian Whates** is the author of ten novels (two co-written), two novellas, and some eighty short stories that have appeared in a variety of venues. In 2019 he received the Karl Edward Wagner Award from the British Fantasy Society, and his work has been shortlisted for the Philip K. Dick Award and on three occasions for BSFA Awards, while his stories have been translated into Spanish, German, Hungarian, Czech and Greek. Ian has served as a judge for the Arthur C. Clarke

Award and for the World Fantasy Awards. In 2006 he founded independent publisher NewCon Press by accident.

**M. R. Carey** is a writer of sci-fi, horror and fantasy across a range of media. He is best known for his 2014 novel *The Girl With All the Gifts* and for the movie of the same name for which he wrote the screenplay. His more recent work includes the Pandominion series, *Once Was Willem* and *The Last Night at the Star Dome Lounge*. Under the name Mike Carey he has written a ton of comic books including critically-acclaimed runs on *Lucifer*, *Hellblazer* and *X-Men*.

**Paul Magrs** was born in Jarrow in 1969 and grew up in Newton Aycliffe, County Durham, where he went to Woodham Comprehensive School. He got a First in English Literature at Lancaster University, and then a Distinction for their MA in Creative Writing, and then did a PhD on Angela Carter. He brought out his first novel in 1995 when he was 26. He was a Senior Lecturer in Creative Writing at UEA and then at MMU. Over the years he has published over fifty books for adults and children and has written many audio dramas for radio and download.

In 2019 he published his book on writing, *The Novel Inside You*. In 2020 Snow Books republished his Brenda and Effie Mystery series of novels. In 2022 he won the Crime Writers' Association Silver Dagger for best short story of the year. In 2023 HarperCollins published his book of cat portraits, *Puss-in-Books*. Under the name 'Elsie Mason' he has written six historical sagas for Orion. He has written many *Doctor Who* stories over the past twenty-five years for BBC Books, BBC Audio, Big Finish Productions and Puffin Books. His latest novel for the series is *Doctor Who: Dracula!*

Last year he began a bookish channel on YouTube where he talks about all the books on his shelves and in his life.

He lives and writes in Manchester with Jeremy and Bernard Socks. Visit him online at Instagram (instagram.com/paul_magrs), Facebook (facebook.com/paul.magrs), Patreon (patreon.com/Paulmagrs), and YouTube (youtube.com/@paulmagrs2474).

**Delilah S. Dawson** is the *New York Times* and *USA Today* bestselling author of *Star Wars: Phasma*, *Galaxy's Edge: Black Spire*, and *Inquisitor: Rise of the Red Blade*, as well as *The Violence*, *Bloom*, *Guillotine*, *House of Idyll*, *It Will Only Hurt for a Moment*, *Mine*, *Camp Scare*, *Ride or Die*, *Midnight at the Houdini*, the Blud series, the Hit series, and the Shadow series (written as Lila Bowen), plus the Arcadia Falls series (written as Isla Jewell). With Kevin Hearne, she writes the Tales of Pell series. She has also written dozens of comics and short stories for children and adults. She lives in Georgia with her family. Visit her online at delilahsdawson.com

**Robert Shearman** has written six short story collections, and between them they have won the World Fantasy Award, the Shirley Jackson Award, the Edge Hill Readers' Prize, and four British Fantasy Awards. He began his career in the theatre, and was resident dramatist at the Northcott Theatre in Exeter, and regular writer for Alan Ayckbourn at the

Stephen Joseph Theatre in Scarborough; his plays have won the *Sunday Times* Playwriting Award, the World Drama Trust Award, and the Guinness Award for Ingenuity in association with the Royal National Theatre. A regular writer for BBC Radio, his interactive drama series *The Chain Gang* won two Sony Awards. But he is probably best known for his work on *Doctor Who*, bringing back the Daleks for the BAFTA award-winning first series of its revival, in an episode nominated for a Hugo Award. His latest books are two *Doctor Who* novels for BBC Books, *Jubilee* and *The Chimes of Midnight*.

**Stark Holborn** is the author of the Factus Sequence, the Triggernometry series and the groundbreaking digital serial *Nunslinger*. Stark's fiction has been nominated for the British Fantasy Awards, the BSFA Awards and the New Media Writing Prize. Stark also works as a games writer on award-winning projects, and is currently lead writer on the SF detective game, *Shadows of Doubt*. She is a Visiting Lecturer in Narrative at Glasgow School of Art.

**Christina Henry** is a horror and dark fantasy author whose works include *The House That Horror Built*, *Good Girls Don't Die*, *Horseman*, *Near the Bone*, *The Ghost Tree*, *The Girl in Red*, *The Mermaid*, *Lost Boy*, the Chronicles of Alice series (*Alice*, *Red Queen* and *Looking Glass*) and the seven-book urban fantasy Black Wings series. Her short stories have been featured in the anthologies *Howl*, *Elemental Forces*, *Cursed*, *Twice Cursed*, *Giving The Devil His Due* and *Kicking It*. She enjoys running long distances, reading anything she can get her hands on, and watching movies with samurai, zombies and/or subtitles in her spare time. She lives in Chicago with her husband and son. Visit her online at christinahenry.net, and on BlueSky (@christinahenry.bsky.social), Threads (authorChristinaHenry), Instagram (@authorChristinaHenry), and Goodreads at goodreads.com/CHenryAuthor

**Una McCormack** is a bestselling and award-winning science fiction writer of more than twenty novels based on TV shows such as *Star Trek* and *Doctor Who*, as well as many short stories and audio dramas. She is an associate fellow of Homerton College, Cambridge, and a trustee of the Science Fiction Foundation. In 2019, she co-founded Gold SF, an imprint of Goldsmiths Press which publishes new voices in intersectional feminist science fiction. A former lecturer in creative writing, she continues to mentor writers, particularly those working towards completing their first novel.

**Jonathan Maberry** is a *New York Times* bestselling author, five-time Bram Stoker Award®-winner, four-time Scribe Award winner, Inkpot Award winner and comic book writer. His vampire apocalypse book series *V-Wars* was a Netflix original series; Alcon Entertainment is developing his YA-post-apocalyptic Rot & Ruin novels for film; and Chad Stahelski, director of *John Wick,* is developing his bestselling Joe Ledger thrillers for TV. Marvel's *Black Panther: Wakanda Forever* was partly based on his work. He writes in multiple genres including suspense, thriller, horror, science fiction, fantasy, and action, for adults, teens and middle grade.

His novels include the NecroTek series, the Pine Deep Trilogy, the Rot & Ruin series, the Dead of Night series, *Mars One*, the Kagen the Damned series, the Sleepers War series, and others. He's written fifty-five novels and over two hundred short stories, and edited many anthologies including *The X-Files*, *Aliens*, *Don't Turn Out the Lights*, *Nights of the Living Dead* (co-edited with George A. Romero), and others. His comics include *Black Panther: DoomWar*, *Captain America*, *Pandemica*, *Highway to Hell*, *The Punisher* and *Bad Blood*. He is the president of the International Association of Media Tie-in Writers, and the editor of *Weird Tales* Magazine. Jonathan lives in San Diego, California with his wife, Sara Jo. jonathanmaberry.com

# ABOUT THE EDITORS

**Marie O'Regan** is a British Fantasy Award and Shirley Jackson Award-nominated author and editor, based in Derbyshire. She was awarded the British Fantasy Society 'Legends of FantasyCon' award in 2022. Her first collection, *Mirror Mere*, was published in 2006 by Rainfall Books; her second, *In Times of Want*, came out in September 2016 from Hersham Horror Books. Her third, *The Last Ghost and Other Stories*, was published by Luna Press early in 2019, and her fourth, *Bleed For Me*, was published by Demain Publishing in 2025. Her short fiction has appeared in a number of genre magazines and anthologies in the UK, US, Canada, Italy and Germany, including *Best British Horror 2014*, *Great British Horror: Dark Satanic Mills* (2017), *The Mammoth Book of Halloween Stories*, and *This Way Lies Madness*. Her novella, *Bury Them Deep*, was published by Hersham Horror Books in September 2017. She was shortlisted for the British Fantasy Society Award for Best Short Story in 2006, Best Anthology in 2010 (*Hellbound Hearts*) and 2012 (*The Mammoth Book of Ghost Stories by Women*). She was also shortlisted for the Shirley Jackson Award for Best Anthology in 2020 (*Wonderland*). Her genre journalism has appeared in magazines like *The Dark Side*, *Rue Morgue* and

*Fortean Times*, and her interview book with prominent figures from the horror genre, *Voices in the Dark*, was released in 2011. An essay on *The Changeling* was published in PS Publishing's *Cinema Macabre*, edited by Mark Morris. She is co-editor of the bestselling *Hellbound Hearts, The Mammoth Book of Body Horror, A Carnivàle of Horror – Dark Tales from the Fairground, Exit Wounds, Wonderland, Cursed, Twice Cursed, The Other Side of Never, In These Hallowed Halls, Beyond & Within: Folk Horror, Death Comes at Christmas, The Secret Romantic's Book of Magic, These Dreaming Spires, Beyond & Within: Witchcraft* and *Best Served Cold*, as well as the charity anthology *Trickster's Treats #3*, and is also editor of the bestselling anthologies *The Mammoth Book of Ghost Stories by Women* and *Phantoms*, and Managing Editor of PS Publishing's award-winning novella imprint, Absinthe Books. Her first novel, the internationally bestselling *Celeste*, was published in February 2022, and a supernatural novella, *Resurrection Blues*, was published in May 2025. Marie was Chair of the British Fantasy Society from 2004 to 2008, and Co-Chair of the UK Chapter of the Horror Writers' Association from 2015 to 2022. She was also co-chair of ChillerCon UK in 2022. Visit her website at marieoregan.net. She can be found on Bluesky @marieoregan.bsky.social, X @Marie_O_Regan and Instagram @marieoregan8101.

**Paul Kane** is the award-winning (including the British Fantasy Society's Legends of FantasyCon Award 2022), bestselling author and editor of over a hundred and sixty books – such as the *Arrowhead* trilogy (gathered together in the sellout *Hooded Man* omnibus, revolving around a post-apocalyptic version of

Robin Hood), *The Butterfly Man and Other Stories*, *Hellbound Hearts*, *Wonderland* (a Shirley Jackson Award finalist) and *Pain Cages* (an Amazon #1 bestseller). His non-fiction books include *The Hellraiser Films and Their Legacy* and *Voices in the Dark*, and his genre journalism has appeared in the likes of *SFX*, *Rue Morgue* and *DeathRay*. He has been a Guest at Alt.Fiction five times, was a Guest at the first SFX Weekender, at Thought Bubble in 2011, Derbyshire Literary Festival and Off the Shelf in 2012, Monster Mash and Event Horizon in 2013, Edge-Lit in 2014 and 2018, HorrorCon, HorrorFest and Grimm Up North in 2015, The Dublin Ghost Story Festival and Sledge-Lit in 2016, IMATS Olympia and Celluloid Screams in 2017, Black Library Live and the UK Ghost Story Festival in 2019 and 2023, plus the WordCrafter virtual event 2021 – where he delivered the Keynote speech – as well as being a panellist at FantasyCon and the World Fantasy Convention, and a fiction judge at the Sci-Fi London festival. A former British Fantasy Society Special Publications Editor, he has also served as co-chair for the UK chapter of The Horror Writers Association and co-chaired ChillerCon UK in May 2022.

His work has been optioned and adapted for the big and small screen, including for US network primetime television, and his novelette 'Men of the Cloth' was turned into a feature by Loose Canon/Hydra Films, starring Barbara Crampton (*Re-Animator, You're Next*): *Sacrifice*, released by Epic Pictures/101 Films. Paul was also asked to pitch, along with a co-writer, for the remake of *Hellraiser* in the 2010s. In 2023 HorrorCon UK screened a retrospective of his film and TV adaptations, and interviewed Paul in front of the live audience. His audio work includes the full cast drama adaptation of *The Hellbound Heart* for Bafflegab, starring Tom Meeten (*The Ghoul*), Neve McIntosh (*Doctor Who*) and Alice Lowe (*Prevenge*), and the *Robin of Sherwood* adventure *The Red Lord* for Spiteful Puppet/ITV narrated by Ian Ogilvy (*Return of the Saint*), plus his plays have been performed at FantasyCon and by Hideout Theatre in London. He has also contributed to the Warhammer 40k universe for Games Workshop and has been asked to pitch on projects for both DC/Warner Bros and Marvel. Paul's latest novels are *Lunar* (set to be turned into a feature film), the YA story *The Rainbow Man* (as PB Kane), the sequels to *RED* – *Blood RED* & *Deep RED*, all collected in an omnibus edition – the award-winning hit *Sherlock Holmes & the Servants of Hell*, *Before* (an Amazon Top 5 dark fantasy bestseller), *Arcana* and *The Storm*. In addition he writes thrillers for HQ/HarperCollins as PL Kane (plkane.com), the first of which, *Her Last Secret* and *Her Husband's Grave* (a sellout on Waterstones.com and at The Works) came out in 2020, with *The Family Lie* released the following year, described as 'Agatha Christie meets *The Wicker Man*' (*all* three novels were Amazon sellouts). His books have been translated into many languages, including French, German, Spanish, Ukrainian, Turkish, Czech, Bulgarian and Polish. Paul lives in Derbyshire, UK, with his wife **Marie O'Regan**. Find out more at his site shadow-writer.co.uk, which has featured Guest Writers such as Stephen King, Charlaine Harris, Robert Kirkman, Catriona Ward, Dean Koontz, Olivie Blake and Guillermo del Toro. He can also be found on X (@PaulKaneShadow), on BlueSky (@paulkane.bsky.social), and Instagram (@paul.kane.376).

# ACKNOWLEDGEMENTS

And now for the important bit – where we get to say an enormous thanks. Firstly, to all the authors for their wonderful stories, to our editor Daniel Carpenter and all the fantastic team at Titan for everything they do. Finally, thanks to our respective families, without whom etc.